Cover design by
www.catherineclarkedesign.co.uk

9781912582747

Williams & Whiting (Publishers)
15 Chestnut Grove, Hurstpierpoint,
West Sussex, BN6 9SS

To Judy.

Very best wishes

Enjoy!.

Marilyn

Also by Marilyn Pemberton
from Williams & Whiting

The Jewel Garden

Also by Marilyn Pemberton

Out of the Shadows: the life and works of Mary De Morgan

Song of the Nightingale: a tale of two castrati

A Teller of Tales

by

Marilyn Pemberton

Book 1 in the Grandmothers' Footsteps series

The world is full of women with tales to tell.

The world needs to listen.

Chapter 1

October 1822

'Boggart, boggart, boggart!'

Three ill-fed and ill-clothed boys encircle us, repeating their cruel words. They pluck at Bobbit's clothes with grubby, calloused fingers, their gaunt faces contorted in spite and their voices shrill with malice. My brother flaps his hands as if shooing away a swarm of wasps and starts to whimper, like a cornered puppy. One of the boys pulls Bobbit's cap off his head and throws it to the ground.

'His name is Bobbit, and he's not a boggart, he's a boy just like you. Leave us be, please, you're frightening him.'

'Boggart, boggart, boggart!'

Suddenly there's a loud 'thwack' as one boy after the other is struck on the shoulder with a cudgel. 'Be off with you, you little vermin. Don't you be insulting the teacher's children. Go on, beat it, before I beat you.' We watch as the boys scamper away, turning only to stick out their pink tongues, probably the cleanest part of their bodies. The stall keeper picks up the cap and tries to brush off the wet mud, only succeeding in making the stain worse. He hands it to me with a shrug of his broad shoulders. 'Are you all right, Miss Hayes? Did they hurt you or Master Robert?'

'No, thank you kindly, they caused us no harm. You would have thought that they'd be used to him by now, but they always make terrible fun of him just because he's ... well, just because he is as he is.'

'Boys can be right cruel oftentimes. Well, as long as you're not hurt. Here, take a couple o' cats' heads.'

I gasp but then smile as he hands two large silvery green apples to me. We have our own apple tree but I am grateful to the man so take them from him and put them in my pocket. I take Bobbit's hand and gently lead him down the road to the canal, one of our favourite places to walk. 'It's alright now; there's nothing to be scared of. They are just little bully boys, and here is another one.'

I grip Bobbit's cold, unresponsive hand and force myself to smile politely at Daniel Sutton, a mine-owner's son of my own age, who is strutting down the towpath towards us. He looks me in the eye as he approaches, his smile more of a leer than a polite greeting.

'Good morning, Miss Hayes, Master Freak. A pleasant morning for a walk, considering the time of year.'

I will not react.

I will not react.

I tilt my head at him for the sake of good manners only and try and walk on but Daniel stands directly in front of Bobbit, preventing him from moving; he turns his gaze from me and slowly studies my brother from head to toe and then back again. 'Such a shame; if he was a puppy he would've been drowned at birth. Still, we can soon rectify that.' Before I can stop him he shoves Bobbit towards the canal, though not hard enough to send him over the edge. A cry escapes from my pursed lips, which amuses Daniel greatly. He shrugs, puts his mouth close to Bobbit's ear and whispers, 'Next time, Freak,' and walks on, thankfully away from us. I watch his receding back until he turns a corner and goes out of sight.

Bobbit's shuddering and mewling belie that he doesn't understand anything, as people, Mama in particular, like to think. 'He's gone. What a despicable boy he is, but he would never actually hurt you, Bobbit. Let's sit here and watch the barges and horses go by.' He doesn't answer, nor do I expect him to; in all of his ten years he has never said a word to anyone, not even me who has cared for him since I was five when I took the little, sobbing one-year old into my bed and calmed him by telling him a silly tale. 'Shall we have a story?'

I take his silence as consent. I have nothing in mind; I just start with a comforting image and let the story reveal itself.

There was once a brother and sister, who lived alone in a little wooden house, deep in a forest. How happy they were! They played all day with their friends the rabbits, squirrels, badgers, foxes and even hedgehogs, though they had to be careful with them. They danced to the birds' merry tunes and swam with the fishes in the wide river. One day the most beautiful butterfly landed on the boy's nose! The boy loved butterflies and would often sit for hours, mesmerised by their colourful displays. He was heart-broken when the butterfly flew off and ran after it, followed by the sister, who didn't want her younger brother to get lost. On and on the butterfly flew; on and on the children ran. They ran down paths they had never known were there, across streams, up hills and down dales. On and on the butterfly flew; on and on the children ran. At last the butterfly landed on a bush growing on the side of a high mountain and waited for the children to catch up. Although they had run all day they were surprised to find they were not tired at all. When the boy went to gently pick up the butterfly it flew away again, into a black hole that the bush had hidden from view. The children cautiously followed, for they were both a little bit afraid of the dark. But they were surprised to find that there was no need for fear, for the walls of the tunnel glittered and shone as if they were made of diamonds, which in fact they were. The two children followed the butterfly deeper and deeper into the mountain-side, their eyes and mouths wide open in wonder. Finally, they reached an enormous cave, bigger even than the whole of Saint Bartholomew's church, imagine that! The walls here weren't made of diamonds but the children realised with joy that they were covered with hundreds, thousands, millions of butterflies, their colourful, iridescent wings shimmering and trembling in a light that-'.

'Ha! Another of your stupid stories, Lizzie?'

It's Jamie, my elder brother by two years. 'I needed to calm him; Daniel Sutton was being his usual charming self. He is such a horrid little boy.'

'He is the same age as you and you are always saying that you are a grown-up.'

'Girls grow up quicker than boys, everyone knows that. What are you doing out of work, anyway?'

'I had to deliver some pamphlets to one of the mine supervisors. Come on. I'll walk back into town with you.'

Jamie is not my favourite brother; Matthew has that special place in my heart. Jamie can often be quite spiteful to me, but today he is good company and as we retrace our route along the canal towpath my anger dissipates. He is also, however, impatient and he soon gets tired of waiting for Bobbit, who always walks more with a sideways shuffle than a forward stride. Jamie gives me a pat on the arm with something akin to affection and walks briskly away.

We pass one of the town's furnaces; the wind carries the sound of muted banging and hissing, of metal against metal and water on burning hot coals. I have never been inside but I imagine a horde of little devils carrying out their satanic business, darting between rivers of molten ore, their black skin shiny and scaly, their eyes glowing red with malevolence. Outside of this man-made inferno, though, I know them to be but ordinary men and boys.

I need to get home; although Mama is always happier when Bobbit is out of her sight, I know that she needs me there to help during the last few weeks before her confinement. My young brother, however, cannot be rushed. We make our way at a tortuously slow pace now past the iron works.

'Look how the smoke comes out of the chimneys like readymade rain clouds. Do you remember what they make in

4

there, Bobbit?' I don't wait for an answer. 'That's right they make nails. Do you think there's a huge beast in there that's always hungry, so they feed it with more and more iron ore until it is so full that it bursts and showers everyone with sharp pieces of metal?' I laugh and wish, not for the first time, that I can make Bobbit laugh too. He shambles on, however, eyes darting from path to canal, from barge to bush.

We have lived in Wednesbury for nearly three years now, having moved from Mancetter, a small village thirty or so miles away, but I am still surprised how the town and the industries that it has spawned and upon which it depends, are impossible to separate, and how but one step takes you from one to the other. We continue along the towpath, keeping pace with a pair of horses pulling a barge laden with coal. Although Bobbit has never communicated with a human through speech, he and the horses exchange quiet neighing sounds and seem to be deep in conversation.

We pass one of the factories built by the side of the canal and I point out a small, square, brick building, as I always do. 'Papa will be in there with his boys, Bobbit. Let's listen to see if we can hear them chanting their letters.' But the noise of industry is louder than that of education. The reason we had moved from country to town was because Papa wanted to use the income from his family to set up a school for the boys of poor, working families, of which there is an abundance in Wednesbury. His dream is to educate them well enough so that they can get jobs that don't involve tearing the coal from under the ground or working in conditions as hot as Hades.

His dream has become my dream. I raise my hand in a silent salute and walk on, Bobbit still engrossed in his equine conversation.

We have to turn away from the canal and Bobbit stumbles as he keeps his eyes on the horses rather than on the path. As we finally near the centre of the town again, the streets become busier with people wrapped in their dark clothes against the grey, autumn weather. Market Place, however, is full of colour from the awnings that cover the stalls and the multifarious goods they protect. It is Friday, market day, and the air is thick with the sound of hectoring traders, the smell of spitted chickens and the dampness of the rain that has just started to fall. I purchase some cheese that Sarah, our housekeeper, had asked for and enjoy looking at the trinkets and fripperies that I never buy; wherever would I wear them?

As we near our house I catch sight of the hem of a black robe as someone rushes through the garden gate. 'I wonder why Papa is home so early?' He has left the front door wide open and as we approach we hear the screams that slide down the banister and tumble out into the open air.

Chapter 2

October 1822

I let go of Bobbit's hand and, God forgive me, leave him alone on the bottom step whilst I race into the house and up the stairs towards my parents' bedroom, from whence the screaming comes. Papa is outside the closed door, his hands clenched behind his back, his head down studying the rug as he paces to and fro. Four strides, turn, four strides, turn. He looks so like Bobbit when he is lost in his own world; when Papa looks up at me and smiles there can be no doubt who Bobbit takes after, although the son is missing the father's intellect and vivacity.

'This one has decided to come a little earlier than expected.' Mama lets out a high-pitched wail and then starts making noises that sound like a dog in pain. 'You shouldn't be here, Lizzie. Go and see if Sarah needs any help. And Lizzie, stay downstairs, there's nothing you can do. Mama is in the good hands of Mrs Dawson and Mrs Foster; and God's, of course.'

I give him a hug and then, accompanied by Mama's animalistic cries, go down the stairs, promising myself that I'll never, ever have children. I hear voices and suddenly remember Bobbit. I rush out of the still-open door and almost collide into a trio of boys - my brothers.

'Ah, Lizzie. I didn't think you would be very far away. We found Robert wandering down the road looking as lost as a motherless lamb.' Nobody except me ever calls him Bobbit, the name I christened him with when I was but four years old. I find I can't speak, so overcome am I with guilt and fear at what could have happened if my elder brothers hadn't come along at that time. I go to Bobbit and hug him tight, managing only a mantra of 'I'm so sorry. I'm so sorry.'

'For goodness sake, Lizzie, has something happened? Why did you leave Robert?' Jamie is two years younger than Matthew but his tone is harsher, less forgiving. His spitefulness, never far under the surface, has returned.

'It's Mama. It's her time.'

Both of the elder boys turn their heads in unison at the sound of a long undulating wail that makes my toes curl and the hairs on the back of my neck bristle. We all remember other such occasions over the past years that have led to nothing but an empty crib. They go into the house leaving me, as always, to deal with Bobbit. I take his limp hand and lead him inside.

'Where were you going, you silly boy? Did you want to finish your conversation with the canal horse? We'll go back tomorrow, I promise. Are you going to help me and Sarah get dinner?'

The kitchen is warm and there's a comforting smell of braised beef and stewed apple. Sarah is standing at the sink deftly peeling potatoes without looking, her focus seemingly on the depleted vegetable patch that is in her line of sight. She is humming quietly to herself.

'Good afternoon, Miss Elizabeth. I have everything under control. Your poor Mama won't be joining us but we must still keep to the pattern of normal life. None of us will go hungry.'

How I love Sarah, her steadiness and sensible outlook. She had been Mama's nanny and then accompanied her as housekeeper when she married Papa. I rarely see either my paternal or maternal grandparents as they both live on the south coast, and I have always looked on Sarah as more of a grandmother than a servant. 'Is there anything I can do? What would Mama be doing if she were here? This one is early, isn't it? Is it too early? Will Mama be all right, Sarah? Will the baby live this time?'

Sarah chuckles, continuing to pare the skins of the pile of potatoes that would surely feed the whole of Wednesbury. 'You have always been the one with all the questions, haven't you? Well, yes, you can go and see if there are any more eggs if you

8

want to do something useful. Your Mama would have been telling me about her day and perhaps helping prepare the vegetables, but they are all done before you ask. Yes, this one is early by a week or two, but I have known many such who are now strapping men or bonny women. Your Mama is healthy, I am sure she will be all right, God willing. As to whether this baby will live, only God knows what His plans are and whether this one stays with us or not. Whatever happens, Miss Elizabeth, it will be up to you and me to keep the family together, well fed and in order.'

I want to move but an unasked question dries my mouth and pins me to the floor. Sarah, who has always been able to gauge my mood often better than Mama, puts the knife down and comes to me, putting her comforting arms around me and pulling me onto her generous bosom that has never nurtured any of her own.

'What is it, my dear?'

'Bobbit was early too, wasn't he? What if ...?'

Sarah waits but I can't put my fear into words, not with him standing but three feet from us. She tightens her grip, making me feel as if I'm being absorbed into her soft, yielding flesh.

'We will love it, Miss Elizabeth, you and I will love it, as we love Robert.' She pushes me away. 'Now, go and get those eggs otherwise there'll be no custard with the apples and you know how the men folk love their custard.'

I take Bobbit's arm and lead him out of the kitchen, down the back garden path and into the chicken coop. The air is warm, thick with the pungent smell of droppings. I remove my gloves and thrust them into my pocket. I look at Bobbit to see if today he will follow suit but he continues to stand, his arms hanging loosely by his side, his head bowed, as if in prayer. I take his gloves off for him then thrust one of his hands under a nesting chicken. He holds it there for a while, perhaps enjoying the warmth, then carefully withdraws his clenched fist, making small clucking sounds as he does so. He allows me to unfurl his fingers, one by one, and then carefully remove the egg. We repeat the process until I have six eggs nestled in the bottom of the basket. I could have done the job myself in a few minutes but I try to make sure that my poor brother manages to do something useful each day. As I reminded Jamie earlier, I have the patience of Job.

Dinner is a strange affair. We sit in our usual seats; I opposite the two boys, Papa, when he is here, at the head of the table and the spirit of Mama at the tail. Papa takes a bite of food followed by a sip of wine, then excuses himself and leaves the table to pace outside the bedroom door until he comes back down to repeat the ritual. Our conversation is sporadic and unenthusiastic, interspersed as it is with Papa's constant comings and goings and the sounds of the two ladies' footsteps as they minister to Mama over our heads. Bobbit eats in the kitchen; Mama has never been able to tolerate the sound nor sight of him eating, so it has always been Sarah who cuts up his food and picks up the pieces that he drops in his clumsiness.

It is not until I have helped Sarah clear away and put Bobbit to bed that I am able to sit and relax. Bobbit shares my room, an arrangement that has been unchanged since I first took him into my bed when he was just a year old, so that I could comfort him in my five year-old way. The only difference is that he now sleeps on his own mattress by my side. I sit on the edge of my bed and watch him. He looks like a normal little boy, although smaller than average. His dark brown hair is curly, like mine and Papa's, and with his eyes closed his habitual vacant look is not evident. His mouth is open and a silver trail threads its way down his cheek. He twitches and makes Bobbit sounds. Does he dream, if so of what? Does he speak and run and have fun like the boys who mock him? Does he remember the stories I tell him, the words swirling in his brain, forming and reforming into new stories that entertain him throughout the night? Or does he just have screaming nightmares that only I can dispel when I hold him, rock him and sing to him?

Could I cope with another such as him? I know Mama would not.

I sit at my dressing table, brushing my hair but something stops my hand at only the count of fifty. I listen but can hear nothing apart from the creaks of the house as it settles down for the night. Then I realise that it is this silence that disturbs me. Why are there no sounds coming from my parents' bedroom? Why can't I hear Papa's footsteps pacing up and down? I start to brush again and the mirror reflects one tragic scene after another and by the count of seventy my vision is blurred with tears. Should I go to her? Should I hold her in my arms as I did a year ago, and a year before that, as her heart breaks all over again and she smothers me with her grief? She needs me but I carry on with my brushing, calming myself with each stroke. I stop at one hundred and decide that I am quite pretty by candle-light.

I should go to her but it's as if I am stuck to my seat. I wonder for one ridiculous moment whether Jamie has been up to one of his tricks and put glue on the cushion. But no, it is fear and guilt that holds me down. Fear at how another loss will affect Mama and guilt at even thinking about how it will affect me. I suddenly stand, knocking the chair over in my haste. Bobbit stirs and coughs but sleeps on. The shawl I am in the middle of embroidering is waiting on top of the sewing basket; yet another to put away in a drawer full of the unfinished.

I open my door and as I do so a sound comes hurtling down the corridor. It's not a wail or a whimper, not a mewl or a moan but a bawl, a bellow, an angry blast of noise from one who demands attention now, right this minute.

I have never heard anything so wonderful.

I am the last to arrive and stand in the doorway surveying the roomful of people. There is Papa with his rugged face almost split in two by his happy grin; Matthew and Jamie, side by side,

11

look both pleased and embarrassed; Sarah, like me, is in her night clothes and tries to plump up Mama's pillow, wipe her face and belatedly braid her hair all at the same time; the two midwives are swaddling the baby and all I can see is a very red face and a black 'o' shape through which he or she is making its existence known. Mama looks dishevelled, despite Sarah's ministrations, but although she is obviously tired, her face still red from her exertions and her hair plastered to her head with sweat, she looks content. She sees me and beckons to me.

'Come and see, Lizzie. Come and say hello to your sister, Dorothy.'

'She's very loud.'

'That's a good sign. She wants to tell the world that she has arrived, that she is hungry and wants feeding this very instant.'

Either Mrs Dawson or Mrs Foster - they are interchangeable in their plumpness, jollity and worthiness - hands the white cocoon to Mama, who takes it with ease. Mama's obvious intent to feed the baby clears the room of the men folk. I turn to go too, but she calls me back.

'Please stay, Lizzie.'

The three older women hover in the background but I sit on Mama's bed and watch as she takes out a plump breast and guides the still open mouth to the source of food. The screaming suddenly stops and is replaced with a wet sound of sucking. Mama grimaces then visibly relaxes and closes her eyes.

'I don't remember Bobbit ever crying so loudly.'

'No.'

'Nor him being so red of face.'

'No.'

'And she's bigger than he was.'

'Yes.'

Slowly all sounds cease but that of six females breathing.

I tentatively put my finger tips onto Dorothy's downy head and for no reason that I can discern, its warmth and softness makes me cry. I put my own head on the bed cover and sob. Mama strokes my hair with one hand and rocks the now sleeping babe with the other.

Chapter 3

October 1822

Bobbit tilts his head to one side and seems to study his younger sister lying in her cradle. The curtains are closed but the morning sun is strong enough to penetrate through the weave and provide enough light for us to be able to see the sleeping mother and baby. Dorothy's mouth twitches as she re-lives her happiest moments.

'Isn't she beautiful, Bobbit?' I whisper so as not to waken them. Bobbit suddenly puts his hand to the baby's face and strokes it, making little cooing sounds, like one of the doves that sit in the apple tree each day and tells anyone who listens of its hopes and fears.

Suddenly Bobbit is pushed away with such a force that he trips and falls heavily to the floor.

'Get away! Get away!' Her voice is raw and full of spittle, fear and loathing.

I look on horrified as Mama grabs the babe and clutches her tightly to her chest, rocking backwards and forwards, muttering to herself. Dorothy sleeps on but Mama is very awake; her cheeks are flushed, her eyes wild, darting from me to Bobbit to the empty cradle and back again. The pounding of footsteps up the stairs heralds Sarah's headlong rush into the bedroom. She is wielding a floury rolling pin thrust before her in defence of her beloved mistress.

'What on earth has happened?' She surveys the room: Bobbit is sitting on the floor, his head hanging down as if in shame; I am standing by the cradle doubtless still looking shocked; Mama and baby are safely in bed, unmolested. She looks at me, 'What's happened, Lizzie? What's all the screaming about?'

Before I can explain, Mama speaks, her voice quieter but still full of venom. 'I don't want him anywhere near her. He mustn't touch her. I don't want ...'

14

'But Mama he'd never hurt her. He was just stroking her cheek and talking to her, in his own way.'

Mama looks at me with such revulsion in her expression that I step back. 'She is perfect. I will not have him touch her and ruin her. I don't want him anywhere near her. Get him away!' Her voice rises hysterically and Sarah goes to comfort her.

'There, there, mistress. Lizzie will take Robert out, won't you, dear? Let's put Dorothy down again, shall we, and see if you can both get some precious sleep. There's no harm done, nor will there be.'

'Come on, Bobbit, let's go and see the horses shall we?' My voice is too loud, with a jolliness that fools no one. I take his hand and help him to his feet. I search his face and for an instant I see a fleeting glimpse of such deep unhappiness and despair that I catch my breath, but then it's gone and there is nothing there but the customary blankness.

I put some apples into our coat pockets but when we go through the garden gate he stands rigid and shakes his head whilst I try and pull him in the right direction for the canal. 'Come on, Bobbit, I thought you wanted to go and see the horses?' He never makes his wants known to me, of course; I can only presume and this time I am wrong. I turn the opposite way and he follows. I notice he is limping slightly. 'Don't worry about what Mama said, Bobbit. She is just very emotional after giving birth and she is so happy that Dorothy is alive and healthy, she just wants to make sure no harm comes to her.' I squeeze his hand. 'I know, and she knows too, that you are the gentlest of boys and would never hurt a baby.'

We carry on along Church Street and then up Church Hill, our pace slowing with each step. Sitting, as it does, at the highest point for miles around, St. Bartholomew's can be seen by anyone who raises their eyes slightly to the heavens and I like to think that in its turn, it casts its benevolent eye over the surrounding countryside and its inhabitants, even the Methodists. I love the way the long, thin pointed steeple points to the skies, reminding us all of our hoped-for destination.

It has not rained since yesterday so the tomb upon which Bobbit and I sit is dry, though cold. It is our favourite place and I have assured Bobbit that Mistress Carmichael, whose bones await the final trumpet, is quite happy for her resting place to be ours also. We sit, hand in hand, me swinging my legs, Bobbit not. Below us the landscape is dotted with fire and smoke, marking the locations of furnaces, chimneys, coke hearths, and charcoal braziers, all of which are necessary for our industries.

'Do you remember me saying how not so long ago all we see before us would have been open countryside and woodland? But they had to cut down the trees to make charcoal and dig up the fields to get at the coal that lies just under the surface? Sometimes they don't have to dig at all; they just bend their backs and pick up lumps of coal lying on the ground. So they say, anyway.'

I continue swinging my legs, as always putting my thoughts into words. 'Just imagine what it would have been like in the days when there was a castle here, rather than a church, and there was forest as far as the eye could see.' I jump down, throw my arms wide open and raise my voice so that it carries back in time. 'Hark to me, people of Wodensbury. I am Ethelfleda, daughter of King Alfred, known as the Great, wife to Ethelred, currently known as the Unwell. It is I, your Lady of Mercia, who will save you from the rampaging Danish hordes, who threaten to burn our villages, rape our women and devour our children. Never mind that I'm a woman; it is I who will lead you, sword in hand, to force the invaders into the sea, never to return.'

I bow to the roaring crowds and bask in their admiration. The applause peters out, except for one person slowly clapping behind me. I turn and smile at my eldest brother.

'I'm right, aren't I Matthew? She did live in a castle on this very spot and she did fight and she did save Mercia?'

'So we are told, Lizzie, but nobody can be sure. It was all a very long time ago and there are no written records. It's not very likely that a woman would do such things, is it? It's just a story that has been told and retold over the centuries to entertain, that's all.'

I feel annoyed that he seems to consider it unthinkable that a woman can be brave or to do anything that is not considered to be 'suitable.' My former exuberance is quashed and I feel as if there is a tight band around my chest. But I cannot be cross with Matthew for long. 'Why are you here, anyway? Shouldn't you be at the school?'

'I was thanking God for the deliverance of a healthy babe.' Matthew has an immutable faith and is never shy to share it with whomsoever will listen. 'I heard what happened this morning. You should have known better than to take Robert to see the baby. You know what Mama thinks of him.'

'Hush! Don't say things like that in front of him.'

'He doesn't understand, Lizzie, you know he doesn't.'

'I don't know he doesn't, nor do you, nor does anyone. Just like we don't know if Ethelfleda really went into battle, we don't know whether Bobbit understands us. *I* believe he does, so I wish everyone would take care of what they say. I want him to feel loved, even if ....'

Matthew shrugs as if to dismiss my wants, as he had earlier dismissed my heroine. 'I need to get to school. Do you want to come along?'

'We'll walk part of the way with you, if you aren't in a hurry. Then I need to get home and see if there are any jobs Sarah wants me to do.'

'Do you mind if we go by the vicarage? I want a quick word with the Reverend Stephenson.'

'He'll surely let you know, as soon as he hears.'

'I know, but he is suffering more and more from the gout and I want to save him having to walk all the way to the house.'

I refrain from suggesting that the said reverend should practice more culinary constraint and, taking Bobbit's arm, accompany Matthew further along Church Hill to where the vicarage stands. It is an impressive building that has more rooms than a single man and a housekeeper can ever have need of. I wait until Matthew has disappeared from sight and sound before sharing my opinion with Bobbit.

'If the good Reverend Stephenson is indeed God's representative on earth, you would think, would you not, that he would share this fine house with some of the families that are crammed six or more to a room in those very houses that he must overlook when he stands at his bedroom window, surveying his spiritual domain? Just because they are called his flock is no reason to treat them like mindless sheep. If you don't agree with me, squeeze my hand.' I wait a few futile seconds. 'There, I knew you'd agree.'

We wait only a few more minutes before Matthew comes out. He seems somehow taller than when he went in and there is a bounce in his step that wasn't there before. His expression is one of forced blankness but he can't hide the brightness of his eyes.

'You've heard, haven't you? Haven't you? They've accepted you and you're going. When? Oh, tell me, Matthew, when?'

He takes a moment to compose his voice and face. 'Stop asking questions. I can't tell you anything before I speak to Papa. Come on, let's go.'

He can't hold himself back sufficiently to walk at our pace, so he rushes on then waits for us to catch up, his impatience evident in his clenched fists and tapping toes. I let him suffer for a while then take pity on him. 'You're making me nervous, Matthew. You go on and speak with Papa. I'll have to be patient, as always, and wait to hear your news later on.'

18

He smiles gratefully and then walks briskly away, his excitement not quite overcoming his obedience to outdoor etiquette, otherwise I'm sure he would have run.

'Well, Bobbit, Matthew is going to university. The Bishop must have liked his testimonial and recommended that Matthew go to Cambridge to learn to be a vicar. Hopefully not like the Reverend Stephenson but a good one. I wonder how long it takes to learn how to be a vicar? Not long, surely? Matthew already knows his Bible so well he has a quote for every occasion and he's very kind. What else do you need to know?' I try and recall how the Reverend Stephenson spends his days. 'I suppose he will need to learn how to write a sermon, and how to baptise, marry and bury. But that can't take long, can it? Maybe he'll only be gone a few weeks then he'll come back and take over from the Reverend Stephenson, who will be sent to another parish, and good riddance.'

I look guiltily around me to make sure no one has heard me criticise the local man of God. At least I know Bobbit won't tell.

We arrive at the centre of the town, now empty of stalls; the only evidence of yesterday's market is the carpet of yellowing cabbage leaves, the curled feathers of deceased chickens trodden into the mud and the piles of dung. It is quiet; the only people about are those who don't work in the mills, refineries, mines or in the shops that line the main streets.

We pass the Cross, an ancient, dilapidated building that has fallen into total ruin. It stands on six pillars, the arches between them high enough for a man to walk under without bending his head. Even standing a distance away, the smell of the putrid rubbish that has been piling up there for years still manages to make my eyes water and my gorge to rise. I pull Bobbit round the building, trying to keep as far away from it as possible. 'Jamie says that at night it is a gathering place for villains, where they plan their next wicked deed. I dread to think how he knows such things but all I can say is that they must have stomachs of iron to stand the smell. People complain about it and say it should be demolished; if they do I wonder what they'll put in its place?'

I hear footsteps behind me but before I can turn someone shoves me hard in the back and pulls my bonnet over my eyes.

'Have you brought my food?'

I rearrange my bonnet. 'Should you be out of the shop, James?'

'Mr Cotterell has gone to Birmingham for the day and has left me in charge. So yes, Elizabeth, I can be out of the shop.' He manages to infuse my name with as much disdain as he can muster. 'So, have you got it?'

'No. I'm on my way home now. Mama sent me out early on an errand. I didn't have time to put together your victuals.'

'Well, hurry up, can't you, I'm starving.'

'I doubt you know what being hungry is, never mind starving.' He doesn't hear; he has already returned into the darkness of the printing shop, where he has been apprenticed for nearly a year. I wouldn't say this to anyone, not even Bobbit, but I don't love Jamie. He is not a good person, not like Matthew, and I suspect he gets up to things that would cause Papa apoplexy. If I cared more for Jamie, I would worry about him and how he might end up.

Chapter 4

October 1822

I leave Bobbit in Sarah's capable hands, put some bread and cheese into a basket and return to the printing shop. There's nobody behind the counter. I call my brother's name but my voice is no competition for the loud thump, thump that is emanating from somewhere at the back of the shop. I have never been inside the print room and I am interested in seeing Jamie at work, so I pull open the door and step inside. The room is large with shelves on each wall, laden with reams of paper, bottles of ink and boxes containing small cubes that I think are probably letters of the alphabet and other paraphernalia necessary for the printing of pamphlets and chap-books. In the middle of the room is the press itself. Jamie is standing with his back to me and I watch fascinated as he winds a large handle that causes a board with the paper attached to move into the right position, then he pulls a lever down hard twice, which forces down the inked press onto the paper. He lifts up the press and removes the paper, studies it then puts it on the counter to dry, along with about twenty others. He then takes another sheet, attaches it to the board and repeats the process. I have never seen my brother so engrossed in something in which there is no mischief. As he returns from laying the next sheet to dry he lifts his head and espies me. I don't expect him to smile at me, but neither do I expect the look of panic that briefly flits across his face before reverting to his normal glower. He strides over to me and pushes me out of the door back into the shop.

'What do you think you're doing, creeping up on me like that? No one is allowed in there but me and Mr Cottrell. It's dangerous.'

Dangerous? What from, paper cuts? I am tired of Jamie's aggression and I don't have the energy to challenge him. I thrust

21

the basket into his hands and walk out of the shop without saying a word.

On my return I go into the kitchen to warm myself from the autumnal chill that has seeped into my bones. I am surprised to see Mama sitting in her rocking chair, nursing Dorothy. Sarah is standing at the table preparing vegetables, her eyes fixed benignly on her beloved mistress. Mama is the daughter and we are the family Sarah never had.

I pull up a stool and sit by Mama's side, stroking Dorothy's head as she suckles. 'Should you be up so soon, Mama? Don't you have to stay in bed for two weeks or more?'

'So some so-called experts say. I think I've had enough babies to know what is best for me and for them. How can sitting here, in the warmth and comfort of my own kitchen, with Sarah tending to my every need, possibly be bad for me?' She takes the sting out of her remarks by roughing my hair and chucking my chin. 'You're a good girl, Lizzie. I don't know what I'd do without you, especially all the help you give with Robert.'

At the mention of his name, I realise that he is not sitting in his usual seat in the corner, out of Sarah's way but in a position to see everything that is going on. He has his own rocking chair and he spends hours just rocking to and fro with his eyes closed. I like to think he is imagining being on a ship, sailing away from his unhappiness, to an enchanted land where boys like him are normal.

Mama notices me looking around; she knows me well. 'Sarah took him upstairs.'

'Oh, Mama, he's no trouble. He would love to sit and just watch you and Dorothy. He would never hurt her; he was only stroking her cheek this morning.'

Mama's face flushes red and she pulls Dorothy even tighter to her breast. 'I've told you, Lizzie. I don't want him near her. He unsettles me and that is not good for the baby. It doesn't matter where he is, he is not aware of his surroundings.'

I want to scream at her, 'Of course he is!' but I say nothing. Mama is dead set against him and has been since she realised, when he was but a few months old, that he was 'not right.' Nothing I say or do will ever change her antipathy towards him, her irrational fear of him. Bobbit only remains in the house because Papa has always refused to send him away and I have always been willing to look after him.

Once Dorothy is replete and winded I hold her whilst Mama goes to her room, followed by Sarah with a jug of warm water and a pile of clean linen. Dorothy is asleep; Mama says all babies spend their first months either feeding, sleeping or filling their napkins. Her hair is almost black, like mine, but Mama says it will fall out and may change colour to the lighter brown of her own, Matthew's and Jamie's. I think Mama would like a little girl that looks like her, what mother wouldn't?

I study Dorothy's face; the more I look the more I am in wonder at her sheer perfection: the arch of her eyebrows; the eyelashes that flutter as her eyes move from side to side - is she dreaming, if so, what of? - the round, pink downy cheeks; the darker pink mouth that trembles and is never still. Her nose twitches, as does mine at the smell that wafts from the nether regions of this perfect specimen.

I take her upstairs. I am suddenly worried that, having never once fallen down them in all my fifteen years, today will be the day when I tumble and Dorothy will smash like a china doll on the hard, quarry tiles. I don't and she doesn't. We arrive at the bedroom safe and sound and I tap on the door, happy to hand Dorothy over to Sarah's welcoming arms. I carry on down to my bedroom, intending to fetch Bobbit back downstairs. The door is ajar but the room seems vacant. Bobbit doesn't normally wander, so I check under the bed, behind the curtains, even inside the blanket box but to no avail.

I hear shuffling overhead and wonder if he has gone up to the next floor. I am surprised if he has, for I rarely go there myself;

it is the domain of Matthew and Jamie. They both have a room up there, another being a store room full of the things we no longer need but can't quite bring ourselves to throw away. Mama insists that the boys keep the rooms tidy themselves, so that Sarah doesn't have to climb up and down another flight of stairs. I hear the shuffling again. There is definitely someone up there and, as far as I am aware, both Matthew and Jamie are still at work.

The stairs are steep and I pull myself up by the wooden handrail. There are only three doors. I am certain that the noises came from one of the bedrooms but I take a peep into the storeroom nonetheless. As expected there is nothing there but dusty old-fashioned furniture, broken toys and stale air that hasn't moved for many a month. I cross the small landing to one of the other doors. It is closed shut so I doubt Bobbit is inside, but I open it even so. If I had not already known it to be Matthew's room I could have guessed from its almost monastic tidiness and austerity. I can see at a glance that Bobbit is not here. I close Matthew's door again and go to the other door, which I now notice is slightly ajar and step into Jamie's space. It reflects his character, just as Matthew's does his: it's untidy, disorganised and has an unpleasant smell.

Bobbit is sitting on the floor, stroking and talking to Thomasina, our cat, so named after we realised that the kitten we thought was a tom, was nothing of the sort. I can see that she is shivering and assume that something startled her, causing her to rush up here in a panic, and that Bobbit must have seen her and followed her. They are not making the purring noise of contented felines, but rather the mewing and clicking of two cats deep in conversation. I can almost see the tenseness leave Thomasina's body as she relaxes into the shape of a crescent moon on Bobbit's lap.

'You're a good boy, Bobbit. The animals understand you, even if humans don't.' Before I can suggest that he brings the cat back down, I hear footsteps coming up the stairs, the door is flung open and Jamie stands, open-mouthed. He drops his leather bag at his feet, the paper contents spilling out over the floor.

'What the hell are you doing in my room?' He is shouting, although there is no need for him to do so; I have perfect hearing and am but a few feet away from him.

I feel guilty for no reason and blurt out my excuse. 'Bobbit must have followed Thomasina up here. I came to bring them down. We will be gone in just a few seconds. There is no need to shout.'

'There is every need to shout. This is *my* bedroom and I don't allow *anyone* in here. Do you hear? Especially not you and not him!'

I now also feel the need to shout. 'Stop it Jamie! Stop being so horrible all of the time. Neither of us is doing any harm, especially Bobbit. He is just comforting the cat. Why are you always so cruel?'

Jamie's face is dark red, 'You think I'm being cruel? What about this?' He turns on me and slaps me so hard that if it had not been for the muscles in my neck my head would have spun round and round, just like the globe in Papa's study. I am shocked into silence, as he is. All I can hear is the ringing in my ears and then a low, threatening growl. At first I think it must be the cat but then I realise it's coming from Bobbit. He has removed Thomasina from his lap and is squatting, like a fox ready to pounce onto an unsuspecting rabbit. He is glaring at Jamie, a ferocious expression on his face, his lips pulled back, revealing his teeth. A small globule of spit falls from his lips and splashes to the floor.

Jamie is looking at his brother, his face a horrified mask. He steps back, getting his feet tangled in the strap of the bag he dropped. I have never seen him look so scared and I cannot resist mocking him.

'You're not frightened of your own, younger brother, are you Jamie?'

'Of course I'm not, but what the hell is he doing? Why is he making that awful sound and sitting like that?'

Bobbit shifts his position and Jamie steps back again, as if he thinks Bobbit really is going to leap up and grab him by the throat.

'He's just showing his displeasure at you hitting me so hard.'

'It wasn't hard, Lizzie, it was just a tap for you being so cheeky.' He raises his voice. 'It wasn't hard, Bobbit, just a loving slap. Stop him making that noise, Lizzie, it's giving me the creeps.'

'You should go to him, help him up. Show you are not scared of him; unless you are?'

He looks at me contemptuously, as I expected he would, and then saunters over to where Bobbit is still crouched, although he has stopped the growling. They both stare unblinking at each other for a moment and I take the opportunity to pick up one of the sheets of paper that has fallen out of Jamie's bag; I'll read it tonight. Bobbit curls one arm around Thomasina and then allows Jamie to help him to his feet. Jamie releases the arm as if it is burning him. 'Take him out of here now.' He looks at me unblinkingly then leaves. Jamie's eyes are the same hazel colour as Mama's and Matthew's. Whenever I look into Matthew's eyes I see dappled sunshine in a woodland glade but in Jamie's I see the cold dankness of rotting leaves.

Jamie is already in the kitchen by the time Bobbit and I get there; he is in full flow, telling the story from his point of view. 'He was like a wild animal, Mama, he was growling, baring his teeth and frothing at the mouth like a rabid dog. I tell you, Robert is getting dangerous and something needs to be done about him.'

I go up to him and punch him hard on his upper arm. 'Stop it, Jamie, stop lying to Mama and Papa.'

He turns on me, his eyes dark with anger. 'I'm not lying. Was he, or was he not, crouched ready to pounce, growling like a wolf. And wasn't he frothing at the mouth?'

'He was squatting on the floor, yes, but he was growling more like old Mr Peters' spaniel, than a wolf. And a dribble of spit is hardly frothing at the mouth.'

I see Papa's lips twitch, but Mama remains stern and unsmiling.

'I don't think he would actually have attacked you.'

'You don't *think* he would have?'

'Did you explain to Mama and Papa why Bobbit acted like he did?' Jamie purses his lips. 'No, I didn't think you had. Jamie slapped me, hard. Bobbit was just trying to protect me. It is Jamie who is dangerous, with his temper and his lashing out at the slightest provocation, not Bobbit.'

Jamie narrows his eyes and glances quickly at the crib where Dorothy is sleeping. 'What if you pick up Dorothy and he thinks she is attacking you? What if he thinks he needs to protect you from her?'

I hear Mama gasp at this ridiculous scenario, and realise that he has added another reason for Mama to revile her youngest son. 'Francis, I knew this would happen one day, but no, you insisted that on keeping him here as if he were normal. Now look at him, a danger to the whole family.'

I am overwhelmed with the unfairness of it all and shout out my frustration. 'You have never loved him as you aught! If you had had your way, he would have been sent to an institution when he was just a baby, or even worse. He is a harmless, caring little boy who saw Jamie hurt me and showed his anger in the only way he knew how. He is no more a danger than Dorothy is. It is Jamie who should be punished; he is the one in the wrong.'

I stop to take breath and Papa steps forward, holding up his hands as if to ward off the onslaught of angry words. 'Enough, all of you! Jamie, you should never have slapped Lizzie.'

'She provoked me. They shouldn't have been in my room and she was cheeky.'

'Silence! There is never a good reason for striking your sister, do you hear me?'

I nod and grin at Jamie, feeling vindicated.

'Lizzie, you should not provoke your brother and Robert acted in an unacceptable manner. You need to control him better and make sure he never acts in such a way again. I will not have your mother distressed in this way.'

Dorothy has woken and is whimpering, doubtless because she is hungry rather than being upset by the antics of her older siblings. I can see that Mama is upset; her pallor is pale and she is biting her bottom lip as if to stop herself from crying.

'Oh, Mama, I'm sorry for my stupid, thoughtless words. I didn't mean them, not any of them. Do you forgive me, please?' I hug her, but she stands as if made of stone and doesn't respond. I look at Papa who nods his head towards the door, indicating that we children should leave.

When Bobbit and I get to our bedroom, Jamie is leaning against the door frame. 'What's that in your pocket, little sis?'

It's the sheet of paper I had picked up from Jamie's bedroom floor; I pull it out unthinkingly. I go to unfold it but Jamie snatches it from my hand, but not before I have seen the words 'REMEMBER PETERLOO!' at the head of the page.

'You've taken to stealing my things, as well, have you?'

'Don't be ridiculous, Jamie. I picked it up off the floor earlier. I just wondered what sorts of things you print. What is it, anyway?'

'It's none of your business, that's what it is.'

'Are you printing off stuff that you shouldn't be, Jamie? Would Papa approve?'

Jamie steps up to me so close that I can feel his hot breath on my cheek and smell the cheese he had eaten earlier. 'I am printing pamphlets for some men who pay me well. That is my job; I print things for other people. They can be selling new-born babies for all I care; all I am concerned about is the money they pay. There is nothing Papa needs to approve or disapprove of. He has enough to worry about at the moment, so you won't say anything will you? Because if you do, I'll tell him that I saw you kissing John in the most brazen manner.'

I gasp at his audacity. 'What do you mean? I have never kissed or been kissed by John, or any other boy for that matter. Why do you always have to tell tales and be so horrible all the time? Why can't you be more like...'

'Like dear brother Matthew? I think God used up all the niceness on him, there was none left for me. Anyway, I have no desire to be an underpaid vicar; I am going to make my fortune in business. So, I won't tell Papa about you kissing John, if you keep quiet about me printing off a few political pamphlets. Agreed?'

Why should I agree with his silly lies? I have done nothing wrong and my instinct is to refuse. But what if Papa believes him and confronts John? That would be too mortifying and John certainly doesn't deserve such treatment. I can't let that happen.

'I agree.'

Chapter 5

October 1822

'Three years? Don't you mean three months?'

Matthew and Papa avoid eye contact but Jamie looks at me directly and sneers.

'Oh, Lizzie, you are such a fool, don't you know anything? It takes years, not months, to get a degree - three to be precise.'

'I'm not a fool, Jamie, don't call me that. Why does it take so long? Matthew, you know as much as the Reverend Stephenson, why do you need to go to university at all?'

'In order to be a vicar I have to be ordained, and in order to be ordained I have to have a degree, which, as Jamie says, takes three years. I don't make the rules, Lizzie, I just have to follow them if I want to serve God.'

'They're not God's rules, though are they? I'm sure God doesn't expect you to go away for three years to learn how to serve Him; He just expects you to have a good heart and to love people, which you do.'

Papa looks at me crossly. 'That's enough, Lizzie. It's not our place, and certainly not yours, to question the rulings of the Church. We will miss him, of course we will, but I can think of no better way to spend some of my grandfather's bequest than on giving Matthew, and James, of course, the opportunity to become whatever they want to be. It will be a wonderful experience for Matthew. He'll meet some fascinating people and learn so much more than I can ever teach him.'

Jamie gives a snort of laughter. 'And, of course, when he does become a vicar it won't be here in Wednesbury. It depends where there is a vacancy but it could be anywhere: Scotland, London, or Cornwall. You had better make the most of him whilst he's here because once he's left you may never see him again!' Jamie leaves the table, chuckling to himself, followed quickly by Papa, who stops and pats my shoulders but then goes to spend some time with his less problematic daughter.

Matthew and I sit in silence until Sarah has cleared away the dinner things.

'I won't be gone forever, Lizzie. I may be able to come home during the three years, but certainly after I have left and before I go to my own parish. Three years is not so long. Maybe you could come and visit me? You might even be able to go on one of those steam trains that they say will soon replace the horse and carriage.'

'Don't be ridiculous; I would never be allowed to travel all that way and anyway, I don't want to have to go anywhere, by horse or by steam train. I don't even want to think of living here when you're not around. You're the only one who listens to me and doesn't treat me like a child; you're the only one that helps me with Bobbit; you're the only one who teaches me things.' I find my throat is too full of tears to carry on listing the reasons why he shouldn't leave me.

'Oh, Lizzie, you don't need me as much as you think. You are a strong girl and will cope perfectly well. Before long you will marry and set up your own home and then you will have someone else to care for you and for you to care for. Wipe those tears now and let's go and spend some time with Mama and little Dorothy.'

#

Bobbit is restless tonight. I believe he senses the atmosphere in the house and today it has been full of disquiet and tension. He has kicked off the covers and his eyes follow me as I move about the room. I read into them a yearning that no one else ever sees. He moans quietly to himself. I put the blanket back over him and he plucks at it as if removing bits of thread. I sit down on the floor next to him and take one of his hands in mine.

'Husha, Bobbit, husha. Shall I tell you a story?' My stories always seem to settle him. It's probably just the sound of my voice but I like to think he understands. I ponder a while then start, the words forming of their own accord.

There was once a family who lived in a small village. The father was a well-liked teacher and the mother cared for two sons and a daughter. They were a very happy family, made even happier when another son was born, who they named Rupert. The baby was healthy and grew well, especially his voice! At only a few months old he was chattering away to himself and to anyone who would listen. One day, the daughter, Emily, was sitting in the sunshine with the baby under an old oak tree. They were listening to the blackbirds singing when suddenly Rupert started singing, just like them. After that they couldn't stop Rupert from singing all day long, not that they wanted to, for he sounded beautiful and he made everyone happy.

One day, the whole family were having a picnic by the river and enjoying the sound of the three year old Rupert mimicking the song birds that lived in the hedges and trees. Suddenly, just when his little mouth was open at its widest, a small sprite dashed out from under a hedge, jumped onto the boy's chest, thrust a hand into his mouth and stole his voice! They all looked in horror as the little sprite dashed back under the hedge and disappeared from view. They all searched high and low for it but they all knew, with heavy heart that it would have gone back to the mountains. They knew the sprites lived in the caves at the top of the mountains and were naughty but surely not this naughty?

From that day onwards Rupert grew thinner and thinner, paler and paler and was as silent as a stone.

Everyone missed his merry chatter and his beautiful singing. Just a few days afterwards they heard that the King and Queen's only daughter had had her voice stolen also and that there was a large reward for anyone who retrieved it. The elder son

32

volunteered to go on the search, his eyes gleaming at the thought of all the gold he would win. So he set off, with a large number of other young men including the King and Queen's only son. Emily's brother had a few coins in his pocket to buy food en-route, and a knife to hold to the sprite's throat.

After just a few days some of the young men drifted back, including the eldest son and the Prince, embarrassed at their failure, telling of the hardships they had suffered, the treacherous mountains that were impossible to climb and the lack of evidence that sprites lived there. Some of the young men never returned at all.

After a few months, when it was obvious that none of the young men were going to return with the voices, the King increased the amount of the reward.

The second eldest son volunteered to go on the search, his eyes gleaming at the thought of all the gold he would win. So he set off, with a large number of other even younger men. He had a few coins in his pocket to buy food en-route, and a knife to hold to the sprite's throat.

After just a few days some of the even younger men drifted back, including the second eldest son, embarrassed at their failure, telling of the hardships they had suffered, the treacherous mountains that were impossible to climb and the lack of evidence that any sprites lived there. Some of the even younger men never returned at all.

After another few months, when it was obvious that none of the even younger men were going to return with the voices, the King increased the amount of the reward.

This time nobody volunteered to go - apart from Emily. Everyone laughed at her and her parents and her elder brothers begged her not to go. All the time the young men and the even younger men had gone off on their searches, Emily had been finding out as much as she could about the sprites, where and how they lived. She was very determined and loved her younger brother very much and wanted him to be happy again, which meant getting his voice back for him. There was no money left and she set off with just a piece of bread and cheese to nourish her and no knife to hold to the sprite's throat – but she had a plan.

At the first village she came to she offered her services at cleaning, laundering and mending, in order to earn a few coins to buy more food so that she could move onto the next village. In this way she travelled slowly but surely, from village to village until she reached the last village before the mountains where the sprites were supposed to live. By this time she had enough food to last her a few days and enough coins to buy a mountain goat that was big enough to carry her on its back. The mountain goat knew all the trails that were invisible to the human eye, and slowly but surely, it climbed up the mountain, bearing Emily on its back. Emily had to avert her eyes as she passed the bodies of the young men and the even younger men, who had had plenty of courage but not enough foresight to have a plan.

After many days the goat led her to the mouth of a cave, right at the top of the highest mountain. Emily hid behind a rock and peered inside. It was just as she had thought; it was an absolute mess and she smiled when she heard some of the younger sprites complaining at how horrid the food tasted. Emily stood up and walked bravely into the cave. The sprites were amazed at a human being coming into their domain and encircled her, prodding at her and quizzing her as to what she was doing there.

Emily smiled kindly at them and said that she was lost and could she stay with them for a while if she promised to tidy up their cave and cook them some decent meals. Now the sprites, as she had learned, were indeed very untidy and not very good cooks and they jumped at the chance of having someone clean up for them and yes, how wonderful it would be to eat a decent meal. So they welcomed Emily with open arms and she spent the next few days sweeping and scrubbing, peeling and baking, gathering and bottling and very soon she was much loved by all the sprite families that lived in the cave. They all agreed that she was the best thing that had ever happened to them and they were very much in her debt.

Of the sprite who had stolen her brother's and the Princess's voice there was no sign, but Emily was patient and had her plan.

Some time later she heard of a sprite, who was going from cave to cave, earning money by his beautiful singing. He was called 'the Blackbird,' because that is what he sounded like. Emily hugged herself in glee - this must be the sprite who had stolen her brother's and the Princess's voice and he was coming to their cave that very night.

Emily sat in a circle with all the sprite families and clapped when the sprite families clapped and smiled and nodded in agreement that yes indeed, the sprite known as 'the Blackbird' had a truly wonderful voice. She served him her tasty broth and offered her soothing drink when his throat was dry. And mopped his fevered brow and cleaned up his vomit when he was violently ill during the night. And continued feeding him her tasty broth and offering her soothing drink over the next few days as she mopped his fevered brow and cleaned up his vomit. Everyone was very worried about him - all except Emily who just smiled gently and carried on looking after him. Everyone agreed that they were all even more in her debt.

After two whole weeks 'the Blackbird' began to feel a bit better and after three weeks he was fully recovered, all, everyone agreed, due to Emily's loving ministrations. 'The Blackbird' was indeed grateful and promised he would give her whatever she asked for in order to repay her kindness. She smiled sweetly. 'You can repay me by giving back to me my brother's and the Princess's voice that you stole.' At first the sprite refused but when the others heard that he refused to honour his promise they threatened to stone him to death, which is the sprite way. So, in the end he coughed up her brother's voice and put it into one box, and coughed up the Princess's voice and put it into another

35

box. He then slunk away never to be seen again, for although sprites were naughty they were not so very naughty as he had been.

Emily stayed a few days more, teaching the sprites how to keep the cave clean and how to cook tasty meals. Then she said her farewells and made her way home, in the same way as she had come out all those months earlier.

The first thing she did when she got to her own village was to go home. She was very surprised to find that she had in fact been away for seven years! Her parents were now white haired and in deep mourning for their daughter, who they were sure was dead. Rupert was still thin and still pale and still silent. The whole family, though, were overjoyed when they realised Emily had returned and even more overjoyed when she gave her younger brother a box and told him to open it near to his open mouth. When he did as he was told out flew his voice and straight down his throat! Rupert was very surprised. He tried to speak. His voice was a bit scratchy but after a bit of practise he sounded just like his old self, just a bit older, and very soon he was singing like a blackbird, like a thrush, like a nightingale, as if nothing had ever happened. How happy they all were.

Then Emily went to the palace. The King and Queen were white haired and the Princess was still thin and still pale and still silent. They were pleased to see Emily and then overjoyed when she gave the Princess a box and told her to open it near to her open mouth. When she did as she was told out flew her voice and straight down her throat! The Princess was very surprised. She tried to speak. Her voice was a bit scratchy but after a bit of practise she sounded just like her old self, just a bit older, and very soon she was chattering away as if nothing had ever happened.

When the King handed over the very large reward, Emily nearly refused it but then she accepted it and spent the money on setting up a school to teach girls how to think for themselves. Her first student was the Princess.

When the Prince asked her to marry him she refused him, for she didn't love him.

Bobbit is still awake. He looks at me with eyes bright with tears then I am sure he smiles before he drops off to sleep.

I have been aware of Matthew standing in the doorway for quite a while. 'You tell a good tale, Lizzie, although your insistence on the hero always being a girl wouldn't go down well with the general public.'

'Why, Matthew? Why shouldn't girls go on quests, vanquish sprites, win rewards, marry who they want?'

'As Timothy says, "Let a woman learn quietly with all submissiveness. I do not permit a woman to teach or to exercise authority over a man; rather she is to remain quiet."'

There are times I wish Matthew didn't have a Bible quote for every occasion.

'Does it really mean in this day and age that all women everywhere have to be submissive to all men everywhere? Surely God must realise that not all men are strong, just as not all women are weak; that women have brains too and can think for themselves?'

'Lizzie! You really must learn not to question God's word. The rules of society, which we all must follow, are based on the teachings of the Bible. Do you remember the story of "Patient Griselda"?'

'Yes, of course I do. If I had been Griselda I would never have handed over my children to be killed with nary a complaint. What a despicable man the husband was! How can anyone say that women should all be like Patient Griselda? Should all men be like the husband also? Where does it say in the Bible that husbands should treat their wives badly; that fathers should pretend to kill their children but actually send them away for years on end; that husbands should pretend to divorce their wives; that fathers should pretend to marry their daughters and all, all just to test the wife? How dare he? The more I think about it, the angrier I get.'

'Oh, Lizzie! You think too deeply. Just accept that God and society desire women to be patient, caring, understanding and quiet. As you are with Bobbit, so should you be with everyone. Let's not argue.'

I don't want to argue with Matthew, but I cannot agree with him.

Chapter 6

December 1822

It's Sunday and we are all going to St. Bartholomew's. Although it's late November and a blustery, drizzly sort of a day, Mama has a sprightly gait and her cheeks are glowing with pleasure as well as with the cold. She and Papa are walking arm in arm at the front of the procession, followed by Matthew and Jamie. Sarah follows carrying a sleeping Dorothy in her arms and I bring up the rear with Bobbit. We are all wearing our best clothes but they are hidden under our winter coats and hats, necessary attire on this typical winter's day. We have plenty of time to get to the church, so the pace is slow, which means that Bobbit and I can keep up with the rest of the family.

'Oh, how good it is to be walking outside and to breathe in the fresh air. I feel as if I have been confined inside for forty months, not forty days. What a lovely day it is.'

We all laugh at Mama's enthusiasm for the cold and damp. Our neighbours smile and wave at us but do not stop to converse, not until Mama has been churched. When we arrive at our destination the Reverend Stephenson greets us and shakes each of our hands, even Mama's.

I had read about the Churching of Mothers in an old book I had found in Papa's study and I whisper to Sarah, 'I thought mothers are considered unclean until they have been churched, but the Reverend just shook Mama's hand and let her straight in. Shouldn't she have been sprinkled with holy water first and then be allowed to enter?'

Sarah shakes her head. 'No, that was what used to happen, years ago, hundreds of years ago. These days we are a lot more modern and churching is now a celebration and a thanksgiving for the mother's survival. Take Dorothy from me please, Lizzie, I need to go and sit with your mother in the churching pews by the altar. By rights, it should be the midwives who sit with her, but the Reverend Stephenson says it is perfectly acceptable for me to do so.'

We are not rich or important enough to have our own pews, not like the mine and factory owners, but we manage to all sit together: Papa, Jamie, Matthew, Bobbit and lastly me, with Dorothy. Bobbit is fidgety and I hope I don't have to take him out. The Reverend Stephenson projects his voice well and his words echo off the stone walls and up into the lofty roof. Once the churching part of the service is over I soon get bored and I amuse myself, as I am wont to do, by giving life to the stone effigies that lie recumbent on their table tombs. I image them standing up, shaking off their marble attire and then carrying on with their lives as if they had not been dead for hundreds of years. I'm afraid I snort with laughter at the image of a knight hobbling around lacking a foot and wielding a pointless sword, both literally and figuratively.

My reverie is interrupted by Matthew reaching over and tapping me on the shoulder. Bobbit is rocking backwards and forwards and kicking the pew in front of him with each swing. A few members of the congregation turn to look, their expressions showing a distinct lack of Christian tolerance and forgiveness. I hand Dorothy to Matthew then take Bobbit by the arm and coax him out of the pew. We walk down the aisle to the back of the church; luckily the hearty hymn-singing drowns out the sound of our footsteps on the tiled floor. I keep my head bowed, not wanting to see any disapproving looks, but a movement at the end of one of the pews near the back catches my eye, and I smile as John steps out, takes Bobbit's other arm and accompanies us.

The door opens with a groan, which reverberates around the church, filling in the silence between the end of the hymn and the start of the Reverend Stephenson's next address. We squeeze out as quickly as we can, letting the door bang behind us, then walk far enough away so that John's and my laughter won't be heard. Bobbit, of course, shows no sign that he is the cause of both my embarrassment and amusement.

'Oh, John, whatever will people think of us?'

'They can think what they like, Miss Elizabeth, they usually do.'

'I do wish you'd call me Lizzie. Surely we know each other well enough after three years for you to call me Lizzie?'

'That would not be right, Miss Elizabeth. You are the daughter of a respected teacher and the granddaughter of the gentry; I am a carpenter and the son of a carpenter; it is only proper for me to call you Miss Elizabeth. The only time when it would be correct for me to call you, well, anything other than Miss Elizabeth, would be if we were married.' He blushes at such a thought.

'I can't imagine anyone ever wanting to marry me. Matthew says I'm too independent and Jamie says I'm too ugly. I'm doomed to stay living at home looking after Bobbit until I die.' I sigh dramatically.

'I know you are teasing with me, Miss Elizabeth. You know full well that there are many families in this town who would be glad to have you as a daughter-in-law one day.'

'You mean the mine owners or the factory owners?'

'Aye.'

'Well I certainly don't ever want to be part of their family. If I ever get married, which I think is most unlikely, it will not be for status or money or any reason other than love. If I love a man, it won't matter if he is a collier or a boatman or a shopkeeper.' Or a carpenter.

We are silent for a few minutes, then I recall something I want to ask John.

'John, could I commission you to make something for me? Matthew is going to Cambridge University in September and I want to give him a gift. I thought a box for his coins, tie pins, cufflinks and crucifix and other small things men have. Do you think that would be useful for a man away from home?'

'It sounds like a very useful gift, Miss Elizabeth. I can make a box about so long,' he holds his hands, about two spans apart, 'and so deep,' he now holds up one hand with his fingers close together. 'I'll make partitions inside so that he can keep things separate. Would you like his initials engraved on the lid?'

'Yes, please. Can you put M. F. H. for Matthew Francis Hayes. Francis is my father's name, you know. Do you want me to write the letters down?'

Today seems to be a day when John is in a perpetual blush. 'There is no need for that, Miss Elizabeth. Do you have any preference for the type of wood?'

'I have to admit that I don't know what types there are. Can I leave it to you to decide?'

'Of course, Miss Elizabeth, we have a good selection in the workshop.'

'Matthew is going in the first week of September, that's enough time isn't it?'

'No problem, Miss Elizabeth. No problem at all.'

We have walked all around the church and are now back at the front door, which is suddenly flung open, releasing a burst of sound as the final hymn is bellowed out by the congregation, doubtless relieved that the end is nigh.

John releases Bobbit's arm and steps out of the way as the Reverend Stephenson stands by the entrance to shake the hand of the congregation as each member exits. I wait a long time for the family to appear; I am chilled to the marrow and stamp my feet to get some warmth into my frozen toes. They eventually come out; Mama is surrounded by a group of women, who are chattering away to her and catching up on over a month's worth of gossip. She looks so happy that I feel a surge of love for her and can almost forgive her for her attitude towards Bobbit.

When we are all back home we sit in the parlour to reminisce about the churching that happened all of two hours previously.

'Did I miss anything when I took Bobbit out?'

Everyone shook their heads, except Matthew. 'There was one interesting thing. The Reverend has invited everyone to a talk next Sunday afternoon, when some men are coming from London. Apparently they're travelling around England trying to recruit missionaries to go to Africa.'

'Missionaries? Why is the Reverend Stephenson letting Methodists into his church?'

Matthew laughed. 'Not all missionaries are Methodists, Lizzie. These men are from the Church of England. I think the Reverend would like as many people to go as possible.'

'Can I go, Mama?'

'Why on earth would you want to know about missionaries, Lizzie? Are you thinking of becoming one?' Everyone laughs at the very idea.

The thought has never crossed my mind, but why shouldn't I be one? 'No, of course not, Mama, but I am interested in learning new things and I would be one more in the audience.'

Mama nods and gives her consent.

'Matthew, where exactly is Africa? Is it much further than London?'

Jamie, who has been silent throughout, suddenly lets out a hoot of derision and eyes me pityingly. 'You are so incredibly ignorant, Lizzie. Fancy not knowing where Africa is.'

Papa looks crossly at his second born. 'That's not fair, Jamie. Lizzie doesn't know where Africa is because she has never been told. You wouldn't know if I hadn't taught you and made you colour all the countries in. Her lack of knowledge is my fault, not hers. Come with me, Lizzie, I'll show you where it is.'

We go into his study and Papa slowly spins the globe then stops it with his finger. 'You see this little pink blob? That's Britain. That dot there is London and we live about here.' He

43

moves his finger very slightly to the middle of the pink shape. He then slowly moves his finger down, across a patchwork of colours. 'This whole area here is Europe and these countries are Germany, France, Spain and Portugal. Jump over this bit of water, which is called the Strait of Gibraltar, and you are in the continent of Africa. There are many countries that make up Africa, but I think the Reverend said they would be sending the missionaries to Sierra Leone, which is here.' He stabs an orange area not that much smaller than Britain, about a third of the way down on the left hand side.

I study the globe intently. The scale is so small that even a town the size of Wednesbury can't be shown. I know that London is many days travel from here but on the map it is less distance than the fingernail of my little finger. 'Africa is a very big place and Sierra Leone is a long, long way away.'

'Yes it is. But the people that live there don't know about God and they need to be taught that He loves everyone, wherever they live and however far from London they are.'

Papa gives the globe a spin and I watch mesmerised as the multicoloured countries merge into one formless, sandy mass.

Chapter 7

December 1822

The church is full, not, I suspect, with people who have any desire to become missionaries themselves, but with those who desire to be on the good side of Reverend Stephenson. Neither Jamie, Sarah nor Mama could be persuaded to come, so it is just me, Papa and Matthew. We are sitting near the back and I take pleasure in focussing on the back of John's head, a few rows in front. His hair curls over the collar of his shirt in a very charming manner. There are three men sitting in a row at the front of the church. All are similarly attired in black suits and tall, black silk hats, but physically they are very different. The Reverend Stephenson has introduced them but I cannot remember their names, so in my head I refer to them as Mr Round, Mr Middleman and Mr Lean.

Mr Lean stands and waits for the shuffling, rustling and whispering to cease.

'Good afternoon, ladies and gentlemen, thank you kindly for coming out on this cold, damp afternoon. We very much hope that you will allow us to plant a tiny evangelical seed that will, in some of you at least, grow to fruition.' He is obviously an experienced orator for his cultured, high-pitched voice can be clearly heard by those of us at the back. 'Many thanks also to the Reverend Stephenson for allowing us to come to this most beautiful church, built to the glory of God many hundreds of years ago, and still continuing to be the gathering place of good Christian souls who want to praise God and thank Him for his bounty.' He holds out a hand, indicated his two colleagues. 'We too are building to the glory of God, not using stone and wood, but rather words. I am sure you all know your Bible, but let me remind you of what John says in chapter 1, verse 1, "In the beginning was the Word, and the Word was with God, and the Word was God," and in verse 14, "And the Word was made flesh, and dwelt among us."' He pauses to allow one old lady to finish her coughing.

'What we want to do, ladies and gentlemen of Wednesbury, is to take those words, those words that offer us all the hope of forgiveness, the hope of the resurrection and the hope of life eternal in the happy embrace of the divine Trinity, Father, Son and Holy Ghost. We don't want to keep those words to ourselves. According to Mark chapter 16, verse 15, Jesus instructs us, "Go ye into all the world, and preach the gospel to every creature." We are here today, ladies and gentlemen to find men who will do as Jesus commands, to take the Word to the world, to those who would otherwise live a life of darkness and hopelessness.'

He stops to take a sip of water, to lubricate his voice which has become deeper over time. People take the opportunity to change position on the hard, wooden pews and to glance at each other.

'So, ladies and gentlemen, as the good Reverend explained, we three are working on behalf of the Church Missionary Society. It was founded in 1799 and was originally called "The Society for Missions to Africa and the East," which I think you will agree, is something of a mouthful.' He pauses for laughter to ripple through the pews. 'So, in 1812 it was renamed and we are now called "The Church Missionary Society," or the CMS, which is even easier to say.' More laughter. 'As members of the CMS we are touring England to try and recruit young men to become missionaries, to go out into the world where they are not yet aware of the one God, His Son and the Holy Ghost. Can you imagine, ladies and gentlemen, not knowing of the Trinity? Can you imagine, ladies and gentlemen, not knowing that God created this world and everything in it? Can you imagine, ladies and gentlemen, not knowing that God sent His only Son to die horribly on the cross for our, yes *our* sins? Can you imagine, ladies and gentlemen, not knowing of the resurrection and the hope of a life everlasting? Can you image, ladies and gentlemen, what it must be like *not* being a Christian?'

I see bonnets and top hats shaking as their owners try and imagine.

'Do not think for one minute, ladies and gentlemen, that taking the Word to these people is an easy task. Let me make it very clear; it is most certainly *not* an easy task. It is hard, very hard. For these people are heathens and believe in multiple gods; they believe in spirits; they believe in good luck charms; they believe in the power of the evil eye.' I smile to myself; most of the congregation believe in these things too. 'We must show these poor people the error of their ways and teach them about the one true God.'

He takes another sip of water, wipes his brow and sits down. Mr Middleman now stands. His voice is deep and pleasant to listen to. I imaging he can be very persuasive. 'And so, ladies and gentlemen, what type of man are we looking for? What type of man will take the Word of God to these poor, unfortunate, ignorant heathens? Well, you can't spread the Word if you don't know the Word, so first and foremost you must know the Bible inside and out and back to front. You!' He suddenly points at someone at the front. 'What's the first verse of the Old Testament?' There is a dreadful silence, broken only by the shuffling of feet and the whisperings of those who know the answer.

'Don't worry sir, I apologise for putting you on the spot. It is, of course, "In the beginning God created the heaven and the earth." In order to be a missionary, you would need to be able to tell me that without thinking. As well as knowing your Bible thoroughly, it goes without saying that you must be christened. Lastly, all we ask is that you have the ability to teach others. We don't necessarily ask for a degree, for, as I like to say, a degree does not necessarily a good missionary make. No! What we insist on is a good Christian soul, who loves God, wants to serve

God and is willing and able to share his love with people who don't yet understand. However, these people will not convert, just like that.' He clicks his fingers. 'You must be tenacious; you must not give up at the first obstacle; you must have faith, not only in God, but in your role as a missionary. You, sir!' He points at a young man sitting about three pews back. 'Do you have the makings of a missionary? Or you, sir?' He points to another. 'Or you, sir?' I feel Matthew stiffen beside me as the finger points at him, then moves on.

'Or madam, do you perhaps have a son or a nephew who might be of the right mettle?' His finger moves along the rows and as he fires out his questions, each person shifts guiltily under his fierce gaze. This is not what they have come for. Then suddenly he drops his finger and smiles. 'Thank you, ladies and gentlemen; are there any questions? If so, my colleague will be happy to answer them.' He sits, takes out a large white handkerchief and wipes his whole face, which I can see is running with perspiration.

It is Mr Round who now stands and waits expectantly. I think everyone is still in shock from Mr Middleman's onslaught and there is an embarrassed silence for a few minutes. Then a hand is tentatively raised. I can't see who it is but he sounds young, perhaps Matthew's age.

'I just wondered, sir, how one would get to Africa? Would one have to pay for oneself?'

'A very good question, sir, and the answer is "no." The Society will pay all travel costs within reason. However, we are totally dependent on donations so we do ask those of you here today, who are not able to take up the challenge of being an actual missionary, to support the Society by making a contribution. It is only by the support of generous people like yourselves that we can afford to pay for our young men to get them to the countries where they can do God's work. If you were to go, sir, we would pay for your travel, but we would not, for instance, pay for your wife, Mother, Father, sisters, brothers or cousins, unless they too had been accepted to be missionaries, of course.' He pauses for laughter that is slow in coming.

Another hand shoots up. 'What do the heathens look like? Are they the same as us?' I see people nodding; it is obviously something many of them want to know.

'They are just like us, dear lady. They have two arms, two legs upon which they walk, two eyes, one nose, one mouth. They have a heart, lungs, liver. The only difference is the colour of their skin.' There is a murmuring and looks of confusion are shared. 'In Africa, the people have dark skin, almost black.'

'Like the miners?' someone shouts out.

'No, sir. Not like the miners, for their blackness washes out. No, the skin of the Africans is black and cannot be made white. Their hair too is black and wiry. But their blood is red, just like ours. It is the blackness of their soul that we can make white, by taking the Word of God to them, for none of us must ever forget that they are still the children of God, whatever the colour of their skin.'

There are more questions on a practical level by men who, I am sure, have no intention of becoming missionaries. I don't really listen as I am trying to pluck up the courage to ask a question of my own. I take a deep breath and raise my arm. I am not noticed and I begin to retract it sheepishly when Matthew calls out loudly, 'Over here, sir, my sister would like to ask you something.' All heads turn in my direction and I feel the heat in my cheeks. Matthew whispers to me to stand up.

'Yes, young lady? What is it you would like to know?'

My mouth is dry and I worry that the words will come out like dust and get blown away by my breath.

'Don't be shy, we are all friends here.'

I swallow, take a deep breath then blurt out, 'Do you accept women as missionaries? Single women?'

I hear snorts and sniggers and the word 'ridiculous'.

49

'That's a very good question and thank you for asking it. The honest answer is that we haven't as yet, but I see no reason why we wouldn't. If a young lady meets all the criteria as already stated and she can prove that she has a true vocation to be a missionary, then I see no reason why she would not be accepted.' He turns to his colleagues, who nod their heads, albeit hesitantly. 'She would have to be a very remarkable woman, of course. Let me assure you that we do not just send people to these countries and leave them high and dry. They are part of a community and often go round in pairs for safety and support. We take good care of them. After all they are God's disciples, doing God's work; they are our jewels. Now, if there are no more questions, I would like to thank you on behalf of my colleagues and of the Church Missionary Society. If anyone wants to come and speak to us please do so now, or we are staying with the good Reverend until Wednesday, when we will be continuing our journey. I am sure he will not mind if you come to visit.' The good Reverend looks as if he does mind but manages a smile to show his generous spirit.

We leave once Papa has put some notes into the collection box; we are keen to get back home, into the warm.

'Well done, Lizzie, for asking your question. It was very brave of you.'

'I am not convinced they would actually accept a woman, are you Papa? Mr Round said she would have to be "remarkable." In what way remarkable?'

'Mr Round? It was Mr Cook who said that.'

'Ah, I couldn't remember their names so I thought of them as Mr Lean, Mr Middleman and Mr Round. Whatever his name, he did not convince me that they would ever accept a woman. I don't see why not, though. I think it would be very exciting to be a missionary. I would love to travel through all those countries you showed me, Papa, and teach the people to read the Bible. I could do that, quite easily. I cannot imagine anyone being black all over, can you? Are their ears black? And the palms of their hands? What about the inside of their mouth, is that black too? Is their hair curlier than mine?'

Both Papa and Matthew laugh out loud and I realise that I am prattling like a small child.

'I have no idea which parts of them are black and which are not, Lizzie. I don't suppose the pictures in books actually show the insides of their mouths. What I do know, though, is that the journey to Sierra Leone would be anything but exciting and that you are far too young to be even thinking of becoming a missionary. By "remarkable", I have no doubt that Mr Cook meant she would be very devout, very educated, twice your age and not needed at home. Now, enough of your questions, let's get back and into the warm.'

'You're very quiet, Matthew.'

'I'm thinking, Lizzie.'

'What about?'

'Nothing of any importance.'

Chapter 8

April 1823

'This one looks a possibility, Beatrice, my dear.'

Mama takes the letter out of Papa's hand, ignores the content and goes straight to the signature. She says you can tell more from the last flourish than you can from the whole letter. 'I know the name Nathaniel Whittaker; wasn't he one of your boys when we lived in Mancetter?'

'Yes, I taught him for about six years until he went to university, which was about seven or so years ago. He was a bright one; I thought he would do well.' Papa scans the letter, picking out the salient points. 'He has been teaching Lord Roscoe's twin boys for the last three years and from what I know of his lordship he wouldn't let just anyone tutor them. Now that the boys are off to Eton, Whittaker says he wants to use his skills to educate the lower classes rather than the upper. He heard of my little school here from a Mr Sutton, who was a guest of Lord Roscoe's a few months ago.' He looks quizzically at Mama and me. 'Who on earth is Mr Sutton that he should know of me and the school?'

Mama shrugs but I am able to answer. 'Mr Sutton owns the biggest iron foundry in Wednesbury. He is said to be very rich but he pays his workers a pittance. He has had that huge house built on the land that used to belong to old Farmer Brook. Some say he stole it.'

Papa frowns at me. 'We don't listen to gossip, Lizzie, and we certainly don't spread it around. Many a man's reputation has been ruined due to prattle taken for truth.'

'He has three sons and a daughter, I think. I know the two younger boys; they are mean and make fun of Bobbit at every opportunity. John Goodman told me about when he went to the Sutton house to deliver some furniture he and his father had made. He was not very complimentary about Mr Sutton or his eldest son, Charles. John says they were very arrogant and treated them like dirt.'

Papa frowns. 'I don't know the man, nor am I likely to, but I am grateful to him if he is spreading the word about the school.' Papa returns to reading the letter. 'Nathaniel seems genuine enough. I'll write to him with a few more questions and explain what I will expect him to do and what his remuneration will be. Depending on his response I hope he can start a few months before Matthew leaves so that he can shadow him. I have had a few other responses, but to be honest, my dear, they are not suitable, either too young or too inexperienced, and some of the letters are so badly spelt that I don't see that they could teach anything to anyone.'

I cannot believe my ears. Nothing has ever been said out loud, but I have always assumed that I would take over from Matthew. Why else would he have given me all his text books and sat with me for many an hour, explaining Latin declensions and testing me on the Kings and Queens of England? I try and speak calmly but there are too many impatient words in my mouth and they come tumbling out. 'But Papa, why can't I teach at the school? My grammar and spelling are good and you and Matthew have taught me lots of things. Matthew has given me his text books and I am reading my way through them all, well most of them. I could teach the basics of reading and writing, even Latin, history and arithmetic and I know all the Bible stories. True, I didn't know where Sierra Leone was, but I am a quick learner, you know I am. You wouldn't have to pay me. I know I would make a good teacher, if you would just give me a chance.'

There is a silence, broken only by Mama scratching at some egg that has congealed on the tablecloth. Scritch, scritch, scritch.

Papa eventually gives a cough, small and quiet but one I know instinctively is a prelude to disappointment. 'You know, Lizzie, that I am a great believer in female education and I have made sure that you know more than just how to embroider and play a tune on the piano.' I take a breath but he raises his hand to block my words before they are even formed. 'But, Lizzie, and this is a very big but, my intention was not to prepare you for employment but to open your mind to the world and to feed your craving for knowledge. One day you will marry and I hope you will be able to support your husband intellectually, as well as emotionally.'

'But, Papa, what if I never marry, what is the point of all that knowledge then? Surely it would be a much better for me to help you at the school now? Mama, what do you think?' She continues to scratch at the tablecloth, although the crust is now nothing but fine dust. 'Mama?'

She finally looks at me. 'If you are not here then we will have to put Robert in an institution. Is that what you want? Is that the price you are willing to pay for your dream?'

'Beatrice, my dear, that is a little harsh.'

Mama's head snaps up and she glares at Papa. 'Harsh? Harsh would be leaving me with Robert. I cannot, nay, will not, have care of him.' She turns her glare on me. 'You want to know what I think? I think you need to accept that you are a girl, soon to be a woman, and that as such you have a role to play in society and in the home. You have responsibilities that you cannot just discard when you feel like it. That, Lizzie, is what I think. Now please leave us, I want a private conversation with Papa.'

I could not have spoken even if I wanted to; the words in my throat are as sand and best kept to myself. My cheeks burn with mortification but I manage to walk out of the room with as much dignity as I can muster and I close the door quietly behind me before the scalding tears give up the pretence. I want to scream as loud as I can, sob uncontrollably, gnash my teeth like the mad women in Bedlam that I have read about in one of Matthew's useless books. Instead, I let the tears flow silently unchecked onto my handkerchief then seek the comfort of the kitchen.

Sarah turns from the range, where she is standing stirring a large pot of stew. 'Goodness me, Miss Elizabeth, whatever is the matter? Have you been crying? Has something happened to Mama?'

'No, Sarah. Nothing has happened to Mama, Papa, Matthew, Jamie, Robert or Dorothy, just to me. Insignificant and totally useless me.'

I wish she would come and hug me but she turns back to the range and continues to stir, slowly round and round the pot, making sure nothing sticks to the side and burns.

'Tell me, then.'

So I relate the unfairness of my lot, interspersed with sobs I cannot control. 'It's just not fair, Sarah. Is that all I'm good for, running a house and looking after a freak?' As soon as I say it I clamp my hand to my mouth, too late of course to stop the wicked words. I see Sarah's back stiffen and she glances at Bobbit, who is quietly rocking in his chair in the corner, in a world of his own. Nothing changes in his expression to indicate he has heard his spiteful, thoughtless sister, who speaks without thinking.

I am momentarily speechless, not knowing how to recover the situation and I just stand, staring at Sarah's back. The only sound is the creaking of the rocking chair and the soft, bubbling of the stew.

'I'm sorry. I didn't mean what I said.'

'Then you shouldn't have said it, Lizzie. Those words can never be unsaid nor forgotten. If anyone else had said what you said, you would have given them what for, just like a mother wolf protecting her young.' Sarah finally stops stirring and turns to face me, her face red from the heat of the range, but her eyes colder than I have ever seen them. 'Did you really think that your Mama and Papa would allow you to teach in the school? You have no need to earn your keep; you are a young lady of good birth and your place is in the home. Even if you did not have

Robert to care for, your role would still be here. You need to help your Mama run this household, especially now that she is blessed with Dorothy. When you are older you will run your own household and bring up your own children. That is the God-given role of women, Lizzie, and it is not for you to question it. If you want to do good, then visit the poor, but what they need is victuals and warm clothing, not education.' She turns back to the range and in a softer, kinder voice, bids me take my brother for a walk, for he has been rocking for the last three hours without cease.

It is a lovely day and the spring sunshine is pleasantly warm on my face. Although I am sure Bobbit did not hear my hurtful words, I feel discomfited and am not able to chat to him as I usually do. We make our way slowly and in silence along the canal towpath, stopping only for me to wave to the passing bargemen and for Bobbit to converse with the horses. I remember that after Church the previous Sunday, John had said that the box I had asked him to make for Matthew is finished and I could pick it up at my convenience, so I decide to walk to the workshop.

There are a number of people dawdling leisurely along the towpath, enjoying the spring sunshine. I exchange greetings with those I know and those I don't; good weather always seems to make people more sociable and courteous. Apart from the Sutton boys, that is. Geoffrey and his younger brother, Daniel, are walking slowly towards us, both with sticks in their hand, both knocking the heads off the cowslips and bluebells that grow in profusion along the sides of the path. Their eyes are fixed on me; I can do nothing to avoid them and am forced to stop.

'Good morning, Miss Hayes. A beautiful morning to be out with your pet.'

'It is not a good morning for those poor flowers.'

'There are plenty of them and they feel no pain. Not like if I was to knock your pet's head off.' Geoffrey leers and Daniel, snorts and repeats, 'knock your pet's head off.'

'How very brave of you, to hurt a harmless, defenceless boy, who is younger and smaller than you. But I believe all bullies are cowards at heart; you two are certainly living proof of that.'

'You have a fine way with words, Miss Hayes. We'd love to stand chatting to you for longer wouldn't we Daniel, but we have flowers to behead and so must be on our way.'

Geoffrey gives me a bow and a smirk I would dearly love to obliterate. Daniel follows his brother and stumbles, falling against Bobbit, who in turn staggers dangerously close to the edge of the water. Daniel pulls him back and slaps him heartily on his back. 'Careful there, freak, we don't want you falling in, do we? Although, perhaps it would be a blessing? What say you, Miss Hayes?'

I don't deign to answer and taking Bobbit's hand I continue walking away from them, my lips firmly shut in case an unladylike word should escape. How I despise the Sutton boys.

My bad temper disappears as soon as I enter the Goodmans' workshop. I love this place. Not only because I take pleasure in seeing John and his parents but because of the atmosphere of the place. I like to think that each smell is the very essence of the woods that have been used and that their spirit lies in the curls of shavings that carpet the floor and the tiny particles that dance in the air whilst deciding where to settle. The shop is poorly lit and I have to lead Bobbit carefully around haphazardly piled planks; cuts of tree that are waiting to be carved into something with no function except to decorate a rich man's house; actual tree stumps showing their age and pieces of finished furniture waiting to be collected. Everything is blanketed with the remains of their arboreal brethren and although I try to avoid touching anything my skirt is soon lightened by a layer of pale dust.

Mr Goodman, John's father, is bent engrossed over the bench and has not heard us, although we have not been silent in our negotiation through the workshop. I stand, Bobbit by my side, and wait patiently, having no desire to startle a man with a very sharp chisel in his hand.

There is whistling coming from the back of the shop, followed by the whistler himself. John is as tall as his father, perhaps a tad taller. His face has grown into one of the artefacts and looks as if it has been lovingly carved from wood, oak perhaps, and then planed to smoothness, with the shavings sprinkled onto his head. He sees me and smiles, causing two chiselled creases, one on either side of his mouth.

'Good morrow, Miss Elizabeth.'

'Good morrow, John.'

Mr Goodman stops working at the sound of our voices and comes over to me and takes both my hands in his warm, calloused ones. 'Ah, Miss Elizabeth, how lovely to see you.' He turns to Bobbit and takes the hand that is hanging limply by his side. 'And you too, Master Robert. Have you come for Matthew's box, Miss Elizabeth? John has done a grand job; I couldn't have done it better myself.'

John goes to a small shelf and fetches down a box, which he hands wordlessly to me, his expression one of nervousness and doubt. It is warm to the touch and feels as smooth as glass. I move to stand under a lamp so that I can see it more clearly and I sigh at the sheer beauty of it. I slide my fingers over the natural swirls in the lid then trace out the gothic-style initials M. F. H. And the year 1823 that are of a lighter wood.

'The lid is made of walnut, Miss Elizabeth, and I have inlaid the letters with linden. I was going to carve some flowers as well but I thought the whorls of the walnut were decoration enough. You don't think it too simple?'

I shake my head, unable to find the words for how beautiful I find it. I open the lid and a smell is released from its captivity

58

that reminds me of the damp woods I used to walk in as a child. I hold it to Bobbit's nose and perhaps imagine him taking a deeper breath. Inside the box there are equal sized partitions that can be removed. I turn the box over and see the initials 'J.G.' neatly engraved in one corner and an acorn in the opposite one.

'The acorn is my signature. Father's is an oak leaf.'

'This is truly, truly beautiful, John; exquisite, in fact. It is much, much better than I imagined, and you know what a good imagination I have.'

He looks both pleased and embarrassed at my praise.

Mr Goodman is nodding in agreement. 'It is a fine piece, Miss Elizabeth. Master Matthew should be well pleased with it.'

'Oh, I'm sure he will be. Now, John, how much do I owe you?'

John glances at his father. 'It was a real pleasure to make it, Miss Elizabeth, and good practice. I don't want paying for it.'

'Oh, but you must, otherwise it would be a gift from you, not me. You must have spent hours on it.' Mr Goodman nods. 'It is a beautiful piece of work and you must have recompense, I insist. I cannot take it unless I pay for it.'

John shuffles his feet, disturbing the shavings on the floor.

'You will never make any money if you don't charge!'

John sighs, twists his mouth and wriggles his eyebrows, all signs, I have learned, to indicate that he is thinking.

'All right, Miss Elizabeth, if you insist.'

I open my little bag in which I keep my coins and take out a shilling. 'Is that sufficient?'

'Goodness, no, Miss Elizabeth, that is far too much. Really just a penny is more than enough.'

'A penny? That cannot be enough. Here, take these.' I drop a small handful of pennies onto the top of a cabinet.

John looks uncertainly at his father, who shrugs and nods his head. 'Alright, thank you, Miss Elizabeth. That is most generous. Will you allow me to escort you and Master Robert back home?'

Chapter 9

June 1823

I have already decided not to like Nathaniel Whittaker.

He has come, as arranged, to meet Papa and Matthew, prior to starting at the school tomorrow. It is just me and Mama at the moment and having paid his respects to Mama, Mr Whittaker is now holding my hand and bowing politely. His hand is cool and his nails clean, short and well-manicured; I doubt he has done a day's hard labour in his life and I compare it unfavourable with those of John's, whose are always warm and look as if they have been hewn out of an ancient oak. Mr Whittaker looks at me with eyes the colour of slate and smiles. Others may think him good looking but I consider him to be unctuous. I learned this word recently and I cannot but smile at its appropriateness. Mr Whittaker's smile widens and I blush in mortification that he may think that I am responding to an attraction rather than to an aversion. I pull my hand away quicker than dictated by good manners, causing Mama to narrow her eyes and purse her lips.

The awkward moment is luckily interrupted by the arrival of Papa and Matthew from school and over the next few minutes Mr Whittaker spreads his unctuousness as they shake hands and ask about each other's health. Everyone is finally seated and I plead with my eyes to Mama to be excused but she chooses not to see. I sit, therefore, with my hands neatly folded on my lap whilst Mr Whittaker, the usurper, casts his spell over my family. Matthew showed me a book recently written by two brothers in which they tell folk tales they have collected from ordinary people. It is in German, but there are pictures: one shows a piper playing his whistle and luring a horde of rats away from the village; the next shows the piper's anger when the villagers refuse to pay for this service and the last shows the children happily following his merry tune but presumably they are never seen again. As often happens, this one thought triggers another and I spend the next half-an-hour physically in the parlour but mentally away in an enchanted land.

Conversation over dinner is all about the marvellous Mr Whittaker but I keep my unasked-for opinions to myself. I plead a headache and go to my room and tell Robert the tale the unctuous man has inspired.

There was once a family who were very poor. Although they all worked hard there never seemed to be enough money. Mama stayed at home and mended clothes, made bread and tended to the bees, whilst the father, the two brothers and the young daughter all worked in the mines that belonged to Mr Sutton, who was a mean and cruel man.

The coal is not near the surface like it is here, so the miners had to go deep underground to dig it out. They had to work in the tunnels every day, from dawn to dusk, so they never felt the warmth of the sun's rays nor had to squint at its brightness. Papa and the two brothers chipped at the walls of the tunnel with their picks whilst Alice, the daughter, put the pieces in a basket. When it was full, Alice carried the heavy basket through the long tunnels to the shaft then climbed up a rope ladder to the top, where she emptied the basket onto an ever-growing heap of coal. It was tiring and dirty work but Alice had a beautiful voice and she would cheer herself up by singing of butterflies and bees, sunshine and rain, laughter and tears.

One morning, the family arrived at the entrance to the mine earlier than everyone else. They saw a piece of paper pinned to a post.

REWARD!!

A reward of one hundred, yes one hundred, gold pieces to the man who can rid the mines of the boggarts once and for all.

One hundred gold pieces was more money than the whole family would ever earn in a life time, ten life times! One of the brothers tore down the poster so that no one else could read it and win the reward. No, the money had to be theirs!

That night, after a hard day's work they sat round the table, eating their bread and honey and discussing how they would rid the mine of the boggarts and so win the reward. The father said he would herd them all into a corner then beat them to death with his pick. The eldest brother said he would herd them all into a corner, build a fence and starve them to death. The younger brother said he would herd them all into a corner then set fire to them.

Nobody asked the mother or Alice what they would do; after all they were only females.

The next night, after a hard day's work, the brothers and Alice went home as usual but the father stayed behind in the mine. When everyone had left he took a candle and went deeper and deeper underground to where the boggarts lived. He saw their heels as they ran from him and heard their mocking laughter, but he couldn't round them up in order to herd them into a corner. He grew more and more tired until he stumbled to his knees, dropped the candle and plunged the tunnel into absolute blackness. He felt something sharp in his legs, his arms, his back and he realised in horror that the boggarts were attacking him with their own little picks, just as he had threatened he would do to them. He was so far underground that no one heard his cries so no one came to save him.

The next night, after a hard day's work, one brother and Alice went home as usual but the elder brother stayed behind in the mine. When everyone had left he took a candle and went deeper and deeper underground to where the boggarts lived. He saw their heels as they ran from him and heard their mocking laughter, but he couldn't round them up in order to herd them into a corner. He grew more and more tired until he stumbled over something, his father perhaps, dropping the candle and plunging the tunnel into absolute blackness. He managed to get to his feet again but he didn't see the opening to a deep pit in front of him and he fell and fell and fell until he hit the bottom. He couldn't climb out for the pit was too deep. The boggarts stood around the opening jumping up and down and laughing with excitement. They didn't have to touch this one, he would just slowly starve to death just as he had threatened he would do to them. He was so far underground that no one heard his cries so no one came to save him.

The next night, after a hard day's work, Alice went home as usual but the younger brother stayed behind in the mine. When everyone had left he took a candle and went deeper and deeper underground to where the boggarts lived. He saw their heels as they ran from him and heard their mocking laughter, but he couldn't round them up in order to herd them into a corner. He grew more and more tired until he stumbled over something, his father perhaps, so that the candle tipped over and the flame caught the sleeve of his shirt. Before he could blow it out the flames spread over his whole body and the last he heard was the sound of the boggarts laughing and cheering as he burnt to death, just as he had threatened he would do to them. He was so far underground that no one heard his cries so no one came to save him.

The next day Alice didn't go to the mine but worked with her mother baking bread and collecting honey from the friendly bees. The next night she waited until everyone had left then she went down the shaft, lit a candle and went deeper and deeper underground to where the boggarts lived. She carried a basket of bread spread thickly with honey and she broke off little pieces and dropped them to the floor, all the while singing. One by one the boggarts followed her, tempted by the sweet smell and the sweet sound. When she stopped singing, they stopped following, *so she sang on, although her throat was dry and sore from the coal dust.*

She walked slowly along the tunnels going up all the time, the boggarts following meekly behind, totally mesmerised by her singing. She led them to the bottom of the shaft and up the rope ladder, the boggarts following meekly behind; she led them along the road and past Mr Sutton's house, the boggarts following meekly behind. She led them up hill and down dale, through forest and across moor, along rivers and around lakes, the boggarts following meekly behind. When she got to the sea she continued walking until the water reached the top of her thighs and the boggarts followed meekly behind. But the boggarts were short, shorter than the top of Alice's thighs and they couldn't swim so quietly and with no fuss, they all drowned.

Mr Sutton and his son, Charles, who was very handsome, had followed Alice when they had seen her leading the boggarts away and when they saw that she had rid their mine of them once and for all, the handsome son carried her on his strong shoulders, telling everyone they met that she was a heroine. When they returned home Mr Sutton gave her a bag of gold pieces (not one hundred though, for remember he was a mean and cruel man), and the son asked her to marry him.

Alice laughed in their faces. 'I don't want the reward Mr Sutton. Instead I want you to give all your workers a decent wage so that they might live in comfortable homes and have enough to eat each and every day. And I won't marry you Charles, not until you prove to me that you are a kind man, care for your workers and admit publicly that a girl can do anything a boy does, often better. Even then I may not marry you, for I will only ever marry for love.

#

'Your Mr Whittaker seems a very personable gentleman, Miss Elizabeth.'

'He is not *my* Mr Whittaker, John, and he is not personable, he is unctuous.'

John repeats the word quietly a number of times, rolling the letters around his mouth as if savouring each one. 'And what does unctuous mean exactly, Miss Elizabeth?'

I think a while but cannot find another word to explain. 'It is just what Mr Whittaker is, John, just what he is.'

John glances at me and then returns his gaze to the jars of conserve I have brought for his mother that he is holding in his hands. 'I take it that it's not a nice word, Miss Elizabeth?'

'No, John it is not.'

'Why don't you like him? Master Matthew came into the workshop yesterday and he was telling me that Mr Whittaker is a pleasant gentleman, a very good teacher and boys already love him.'

'Well that just proves my point. That is what happens when someone is unctuous, they wheedle their way into peoples' affections and blind them to their faults with their, well, with their unctuousness.'

I wait for John to show some understanding but the jars of conserve bouncing in his hands reveal his poor attempt not to laugh. 'It's not funny, John. Everyone thinks he is so wonderful but he is doing the job I wanted to do. I could have done it, John, you know I could.'

John suddenly stops laughing and looks at me seriously. 'I know you could, Miss Elizabeth, but, well, it's just not done is it, a young lady like yourself working and in such a place?'

'Who says it's not done, John, who makes these stupid rules? Men, that's who! Women may not be as physically strong as men but we are not stupid, John, and some of us could do so much more than make conserves and tell stories to boys who probably can't hear.'

John remains silent, looking at his feet, which he is shuffling in embarrassment. I replay the words I have said in my head and I realise I sound like a spoilt child who has had her favourite toy taken away. 'Oh don't listen to me, John, I'm being childish. Please don't think that I did not take great pleasure in making the conserve that you are holding in your hands or that I don't love Bobbit dearly, it's just that....'

He takes my hands in his for a second only, then releases them. 'It's just that you want to be the heroine in one of your own stories?'

'Oh, John, that's exactly it.'

Chapter 10

June 1823

Today is my birthday. I have been sixteen years on this earth. Sarah picked some flowers from the garden and put them in my bedroom so that they were the first thing I saw when I awoke. Over breakfast, Mama gave me a cotton handkerchief she purchased from Mrs MacDonald's haberdashery shop, upon which she had embroidered the letter 'E,' in case I should forget who I am.

It has been a week since Mr Whittaker came to Wednesbury and the other members of the family consider him to be the saviour, if not the Saviour. Papa has nothing but praise for his teaching methods, his engagement with the boys, his intellect, his ability to enforce discipline with compassion, even his attire, with Matthew offering no contradiction. My daily habit, weather permitting, was to take Bobbit to meet Papa and Matthew from school and walk back home with them. I saw no reason why the presence of Mr Whittaker should alter my routine, but it has. Mama insists that Mr Whittaker joins us for the evening meal and the three men now stride ahead each day, discussing things edifying and educational no doubt, whilst I fall behind with Bobbit, trying not to drag him faster than his poor legs can go, in an attempt to keep up. I know that I'm a fool to think that they would include me in their conversation, but I am cross that Mr Whittaker has ruined the familial time that I used to enjoy and look forward to.

'Matthew tells me that you are a teller of fairytales, Miss Hayes.'

I am startled from my bitter musings by the voice of Mr Whittaker himself, who I am surprised to see is walking on the other side of Bobbit with one arm linked to his. I do not return his smile. 'I wonder that my brother should talk about me with you Mr Whittaker. You surely have far more interesting things to discuss.'

Bobbit suddenly stops dead, as he is wont to do, and we have to wait whilst he watches as a shaggy mongrel runs past us with a chop in its mouth, followed closely by an irate butcher. Is it my imagination that the dog is grinning as the gap between man and beast gets ever wider? Only when Bobbit is sure that the dog is in no danger of being caught does he restart his slow amble.

'You have an admirable sympathy for Master Robert's needs, Miss Hayes. There are not many who would be so patient.'

'If I didn't care for him, he would be shut away somewhere awful, where there is no sunshine or freedom of any sort and he would be treated like an animal. He may not be like you, Mr Whittaker, but he is still just a boy, one of God's treasures.'

Mr Whittaker looks at me in consternation. 'Please forgive me, Miss Hayes, I was not being facetious in the slightest and meant no offence. My words were most sincere; I have nothing but admiration for you. For the way you care for your brother, I mean.'

I snort internally but tilt my head to indicate acknowledgement of his apology.

'I would be most interested in hearing your fairy tales, Miss Hayes. Matthew says they are, well ...' I do not offer Mr Whittaker any assistance in finding the appropriate word. 'He uses the word "controversial," but perhaps you prefer the word "challenging"?'

I am surprised at his discernment but have no desire to encourage him. 'They are just silly stories, Mr Whittaker, just silly stories written by a silly girl.' We glance at each other at the same time and then quickly away in embarrassment.

'Matthew also says...'

'My goodness!' the words explode out of my mouth, cutting off Mr Whittaker's reminiscences. 'Has Matthew nothing better to do than gossip to a complete stranger about his younger sister?'

We are now at the gate to our house and Mr Whittaker releases Bobbit's arm and quickens his step, his stiff body and clenched fists indicating his anger. He then suddenly stops and turns to me, barring our progress, the colour in his cheeks heightened by more than just fresh air. 'I know you don't like me Miss Hayes, and I know why. Matthew was not gossiping about you, he was merely trying to explain your antipathy towards me, which, I assure you, I do understand. But, Miss Hayes, you cannot blame me for wanting to come and teach at your father's school, nor can you blame me for accepting your father's offer. I have a tremendous respect for him and the life he has chosen for himself and his family. I assure you, Miss Hayes, that there is very little satisfaction in cramming facts into the heads of rich boys, who will use their knowledge as a sign of their supposed superiority rather than using it to improve the conditions of their workers. Your father taught me many years ago that all children, not just those of the moneyed classes, should have the opportunity to be educated. I have been tutor to the rich in order to earn some money but now I want to take an active role in your father's new world. Why should the poor not learn to read and write so that they too may one day enjoy Shakespeare's sonnets or maybe even write their own; why should they not know how many pennies they have in their pocket and what they might purchase with them; why should they not have an understanding of the history of this great country we all live in together? I am sorry you cannot follow your dream, Miss Hayes, and I cannot begin to appreciate the constraints females have to suffer, but hating me will not change anything. I would very much like us to be friends, Miss Hayes, once you have grown up.'

He turns and walks briskly away, leaving me standing bemused and chastened. He stops at the front door, however, and holds it open for us. As we walk past he says quietly, 'I apologise for my words, Miss Hayes, they were said in haste and without thought, please forgive me. What Matthew also told me was that today we are celebrating the day of your birth and I wanted to offer you my felicitations, that is all. I hope you will accept them?'

I nod and offer back a tentative smile, my first small step towards growing up.

Chapter 11

September 1823

'I have a gift for you, Matthew.'

I hold out the wooden box that I had commissioned John to make, as I imagine the magi presented their gifts to the baby Jesus. 'I had this made for you - it is for your small trinkets. Look,' I open the lid for him, 'it is divided so you can keep your odds separate from your ends. It has your initials and the date and,' I turn it over for him, 'it has John's initials on the bottom. You see that acorn, that is his sign and his father's is an oak leaf. That's clever isn't it, John being Mr Goodman's son, and the acorn being -'

'Lizzie, Lizzie, slow down! Let me have a look at it.' He strokes it, as I did when I first held it and holds it to his nose and breathes in deeply. He studies every inch of the outside and then opens the lid, takes out the partitions and puts it back again, nodding all the while. 'An excellent piece of work, just excellent. John is a good craftsman, almost as good as his father.'

I feel as proud as if I had made it myself. 'I'm glad you like it. I'll tell John what you said. Every time you open it I want you to think of me.'

'You silly goose. I don't need anything to remind me of you; you will always be in my heart and mind.' Matthew hugs me and I use his shirt to absorb the unbidden tears. 'Now, I have something for you too.' He picks up something from the table and holds it on the palm of one hand. It is loosely draped with a cloth, which he pulls off with a grandiose flourish. It is a pile of paper, three or four quires thick. Lying on the top is a beautiful quill pen made out of a perfect white feather. I must look puzzled. 'I know you will write to me as part of Papa's letters, but I want you to use these to write down your stories. Some of them are real gems, Lizzie, and should be saved for posterity.'

I pick up the quill and stroke the back of my arm, my skin tingling at the soft caress. I write 'Lizzie' in fancy script in the air, the shaft already like an extension to my hand, so right does it feel. 'Oh, I will! It's a perfect gift, thank you so much, Matthew.' It must have cost him a lot of money.

'All I ask is that you don't make them too outrageous, Lizzie. No number of fairytales that tell of girls doing what boys should do by right, will change the ways things are. You tell a good story but they need to be tempered with a dose of reality and not be too far-fetched. Do you promise?'

I don't want to argue with Matthew on his last day nor do I want to promise something I cannot keep, so I don't reply. Instead I hug him tight, trying to memorise every small detail: his smell; the feel of his bristly chin resting on the top of my head; the strength of his muscles as he embraces me; the sound of his breath. We stand for quite a few minutes, swaying together slightly to music only we can hear. Then he kisses my forehead and pulls himself away.

'I need to finish my packing and I must spend some time with the rest of the family. Remember that I love you and I will be home before you even know I have gone.'

I stand for a moment longer, still feeling his arms around me, the pressure of his lips on my skin, the warmth of his breath on my ear. Oh, Matthew, what am I going to do without you?

#

His departure is a far merrier occasion than any of us thought it would be. The neighbours that congregate outside the Turk's Head, where the stagecoach will leave from, have come to wish him good luck, not to mourn his leaving. They are a jolly crowd, many of the men having already drunk to Matthew's health, many times over by the reek of them. Matthew's face is flushed and he looks a little wild-eyed as he shakes people's hands, kisses proffered cheeks and thanks everyone over and over again for their good wishes and for bothering to come to see him off. He said his farewells to Mama, Dorothy, Bobbit and Sarah back at the house, the weather being too inclement for them to stand outside for too long. Papa is bustling around making sure Matthew's trunk is stowed securely and Jamie is leaning against the side of the coach, his face a picture of indifference and ennui. How I wish it is him leaving and not Matthew; how happy I would be then.

Mr Whittaker is there also with the boys from the school. Despite their number, their natural aptitude for mischievousness and inability to stand still, they are in fact in a controlled line, clapping with great gusto and some, I notice, wiping their snot and tears on their none-too-clean sleeves. Matthew goes to them and shakes each one by the hand and each boy grins at whatever he says to them.

I catch Mr Whittaker's eye and give a small wave. It did not take me long to grow up and realise that I was behaving like a child and that the inequalities of the sexes cannot be lain at his door. I know that Papa was quite right to employ him and he is already a great asset to the school. He is a good conversationalist at the dinner table and, as evidenced by the titters and blushes of any female he comes into contact with, considered to be good looking and a good prospect. I am happy that I now consider him to be my friend.

The driver comes out of the inn, wiping his mouth and pulling his thick coat around him. The crowd pulls back leaving space for father and son to shake hands one more time and for the elder to give a final piece of advice to the younger. Before climbing into the coach Matthew looks slowly around until he finds me. He nods slightly, winks then disappears inside and without any further delay a whip is cracked, the horses roused and the coach trundles off down the road.

My heart suddenly beats like a trapped moth inside a bell jar and without any pre-thought I start to run as fast as my skirts will allow. I push my way none too gently through the people who are still loitering, shouting 'Excuse me, excuse me!' The coach is not going fast and I catch up with it just as it slows at a crossroads at the outskirts of the town.

I have a stitch in my side and my breath has turned into splinters that tear at my lungs but I have enough energy left to beat on the window to get my brother's attention. He looks surprised then concerned and slides down the window. 'What is the matter, Lizzie, has something happened? Lizzie, speak to me!'

I shake my head and try to wear a beatific smile. My words come out interspersed with gasps, 'I never said goodbye and good luck. I just wanted to say goodbye, that's all.' He puts his hand out to me but the driver, not knowing of the drama being enacted behind him, clicks to the horses to move on and I never receive that last caress. The last thing I hear is someone complain, 'Shut the window, it's damnably cold'.

I watch as the coach rattles down the road and finally disappears around the corner. I am surprised to find that I am still smiling, though my heart is sinking with every hoof beat.

Goodbye Matthew, goodbye.

Chapter 12

October 1823

Jamie's singing wakes me.

> *At Wednesbury there was a cocking.*
> *A match between Hayes and Sutton,*
> *The colliers and nailers left work,*
> *La di da di la la la la.*

Papa must have stayed up, waiting for his son to return home. I hear his angry voice quite clearly, although he is downstairs. 'What in God's name are you about?' Jamie giggles and I hear the clump of footsteps as the elder pulls the younger up the stairs.

They are right outside my bedroom door. Jamie giggles again and his words are slurred, 'Hush, father dearest, else you'll wake the household.' There is a yelp of pain. I imagine that Papa has grabbed Jamie's arm tighter than his inebriated state probably warrants.

'You've already done that, James. Collect yourself and get you to bed. We'll talk tomorrow when your brain is not fuddled with alcohol.'

'We'll talk tomorrow when your brain is not fuddled with alcohol.' Jamie mimics Papa in a high-pitched and mocking tone. I am not surprised to hear the slap of a hard hand against a soft cheek. There is a moment's silence then the sound of a scuffle and I assume that Papa is finding it hard to control his wayward son. I get out of bed and step carefully using the wavering light under the door as my guide. I open it tentatively and peer out. Papa is holding a candle in an outstretched hand, as far away from Jamie as possible, whilst with the other he is trying to drag him along the corridor to the stairs up to his room.

Without saying anything I take the candle from Papa's hand, allowing him a firmer grip of Jamie's arms and better able to haul the unwilling body in the right direction. I step in front of them to lead the way and my nose instinctively wrinkles at the stink of alcohol emanating from Jamie. We pass Sarah's bedroom; she is standing in the doorway. 'Can I be of any assistance, sir?' Papa shakes his head and Sarah and I share a wry grimace. I go first up the stairs and into Jamie's room. I pull down the covers on the bed and look for a nightshirt. Papa drops Jamie, now seemingly fast asleep, onto the bed and steps back. I go to lift a dangling leg onto the mattress, with the intention of getting him into a comfortable position but Papa snaps, 'Leave him.' He answers my quizzical look with a glare. He waits for me to leave the room before following, as if he suspects I might ignore his command. He accompanies me to my room then goes downstairs to lock the front door before retiring to his bed.

I am chilled and lie shivering, listening to the house finally able to settle down for the night, waiting for the blankets to do their job and warm me so that I can get back to sleep. I know Jamie has been staying out later and later recently, but until now I don't believe that he has ever come home drunk. I think back and realise that this behaviour only started after Matthew left for university. I never considered that the two brothers were particularly close, but perhaps Jamie's bond with his elder brother is stronger than I appreciate. I feel no sympathy for him, however. My attachment to Matthew is much stronger than ever Jamie's could be; I miss Matthew terribly but I have not resorted to carousing and drinking to excess.

Bobbit wakes me at his normal time. I would have been thankful for a longer sleep but the daily chores still need to be done so I get up, albeit unwillingly. There is an autumnal chill in the air and I start to get myself and Bobbit dressed as quickly as I can. Whilst doing so, I hear firm, booted footsteps pass my door and go upstairs, then raised voices. I cannot hear the words but I can imagine the angry exchange between disappointed father and truculent son. I finish our dressing and take Bobbit downstairs into the kitchen so that I can assist Sarah with the breakfast. Although Matthew is no longer here, we are still the same number as Mr Whittaker now joins us in the morning as well as in the evening. He seems to like the way I cook his eggs.

'Your Mama is staying upstairs awhile. Dorothy has a slight teething fever and will only sleep in the mistress's arms. I'll take up their breakfasts if you can continue with the eggs and bacon. I don't know if Master James will be down.'

'Oh, I think he will. Papa is upstairs with him now and I cannot imagine he'll come down without him.'

There is a knock on the front door but before I can go to open it I hear Papa's welcome to Mr Whittaker. Papa pops his head in on his way to the dining room. 'Just the three men folk this morning, Lizzie, my dear, your mother is staying upstairs with Dorothy a while longer. I hope your sleep was not too disturbed last night?'

'No, thank you Papa,' I lie. 'Is Jamie all right this morning?'

'It matters not whether he is all right. He is up and he will go to work on time and do a full day. How he feels is of no interest to me.'

I almost feel sorry for Jamie.

As Sarah is still with Mama, I take the plates of food into the dining room. We could afford a kitchen maid, even two, but I have grown up knowing that our household is different and that the money that might have been spent by others on servants, coaches, fine clothes and fripperies, is instead spent on Papa's school. We do not suffer; we live in a pleasant house, have sufficient clothes and food to eat but we are not part of the society into which both Mama and Papa were born, but which they both agreed to forego. I have never yearned for satin frocks, glass slippers or a life of idleness and if I marry, it will not be to one of the 'ton' but rather to a man just like Papa. Or Mr Whittaker.

77

Mr Whittaker stands when I enter and gives me his ritual morning bow, which always makes me smile. Some might say that I am doing the job of a serving wench but he still treats me like a lady. Papa is straightening his cutlery and humming tunelessly to himself and Jamie is slouched in his chair, barely upright. He has changed his clothes, or had them changed for him, I am glad to see, but there is still an alcoholic miasma around him. Papa and Mr Whittaker come to the sideboard to fill their plates, but Jamie remains immobile. I load a plate with eggs and bacon and pour the fat liberally over the top and, with what I hope is a saintly expression, waft it under Jamie's nose and put it down in front of him. I watch with interest as his face changes from white to green and step briskly aside as he suddenly stands and lurches out of the room. As I turn to go I think I see the corner of Mr Whittaker's mouth twitch.

Bobbit is capable of feeding himself slices of bread and strips of bacon without making too much mess; he does this whilst I consume my own breakfast, sitting in the kitchen so that I can keep an eye on him whilst Sarah is still upstairs with Mama. I hear the men in the hall putting on their coats then the door opens and Mr Whittaker stands in the doorway, half in and half out. 'Good morning to you, Master Robert, I see you are enjoying your breakfast. I'm afraid Master James was not able to eat your excellent eggs and bacon, Miss Hayes; hopefully he will feel more like eating later in the day.' His expression is completely serious but his voice has a smile.

'I'm sure he will, Mr Whittaker. I believe the ailment from which he is suffering is usually of a short duration.' I hand him the packages of food for them to eat at mid-day and then nod a farewell as Papa calls to him to come along. Is that a wink he gives me?

The weather outside is windy and wet and I am happy to stay indoors. When we women are in the kitchen together we chatter about all sorts of things except the one that is uppermost in all our minds. I know from my reading that the after effects of too much alcohol are both nausea and a headache. I wonder how Jamie will cope with the constant pounding of the printing press; I doubt it will be recuperative.

Papa and Mr Whittaker come home first, as school finishes earlier than the print shop. As always, they go into the study to discuss the day's events and to plan for the next. I take them both a glass of beer.

'Thank you, Lizzie. When Jamie comes, tell him to come directly to the study.'

But Jamie doesn't come.

As the minute-hand on the longcase in the hall creeps inexorably round, marking his tardiness, the tension in the house increases. The murmurings from the study gradually cease. We are all waiting for Jamie's return. I imagine the Sword of Damocles swaying over the front door and as soon as he opens it, the thread will break. What then?

Routine is maintained but dinner is eaten in almost complete silence. Jamie's presence is far more evident by its lack than if he were physically sitting at the table. I feel an inexplicable nervousness that I cannot explain and I have no appetite; nor, it seems, does anyone else. Mr Whittaker looks understandably uncomfortable throughout but Papa does not agree to his suggestion that he leaves directly after the meal. Instead, they both retreat to the study and I hear the clink of glasses as I go about my evening chores.

I hear the creak of the Sword as it, like us, waits.

I have a very low opinion of my brother but even so I am aghast at his blatant disrespect and ill manners. He is not yet a man of independent means and will have need of his father's financial support for years to come. What on earth is he thinking of?

I happen to be in the hallway as the front door opens and Jamie comes in, looking as if he has nary a worry in the world. I wait for the sound of a falling Sword but only hear Jamie's cheery, 'Good evening, sister mine.'

'What on earth are you thinking, Jamie? To be so late after last night; have you completely lost your senses? You need to go straight to the study, but I warn you Papa is beside himself. What on earth,' I repeat, 'are you thinking?'

Jamie looks puzzled. 'I sent a message to say that I would be dining at the Suttons.' He pulls a face. 'I assume you did not receive it?'

'Only the butcher has called today. Who did you give the message to?'

'Some little urchin in the street. I wrote a message on a piece of paper and made him repeat the address three times to make sure he remembered it. I even gave him a couple of farthing. Wait till I see him again, the little thief.'

'You are such a fool. It would have been no trouble to come here first, would it? We have spent a dreadful evening, all assuming that you have disobeyed your father and gone drinking again. You surely didn't go to dinner in your work clothes?'

'No, I borrowed an outfit from Geoffrey and to be honest, I didn't feel up to facing Father.'

'Is that you, James? Get in here, now!'

'Well, you're going to have to face him now.'

As I shut the front door I notice a small piece of paper lying on the front mat, held down by a stone. The ink has run but I can just make out Jamie's message. I take it into the house as evidence, should it be needed.

Chapter 13

November 1823

'Master James has gone then.' A statement, not a question.

John and I are standing outside the church, waiting for our respective families; my own much depleted now that both elder brothers have left home. It is not raining but we stand under one of the yew trees to give ourselves some privacy whilst remaining in public view.

'Yes, he left yesterday. He travelled in great style in the Sutton Coach along with Charles and Mr Sutton. Mama shed a few tears but I think it was just for show. I certainly didn't. I'm glad he's gone and will not miss him at all.'

'He came into the workshop a few weeks ago to place an order from your father for some more benches for the school. He told me all about it. He seemed very excited about his new position and saw it as a great opportunity.'

'He is the only boy I know who can act despicably one day and then get his heart's desire the next. It really is most unfair.'

'Why, Miss Elizabeth? Is it your heart's desire to move to London and work for a publisher? I thought it was to teach.'

I punch him on the arm in a most unladylike manner. 'You know what I mean. He is going on an adventure, seeing the world that I can only read about. He's escaping.'

'Escaping from what?'

'Here.'

'Do you want to escape from here?'

Do I? Or do I just want to escape my dreary life that consists of nothing but household duties and caring for Bobbit, who seems to be taking up more and more of my time?

'No, of course not. I might as well be here as anywhere.'

'Didn't you want to give Master James a box like the one I made for Master Matthew?'

'Good grief, no. I have no desire for him to think that I care a fig that he is going; good riddance, I say.'

'He told me that he is going to work for the elder Sutton son, who will be running the publishing company his father has recently acquired. I have only met Master Charles the once, when I delivered some furniture with father. He was ...'

John is far too polite to be honest and struggles to find an appropriate word, so I volunteer my own. 'Arrogant? Proud? Obnoxious?'

'What was that word you once used to describe Mr Whittaker when he first came? Unc something?'

'Unctuous! Oh, how terrible of me. Please don't ever tell him I called him that.'

'You don't think him unctuous any more then?'

'No, he's a good teacher and I like him.'

John studies the toes of his shiny, Sunday shoes. 'Well, I think Charles Sutton is unctuous and I personally would not like to work for him but I am sure it will be different for Master James. I have heard that the younger boys, Masters Geoffrey and Daniel, are trouble.'

'Yes, they take great pleasure in plaguing Bobbit whenever our paths cross. It was apparently Geoffrey who took Jamie to the cock fight and got him drunk. But it was also Geoffrey who invited him to dinner the following day and persuaded his father and Charles to offer him a post. As I say, he was born under a lucky star.'

'I wouldn't have thought you believed in astrology, Miss Hayes.'

Both John and I jump. 'Why, Mr Whittaker, you startled us.'

'Forgive me, next time I will stamp my feet loudly to give you warning.' He nods at John, who nods back with a rather fierce expression; neither smiles; neither seems to like the other, although I don't know why.

'Ah, here are Mama and Papa at last. I can't think what they have to say to everyone that takes so long. I will bid you both good day.'

They both say their farewells. When I go through the church gate I look back; they are still standing stiffly side by side under the yew tree; they do not appear to be talking.

Chapter 14

August 1824

There is a tension in the air that I sense but cannot explain.

I have come up to the churchyard to read in the hope that it will be cooler but although there is a slight breeze it is too warm to offer much of a respite. I am alone today as I have left Bobbit contentedly sitting in the garden with Sarah, his arms spread wide whilst she winds a skein of wool into tight balls that she will later magically transform into socks. I am sitting on Mistress Carmichael's tomb, our favourite outside place, and the vista beneath me shimmers in the summer heat but it is not this that disconcerts me; there is something else that is distracting me from my reading.

The sunlight reflects off the canal and I follow it with my eyes as it meanders its way from the town through the countryside all the way to Birmingham over the horizon. It takes a while for my brain to process what I see, or rather what I don't see: there are no barges moving on the water and no men leading the horses along the towpath. There is always something happening on the canal during the day - but not today.

I shift my focus nearer home, to the industrial area. Most of the workers are usually inside or underground, of course, but there are always people walking or running from building to building; teams going on or off shift; horses pulling carts to be emptied or filled – but not today.

Where is everyone?

Something catches the corner of my eye. It is a black mass that looks like a colony of ants or a murmuration of starlings. Not insects or birds, but men, hundreds upon hundreds of them.

These must be the missing colliers, miners, bargemen and foundrymen. I sit perfectly still and listen. I can hear my own breath, birds twittering in the yews, the bark of a dog but there is something else that makes the air tremble and the hairs on the back of my neck bristle. It is the far-off sound of a thousand angry men.

'What on earth is going on, Mistress Carmichael? You don't know? In that case, I will have to go and see for myself.' I jump down intending to make my way to the Turk's Head, which I think is where the men are gathering.

I'm not the only curious person and I join a throng of men, women and children, all running in the same direction into town. Some of them are shouting and their angry words hang in the hot air: 'wages'; 'colliers'; 'greedy'; 'bastards'; 'riot'; 'Peterloo'. It's as if I'm caught in a strong current and I couldn't stop now even if I wanted to. As we flow into Market Place those of us at the rear find ourselves bumping into the backs of the people in front of us, who are now standing stock still. Their way is barred by a line of cavalrymen looking like Jamie's toy soldiers; all dressed exactly alike in their dark blue uniform with white cording and their white-plumed helmets. Their faces have been painted with the same stern expressions and they and their mounts are absolutely still. The only sound is the heavy breathing of the crowd.

I sense the crowd is becoming restless and there are murmurings of discontent that turn into screams when a soldier raises his musket into the air and fires. Everyone takes a few hurried paces back, stepping on the toes of those behind and I see a woman fall to the ground in a faint. My own heart is racing and the air seems too thick to breathe in. I remember the horrific stories I have heard about the massacre at Peterloo and I feel a stab of fear twist into my stomach.

'Silence!' One of the soldiers in the middle of the line has stepped his horse forward and is holding up a piece of paper in one hand. 'I am Captain Frobisher of the Staffordshire Yeomanry and we have been sent to quell a riot.' The word 'riot' ripples through the crowd, which sways like weeds under moving water. 'This piece of paper I have here,' he waves it so everyone is clear which piece of paper he is referring to, 'is the Riot Act, which has been read to the men who have congregated together unlawfully. They have been given one hour to disperse.'

'What if they don't, you going to shoot them all?' a man shouts out.

The Captain searches the crowd but luckily can't pick out the culprit. 'If the men do not disperse then we are authorised to use whatever force is necessary to ensure they return to their workplace.' As if this is a cue the soldiers raise their muskets and we all take another few paces further away from them, as if this will save us.

'Go back to your homes and stay there until the men have returned to work and we have left the town. That is an order, not a request. We have no desire to hurt anyone but the law is clear.' Nobody moves until another shot is fired, after which everyone turns and starts to run back from whence they came, me included. I have only taken a few steps when someone grabs my arm and pulls me into a doorway.

'For goodness sake, Miss Hayes, what on earth are you doing here?'

'For goodness sake, yourself, Mr Whittaker. I was sitting up at St Bartholomew's and could see that something was amiss, so I came to see what it was.'

'Your curiosity could have got you killed.'

'I don't think so; they would have had no reason to shoot me.'

'Once the command has been given to fire there is no selection, merely slaughter.'

'Do you know why the men were rioting?'

'Yes. The owners are reducing the wages of the colliers for no apparent reason, other than greed. The men have all gathered together in Turk's Head field and have persuaded the other workers to join them.'

'What do you think will happen if the workers don't go back to work? Will the soldiers really shoot them, like they did at Peterloo?' An image of the pamphlet that I took from Jamie flashes into my mind, but that was many months ago before the owners had got together and agreed to pay their workers even less.

'I don't know. I think the colliers have every right to object to the wage reduction and to ask for support from other workers. God knows they get paid little enough now; certainly not enough to keep their families sufficiently warm, clothed and fed. But I also think that today will achieve nothing other than to make the owners even more determined. Whoever organised this gathering should put their efforts into starting a trade union; they are now legal although not loved by the employers, of course.'

I look at him in surprise. I have never heard him speak so passionately and his eyes are shining with anger. He notices my glance and gives me a sheepish grin. I turn to look back down the street towards where the cavalrymen had been lined up against us. They have gone, as has the crowd, who have scuttled back home, leaving the street deserted and strangely hushed.

'Come, Miss Hayes, I'll walk you back home.'

Before we even leave the protection of the doorway, the silence is broken by the pounding of hooves on cobbles as cavalrymen ride round the corner towards us, six abreast, the horses trotting in perfect harmony; even their tails and the plumes on the helmets sway in unison. The sun is reflected off the rumps of the horses, the brass harness buckles and the polished boots of the riders. It is an impressive sight that I find quite exhilarating until a caged cart passes by. Inside there are six men, all miners by the look of them, shackled to the metal bars of the cage as if they are dangerous beasts.

I look at Mr Whittaker in consternation. 'Who are they? Where are they taking them?'

'I expect they are the ring leaders. God help them.'

'Oh, look!' There are women and children running alongside the cart trying to grab hold of the men's hands that are poking out through the bars. One woman stumbles and I instinctively take a step to help her but before I can do so Mr Whittaker rushes forward, grabs hold of her and leads her back to our refuge. She struggles briefly but then collapses against him, her sobs matching those of a young child she holds close to her breast.

'Oh my poor man, my poor man. Where are they taking him? What will become of him? What will become of us? We should be with him, let me go, please.'

'You won't be able to keep up with them, mistress, and they won't let you go with them.'

'Where will they take them? Perhaps she can visit later on?'

Mr Whittaker shakes his head, for my eyes only. 'We can find out where they are going later on, but, mistress, you need to get home and look after your son. What's his name?'

The woman has stopped crying and she puts the boy onto the ground. He runs to stand behind her threadbare skirt, his bare feet making little footprints in the dust.

'I'm Mrs Morgan and this here is our William.' Now she is unburdened I can see that she carries an unborn child. 'Say hullo to this nice lady and gentleman, William.' William sticks a thumb into his mouth as greeting. 'Thank you kindly for pulling me away from them hosses feet. Oh, look, here are the others coming back. I'll walk back with them. Thank you again.'

We watch as she joins the other women and children walking dejectedly, still red-faced from their exertions. One older woman puts her arm around Mrs Morgan and then picks up William who continues to suck his thumb and stares at us over the woman's shoulder.

'What will happen to the men?'

'At best they will be transported to the other side of the world, at worst hung. Either way their families have now lost their main wage earner.'

'And a husband, father, brother or son. Those families will need all the help we can give them.'

'That's what the Poor Fund is for. I expect the mine owners will give generously and think they are being good Christians.' He gives a wry smile which quickly turns into a scowl when he sees John approach us.

'Are you alright Miss Hayes? Have you been hurt?'

'No, I'm perfectly well, thank you. Mr Whittaker has just saved a young woman and child from being trampled to death. He was very brave. He's going to walk me home now. Send my greetings to your mother and father, please, John.'

I take Mr Whittaker's arm; when I turn to give John a farewell smile he is glowering at Mr Whittaker's back.

'What is that you are reading?'

I show him the book I am still clutching in my hand. 'These are Perrault's fairytales. He was French but Matthew found an English translation when a fair came to Wednesbury a few years ago and he bought it for me. I only read them to remind me what my own little stories should *not* be like. Most of these make me very angry.'

'Angry? That surely is not the purpose of fairy tales?'

'What do you think their purpose should be?'

He pauses to consider, then continues walking. 'I suppose they are stories that tell us how we should behave but in an entertaining way?'

'And how should girls behave, Mr Whittaker?'

'I suspect this is a trick question, Miss Hayes, and that whatever I say will be wrong.'

'Do you know the story of *Little Red Riding Hood*?' Mr Whittaker nods. 'What do you think the moral of that story is?'

'Oh dear, I'm bound to say the wrong thing, aren't I? Well, from what I remember the wolf eats both the grandmother and the little girl. I can't recall all the details, I was told it over twenty years ago. Remind me, Miss Hayes.'

'You are correct, Mr Whittaker, that the wolf eats both the grandmother and her granddaughter. I'm not sure why the grandmother has to die, but Monsieur Perrault says that because the young girl is undisciplined enough to talk to a wolf, which she should not have done, then she must be punished with death.'

'Surely Perrault is just warning girls to be careful of wolfish men?'

'But why is she so helpless? I agree that she should not have spoken to him and told him where she was going, but why did she not see that it was a wolf underneath the nightgown and why, oh, why did she not just run away? Or perhaps she could have killed him, he certainly deserved it. The wolf is the villain but he gets his prize, whilst the girl, who has made one mistake, dies. It just makes me so cross that all the girls in these fairy tales are described as being so, well, so stupid! These stories, Mr Whittaker, tell a girl that she must be virtuous, patient and subservient with not one jot of intelligence in her pretty little brain. She must do as she is told, by a man of course, and if she does, only then will she get her heart's desire, which is invariably to marry a prince.'

'Don't all girls want to get married? Don't you, Miss Hayes?'

I ignore his question. 'I want to read stories that tell of brave girls; girls that are intelligent; girls that go on adventures; girls that make their own decisions and their own mistakes; girls that rescue boys; girls that marry on their own terms.'

'And those are the stories that you write? You are unique, Miss Hayes, quite unique.'

I know he is trying to flatter me but all I feel is annoyed. 'We are all unique, Mr Whittaker, each boy and girl, man and woman, is unique and should not be made to behave in a single way just because of their sex.'

We continue home in silence and are greeted with relief by Papa, who has closed the school and sent the boys back to their families; some of whom will have to be added to the Poor List.

During the meal I only half listen to the conversation; instead in my head I write my own version of *Little Red Riding Hood*.

Chapter 15

September 1824

54 Leadenhall Street
London
27th September '24

My dear Mother, Father and Lizzie,
I'm always amazed when it's time to write my monthly missive to you again; time seems to go much quicker here in London than in Wednesbury. I think I said a few months ago that we were exceedingly busy? Well, we are even busier now, but I love it. Charles has just promoted me to his assistant and he is teaching me how to select a book that will sell well, how to edit it to remove any spelling, grammatical or other errors, and how to lay it out ready to be sent to the printers. In the last month alone I have read and helped prepare books on the 100 Days War, the Battle of Waterloo (bigger than the one on the whole war!), a travelogue by a man who journeyed through India (very interesting), the life stories of saints whose names I can't even recall (not so interesting) and a collection of short stories that are nowhere as good as Lizzie's.
My rooms are adequate but I spend much of my time at the Suttons'. Geoffrey is down here and we socialise a lot together. His twin sister, Alice, is also here.
I am eating well, working and saving hard. I hope you are proud of me.
Lizzie, Matthew has given you some paper, hasn't he? Write down your stories and send them to me, I am sure I can persuade Charles to publish them.
Your dear son,
James

'Short and to the point,' is Papa's only comment.

'Oh Francis, I know he doesn't write such long letters as dear Matthew but he is obviously working hard and I think we should be proud of him. What say you, Lizzie?'

I find that I have become fonder of Jamie the longer he is away. 'It does seem as if he has found his forte. I'm sure he will do well for himself, his sort always does.'

'What on earth do you mean, "his sort"?'

'Oh Mama, you know what I mean. He was born under a lucky star and always manages to fall on his feet.'

Papa gives me a crooked smile but says nothing.

'What do you think about his suggestion that you send your stories? It's very generous of him. It sounds like they have plenty of books but he is still willing to try and get yours published. Just think of that, seeing your name in print. Are you going to send them?'

'I might, but I don't think for one minute that he is making this offer out of the goodness of his heart, Mama. He only ever does anything if it benefits James Hayes. However, I have been writing some out on the paper Matthew gave me. I'll finish them and then I'll see.'

Papa gives me another smile. He sees right through my pretended ambivalence.

#

We are walking home from church after a very uninspiring sermon. John and I are dawdling at the back and taking the opportunity to have a long talk, something we haven't managed for quite a while.

'Look, the leaves are beginning to turn. This is my favourite time of year; I love to see the greens slowly disappear and being replaced by every conceivable tone of yellow, orange and red. I even love getting out the warmer clothes and boots. I am quite happy to exchange the summer warmth for the autumnal chill.'

'I prefer the spring and summer months if I am working outside, but there is beauty in all the seasons, Miss Elizabeth and each one has a benefit for someone, somewhere. We might as well enjoy each one as we can't stop the natural cycle. Just think if there was no summer, how would the crops ripen? And how would the earth recover itself if there was no winter? Maybe you should write one of your stories, Miss Elizabeth, about a land where there are no seasons. What a strange place that would be.'

'That would indeed make a very interesting tale but I prefer to write about people. In fact I have just written a story that is based on a fairytale told by a Frenchman. I have changed it slightly as I didn't like his ending. Do you want to hear it?'

'I always love to hear your stories, Miss Elizabeth.'

There was once a little girl who was by no means the prettiest in the village, but she was a good girl and helped her mother with the chores, went to school and learned her lessons well and was much loved by her mother and grandmother. Her mother was a seamstress and made her daughter a red cloak with a hood, which she wore all the time so that everyone in the village forgot what her real name was and called her Little Red Riding Hood instead. But we shall call her Eleanora, because that was her name.

One day, the mother received a message saying that the grandmother was sick, so she gave her daughter a basket of biscuits she had just baked and asked her to take them to her grandmother and make sure she was all right. So Eleanora put on her red cloak and gladly took the basket and set off to her grandmother's. She had to walk through a big wood in order to get to the house, but she knew the route and took pleasure in picking some flowers and listening to the birds trilling in the trees. She also knew that wolves lived in the wood so she carried a hefty stick and kept a sharp lookout. She didn't see any wolves but one saw her. He was a sly fellow and recognised the red cloak and knowing where she was going, he ran to the grandmother's house in order to get there before the girl.

The wolf pretended to be Eleanora so that the grandmother let him in, but regretted it immediately because the wolf attacked her and ate her up. He then dressed himself in one of the grandmother's nightdresses and put a night cap on his head. He closed the curtains so that it was quite dark and then got into bed and waited for Eleanora to arrive.

When the girl knocked on the door and said who it was, the wolf pretended to be the grandmother and said in a very high-pitched voice, 'Come in my dear. I am not feeling very well and am in bed.'

Eleanora put the flowers she had picked into a vase and the biscuits onto a plate and then started to make a cup of tea. The wolf was impatient because he was still very hungry, despite having just eaten the grandmother, and said, 'Leave that my dear. I'm not very thirsty. Come and sit by me on the bed and tell me all your news.'

Now the wolf couldn't keep his voice at a high pitch and it had become quite hoarse.

'Why is your voice hoarse, grandmother?'

'Oh, because I have a bad chill but I am quite able to chat with you. Come closer, my dear.'

When Eleanora sat on the bed, she could not see her grandmother very clearly because the curtains were closed but did think that she looked a bit strange.

'Your arms seem very long, grandmother.'

'Oh no, they are not long, come, let me hug you, my dear.' Which he did. Eleanora was puzzled by the feeling of fur on her grandmother's arms and pulled away quickly, before the wolf had time to hold her tight enough to eat. And what, thought Eleanora, were those sticking out of the top of her night cap?

'Are those your ears, grandmother? They look very long and are they furry?'

'Oh, they are the decoration on my night cap. I can hear you perfectly with my own ears, my dear.'

Now, Eleanora was not stupid and by now she realised that this was not her grandmother in the bed, but a wolf. But she played along with the wolf's game and made her own plan.

'Could I get myself a glass of water, grandmother? I am rather thirsty.'

The wolf sighed but agreed. When Eleanora had got herself a drink she sat back on the bed and continued the silly game.

'What big eyes you have, grandmother.'

'All the better to see you with, my dear.'

'What big teeth you have, grandmother.'

'All the better to eat you with, my dear!'

Eleanora knew what the wolf would answer and that he would try and grab her and eat her, so whilst the wolf was talking Eleanora bent to pick up the heavy stick that she had brought from home and which she had picked up when she had got herself a glass of water and before the wolf could sink his teeth into her tender, pink flesh, she beat him over his head again and again, until he dropped down dead. It was a good thing that Eleanora's cloak was red.

And the moral of this tale? Boys, do not underestimate the female sex and girls, take control of your own life and save yourself.

John chuckles. 'Oh, Miss Elizabeth, you really are unique.'

I'm surprised at John's turn of phrase and remember how Mr Whittaker had also named me as such. I had felt irritated with him but I feel pleased that John thinks me so.

'It's a shame she couldn't save her grandmother.'

'Maybe I could change it so that the wolf just locks her in a cupboard?'

'No, a wolf would not show such mercy. It's a good tale, as usual. My sister will like it.'

96

'I've written it down; it's one of the ones I'm going to send off.'

'Send off? Where to?'

'Didn't I tell you? James has suggested that I send my stories to him and he will see if Charles will publish them. He probably won't but I might as well send them, there is no harm in doing that is there?'

'Goodness no, and just think if they are published, everybody will know of the great teller of tales, Miss Elizabeth Hayes, and marvel at her works!' He laughs, 'And all the girls in the land will throw down their embroidery and pick up big sticks and woe betide all the menfolk.'

I cannot help but join in his laughter. 'Oh, fie, John.' I'm secretly thrilled at his words and can feel my cheeks redden with pleasure. 'Be off home with you. Oh, and I nearly forgot. Could you come to the house over the next few days? A couple of the chairs in the dining room need mending. Poor Mr Whittaker nearly fell to the floor the other evening when one of the legs fell off.'

'Oh dear, I'm sorry about that. I do hope he didn't hurt himself too much.'

'Are you laughing, John? No? You'll be glad to hear that he was not hurt at all, perhaps just his pride. Papa would like you to take a look and give a price. You or your father, of course.'

'Tell your father it will be my pleasure. I'll come tomorrow if that is convenient?'

I nod, knowing that it is convenient for me at least.

Chapter 16

March 1825

There is a letter from Matthew. Although it is always pleasant to hear from him, there is by now very little to excite. Papa usually reads it to himself first and then out loud but today, whilst still silently perusing, he gives such a shout that Mama and I both jump and I choke on a piece of toast.

'Goodness, Francis, you quite startled me. What on earth has Matthew written? He's not ill is he? Oh, Francis, there's nothing wrong is there?'

'No, dearest. I apologise for alarming you both. Lizzie, you have some conserve on your cheek. I will read you his letter, then you'll see. "*My dear family, I pray that you are all in good health and that the commencement of spring cheers both your bodies and souls. The blossom is just opening on the trees along the Cam and it makes for a very pretty sight. Your tutoring in mathematics, Papa, is of great benefit and the tutor says I am one of his best students, though I hasten to write that it is gratitude to you that I feel, rather than pride in myself."*'

'Gracious, he gets more and more pious. He'll end up as the Archbishop of Canterbury at this rate.'

'Stop interrupting, Lizzie. Francis, read on.'

Papa winks at me before returning to the letter. '*"I think I told you in previous letters that I have made a few good friends, one in particular is called Mr George Docherty. He too has been called by God and we attend meetings together."*'

'A meeting isn't the same as a lecture is it? What does he mean?'

'I don't think so, Lizzie, but he doesn't say anything more about them. Can I continue?'

'Please do, Francis. I'm struggling to see what you got so excited about.'

'Just be patient, my dear, it is worth the wait. *"I have actually moved to his rooms, which are actually   cheaper   than   my previous ones, so you will be pleased at   that, Papa. There are four other students who reside here but they are all older and we don't mix with them very   much. The food is acceptable, though not as good as Sarah's. I hope you are all well and please pass on my best regards to Mr Whittaker."* A reassuring letter, don't you think?'

Mama and I glare at him in consternation then irritation as he looks at us both with an expression of great superiority, as if he knows a secret that we don't know, which is, of course, the truth of the matter.

'That is all really, except for the closing sentence.' He pauses, Mama's cheeks redden, I restrain myself from screaming, he continues. 'Where was I, ah yes. *"By the way, I am coming home for a few days at the end of April; the coach will arrive in the afternoon of the 12th. I   will   be bringing my friend, Mr Docherty, and he can sleep in Jamie's room if it can be prepared for him? There is no   need to write a reply, I will probably see you sooner than a letter will get here. I send all my respect, love and prayers,   your loving son, Matthew."'*

Papa sits and smiles at us as I clap and squeal like a small child and Mama puts a hand first to cover her open mouth and then to wipe away a tear.

'Oh, Francis, he's coming home. Matthew's coming home. You must write back immediately, even though he says not to, and say that he can come whenever he wants, for however long he wants and he can bring whomsoever he wants. Lizzie, we will have to clean James's room out and make it into a decent guest room for Mr Docherty. I must tell Sarah, she will be thrilled. I expect she will start cooking this afternoon. Oh, Francis, Matthew is coming home.' She leaves to go into the kitchen, still wiping her eyes.

Papa is rereading the letter, still smiling.

'Will you write Papa? Oh, I can't wait to see him. He has always said he couldn't come whilst he was at university; I wonder why he can now? Oh, it doesn't matter does it? He'll be here in just a few weeks. Will you write?'

'No, my dear, Matthew is right. There is no point in wasting paper; the letter most likely won't get there before he has left. It's a shame he will only be here for a few days, but we will make the most of it. Dear boy, dear boy.'

I start to tidy up the breakfast things and try and work out how long it has been since I last saw my beloved brother.

'It's seventeen months, Bobbit. Seventeen whole months since we last saw Matthew. I tried to reckon how many weeks that is but my mathematics is not as good as Matthew's, more's the pity. Do you think he'll have changed very much? It sounds as if he is even more religious than he was before he left, but that shouldn't change his look, should it? What if it has and I don't recognise him? Oh, I know I'm being ridiculous; he will just look a little older, as we all do, even you.'

Bobbit continues rocking gently, keeping his excitement deep inside himself. I like to think that he gets it out when he is alone and rubs it until it shines, rather like Aladdin and his lamp as told in Scott's *Arabian Nights Entertainments*, another book Matthew bought me to inspire my own little tales.

Mr Whittaker is allowed to read the letter, and he is, of course, not as excited as we are. He knew Matthew for only a few short weeks and perhaps he is worried that he will criticise his teaching methods, although there is not much fear of that as Papa is always praising him. He reads the letter twice, with a frown fluttering between his eyebrows. He does not smile, not even at the last sentences and I suddenly feel cross with him and snatch the letter out of his hand and hold it to my breast, as if it is a secret love letter.

'Are you not pleased for us, Mr Whittaker? You do not seem so.'

'Of course, Miss Hayes, of course. You must be very excited about seeing him. It's just that, oh, no matter; it is nothing.'

Before I can question him further Papa offers him a port in a rather loud voice and the conversation changes to one of mundane daily topics.

Chapter 17

April 1825

'Matthew's coming home, Matthew's coming home,' I sing as I alternate between sitting at the table peeling the potatoes, giving Bobbit another carrot to skin and standing at the range to stir the simmering sauces.

'Good gracious, Lizzie, you running to and fro in such a manner will not make the coach arrive any earlier. It will be this afternoon, unless the poor horses have grown wings.'

'You mean like Pegasus in Greek mythology? Wouldn't that be grand, if all the horses could fly? The roads would be much easier to walk down, wouldn't they?'

'Not so grand when a horse makes a pile. It would fall on your head!' We laugh at the image Sarah has conjured, which gives vent to some of my pent up excitement, so that I now settle at the table to complete my task. Dorothy, now two and a half years of age, is helping Mama shell peas, although there are far fewer in the bowl than is warranted by the size of the pile of pods.

Sarah is looking at the youngest Hayes with a slightly sad expression. 'Just look at young Dorothy, mistress. She looks just as you did at that age; although she is much better behaved as ever you were.'

I laugh and Mama throws a pod at Sarah in mock anger, but it makes me think.

'You have been with Mama almost all her life, Sarah. That's a very long time.'

'Thank you, Lizzie, for reminding me how old I am. But you are right, Sarah was my nurse when I was a year old and has been with me ever since. More a companion now and part of the family, as you well know.'

'Have you no family of your own, Sarah? I have never heard you speak of any.'

'I had parents, as we all do, but they passed away many years ago, as have four of my siblings, God bless them all. There is only Esther left now and I have not seen her for many a year. She is very much younger than me; she was still clinging to mother's skirts when I left home. But we exchange letters each year, hers written by the local vicar and mine by your Mama. She is always asking me to go and stay with her but, well, I haven't as yet.'

'But that's terrible! Mama, you must let Sarah pay a visit to her sister.'

Mama looks at me crossly. 'It is not for want of my encouragement. Sarah knows full well that she can visit anytime she wants; she is not a prisoner here. If she chooses not to, then that is her decision and one which we should all accept without argument.'

'But...'

'Without argument, I said.'

'It's all right Miss Elizabeth. I did mean to go a few years ago but then Miss Dorothy was born and, well, time has just flown by. Perhaps I'll go this summer, or maybe next. There's plenty of time. She and her husband are in service for the Tregonwell family, who have just had new houses built in a place called Bournemouth. It is by the sea and meant to be a good place to go if you are not well. Esther says they have planted hundreds of pine trees which make the air especially beneficial for those with breathing ailments. So she says, anyway.'

'Oh, it sounds wonderful, Sarah. You must go and we shall all accompany you and go sea bathing! You'd enjoy that, wouldn't you, Dorothy? Just think how you would enjoy splashing in a giant bathtub with water that doesn't have to be carried from the pump.' Dorothy squeals in delight, though I doubt she understands.

'Get away with you, Miss Elizabeth. You do let your imagination run away with you sometimes. Mind you, I like the idea of breathing in the smell of pines rather than coal, like we do here. I have no intention, though, of putting more than my toes into the sea.'

We have finished our tasks and I am restless, waiting for time to pass so that I can go down to the town with Papa and Mama to meet the coach. I check the bedrooms that I have already checked twice this morning and rearrange the already rearranged flowers I had picked from the garden at dawn. The dew has dried now and they are beginning to wilt. I remove them from their vases and take them downstairs, meaning to throw them onto the heap in the back garden where we throw all our waste and then to pick some new ones. As I go into the kitchen, though, Papa is waiting for me so I put them on the table. I don't want to be held back by Bobbit today, so I leave him with Sarah and I lift Dorothy into my arms and almost skip down the road with her, acting more like a seven year old than one ten years older.

When we reach the Turk's Head there is no coach but there are family members, like us, waiting for the arrival of their loved ones. John and Mr Whittaker are standing some feet apart, ready to help carry the trunks. John has a wheeled box and Dorothy giggles hysterically when I put her in and John runs up and down the street with her.

Suddenly Mr Whittaker puts up his hand, cocks his head and shouts 'Listen!' We all stop what we are doing and stare at him; we look like the people in *The Sleeping Beauty in the Wood*, who are frozen in their last position for one hundred years.

'I can hear the coach.'

We all cock our own heads in unison and then I too can hear the distant rumbling. I long to run towards it, pull open the door and drag Matthew out, but I patiently stay where I am and wait for him to come to me. Dorothy does not know Matthew; she was not even one when he left, but she senses our excitement and jumps up and down and squeals, just as I want to do.

At last I see the horses and then the coach turn the corner and make their slow way to the inn. White froth and patches of dust

104

cover the coats of the horses so that they look piebald rather than plain black. Steam is rising from their heaving flanks; poor things! I wish Bobbit were here now, so that he could talk gently to them and calm them down.

The doors on either side are thrown open and it is chaos as men, women and children tumble out, calling out greetings to those waiting for them, shouting to the driver to be careful getting their boxes and trunks down and generally just releasing their energy after hours of being trapped in a shaking, hot, metal box.

I can't see Matthew. Where is Matthew?

I race around to the other side but he's not there either. I begin to feel quite panicky, when I hear a voice from the heavens. 'Lizzie, we're up here.' I look up and see two gentlemen, looking as if they have rolled in the dust, sitting quietly on the seat whilst all beneath them is disorder. 'We were waiting for things to quieten down a bit. We'll come down now.'

They clamber down and then they are there, standing side by side, the dust on their cheeks cracked by the big grins on their faces. Papa pumps their hands up and down, Mama hugs them both, disregarding the dirt that transfers from their shirts onto her blouse, Dorothy runs around their legs like some maddened dog and I just stand watching them, biding my time.

Matthew looks as if someone has stretched him so that he is taller, but also thinner, and he looks older, more serious, despite his wide smile. His friend, Mr Docherty is shorter and of a more solid build and seems to be pleased with being included in the familial welcome. Matthew catches my eye and winks and, as if this is a sign, I hurl myself at him and throw my arms about him, laughing and crying at the same time, using his shirt as a kerchief for both my eyes and my nose.

'Careful, Lizzie, you'll knock me over. Come now, control yourself. Let me introduce my good friend. Docherty, this is my sister, Miss Elizabeth Hayes. Elizabeth, this is Mr George Docherty.'

He holds his hand for me to shake, which I duly do. 'I'm very pleased to finally meet you. Miss Hayes. Matthew entertained me often with anecdotes of his family life during the first few months when I sorely missed my own. He tells me, however, that his stories are not as good as your own. I hope you will share some of them with me whilst I am a guest at your house.' He has a lovely lilt which I assume to be Irish.

'You are most welcome, Mr Docherty, and very glad that we were able to act as your substitute family. I doubt that my little stories will be of much interest to you, though. Not when you have a library with all the world's books at your finger tips.'

We can speak no more as the trunks are now loaded precariously in John's wheeled cart and we all make our way slowly back home. Papa is politely walking with Mr Docherty and Mama with Matthew, who is carrying a Dorothy too tired to even wake to his kisses on her cheeks and forehead. I walk behind, happy just to have Matthew in my sight. Mr Whittaker, who is carrying a leather case in each hand, walks with me.

'How long are they staying, Miss Hayes?'

'Matthew said just a few days in his letter, but they do seem to have rather a lot of luggage for a short stay.'

'Indeed.'

We are at the house now and Mr Whittaker quietly leaves the cases in the hallway, excuses himself to Papa and leaves. He has absented himself from joining in our evening meal, which I think is very polite and considerate of him. John helps the two men take their trunks upstairs and when Mr Docherty tries to give him a tip, he puts his hands behind his back and blushes terribly, which is quickly equalled by Mr Docherty's own cherry cheeks when Matthew whispers in his ear, explaining that John is a friend and expects no payment. I suddenly remember I have not placed new flowers in the vases and I apologise for the lack.

'Please do not worry, Miss Hayes, I prefer to see God's gifts alive as he intended rather than dead just to decorate a room for a short period.'

Dinner is a merry affair and Mr Docherty regales us with stories of their student lives, the eccentricity of their professors and the dreariness of their lectures, which I am sure are highly exaggerated. Matthew laughs along with the rest of us but I cannot help but notice that there are lines of strain around his mouth and his eyes are dark with an emotion that is not one of humour. There is a lull in the conversation and I ask a question I have been wanted to pose all evening.

'In your letter you mentioned that you attend meetings with Mr Docherty. What meetings are these, Matthew?' Do I imagine the glance between the two men?

'There are often student meetings; I expect I meant them. We often meet to discuss different topics, maybe one of the books we are studying, or a philosophical conundrum or, I don't know, how many books there are in the library.'

'Did you decide how many books there are? Hundreds?'

'Oh, Lizzie, even you cannot imagine how many there are. The walls are higher than this house and run the length of half this street, every wall is shelved from floor to ceiling and every shelf is filled with books. There must be thousands upon thousands of them.'

'It's a jolly good job we don't have to read all of them, Miss Hayes, otherwise we would never finish our degree.'

'Some are so old, Lizzie, that we are not allowed to handle them ourselves and must ask one of the librarians, who wear thin, cotton gloves and it is they alone who are allowed to turn the pages. I can't even begin to describe the smell. It is a mixture of leather, mould, dust, oil and wood.'

'Some smell of vanilla, for some reason, and in the Far East section I am convinced I can smell spices, but that is probably just my imagination. I suppose it is the smell of the world's knowledge.'

'Oh, how lucky you are. It is so unfair that women are not allowed to go to university or even just use the library. How I would love to read books that tell the stories of hundreds of years ago.'

'Oh, don't start, Lizzie. Mr Docherty doesn't want to hear about the injustices faced by women. The university was founded, as we are regularly told, in 1209 and has never had female students and never will. It is a known fact that women's brains are much smaller than men's and that they will never be academics. What would you do with a degree anyway? It is a truth that you should accept that a woman should "be sensible, pure, workers at home, kind, being subject to their own husbands." You are far better suited to domesticity; nothing you say or do will ever change that.'

I am mortified at Matthew's disdain and feel a ball of anger knot in my stomach. Mr Docherty nods in agreement but stops and blushes under my glare. 'My brain may well indeed be smaller than yours, for instance, but I cannot believe that every man in the world is cleverer than every woman in the world; I just don't believe it. And anyway, doesn't it say in the Bible somewhere, "ask and it will be given"?'

'John 15:7, "If ye abide in me, and my words abide in you, ye shall ask what you will, and it shall be done unto you." You need to work on the first part, Lizzie before you ask for God's help in allowing women into universities.'

'I have five sisters, Miss Elizabeth, and they all complain that they do not have enough lace or buttons, or that their bodice is not low enough, or is it high enough, I cannot for the life of me recall. But I have never heard any of them complain that they cannot go to university or take advantage of their libraries.'

'Not all women are the same, Mr Docherty, and I for one care nothing for fashion, but I do for knowledge.' There is an embarrassed silence which I feel obliged to break. 'But Matthew, is right, you don't want to listen to me, pray, tell us more about your sisters; they sound delightful. Would you not have preferred to see your family rather than come here? Not that you are not most welcome, of course.'

Why does he blush? 'No, Miss Elizabeth, it is too far. And...'

'And what?'

His blush deepens. 'I'm sorry. Mrs Hayes, Mr Hayes, Miss Hayes, forgive me. I find I am rather tired after all the travelling; I am talking nonsense. I thank you for your hospitality but I ask for your indulgence in allowing me to retire now?'

We all stand and bid Mr Docherty goodnight. Matthew speaks quietly to Papa and then departs also.

We three remain a while longer, not having an arduous journey to tire us out. I work on embroidering a handkerchief that I intend to give to Sarah, Mama reads and Papa stares into the flames of the fire, still necessary to take away the evening chill.

'Matthew wants to speak to me privately tomorrow morning. He didn't say what about.'

'Maybe he has run away from university, Papa. Would that be so awful? He could be a teacher again at the school. It would almost be like the old days, without Jamie to ruin it.'

'Hush, Lizzie, don't speak about your brother like that. I really don't know what he wants to say. All I know is that it is serious and I sense that he is worried about telling me.'

Chapter 18

April 1825

Breakfast is a quiet affair. Matthew seems nervous and eats little. As soon as Papa finishes they both go into the study and we can hear the murmur of their voices over the noises of our eating. Mama leaves the table to see to Dorothy, leaving just myself and Mr Docherty, who does not deign to look at me but concentrates instead on the leaf-pattern of the white linen tablecloth.

'It is indeed a pretty design, isn't it, Mr Docherty. Perhaps your Mama has something similar at home in Ireland and you are wishing you were there?'

He looks at me sheepishly. 'I apologise, Miss Hayes, please forgive my rudeness. I wonder whether you would be kind enough to show me around the town? I could do with stretching my legs and breathing in some fresh air.'

'I doubt the air is all that fresh once we get into the town, but I am happy to accompany you. Would you mind if I take my younger brother along? He too enjoys a walk, especially along the canal. Has Matthew mentioned him?'

'Yes, he's told me of the brother afflicted from birth and of your unselfish care of him. Do you not think you are serving God by loving one others cannot? Far better, for instance, than going to university for your own gain?'

'Oh, you're as bad as Matthew. You always have an answer that makes me sound selfish and ungodly. But God Himself gave me my brain; surely He cannot object to me wanting to use it? Oh, never mind, we will never agree. Come, I will show you the wonders of Wednesbury. We will start with St. Bartholomew's; I expect that is what interests you the most.'

We walk at Bobbit's pace and I entertain Mr Docherty with describing the antics of our neighbours, or at least what I imagine they get up to behind their closed front doors. We look inside the church, which Mr Docherty agrees is worthy of much praise and then we walk outside.

'Ah, good, our favourite place is free; please take a seat Mr Docherty. May I introduce you to the most accommodating Mistress Carmichael, to whom we are eternally grateful for allowing us to sit on her head?'

Mr Docherty hesitates. 'I prefer to stand, thank you, Miss Hayes.'

'Oh, fie, sir, she doesn't mind, really. Ah well, suit yourself.' He asks what the tall chimneys are that we can see below us and I tell him what men, women and children are doing in each building and underground. 'It is not work many would choose to do but it's work for which they get paid, although too little.'

'It is the boys of these people whom your father teaches?'

'Yes, it is. Hopefully they will be able to get better jobs than "these people," as you call them.'

'But if all the children get so-called better jobs, who will mine the coal and smelt the iron? Our industries will die, the country will become poor and there will be no better jobs.'

'I don't have the answer, Mr Docherty, as I expect my brain is too small. All I know is that no person should be made to dig underground like a mole or work in a foundry that is as hot as hell. They get so little for their hard work and have to see their own children starve whilst the owners and their families get fatter and fatter.'

We silently look at the vista before us, each with our own thoughts.

'Do you know what Matthew is speaking to Papa about, Mr Docherty?'

He continues to gaze out and I think he will not answer. 'It is not my place to tell you, Miss Hayes. Matthew or your father must.'

'Have you left university? Has Matthew fallen in love with a bar maid and married her? Are you running away from some dastardly men you owe money to?'

Mr Docherty throws his head back and laughs. 'You do indeed have a very fertile imagination, Miss Hayes. Please do not tease me; I cannot tell you. Come, lead on and let us walk along the canal.'

Mr Docherty is very pleased with Wednesbury. We look in all the shop windows, say a quick 'Good morning' to Mr Whittaker and the boys, and stroll along the towpath. He is at first amused and disbelieving when I tell him that Bobbit converses with the barge horses but he soon realises that it is really so, and thereafter he takes my brother's other arm and listens intently to the soft murmurings, though I can tell he understands nothing.

I feel nervous as we enter the house; surely I will find out Matthew's news and I cannot but feel that it will not be good. I go towards the kitchen and Mr Docherty goes upstairs to his room. I suspect he is keeping himself out of the way and I do wonder why he is here. Is it just to support Matthew or is he part of the story.

They are all here. Mama, Papa and Matthew are sitting round the table, Matthew is holding onto Mama's hands. Mama has been crying. Sarah is at her station by the range and Dorothy is playing under the table. They all look at me whilst I walk Bobbit to his rocking chair and make sure he is comfortable.

'Come and sit down, Lizzie. Matthew will explain what he has decided to do.'

I don't want to sit down. I don't want to know.

'Please, Lizzie. Come and sit next to me.'

I sit and Matthew now takes my hands in his.

'Do you remember a few years ago we went to hear a talk about being a missionary? You were very cross because you thought you might want to be one but they said they wanted women who were remarkable, and you wanted to know what that entailed?'

I nod. I look at his dear face, into his eyes the colour of autumn leaves, and I know.

'When are you going? And where?'

'Oh, thank you, Lizzie, for understanding.'

'I didn't say I understood. I am just asking how much longer you will be staying with us and how far away you will be.'

He squeezes my hand as if that will reassure me. 'We are going to a London training college for a few months first and then we are to set sail to Freetown probably in October. It is still to be decided.'

'We. Has Mr Docherty put you up to this? If he wants to go, that's his business, but why must he drag you there as well?'

'Oh, Lizzie. The seed was sown at the talk we attended at St. Bartholomew's. I have prayed and argued with God over the last few years; Docherty has tried his hardest to dissuade me and I him, but we are both absolutely certain that this is truly what God wants us to do. I feel so blessed that God has shown me the path He wants me to take so clearly.'

'And where does this path lead? Where exactly is Freetown and why do they need missionaries, anyway?'

'Freetown is in Sierra Leone. Do you remember when Papa showed it to you on the globe? It is on the west coast of Africa. Slavery has just been abolished, thank God, and there are many freed slaves and indigenous peoples who live there in darkness. Missionaries are needed to lead them out of that spiritual night into the Christian daylight. It is my calling. Mother and father understand; I very much hope that you can, Lizzie. I cannot refuse to do God's will because my little sister won't let me.'

I laugh although I don't want to. 'So I suppose those were the meetings you went to; meetings about being a missionary?' He nods. 'Will we ever see you again?'

'Of course you will. I won't stay out there forever and I will write.'

'Do they have paper out there? Will you be able to send letters? How will they ever get to us?'

'I will make sure I take lots of paper with me, a whole trunk full of it. There are regular mail boats between Sierra Leone and London so we can all send letters. It will take a while for them to be received so any news will be old news, I'm afraid.'

I suddenly have a wonderful thought. 'Now that I'm older, I could come with you! I could look after you and Mr Docherty if I need to. I could teach the little children their letters and read them stories. I wouldn't eat much and not take up any space at all. Maybe that is what God wants me to do?'

'Lizzie, oh, Lizzie. God doesn't want you to be a missionary. God wants you to stay here and look after Bobbit and help mother with Dorothy; to marry and bring up your own children as good Christians. I love you for wanting to come with me, but it is not the answer. Be content with being needed here. God needs his missionaries in Wednesbury as well as in Sierra Leone.'

Mama and Papa have been silent all the time Matthew and I have been talking, apart from a grunt from Papa when I suggested going to Africa, but now Papa speaks. 'It will be hard knowing that Matthew will be so far away, but we trust him, Lizzie, and trust in God, who is asking him to go. We will make the most of him whilst he is here, support him in any way we can and we will certainly make sure we give him a splendid send off when he goes. Do you know where you will be sailing from?'

'Bristol, I believe. It would be wonderful if you all came. Maybe you can persuade Jamie to come as well?'

A thought occurs to me. 'Why hasn't Mr Docherty gone home, Matthew? Is he scared of telling them?'

'Not scared, no, but we need to be in London in a few weeks and he really wouldn't have had time to travel to Ireland and back

114

in time. He has written them a very long letter and maybe some of them will manage to come to Bristol as well.'

'You had better go and fetch him; he is upstairs in his room. You should tell him it's safe to come down now.'

Mr Docherty does indeed look a little wary when he comes in but he soon relaxes as he is included in the conversation and he realises that Mama and Papa, at least, have accepted Matthew's decision.

But I haven't.

Chapter 19

April 1825

I feel the need to shout and scream at someone, so I excuse myself and go to the Goodmans' workshop to see if John is there. He is sitting outside on a log, eating a thick sandwich, which makes my mouth water. He breaks me off a piece.

'Why do you look so melancholy? Are you not pleased to have Master Matthew back? And his friend seems friendly enough.'

I finish chewing. I don't want to say the words out loud as it will make it a reality, but I say them anyway. 'Matthew is going to Sierra Leone as a missionary.'

'Ah, so that's it. A missionary. Where is Sierra Leone? Is it far?'

'Oh, John it is so far away it takes weeks and weeks, months even, to get there. It is in a place called Africa and the people are black and don't even speak English. I don't think they do anyway.'

'Black? What do you mean black?'

'I mean, their skin is black, whereas ours is pink. Or brown like yours because you go in the sun.'

'Is their blood black?'

'Oh, I don't know, John. Does it matter? The point is, Matthew thinks God is telling him to go, so he's going. How can I persuade him that it is probably the devil rather than God that is tempting him there? If he goes I'll never see him again, I know I won't.'

John sits awhile, scuffing his shoes in the earth.

'And he won't take me with him because I'm a woman and must stay in the house. Apparently that is what God wants for all women. Because we have small brains.'

John looks at me with a confused expression. He shakes his head like a wet dog.

'Say all that again.'

'Oh, never mind. I'm just cross because I don't want Matthew to go and know I won't be able to stop him, and all I have heard recently is how I should be happy to look after the house and all I can look forward to is marriage and having children.'

John's expression has changed from confusion to consternation. 'Men wouldn't be anywhere without women. How will the world go on if women refuse to have children? Is looking after a house, marriage, having children such a bad thing?'

'It just seems so inconsequential, so insignificant, so unworthy. Is that all I'm good for?'

John looks at me angrily, 'Miss Hayes, you are the cleverest, funniest and most capable person I know. I don't think being a homemaker is inconsequential; I don't think being a wife is insignificant; I don't think being a mother is unworthy. They only are if you think they are.'

'Oh, John, you are such a good person. You will make someone a very fine husband someday.'

'I hope so, Miss Elizabeth.' He stands up abruptly. 'Now, shall I ask mother to make another sandwich, as you have eaten mine?'

I spend a happy hour in the Goodmans' cosy kitchen, telling Mrs Goodman all about Matthew's plans and afterwards I walk slowly back home. The mention of black skin, John's homily and my own unreasonable discontent tickles my imagination and I think of a story I will tell it to Bobbit later on then write it down.

There was once a perfect village where everyone was as happy and healthy as can be; nobody was rich but everyone had just enough so that they were never cold or hungry. Everyone was content with what they had and thanked God every day. Everyone, that is, except for a young girl called Bess. Bess was always looking out of the window, wondering where the road went after the bend and what was over the hill. She wished she could go and find out. She was always day-dreaming of being somewhere else and imagined how exciting it would be to see different places. Maybe the people in these other places had different coloured skin or strange animals that made her laugh so much she had to hold her sides. Once, she walked to the next village, which was round the bend and over the hill, but she was disappointed to find that it was no different from her own. Maybe she had to go even further.

Bess was betrothed to a man called...'

I can't call him John or Nathaniel; that would be too presumptuous. I'll call him William, I don't know anyone called William.

Bess was betrothed to a man called William. He was a kind, gentle man who loved her very much and wanted nothing more than to get married and have lots of children. Although she had agreed to marry him - for what else was there for her to do? - she felt she was missing out on something, something she might find round the next bend or over the hill, or even across the waters.

The morning of her wedding, Bess went for a walk to pick some flowers for a garland. She strolled by the stream, which was giggling and chortling as it went on its merry way, where to? On an impulse, Bess thought she would follow the stream for just a little way, to see where it went. She walked and walked until the stream joined a large river, which didn't giggle and chortle but gave a deep, sonorous laugh as it slowly rolled on its way. Bess should have turned back, there was still time, but instead she carried on walking until finally the river joined the sea, which shouted and screamed at the top of its voice as it hurled itself against the rocks in frustration. Bess knew how it felt.

Bess did not know what was over the other side of the sea. Perhaps a land peopled with different coloured skin or strange animals that made her laugh so much she had to hold her sides. So she went to the port and got on a boat, paying her passage by telling stories to the sailors and helping to cook their meals. She didn't think of home or William once. After many days and nights of being tossed on the giant waves, the boat arrived at another country where Bess was thrilled to find that the people had skin as green as a newly opened leaf. Bess tried to speak to them but they didn't speak her language and they just laughed at her, thinking her quite an oddity with her pink skin.

She wandered through the country earning her keep by entertaining the green people with her dancing and singing, and she saw strange animals that made her laugh so much she had to hold her sides. Bess never once thought of home or of William. Each night she had a dream of a woman, plump and very happy, who lived in a pretty cottage with her husband, who was stout and very happy, and two lovely children, who were chubby and very happy. She never saw their faces but she always woke with a smile on her lips, she knew not why.

After a few days she came to a country where the people had skin as blue as the summer sky. Bess tried to speak to them but they didn't speak her language and they just laughed at her, thinking her quite an oddity with her pink skin. She wandered through the country earning her keep by entertaining the blue people with her dancing and singing, and she saw strange animals that made her laugh so much she had to hold her sides. Bess never once thought of home or of William. Each night she had a dream of a woman, stout and not very happy, who lived in a pretty cottage with her husband, who was stout and not very happy, and one lovely child, who was chubby and not very happy.

119

She never saw their faces and she always woke with tears in her eyes, she knew not why.

After a few days she came to a country where the people had skin as black as coal. Bess tried to speak to them but they didn't speak her language and they just laughed at her, thinking her quite an oddity with her pink skin. She wandered through the country earning her keep by entertaining the black people with her dancing and singing, and she saw strange animals that made her laugh so much she had to hold her sides. Bess never once thought of home or of William. Each night she had a dream of a woman, stout and really quite sad, who lived in a pretty cottage with her husband, who was stout and really quite sad, perhaps because there were no children. She never saw their faces and she woke crying, she knew not why.

After a few days she came to a country where the people had skin as pink as hers and who spoke the same language. They did not laugh at her, not even when she danced and sang because they didn't have enough to eat and had no money. The only animals that were there were too skinny to eat and too weak to work and it made Bess cry to look at them. Bess never once thought of home or of William. On the first night she had a dream of a woman, stout and sobbing uncontrollably, who lived in a pretty cottage all alone. For the first time she turned around so that Bess could see her, and she woke sobbing uncontrollably because the woman was her!

Bess realised that none of the countries had made her happy and that it was her own village and her own William that she yearned for, so she ran back through the country with people with the skin as pink as hers, through the country with people with the skin as black as coal, through the country with people with skin as blue as the summer sky and through the country with people with skin as green as a newly opened leaf.

She caught the first boat that was sailing to her own country and earned her keep by telling stories about the countries she had visited. When the ship docked, she ran and ran, away from the shouting and screaming sea, along the river with its deep, sonorous laugh, and along the giggling and chortling stream, until she was on the outskirts of her own village. She was exhausted and so stopped for a while, resting against the trunk of an oak tree.

The laughter of children woke her and she was astonished to find that they had come to help her pick flowers for her wedding garland. So she ran to the church and married William and was as happy and contented as everyone else in the village. Over time, Bess grew plump and William grew stout and they had two lovely, chubby children. They were very happy every day and Bess always woke with a smile on her lips – and she knew why.

This story surprises me; it is not the ending I would have expected to come out of my imagination. Matthew will approve but I am glad it is not one of the ones I sent to Jamie.

Chapter 20

April 1825

When I return home Papa has gone to the school and Matthew and Mr Docherty have gone to pay a visit to the Reverend Stephenson, whom I blame unequivocally for inviting the men from the missionary society to talk to his congregation in the first place. If it wasn't for them, Matthew would not now be preparing to travel to the other side of the world to a land where the people have different coloured skin and there are no doubt strange animals that will make him laugh so much he has to hold his sides. But such an adventure is not for me, for I am a woman with a small brain and must remain at home.

I suddenly feel guilty that I have neglected my duties today, so I go into the kitchen to offer my hands for peeling, scrubbing or chopping. But only Bobbit is there, rocking slowly and holding one of Dorothy's rag dolls that had once been mine. He is holding it as if it is a babe and humming a tune I do not recognise; his eyes are closed and he has a sweet smile on his lips. My heart lurches and I feel tears form that I let flow as there is no one to see me. How can anyone say that he doesn't understand anything? That he has no feelings? My poor, beautiful boy.

There is suddenly a loud rap on the door that startles us both. Bobbit's eyes spring open and he clutches the doll to his chest.

'It's all right, Bobbit, dear. It's only someone knocking at the door. Go back to singing to your babe.' But his expression has become blank and he drops the doll onto the floor, where it lies like the pile of old rags that it is. I hear Sarah coming down the stairs and the murmur of voices as she talks to whomsoever knocked with such gusto. The kitchen door opens as Sarah pops her head round.

'Can you come to the door, Miss Elizabeth? The gentleman says he must give the parcel to you alone.'

'Parcel? For me? Who's it from? What is it?'

Sarah chuckles and just shakes her head.

It is Master Geoffrey Sutton who is standing at the threshold, grinning like an idiot. In his hand he is holding something wrapped in blue paper.

'Good morning Miss Hayes. I am on my way home from a visit to London and your brother asked me to give this to you, and only you.' He hands me the package, bows to us both and turns to leave.

I suddenly remember my manners. 'Master Geoffrey, forgive me, please come in for some refreshment.'

'Thank you, but I will decline. My sister Alice has stayed in London for a while longer; she enjoys the company there. But it means that poor Mama has only had young Daniel for company for two weeks and I know she is impatiently waiting for me to tell her all the society and family news.' He bows again and departs to the coach that is waiting on the street outside.

'Well, Lizzie? What is it? What has James sent you?' Mama has come downstairs, her arms full of sheets that are to be washed.

'It feels like a book. Why would Jamie be sending me a book?'

'For goodness sake, Lizzie, are you going to just stand there wondering, or are you going to open it?'

'I need a knife, the string is bound too tight and I can't undo the knot as it is covered in sealing wax.'

Once I have cut the string the paper flutters to the floor like blue blossom and I am left holding a book in my hand. The pages are protected by brown paper-covered boards and words have been neatly scribed by hand on the front, but they might as well have been written in a foreign language for I seem to have lost my ability to read.

Mama sighs impatiently and takes the book out of my hands. 'Fairytales to Entertain.' Her eyes move to the bottom. 'By E.

Hayes. E. Hayes. My goodness, that's you Lizzie! Oh my word, James has got your stories printed in a book, a real book!'

I, whose words have been reproduced for all to read, am so overwhelmed that I can think of nothing to say. I take the book back and gently stroke the cover but still cannot make out the words; they are blurred through my tears. I hug it to my breast, just as Bobbit had done with Dorothy's rag doll and, still without saying anything, I go outside to sit and read my book.

My book.

I open the cover and see that Jamie has put a letter inside. I will read it later. The title and author are repeated on the front page, along with the publisher's and printer's details. Then comes the list of fairytales; I don't recognise the titles. The first one is called 'Edward's Quest.' I start to read. I recognise the story, it is the one I called 'Emily's Quest,' and most of the words are mine, but not all. Why is there no daughter called Emily but instead a son called Edward? Why is it Edward who goes in search of the voices? As I read on, my confusion turns to certainty and I feel chilled, despite the warmth of the sun. The ending is changed and as I read it I feel the bile rise in my throat.

When the King handed over the very large reward, Edward accepted it gratefully and was even happier when the Princess agreed to marry him.

No school for girls, no refusal to marry without love. What is the point of the story now? I can hardly bear to do it, but I turn to the next story, called 'Reward!' but it is a boy called James who leads the boggarts into the sea, and he does not refuse the reward and demand that Mr Sutton increases the men's wages as I had written, but instead he accepts it and is also given the hand of Alice, Mr Sutton's daughter. I cannot read any more, my hands are trembling and tears of anger blind me. How could he? How dare he? The book turns into a writhing snake on my lap and I throw it to the ground, the loosely bound covers coming apart, as if they too do not want anything to do with the contents.

Jamie's letter lies at my feet. I want to both tear it up unread, and read it. I stare at it for a while not even wanting to touch paper my despicable brother had handled but I cannot make out the words, so I lift it with two fingers and hold it as far away as possible whilst still close enough to read his poisonous words.

Dear Lizzie,

Well, what do you think? Doesn't it look grand? It will look even better with a leather cover and the words embossed in gold. This will be done once you have given your approval. Also, we are trying to get someone to illustrate the stories, which will not be cheap but Charles is very confident we can sell enough to cover the costs and more, and he already has a couple of booksellers interested.

You may not notice, but I have made a few small changes. Both Charles and I agree that the main characters need to be male and that the endings are the ones expected by the readers; that is wealth or marriage, preferably both. But the stories are still yours and I said you wouldn't mind, if it means getting the book published and sold.

You owe me a letter anyway, but can you write as soon as possible saying you are happy to have the book published?

Must dash, off to the theatre with the Suttons – Geoffrey has probably told you that Alice is here and we have to entertain her.

Write soon! J

'Small changes! I probably won't even notice! I won't mind! You, you, stupid, arrogant, useless...'

'Lizzie, Lizzie, whatever is the matter? Mama said you had something wonderful to show me. Why are you shouting so angrily? Please, remember we have a guest.' It is Matthew, looking both curious and concerned.

'I have every right to be angry. Look what he's done.' I pick up the unbound book and hurl it at him, the pages going in every direction. For some reason the sight of Matthew standing there looking so shocked makes me burst into tears and I rush past him and run up to my bedroom, where I lie on the bed and wet my pillow with my hot, angry tears. Every time my sobs subside I remember what Jamie has done and I start all over again, until I run out of energy and just lie, hiccupping.

There is a knock on the door and it opens.

'Can I come in, Lizzie?'

I shrug and keep my swollen eyes and running nose buried in the pillow.

'I take it that you don't think his changes are better, even though they will make the book more likely to sell?'

My throat is dry and sore after all my crying and I can only manage a rough, 'No.'

'But they are still your stories, written from your wonderful imagination. All he has done is change a few names and the endings. That is not too much, surely?'

My anger gives me the energy to sit up and I no longer care if Matthew sees the devastation of my face. 'I might have known that you would take his side, for you have always said that my stories should have brave men and not brave women, and that a bag of gold is a much better prize than a school or a decent wage.' I can feel the ire building in me again and it spills out of my mouth. 'I will not give my approval for those stories to be published. I will not have my name against them, I won't allow it.'

Matthew comes and sits on the bed and tries to take my hand, but I am in no mood for fraternal platitudes. He puts the book,

126

which he has collected together, on the bedcover. 'Don't be too quick to dismiss his offer, Lizzie. It is a great honour to have your stories published, even though they are not exactly as you wrote them. Just think how many people will be entertained. Isn't that what you want?'

'No! You have never understood, have you? I don't just want people to be entertained, I want them to have to think; I want them to realise that girls have brains, can be brave and can make a difference; I want them to understand that a prize for a girl can be something other than just marriage.'

'Oh, Lizzie, you can't change the way of the world with fairytales. The stories as you wrote them will never be published, these that James has changed will. Don't throw away this opportunity by your childish pride and stubbornness. Come downstairs now and walk with us into the town. I want to show Docherty the school.'

'I'll come down shortly. I need to tidy myself and I'll write to Jamie.'

'Good girl, Lizzie.'

13th April '25

James,

I cannot bring myself to call you dear at present, maybe I will again in time. I cannot like the changes you have made to the stories and I no longer consider them to be mine. If you want to publish them then please change the name on the front to J. Hayes, but I want no credit for them.

Please send the originals back to me.

Your very angry sister, Elizabeth Hayes.

I fold the paper and seal it with some wax. It will get included in the next letter Mama and Papa send to him but I don't want them to read it, for I know it is curt to the point of rudeness and they will try and make me write something less harsh. But Jamie needs to know that what he has done has hurt me terribly and I cannot forgive him. I wash my face with cold water and re-pin my hair. My eyes are still swollen and the smile I practice in the mirror looks instead like a grimace. I don't feel like smiling anyway.

When I go into the kitchen, Matthew, Mr Docherty, Mama and Sarah are all deep in conversation, which stops abruptly at my entrance.

'Ah, Miss Hayes. I hear congratulations are in order.'

'Hardly that, Mr Docherty. Just to let you all know, I have written to James to say I don't want the stories published under my name but he is quite welcome to do so under his own.' I put my hand up to stop the reproaches that everyone opens their mouths to utter. 'My mind is quite made up, so please do not ask me to change it.' I avoid looking at anyone so that I do not see the hurt and disappointment in their eyes. 'Now, Mr Docherty, I believe you are interested in seeing our little school.'

Chapter 21

April 1825

'Master Matthew looks very well.'

John and I are standing in our usual 'after Church' position under the yew tree, waiting for our families to finish their own catch-up with friends. Mr Whittaker is standing with Matthew but keeps glancing over to us as if he would prefer to join in our prattle.

'I don't think they ate very well at university. He and Mr Docherty have done nothing but eat since they have been here. Sarah made a multitude of pies before they came, but she still has had to do lots of baking to satisfy their appetite.'

'I suppose they want to make the most of it whilst they can. The food may not be so good in that country they are going to.'

'It's called Sierra Leone, John, and it's in Africa, which is a long, long way away.'

We both stare at Matthew as if to memorise how he looks in the English sunshine, having eaten sufficient good, English food.

'Master Matthew came into the workshop yesterday. He wants me to make a box for Mr Docherty, like the one I made for him. He said that his friend had admired it and so he wants to give it to him as a gift. They seem very good friends. I suppose they have to be if they are going to be missionaries together.'

I feel a stab of jealousy. I had had the box made especially for my brother as my gift to him when he left for university. I wanted him to think of me every time he put a cufflink, crucifix or coin into one of the partitions. I didn't want John making a similar box for just anyone else, not even Matthew's friend.

'Don't worry, Miss Elizabeth, I'll just make a plain box out of cherry wood and I won't make the initials as fancy as I did on Master Matthew's. It will be well made, for I can't make anything else, but it will be simple and functional, which is what Master Matthew asked for. In any case, I only have a few days to make it as he wants to take it with him to London.' John seems to understand me better than I do myself. 'Have you forgiven him, Miss Elizabeth?'

'Yes, I have. I can never be cross with him for long and I have to admit that he will make an excellent missionary. He said he would probably be allowed to come home after a couple of years. That isn't so very long to wait, is it? I'm used to being patient; it's one of the things I'm good at.'

'He's a good man, Miss Elizabeth and you should be very proud to have him as a brother. I always wanted a brother but it is my fate to be one to a younger sister. '

How I love John's smile. 'And I am sure she is proud that you are her elder brother, John. I wish you were my brother, rather than Jamie.' John's smile disappears. I could kick myself but cannot unsay the words, as much as I would like to.

'What has Master James done that is so bad that you want to disown him?'

I tell him and wait for him to say that I have made a mistake by refusing to give my approval for the stories, no longer my stories, to be published.

'I think you did right, Miss Elizabeth, if that means anything. He has no right to change your stories like that. The stories are wonderful because they are about strong girls who care about things other than money and marriage. Having those stories published under your name would be like,' he considers for a moment, 'like the good Reverend Stephenson rewriting some of the Bible stories so that the message is more palatable to us poor sinners. Does that make sense?'

'Oh, John, that means such a lot to me, thank you. Matthew says things will never change because of a fairytale, but I disagree. It is through telling stories that ideas form and alternative ways of life can be explored.'

'You keep telling your tales, Miss Elizabeth. One day you will tell them to your own children, who will tell them to theirs, and they to theirs. And maybe it will be one of your great-great-granddaughters who will change society because she was told one of your stories. Just think of that.'

'Oh, John, what a wonderful thought. You are the only one who understands. I don't want you as a brother, after all, I want you to stay as my friend. A very good, dear, friend.'

'Good morning, Miss Hayes, Mr Goodacre. I hope I'm not disturbing your private little tête-à-tête but your mother asked me to walk home with you, Miss Hayes, as she has kindly invited me to share your Sunday meal.' John doesn't respond verbally but his glower says a lot.

'Good morning, yourself, Mr Whittaker. And it is Mr Goodman, as you very well know. There is nothing private about our conversation; we are in full view of all and sundry and anyone is quite welcome to join us in discussing the making of wooden boxes and the telling of fairy stories. I will bid you good morning, John, and I thank you again for your reassurance.'

Mr Whittaker and I walk slowly home, discussing the Reverend Stephenson's sermon on the wrath of God, and then of other inconsequential things, until Mr Whittaker bursts out, as if he can hold the words in his mouth no longer, 'I am sorry that you need reassurance from a carpenter, Miss Hayes. It is surely something your family should provide? Or perhaps I?'

'It is one of the members of my family that has caused me to seek reassurance. John's job of work is of no relevance; he gave it as a friend, which is what he has been for many a year.'

'Matthew told me what James has done to your stories, for which I am sorry and I meant no disrespect to young Goodman's skills. I hope you also consider me as a friend, Miss Hayes? Maybe not one of such long-standing, but we are more akin as far as superiority, education and social standing. Can I be of any service? I like to think that I am a very reassuring person.'

I make no effort to keep the anger out of my voice and I stop and glare at Mr Whittaker with such ferocity that he steps back.

'John Goodman may not have grand-parents that are of the gentry, but then my parents have rejected that lifestyle and the Hayes of Wednesbury do not consider themselves superior to any family in this town; John Goodman may not have been educated to the highest level but that is for want of opportunity, not intelligence; John Goodman may not be invited to the houses of the wealthy as a guest to be entertained by silly dances and mediocre musical recitals, but he *is* invited to their homes because he is a master of his craft and can produce things of great beauty and function that are much sought after by people of all ranks.'

Mr Whittaker looks abashed; I take a deep breath and continue. 'John Goodman is the only person who understands why I write what I do. He believes in me, which is more than any of my family does. He agrees that I shouldn't put my name to the stories Jamie rewrote and I should carry on telling my own stories, even if no one wants to publish them. People may not be ready to read about my girls today, and maybe not for many years, but one day they will. So, Mr Whittaker, would you have reassured me in a similar manner? Or do you agree with Matthew, Mama and Papa, that I should be grateful to Jamie for re-writing my stories to being just ordinary so that they are sellable?'

Mr Whittaker does not answer immediately; he seems to be chewing a piece of gristle that he cannot swallow. 'I for one very much enjoy your stories, Miss Hayes, and I'm sorry for you that the publisher doesn't think they will sell in their current form. As your aim does not seem to be to sell them, then I see no reason why you should not continue telling your stories any differently than you do now.'

'A very diplomatic answer, Mr Whittaker. Now, shall we proceed otherwise we will have Sarah's wrath to contend with, which I assure you is far worse than God's.'

132

Chapter 22

October 1825

I have been dreading this day for so long and although I have packed my small trunk and walked down to the Turk's Head, where it is now in the process of being loaded onto the coach, I want to turn back home dragging Mama and Papa with me. Matthew wouldn't leave if we weren't there, surely? Could I pretend to be ill? But no, Mama would just ask Sarah to look after me, as well as Dorothy and Bobbit. Even if Mama stayed with me, Papa would still go to Bristol and Matthew would still sail to Sierra Leone and I would become really ill with guilt that Mama had not been able to spend time, maybe the last time ever, God forbid, with her first-born son. Oh, what a horrible person I am. I know I can't stop Matthew going, that my small voice will never be heard over 'His voice, and that a mighty voice.' I smile to myself despite my deep unhappiness; Matthew would be proud of me knowing an appropriate quote from the Bible. I go and stand next to the family group, where Mama is fretting.

'Oh, I do wish we were taking Dorothy. Is it too late? Can she not come?'

Mama has only just put Dorothy back into Sarah's arms, but she takes her again and holds her tight, smothering the poor child with more kisses. Dorothy wriggles until Mama has to put her down onto the ground and Sarah grabs her arm before she can run off.

'Beatrice, my dear, we have discussed this and we both agreed taking a three year old to Bristol would be too taxing for you, for her and for everyone else. She cannot sit still for three minutes, no matter about the two or three days it will take to get there and the same back again.' He takes both Mama's hands in his. 'She will be perfectly happy with Sarah and young Emily Goodman looking after her. I expect she will be badly spoiled and petted and you will have a hard time instilling discipline again when we return. Come, let us enjoy ourselves, just the two of us.'

'And me.'

'Well, yes, Lizzie, and you, of course. But you are an adult and don't need looking after. This is the first time I have had your mother to myself since Matthew was born. I intend to take full advantage of it.'

Mama blushes like a young maiden.

I see John standing on the outskirts of the crowd and go to him.

'How nice of you to come and see us off, John, thank you.'

'My pleasure, Miss Elizabeth. I know it is not a visit you are looking forward to, but would you write down everything you see, on the road and in Bristol? I want to know all the details.'

'You are right, my heart is too heavy to enjoy the journey but it might take my mind off things if I have the task of remembering everything so that I can write it down for you. It is a pity that my sketching skills are non-existent.'

'You paint pictures with your words, Miss Elizabeth and I know when I read them it will be as if I was there. I would especially like to see the ships. They are made out of wood, you know. I can't begin to imagine how many trees are needed. Will you find out for me, Miss Elizabeth?'

I can't help but smile at his enthusiasm. 'I will find out how many trees, how many planks, how many nails.' I put my hand on his arm and am surprised that the feel of his strength under my fingertips makes my toes curl. 'Will you do something for me? Will you go and see Bobbit when you can and take him for a walk? I am sure that your Emily is a good little worker but I am worried that she and Sarah will be too busy with Dorothy and the household tasks to spend any time with him. He needs his exercise and you know that he is no trouble at all.'

'Of course, Miss Elizabeth. I had already planned to do so. We two get along well together and I will take him to the stables so he can talk to his friends. Don't worry yourself about him. How long will you be gone, do you know?'

'We will be back before the end of two weeks.' Papa calls to me to come along. I realise I still have my hand on John's arm and quickly pull it way. I turn but not before I see his fingers stroking where my hand had touched his sleeve.

I have to wait whilst a large lady tries to force herself into the door, wriggling her well-endowed hips this way and that. I am sorely tempted to put my hands on her rounded rump and push hard but before I can do so another hand takes one of mine and holds it tightly.

'I wanted to say goodbye, Miss Hayes and wish you and your parents a safe journey.'

'Mr Whittaker, how kind of you. I wish the journey was for another reason so that I may enjoy it more.'

'My dear Miss Hayes, I do hope you don't distress yourself too much. As well as bidding you and your parents farewell, I wanted to reassure you that I will visit Master Robert each day and take him for a walk around the garden or perhaps up to the church. I hope that pleases you?'

The Large Lady, as I call her in my head, suddenly falls into the carriage, which rocks in protest, and it is now my turn. 'That is most kind, Mr Whittaker. I have already asked Mr Goodman to walk with Master Robert, but I'm sure he will be more than happy to share the task with you. May I have my hand back? I need to get in now.'

He releases my hand, we look at each other and then without any forethought I go onto my tiptoes and kiss him lightly on the cheek. He bows to me, but not low enough that I don't see his smile. Being the last to take my seat, I have no choice but to position myself between *The Large Lady* and a gentleman whose face I cannot see, but whose demeanour is one of anxiety and nervousness. His nails are bitten to the quick and though his upper body is perfectly still, his hands flutter on his lap as if he is playing an invisible instrument and one of his legs bounces up and down like a puppet's whose knee is being pulled constantly up and down by an invisible puppet master. *The Large Lady*, who takes up two seats, sits opposite Mama and Papa; they are holding hands in a most romantic way and I can tell that Papa is trying not to laugh at my obvious discomfort. Next to Papa is a father and son, their relationship evident by the likeness of the younger to the elder. Their clothes are of poor quality and have had many years' wear, but they are clean. It is clear that they have both recently bathed, so pink and scrubbed looking are their faces, although the father's hands cannot be cleansed of the coal dust that is engrained in the cracks and creases of his skin. The boy looks at me and smiles shyly; his excitement is almost physical and I wonder where they are going and why. Suddenly there is a shout of 'Walk on,' the crack of a whip and the coach lurches, as does my heart. I can only look out of the window where *The Nervous Man* is sitting as *The Large Lady* blocks my view of the other. I can't see anyone I know but I am pleased that *The Excited Boy* is able to give one last wave to his mother, who is smiling through her tears, unable to wave back burdened as she is with a baby in one arm and two youngsters clinging to her other.

I look out of the window as the shops and smoking factories quickly pass by and in a very short space of time we are into the open countryside. I describe what I see in my head so that I might remember and write it down accurately for John.

'Would you like to sit here, my dear? You will be able to see better if you are right next to the window.'

It is *The Nervous Man*, whose quiet voice I can hardly hear above the rattle of the wheels over the stones, but is heard perfectly by *The Large Lady*.

'Don't you dare move Father. You'll upset the balance and cause the coach to tip and we'll all get broken bones or worse. Just sit still. Here, have a crystallised fruit. No one should change seats whilst we are moving.' She glares at everyone, all of whom look down sheepishly as if they are children caught out in stealing. An arm is suddenly thrust before me with no apology offered and a dainty is dropped into *The Nervous Man's* hand, which he proceeds to nibble, like a little mouse.

So, they are wed; what an unlikely pair. The thought of them as a married couple reminds me of the effect of my touch on John's arm and the not unpleasant feel of Mr Whittaker holding my hand. I am not an innocent and know full well the reason for their animosity and refusal to be friends. A thought suddenly pops into my head unbidden, as thoughts are wont to do. What if both men asked me to marry them, would I accept either of them and if so, which one? John is a good, kind man, who I believe loves me but who also respects me and understands my belief that women are capable of much more than just keeping house and rearing children. Our marriage would be one of equality and partnership, but could he offer me a life that allowed me to live out my beliefs? Mr Whittaker is certainly more ambitious than John and if we were to marry then there could be opportunities for me to break the mould; perhaps teach at the school or maybe even open a new one together. They are both good looking in very different ways and both would make a good husband, again in very different ways.

This stretch of road is rutted and I am suddenly jolted out of my reverie; here am I dreaming of two husbands when I have not had one offer, and am not likely to for many a year. We are passing through a small town and I wave back at the children as they run alongside, totally oblivious to the mud that the wheels spray over their bare, skinny legs and tattered clothes. I have no idea where we are and ask Papa.

'This is Smethwick, Lizzie. We'll be in Birmingham in under an hour, I should think.'

The Large Lady leaches disapproval and censure that inhibits conversation, so I smile my thanks and revert to looking out of the window, realising that I have been too busy with my ridiculous imaginings to take any notice of the scenery. I will need to be more alert on my way back so that my account to John does not have big gaps in it. We are through the village in a matter of minutes and back in countryside that is flat and dull. Soon, however, the open fields and leafless woodland turns into smaller, distinct patches of land, each being worked by men and women bent almost double. I look to Papa and raise my eyebrows, knowing he will understand my silent question.

'These are small holdings where they grow vegetables and fruit for the Birmingham markets. They are on the outskirts of the city, so we will be there soon.'

In fact the view is already of factories and terraced houses, the buildings wreathed in smoke that creeps into the coach, despite the windows being closed. The smell is a familiar one that reminds me of home. The sound of the wheels changes as we cross a wooden bridge that spans a canal.

'That's our canal, Lizzie. This is where a lot of the barges come with the output from the iron foundries.'

The Excited Boy sits even further forward on his seat and grins; it is a link with home. The coach slows and finally stops. I can see nothing except a swarm of people all of whom seem to be intent on getting to their destination as quickly as possible. The doors are flung open, letting in a bedlam of noise that is so loud I want to put my hands over my ears: horseshoes and iron wheels on cobblestones; the shouts of men advertising their wares in market stalls I cannot yet see; dogs barking and horses neighing, caged chickens squawking; the drone of conversations as the crowd moves past like a swarm of bees.

The Nervous Man jumps down and runs round to the other side to help *The Large Lady* down. In the time it takes him to do so, we have all dismounted by the other door and are waiting for our luggage. I find myself standing next to *The Excited Boy*, who is looking around with eyes as round as marbles.

'Are you staying in Birmingham or are you going on?'

'I'm staying here, missus, I'm to be apprenticed to a silver maker who's an uncle or summat like.'

'Don't mither the lady, boy. She's not interested in the likes of you.'

'Oh sir, you are quite wrong. I am most interested and have been wondering throughout the journey what great adventure he is about to embark on. Well, I see you have your trunk. I wish you well and every success.' I shake the boy's hand, which surprises him a little and give the father a small curtsey, which surprises him even more. Then they disappear into the crowd, one tall, one short, carrying the trunk between them; the boy constrained from skipping only by its weight.

Chapter 23

October 1825

We have been deposited outside St. George's Tavern, a large, white, three-storied building, from which we will depart on another coach to Worcester later in the afternoon. Having a few hours to while away, we leave our trunks under the watchful eye of an elderly man, once a soldier if he is to be believed, and go into the inn to find somewhere to sit and eat. I had put together a basketful of food this morning and I am surprised that sitting relatively still for two or so hours, apart from being bounced up and down due to the roughness of the road, has made me hungry. The room is the full width of the building and is filled with long tables, at which people sit, all of whom I assume to be in the same position as ourselves. The noise is such that we eat in silence, the effort to make ourselves heard too great. I study the other travellers so that I might describe them to John. There are groups of working men, perhaps small holders having delivered their products to the market, tucking into their bread, cheese and meat pie and obviously enjoying their flagons of beer, if their loud outbursts of raucous laughter is any indication; gentlemen of business, identifiable by their black, shiny top hats, gold-topped walking sticks and obvious contempt of everyone not of their ilk; families, from the common folk whose children are allowed to run around screeching at the top of their voices and getting in everyone's way, to the gentry whose off-spring sit passively, backs ram-rod straight, but whom I imagine would dearly love to throw off their tight apparel and have a good romp with the others.

Having finished our repast we agree to take a walk around the market for a little exercise and conversation. Papa makes sure the entrance to the inn is still in view.

'I need to be able to see when our coach arrives. It will have come from Coventry and it will only take a few minutes to

replace the horses and refresh the driver before they are
leave again. It's not too far to Worcester, so we should ḷ
in time for supper this evening. We will need to retire eȧ.ɹy as
we have to be ready to leave again at five o'clock in the morning.
The coach won't wait; it's a long journey and they have to get to
Bristol by the evening.'

I know all this, for it has been repeated almost every day
since the arrangements have been finalised. 'Just think,
tomorrow evening we will be seeing Matthew. He will be there,
won't he Papa?'

'I'm sure he will. He said in his letter that he expects to arrive
tomorrow morning and there is no reason why he will not.'

We have markets in Wednesbury, of course, but this one is
three or four times larger. I lift my skirts to avoid the excretions
of the live animals: horses, donkeys, dogs, sheep, goats, geese
and pigs. Those not so fortunate to be roaming freely are caged
and making their indignation known by loud brays, bleats,
squawks or squeals. Those not so fortunate to be alive are
hanging feet first from poles, their blood dripping slowly into the
mud, forming a russet-coloured puddle beneath, or being rotated
slowly on a spit with their fat dripping into the fire beneath and
their skin cracking and spitting into the faces of the boys slowly
turning the handle. The warmth is gratifying and the smell
mouth-watering. There are stalls selling vegetables picked this
morning but now beginning to wilt and also the 'crop' from the
local factories: buttons, buckles, silverware and snuff boxes, all
of which shine even in the dull, October gloom. I am tempted to
buy some buttons that will look very pretty on a bed jacket I am
knitting for Sarah, but before I can do so Papa diverts my
attention and says our coach is being loaded ready for our next
part of the journey.

This coach is slightly bigger than the one we took from
Wednesbury and at full capacity will take eight people inside and
ten outside plus the coachman and guard. The four new horses

being attached to the coach are fresh and eager to be on their way, their restless hooves scraping at the cobbles. Papa makes sure that our trunk is securely stowed in the rear baggage boot and then we climb the steps into the tin box, which, after all, is basically what the body of a coach is. We are the first passengers so we are able to sit where we want; Papa sits by one window and Mama opposite him and I choose to sit by the other window, the better to see out of. I have a sudden moment of horror when I wonder if *The Large Lady* and *Nervous Man* will be our travelling companions, but no, it is another family that mounts. The father, who has the bearing of a soldier, sits next to Papa and the mother opposite him and the two children sit next to their father, opposite me. Their outer clothes are of a good quality and the boy, aged about eight and the girl, who is a couple of years older are, at present anyway, well behaved. Papa introduces us to the family and the man, military as I suspected, shakes Papa's hand and says his name is Captain Cartwright, then introduces his wife, Mrs Francesca Cartwright and his son, Stephen, and daughter Abigail.

Whilst we are all politely nodding and smiling at each other, the coach rocks, causing us all to laugh nervously, as the remaining passengers clamber up to the outside seats, some at the back, some the front and some directly on top. These seats are much cheaper but I don't envy them their precarious position, hanging onto the rails for dear life, being buffeted by wind, drenched by rain and covered by the mud and dung flung up by the horses' hooves.

Before long we are on our way. I soon tire of the industrial scenery and turn my attention to the inside. Papa is in quiet conversation with the Captain and Mama and Mrs Cartwright also seem to have found a common interest and are sitting with their heads together. The children are engrossed in a game of Fox and Geese, which results in periods of deep, silent concentration interspersed with giggles and painless pinches. I watch them for a while, remembering when I used to play with Matthew, who always let me win, or Jamie, who never did.

We are out into the countryside again, but I don't find it very interesting, deciding that one tree looks very much like another, and one field indistinguishable from its neighbour. I take out my book and settle down to read, making use of the remaining daylight. It is *Pride and Prejudice* written, according to the front-piece by the author of *Sense and Sensibility*. We now know this to be a Jane Austen, who has written other novels, many of which I have read and found very satisfying. I am particularly enjoying this book because Elizabeth Bennett is a woman after my own heart: strong, independent and determined to marry for love, regardless of any economic factors or social expectations. We stop after a few hours at Bromsgrove to allow the passengers to stretch their legs and the horses to eat some hay and drink from the stone trough by the side of the road. There is no time to wander around but I have no desire to; the small cottages are crowded together and don't tempt exploration. Everything looks dirty in the half-light and there is a constant hammering that makes my head ache, which Papa says comes from the nailers in the tiny sheds attached to their cottages.

We are soon on our way again. The light is too poor for me to read so I put it back into my reticule and close my eyes, meaning to draft a letter to John in my head, describing my journey thus far.

Maybe I did but I have no memory of it and the next thing I am aware of is Mama touching my arm and telling me to wake up for we have arrived at Worcester. It is now night-time and apart from the passengers milling around waiting for their baggage, there are few people on the street. The door to The Talbot, the coaching inn where we are staying, is open and the light spills out, along with the murmur of diners and drinkers enjoying their evening meal. Looking away from the inn there is a huge, towering mass that is blacker than the black sky.

'That's Worcester Cathedral. It was built over a millennium ago and has the most interesting history. I wish we had time to visit it for I am told it is exquisite inside.' Papa looks wistful at the missed opportunity but then busies himself with putting a coin into the hand of the coachman and guard and telling the porter where to take our trunk.

Only our inside travelling companions are staying at The Talbot; the others are drifting off, I know not where. I watch them disappear into the gloom and, perhaps because I am far from home and out of my normal routine, I am suddenly struck by the thought that each of them, regardless of age, sex or social position, has dreams and fears, prayers they want answered, a past and a future which are unique to themselves and which they take with them into the dark. My own sorrow at the prospect of Matthew leaving and my frustrations at the unfairness of life are, I realise, small and insignificant and of no interest to anyone else. I see myself as God must see me, one small person; it matters not whether I am a man or a woman, in a village or a city, I am just one of a world full of people all wanting their lives to be meaningful and fruitful. I know now that it is impossible for God to answer my prayers and for my dreams to be fulfilled without having to deny others theirs. Worcester Cathedral has stood for a thousand years and will have watched with its stony face generations of men and women live their lives, most of who never changed the course of history nor were remembered once they had died.

'Come on, Lizzie. Don't stand there daydreaming. Get inside and let's get settled and then we can have a meal and get to bed. We have an early start tomorrow, remember.'

Papa frowns as he stands by the door, waiting for me to move but my heart seems so heavy I can barely find the strength the bear it. How I wish I wasn't here; how I wish I was at home; how I wish I hadn't realised how unimportant I am and how impossible it is that I will have my prayers answered or my dreams realised.

Chapter 24

October 1825

A tap on the door rouses me from a slumber I am sure I have only just fallen into. Because of the deep melancholy I had sunk into, I had not managed to sleep straight away, but had lain in my narrow bed staring into the void. I could have lit a candle but my surroundings would not have cheered me, clean and neat though they were. No, my thoughts needed to be chewed by the black teeth of the night and swallowed down its dark gorge. I have no time for further introspection and quickly get dressed, leave a coin for the chambermaid and go downstairs where the inn keeper has put out some meats, cheeses and bread. I am not hungry but eat anyway, Papa having said that we will probably not stop again until lunchtime, when we get to Cheltenham.

'This is an interesting inn, Lizzie. I stayed up a little while last night and the keeper told me and the Captain here how one of the back rooms was used by Charles II as his headquarters during the Battle of Worcester. Just think of it, nearly two hundred years ago the King of England might have been sitting where you are, eating the same sort of food and planning how to defeat Cromwell.'

'He didn't though, did he? Didn't he have to run away and all his troops got killed or taken prisoner? Or was that a different battle?'

'No, you're correct. I'm pleased that you listened to your history lessons. This was the last battle of the Civil War and led to Charles's exile, the rule of Parliament and the rise of Protestantism in England. An important time in our history.'

'Would you have been a Roundhead or a Cavalier, Papa? A Royalist, I fancy. I can just see you in a wide lace collar, a broad brimmed hat with an enormous feather and an upsweeping moustache and a neat beard.'

146

Papa has no time to answer as the guard comes into the room and asks us to get a move on. It is cold and damp outside and still dark; our chatter ceases and we all clamber into the same coach seats we had yesterday and sit huddled in our coats, the only noise being our blowing onto our hands to warm them a little. Others emerge from the murk and climb unenthusiastically to their outside places. The lanterns hanging on the outside of the coach benefits the coachman only and soon those of us inside succumb to the steady movement, the lack of anything to see and the chill.

It never really gets light all day. There is an autumnal mist that smothers the landscape and I get a headache trying to pierce its veil. We stop at Cheltenham for some refreshments and to change the horses. There is a lot of building going on with a preponderance of curving crescents of large houses with columned porticoes - of the Greek Ionic style Papa informs me - and wrought-iron balconies. Even the white stucco appears grey in the not-quite-daylight. The streets are busy with visitors partaking of the healing waters, the builders of the aforementioned houses and the carts laden with all the paraphernalia required by these workmen.

Back in the coach, I revert to my day-dreaming. I am tired of my own emotions and want to try and imagine how Matthew is feeling, so I picture him, having just arrived at Bristol, in a small, room similar to the one I slept in last night. He will be laying out a clean shirt ready to change into later on, putting the wooden box that I commissioned John to make onto the chest of drawers along with his hair brush. There will be a bowl and jug of hot water, so he will wash his hands and face of the grime picked up from his journey from London. He will be looking forward to seeing his parents and sister in the evening but his thoughts will not tarry with them for long. Instead, he will take out his Bible and read it to remind himself why he has chosen, or rather been chosen, to travel to a distant country in order to evangelise to the heathen. He will perhaps imagine himself standing at the front of the ship, the sea spray in his face, the sails filled with the wind taking him to Africa, his eyes searching for the first hint of land on the horizon. He will see himself surrounded by a group of smiling men, women and children, all with skins as black as coal, all hanging onto every word out of his mouth, out of His mouth.

The anticipatory excitement that he must be feeling courses through my own veins and quickens my heart. How could I be so selfish as to make him feel guilty at my misery at his going? No, I decide there and then, that I will be happy for Matthew; that I will be proud of him; that I will never bemoan his going, but rather rejoice in it. I feel so relieved, as if a great load has been lifted from my shoulders. I am pleased for him; I am excited with him; I will send him off with a genuine smile on my face and a blessing in my heart.

The day seems brighter, although there is still no sign of the sun and I bring my thoughts back to the here and now. I smile at Master Stephen and ask him if he would allow me to beat him at a game of Fox and Geese. He accepts my challenge with a wide grin, his sister comes and sits next to me – *The Large Lady* would have been horrified at her moving whilst the coach is in motion – and we spend the remaining hours very pleasantly, with the boy always the victor whether in the role of fox or geese.

We arrive at Bristol at around seven o'clock, as promised. We are deposited outside a coaching inn called The White Lion and bid our fond farewells to the Cartwright family. We are not staying here, though, so Papa calls for a porter and we follow him trundling along the street with our chattels loaded into a small cart. It is only a short distance down Broad Street and round the corner to Corn Street and The Bush Tavern. I am too tired to take much notice but am aware of a well-lit street with people still milling about, despite the hour. Soon we are being greeted by the very short, wide, buxom innkeeper's wife, who assures us that two 'gennlemen' from London arrived earlier in the day and are eagerly awaiting our arrival in a private dining room.

Papa has to hold me back from rushing there directly.

'Another ten minutes is of no matter, Lizzie. We will go to our rooms, change and refresh ourselves and then we will be in a fit position to be seen in company. The journey has left us all looking somewhat unkempt. Your mother and I will call on you when we are ready so that we can go down together.'

I am ready within minutes and then sit tapping my foot impatiently waiting for Mama and Papa to arrive. When they do so, I can see by their bright eyes and wide smiles that they are as excited about seeing Matthew again as I am, but we are quite decorous in our descent and walk serenely to the room where we are to dine as if we are about to meet someone of no interest to us.

When we open the door it is like walking into Bedlam at the full moon and we stand in the doorway a little bemused. I had expected just Matthew and perhaps Mr Docherty to be there, but the room is full of people unknown to me. Mama and Papa seem as confused as I am, but then a familiar figure strides towards us, arms held out to embrace Mama, shake Papa's hand and hug me so tight that all the air is forced out of my lungs.

'Oh, Mother, Father, Lizzie, it is so good to see you. I had planned just a quiet meal but look, Docherty's whole family have come from Ireland after all and we thought we would have a celebration meal together. That is all right with you, isn't it? Please, just say if you would prefer something a little less boisterous. We can always go into another room if that is what you prefer.'

'Of course not, boy. It will be a great pleasure to meet Mr Docherty's family and to share the occasion. Come, make the introductions.'

It is easy to see what the younger Mr Docherty would look like in twenty years or so should he have chosen to remain in

Ireland and live the gentrified life that his father probably wanted him to. The older Mr Docherty has the look of his son in the face from what I can discern under the long, thick sideburns that he sports. They are both short in stature but whereas I describe the son as being solidly built, the father can only be described as fat. He has the most rotund stomach I have ever seen and I applaud the tailor who has made the waistcoat with such robust seams and buttons. The cravat is not sufficient to cover his multiple chins. When he bows deeply over my hand I am presented with his shiny bald crown and a waft of pomade that makes me cough. He is however, utterly charming in a sincere way and I decide that I like him very much.

Mrs Docherty is almost, though not quite, as round as her husband and is dressed in a rather startlingly pink dress that reveals far too much of her ample bosom. Her hair is red, a common colour in the Irish I believe, her white skin freckled and her eyes the same colour as our cat, Thomasina. She, like her husband, has the most friendly of dispositions but I am glad she is not my mother.

The daughters, just the three older ones as the two younger ones, as Mrs Docherty breathlessly explains, are too young to be in company, range from the ages of fourteen to eighteen and are all silly. I cannot easily tell them apart for they all look alike with their mother's colouring, the same elaborate curls tumbling down and dressed in evening dresses of white and far too much pink lace, ribbons and bows. They look so much like three meringues that I am ashamed to say that I giggle when I am introduced, but as they do nothing but giggle themselves, my own goes unnoticed.

Once all the introductions have been made we sit at a large circular table for a supper prepared by the innkeeper's wife. I am placed between the two older Docherty girls, whether Aileen, Cathleen or Coleen I am uncertain. I feel quite dull and plain next to them; like one of Sarah's fruit cakes between two elaborate dainties. Although both my grandparents are of the gentry, my father, the third son, chose a life in which he gives rather than takes, and my mother, one of many daughters, was happy to join him. Our life, therefore, is not one of genteel soireés and pointless pursuits and although my neighbours try very hard to involve me in their discussions of current fashions, it is clear from my own dress and lack of knowledge that we have nothing in common. Very soon the Miss Docherty on my left turns her attention to her other sister and the Miss Docherty on my right to my brother.

I read novels and recognise flirtation when I see it and Miss Docherty is most decidedly flirting with Matthew, although I am at a loss as to why, as he will be gone in a few days' time, but that may indeed be the very reason. Everyone is talking at once and their words fill the room and my head and getting louder and louder. A burst of laughter makes me jolt upright and I realise in horror that I have dozed off. I look around to see if anyone has noticed; Mama has. She stands and the conversations die down.

'It has been the greatest of pleasures to meet you all and share supper with you but it has been a very long day and I really feel the need to retire. Please do not let me spoil the rest of your evening. Elizabeth, would you care to accompany me?'

I gratefully curtsey to the men who stand as we leave and to the ladies, who remain seated but who wish us a good night's rest. I take Mama's arm and walk her to her room.

'Come in with me for a few minutes, Lizzie and brush my hair for me. I know you're tired but I want to ask you something.'

I help her out of her dress and into her nightshift then unpin her hair and start to brush, a task I used to do willingly when I was a child. I notice that there is now grey among the brown. Mama looks at me in the mirror a frown creasing her brow.

'Have we done wrong by you, Lizzie?'

'Wrong by me? What do you mean?'

'Bringing you up as we have. Would you prefer a life like the Docherty girls?' I am so surprised that I stop brushing and stare at her in the mirror. 'Because if you do, my sister will be more than happy to introduce you into society, if that is what you want.' I am still standing like a statue, hand raised mid stroke, mouth slightly open. She smiles hesitantly. 'I just wondered whether you would like to be able to discuss the current fashions with other young ladies; to wear pretty dresses and curl your hair with papers; to know how to dance and to flirt.'

I start to brush again, harder than before until Mama gives a small yelp of pain. 'Why would you possibly think that I wanted to be anything like the Docherty girls, or anyone of that sort? I can't believe that you would. Have I ever said that I wanted to?'

She shakes her head. 'It's just seeing you tonight with the other girls reminded me what sort of life your father and I chose to walk away from. But our choice may not be yours. It doesn't have to be.'

'You mean it doesn't have to be if I desert my family; abandon my care of Bobbit; renounce my love of writing and story-telling; turn my back on everything you and Papa have taught me?' I walk to her side and gently take her chin and turn her head so that I can look at her eyes directly, not through the distorting mirror. 'I have dreams, yes, but none of them involve dancing, giggling or flirting. Or looking like a meringue. Does that answer your question, Mama?'

We silently look at each other and then both burst into laughter, Mama gasping the word 'meringue' over and over again.

Chapter 25

October 1825

There was once a King whose beloved wife had died giving birth to their only child, a daughter whom the King could not bear to name. The King knew he needed someone to bring the child up as a Princess so he put an advertisement into the local newspaper asking for nannies.

The first girl he interviewed was very pretty with an oval face and long, black hair and long, black eyelashes that she fluttered at the King. She was tall and willowy and as dainty as dainty could be and the King was quite convinced that she had wheels rather than feet under her layered, taffeta skirts.

'And what will you teach my daughter?'

'Oh, your Majesty, I will teach the Princess to dance so that she is always the belle of the ball. She will be able to pirouette, skip, twirl and glide. She will know how to dance the cotillions, reels, waltzes and quadrilles and she will never be without a dancing partner.'

'Can you teach her anything else?'

'Dancing will be enough for her to ensnare and marry a Prince, and surely that is all you want for her? And I will always be happy to teach you to dance, your Majesty, and to be on hand to help you to entertain.' She fluttered her long, black eyelashes again and gave the most spectacular curtsey and the King said he would let her know, although he realised he didn't know her name.

The next girl was very pretty with a round face and long, golden hair and long, golden eyelashes that she fluttered at the King. She was tall and dressed in a black and white dress that showed off her impressive bosom and she trilled as she walked.

'And what will you teach my daughter?'

'Oh, your Majesty, I will teach the Princess to sing and play the pianoforte so that she is always the main attraction at every

153

musical evening. It will be as if she was a pupil of Bach, Mozart and Haydn themselves and she will sing a Scottish and Irish ballad as if she had been born in those distant lands.'

'Can you teach her anything else?'

'Music will be enough for her to ensnare and marry a Prince, and surely that is all you want for her? And I will always be happy to teach you to sing and play the pianoforte, your Majesty, and to be on hand to help you to entertain.' She fluttered her long, golden eyelashes again and gave the most flamboyant curtsey and the King said he would let her know, although he realised he didn't know her name.

The next girl was very pretty with a heart-shaped face and long, auburn hair and long, auburn eyelashes that she fluttered at the King. She was tall and had long fingers and a dress of all the colours of the rainbow.

'And what will you teach my daughter?'

'Oh, your Majesty, I will teach the Princess all about art and to paint like one of the masters. She will capture each petal of one of the roses plucked from your garden, each whisker on one of your favourite hounds, each hair on the head of your majesty. Everyone will be amazed and say that they have never seen anything so life-like.'

'Can you teach her anything else?'

'Art will be enough for her to ensnare and marry a Prince, and surely that is all you want for her? And I will always be happy to teach you to paint, your majesty, and to be on hand to help you to entertain.' She fluttered her long, auburn eyelashes again and made the most exuberant curtsey and the King said he would let her know, although he realised he didn't know her name.

By now, the King was very tired and really didn't want to have to face yet another simpering maid, but he was a King after all and had to rise above such feelings, so he asked for the last one to be brought to him.

She was, well, what was she? Scruffy certainly and she might have been pretty if she had washed the mud off her face. Her hair looked like straw, my goodness, it was straw peeping out from under her slightly askew bonnet. The King did not notice whether she had long eyelashes for he was mesmerised by her blue eyes that pierced him as if he was a butterfly pinned to the wall. He felt unaccountably nervous.

'Er, and what will you teach my daughter?'

'Does your daughter not have a name?' The King sadly shook his head. 'Then the first thing I will do is to name her so that she knows who she is. Do you like the name Flora?' The King suddenly realised that he loved the name and nodded his head.

'Just so you know, my name is Marigold.' She surprised the King by stepping up to him unbidden and firmly shaking his hand. 'And I will teach Princess Flora where the worms live and where the stars go in the daytime.'

'And what else?' He felt a little braver.

'I will teach Princess Flora how to feed a motherless lamb and what tadpoles grow into.'

'What about dancing?'

'Princess Flora will study the bluebells and the snowdrops, the foxgloves and the lilies of the valley and when they dance in the breeze, so will she.'

'And what about singing?'

'Princess Flora will befriend the birds and when the robin twitters and the blackbird chirrups, when the blue-tit whistles and the little wren flutes, then so will she.'

'And what about art?' The King felt he had to ask.

'Princess Flora will learn very early on that God is the one and only artist and that it is sacrilege to even try and copy Him. No person can better the colours of Nature; flowers should be left to grow, not torn from mother earth to die in an ugly vase.'

155

The King felt inexplicably ashamed. 'And will she learn to be a suitable wife for a Prince?'

Marigold tilted her head and looked at the King with a disappointed expression. 'I think the question should be whether there is a Prince who will make a suitable husband for the Princess Flora, don't you?'

The King realised that, yes, that is the question he should be asking. He also realised he didn't know where worms lived or where the stars went in the daytime. 'Can you teach me all these things?'

Marigold smiled. 'Of course I can, your Majesty. As long as you are happy to get up and come outside as soon as the sun stretches her rays, whatever the weather is; as long as you don't mind lying in the mud waiting for the worms to peep out; as long as you don't mind climbing a tree to put a fledgling bird back after he has fallen out of the nest; as long as you are content to take your shoes and socks off and dangle your toes in a river and listen to it as it tells you of its life.'

The King looked at Marigold and Marigold looked at him. Marigold did not flutter her eyelashes, which, the King noticed, were long and brown; Marigold did not make any sort of curtsey but stood upright and the King did not think he had ever seen a girl so beautiful.

'When can you start, Marigold?'

The King and Princess Flora learned together and when the King died, as Kings invariably do, he was quite happy to hand over his kingdom to his daughter, knowing that she would reign with patience, love and respect. Princess Flora had not married for she had not yet found a Prince whom would make her a suitable husband. Neither had the King remarried. What? You expected him to marry Marigold? The girl with the muddy face and straw in her hair? Don't be ridiculous, that sort of thing only happens in fairy tales!

It is quite late in the morning when I go down to break my fast and I assume the rest of the family are already there, but when I enter the room where the food is being served I am surprised to see Mr George Docherty sitting alone at a table, looking rather wanly at a plate of kippers.

'May I sit with you, Mr Docherty? Will the rest of your family be joining you soon?'

Mr Docherty half stands and gives me a slight bow, before sitting heavily back down. He grimaces as someone else scrapes his chair along the floor, the noise seemingly too loud for him to bear.

'Please do, Miss Hayes. No, my family are not staying here; this place is a bit beneath them and so they are ensconced at a nearby hotel.' He seems to realise what he has inferred and blushes deeply. 'Oh, forgive me, Miss Hayes. That did not come out as I intended; I meant no offence. My sisters are prigs, as I am sure you have discovered for yourself, and wanted to stay somewhere where they might bump into the aristocracy. The older two are on the lookout for husbands, d'you know.'

'No offence taken, Mr Docherty. Did supper go on for much longer after Mama and I left? You seem somewhat, how can I say, weary?'

He manages a grin. 'Mother and the girls left soon after you, but the men folk remained and drank more port than they probably should have. I know I did.'

This surprises me, for I have never seen either Papa or Matthew drink more than one glass. 'Your plate of kippers looks most appetising, I think I will order myself some,' to which Mr Docherty merely responds with a grunt. No sooner had he done so than the door opens and Mama, Papa and Matthew come in, looking far more refreshed than poor Mr Docherty, who manages to stand upright to bid them all the top 'o the morning.

'My appetite is not great this morning so if you do not think me too rude I will take my leave. Mr Smith said he would meet

us at the Cathedral at midday, Matthew. I'll see you all there.'
He bows his farewell and leaves.

'What is happening at the Cathedral, Matthew?'

'There is a service of thanksgiving for the new missionaries - and their families and friends, of course. Mr Docherty and I, along with a few others, have been staying with Mr Benjamin Smith whilst we have been in London. I suppose you could say he is our sponsor and he has been instructing us on what is expected of us and what we can ourselves expect. He has come to Bristol to make sure we get on the boat!'

'I think you'll find they are called ships, Matthew. You don't want to go upsetting the captain by calling his vessel by the wrong name. Let's have a hearty breakfast and then make our way to the Cathedral. I understand it is possibly the most beautiful example of a medieval church in England, if not in Europe. Although it was originally an abbey, it didn't get destroyed as part of Henry VIII's acts of suppression but the nave never got finished. I am looking forward to seeing the inside.' Papa, ever the teacher.

We are in the process of ordering our food when the outside door is flung open, letting in a blast of cold air and a shower of rain. Someone comes in, stamping his feet and laughingly shaking his head, scattering wet drops over the floor. I am focussed on extricating my skirts from a kitten's sharp claws and take no notice of him.

'My God, James! Is that really you? You came after all, you old devil!'

James? Brother James? It is indeed he, grinning from ear to ear as he hands his sodden cape to the innkeeper's daughter, who bobs a curtsey, straightens her mob cap and giggles all at the same time. There is a flurry as Mama rushes to hug him, Papa slaps him soundly on the back and Matthew pumps his hand up and down. Jamie greets me with a raised eyebrow, to which I similarly respond. I have not forgiven him, nor ever will, for what he did with my stories and I have no intention of being anything more than merely polite to him.

'Mama, please, you are squeezing the life out of me. You don't think I would let my elder brother depart this land without me waving a fond farewell? Geoffrey Sutton has relatives here and he felt a visit was due so he was kind enough to bring me. We are staying at his uncle's place. We arrived last night but I didn't want to disturb you as it was unsociably late.'

Mama reluctantly releases him from her embrace. 'It is wonderful to see you James. Have you breakfasted? Either way, come and sit with us and eat or not as you wish. Afterwards we are all going to the Cathedral for a thanksgiving service. Where does Mr Sutton's uncle live, is it far from here? How was the journey from London? Oh, it is so lovely to see you and you are looking well, life in London obviously suits you.'

'Mama, Mama, no I haven't eaten and some eggs and kippers would be much appreciated. Let me sit down and I will answer all your questions and more.'

So, what is meant to be Matthew's day has suddenly become James's, how very typical. I am sure he has not come to Bristol just to see his brother off; there will be another reason, one that is only of benefit to Mr James Hayes.

Chapter 26

October 1825

The chapel is bitterly cold, colder than it is outside. Any air warmed by the candles rises up and is lost in the high, vaulted roof and offers no comfort to the people sitting in the pews. Why on earth do the architects never include a roaring fire in such places? We are waiting for the service to begin and, like most of the congregation, I take the opportunity to look around at what the architects *had* concentrated on: the stained glass windows depicting Marion scenes; the fluted stone pillars and gothic arches; the statue of Mary holding baby Jesus that looks benignly but indifferently down upon us all; the elaborate medieval tombs containing the bones of people who had once mattered; the colourful icons of saints.

The priest finally arrives and we all stand to sing the first hymn. Our unconfident voices are not loud enough to cover the sound of latecomers, who, rather than slip sheepishly into seats at the back as most other people would have done, stroll down the central aisle looking for spaces. I am not surprised to see that one of the party is Jamie; I *am* surprised to see another is Miss Lucy Sutton.

There is more disturbance as people move up a couple of rows in front of us to make room but all are settled by the time the last note is sung. Apart from Jamie and Miss Lucy, the latecomers consist of Geoffrey Sutton and an older lady I do not know; there, no doubt, to act as chaperone. I wonder why the Sutton contingent is there; I am not aware they had even known Matthew, never mind care that he is leaving for Sierra Leone. The quick look Miss Lucy gives Jamie as they sit, provides me with a clue. The priest reads a passage from Mark in which Jesus calms a storm at sea and I ponder on what that surreptitious glance can mean. I can understand why Jamie wants to inveigle himself into the Sutton household; they have everything he desires: wealth, power, influence, respect. But what has Jamie got to offer the Suttons? The answer is nothing, other than ambition and good looks; perhaps that is enough.

The priest progresses to the sermon, which is about the storms all of us face in life and the role of the missionary to calm them; a little contrived, I think. The missionaries-to-be are sitting together on the front row and they are called up to the front to be blessed, to take the sacrament and to be given a Bible, inscribed with their names, the date and a personal message from Mr Benjamin Smith, their sponsor.

The service finishes with a rousing well-chosen hymn:

Ye Christian heralds, go, proclaim
salvation through Emmanuel's name!
To distant climes the tidings bear,
and plant the Rose of Sharon there.

The congregation drifts out of the chapel into the vast body of the Cathedral whilst the young men remain huddled around Mr Smith as he gives them final instructions. We are introduced to the unknown lady, who transpires to be Lady Sutton, wife to Lord Walter Sutton, the elder brother to the Mr Sutton we know, who is father to Charles, Geoffrey, Lucy and Daniel. Matthew eventually joins us and introductions are made again. Is it my imagination or has he changed since he entered the chapel just an hour or so earlier? Where this morning I had merely seen my elder brother, I now see a man, literally and figuratively, on a mission. His mouth is set in a determined line and he does not look at me but through me, as if to a distant land. I realise with sorrow that he doesn't want to be here with us; that talking politely about social trivia is burdensome to him. He just wants to be on his way.

Jamie has been the main conversationalist and now turns to Mama and Papa, with an ingratiating smile on his face.

'Lady Sutton has very kindly invited you all for refreshments at Sutton House this afternoon, a very great honour, I assure you.'

There is a silence that lasts just a little too long but Papa chooses politeness over preference. 'That is indeed extremely kind, Lady Sutton, and we are indeed greatly honoured by your invitation.' A time is agreed to allow the Hayes family, except for Jamie, to change into attire more suitable for visiting.

This is not how we had imagined spending our last afternoon with Matthew, a fact I loudly point out as we walk back to the tavern. 'The invitation was prompted by James for James's benefit. I cannot imagine Lady Sutton has any interest in us at all. This is all about James, James, James.'

'Hush, Lizzie, I couldn't refuse the invitation.' Papa, ever the diplomat.

'We will still all be together and we need not stop for long.' Matthew, ever the peace-maker.

'Why would James initiate the invitation?' Mama, ever the innocent.

'Do you not see how Miss Lucy looks at him? How she clings to his arm? How she agrees with everything he says? If he said up is down and left is right, she would nod sagely and say that it is indeed so.'

'Oh, I'm sure you are mistaken, Lizzie. They are both far too young to form any sort of attachment and James is an employee and not of her rank at all. Francis, what say you?'

Papa glances at me with a frown, obviously annoyed that I have said anything, but he cannot lie. 'You are correct in what you say, my dear, but I think Lizzie is also correct in saying that Miss Lucy is fond of James. But I am sure he is too much of a gentleman to take advantage of a young girl's childish affection.'

'I disagree, Papa, they are neither of them too young to marry,' Mama gasps. 'And Jamie knows exactly what he is

162

doing. He has set his sights high and, knowing him, he will not waiver until he gets there.'

'Silence, Lizzie! I will not have you talking in such a way about your brother. Now go and get changed not just your clothes but also your attitude. I will not tolerate any rudeness when we are at the Suttons'. You will be the epitome of decorum, genteelness and femininity. Do you understand?'

'Yes, Papa.'

Before I can proceed up the stairs Matthew holds me back.

'Don't be hard on Jamie, Lizzie. He has a dream, just as I have; just as you have.'

'I did have a dream once, until Jamie crushed it, if you recall.'

'He was merely being realistic and meant no malice. He was trying to make your dream come true.'

'You and I see our brother through very different eyes.'

Matthew smiles sadly and puts a wayward curl behind my ear. 'I don't ask much of you, Lizzie, but I do ask that you forgive him. Will you? Not just for me but for the whole family and especially yourself. Such negative thoughts are sinful and do you no credit. Forgive and forget. I don't want to be worrying about the two of you whilst I am away.'

He looks at me, not through me, so lovingly and seriously; it really matters to him. 'I'll try, Matthew.' Just not very hard.

When I come back down Papa has ordered a small coach so that we can arrive dry and mud-free. Sutton House is one of a crescent of similar large, white stuccoed, three- storied buildings inhabited, no doubt, by other wealthy Bristolians. The door is answered by a footman, whose uniform is of a far superior quality to our own clothes and certainly more colourful. We are led through a hallway with a black and white marbled floor; I imagine ourselves as chess pieces, pawns most likely, being manipulated by unseen players.

We are ushered into the drawing room and to our hosts, who are standing by an enormous fire. We are greeted first by Lord Sutton, who looks very like his younger brother, but ruddier and fleshier, then by Lady Sutton, who has changed into a very elegant pale blue silk dress. Mr Geoffrey and Miss Lucy are also there, as is Jamie, who looks very much like our Thomasina when she has just finished a plateful of fish. We are invited to sit on an over-large sofa that almost consumes us in its deep, soft cushions; I do not think I could get out of its embrace quickly.

I leave the polite conversation to the others whilst I take the opportunity to surreptitiously look around so that I can describe it all to John. It is a large room but seems small, so crowded is it with furniture and ornaments. Without even moving my head I can see five elegant side tables, Queen Anne perhaps, each bearing a blue and white patterned vase that holds the most colourful exotic blooms, plucked that day, no doubt, from an English greenhouse. Along the walls are plinths upon which rest the marble heads of Greek philosophers and Roman emperors; alcoves display small wooden statues and masks that I am surprised to see have been roughly carved, not by a hand as skilled as John Goodman's; silk brocade curtains of peacock blue, emerald green, ruby red and gold hang either side of the tall windows, waiting to be pulled to shut out the darkness and keep in the warmth.

My inspection of the intricate design of the carpet at my feet is interrupted by a gentle tap on my arm by Mama, who raises an eyebrow at me and glances at the cup and saucer being proffered to me. I take them from a hand the colour of ebony. My eyes follow the arm, encased in a dark blue sleeve edged by gold piping and topped with a gold tassel that sways as its wearer bends to pass me a silver cake stand. I look at the man, who is probably about twenty, in his round, plump, black face and say, 'Thank you, kindly.' He doesn't react other than lifting his eyes to mine for the briefest second and blinking twice quickly.

My eyes follow him as he bows to Lord and Lady Sutton and walks out of the room, backwards, his eyes firmly fixed on the carpet where he has just trodden.

Lord Sutton is beaming and his jowls shake as he chuckles. 'I can see that you are interested in our Abraham. A luckier man you will never meet, not of his sort, anyway.' I feel Matthew stiffen beside me, 'Let me tell you how we come to have him; it's an interesting story. His mother gave birth to him at sea when she was being brought over from Africa, or wherever it was. She died, as many did, but the baby survived, kept alive by the milk of women who had lost their own. When they docked, the Captain came to me to ask me what to do with him.'

'What do you mean? Couldn't he stay with his family?'

'Ah, Miss Hayes. There is no knowing if he had any other family and even if he did, they were quite likely on a different ship. The Captain knew that if he went onto another ship to America, which was the blacks' destination, then he would likely die. The Captain felt sorry for the boy and asked if he could leave him with his wife to bring up, as she had had no luck keeping a child of their own for more than a few days. I thought it was a ridiculous idea and said so, but he pleaded and pleaded and in the end I gave in.'

Lord Sutton pauses to sip his tea, his face glowing with pride at his act of generosity all those years ago. 'About six years later the Captain died and his wife brought the boy here and said she couldn't afford to look after him anymore. Made quite a fuss in fact. She was a sickly specimen but she had done a good job and he was a fine, strong boy. Lady Sutton, soft-hearted as she is, felt sorry for the boy and so Abraham came to live here, first as a scullion and now as a very competent footman. I allow him to serve at dinner parties, sometimes, as my guests find him quite entertaining.'

'Doesn't he want to go home, back to Africa?'

'This is his home, Miss Hayes, the only home he knows. He never knew his mother and has no idea where she came from and he knows only English ways. Why would he want to go to a backward country to live amongst heathens?'

'Is he a slave then?'

Lord Sutton's smile slips and he looks angry. 'Most certainly not. Slavery, as you well know, Miss Hayes, is illegal, more's the pity.' He extends his arms to encompass the room. 'Transporting those blacks paid for all this; it was a very lucrative business but luckily there are other goods that need to be shipped.'

'But wouldn't he be happier with,' I glance at Matthew, 'with his own kind?'

The Suttons and even Jamie, laugh. 'Oh, my dear. They are not the same as us and don't have the same feelings. He has nice clothes to wear, somewhere to sleep in the warm and dry and food to fill his belly. What more can he possibly want? If it wasn't for us he would have died, there is no doubt about it.'

All this time, Matthew has been sitting straight-backed, fists and jaws clenched. He exhales loudly. 'If it was not for people like you, Lord Sutton, his poor mother would not have been torn from her home and family, crammed into the hold of a ship for weeks on end, lying in vomit and worse, eating maggot-ridden food. If it was not for people like you, she would not have had to give birth to her child in conditions you cannot even begin to imagine; if it was not for people like you, she would not have died a horrible, painful death and been flung into the sea like just so much garbage.' Matthew suddenly stands, managing to deftly get out of the cushions' grip. 'I thank you for your hospitality but I cannot be in the same house as you for a moment longer. Those that you so blithely dismiss as having no feelings, as being different from us are human beings. They have families, they have hopes and fears, they bleed when they are cut and they are God's children. I feel honoured to be allowed to go to their country to tell them of the love of God and of His son, Jesus Christ and I will cast myself at their feet and ask for their forgiveness for the actions of people like you, Lord Sutton; for your arrogance and misplaced sense of superiority, your inhumanity, you lack of Christian spirit and for doing the work of Satan.'

Mama, Papa and I are now also standing and I am sorely tempted to clap when Matthew's tirade comes to an end. Papa and Mama are nodding, no longer torn between politeness and preference. Papa turns to Jamie. 'We will go now. Are you coming?'

Jamie looks horrified. For a moment I think he is reacting to the Sutton's lack of humanity and will walk away from them and their lifestyle bought by the lives of men, women and children, but I am soon disabused. He turns to Lord and Lady Sutton. 'I must apologise to you most profusely for my family's extreme insolence and discourtesy. I can only suppose that this outrageous outburst is caused by their anxiety at my brother's imminent departure.' He turns to his parents. 'I have never been shown anything but courtesy and kindness by any of the Sutton family and Lord and Lady Sutton have treated me like a son. I very much hope that they will not tar me with the same brush and that they will still welcome me into their home. Your outburst today, Matthew, was inexcusable and you should indeed leave immediately. And no, Father, I will not be coming with you.'

Everyone is now standing, separated by a table upon which the tea, like our goodwill, has gone cold. We see ourselves out of the room but it is Abraham who helps us on with our outer clothes; Abraham who opens the front door and sees us off the premises; Abraham who shuts the door firmly behind us.

I take a deep breath trying to fill my lungs with air only contaminated by smoke, horse dung and the autumn drizzle.

'Oh, Matthew, you were wonderful. I am so proud of you.'

'Oh, Matthew, what you said was right but I do wish you hadn't said it. I think you have upset James greatly. I am a little surprised that he chose to remain with the Suttons, perhaps he did not want to seem ungrateful if they have been good to him.'

'Well, Matthew, it is probably a good thing you are leaving the country tomorrow for I fear you have made an enemy out of Lord Sutton.'

Matthew looks crestfallen. 'God forgive me for not holding my anger in; I just could not keep quiet any longer. I do hope I haven't made things difficult for you all. I will write to Lord Sutton tonight and apologise for my rudeness, but not for the substance of my words. I must admit I am disappointed in Jamie, but I expect he has his reasons.'

Why has no one listened to me? 'I keep trying to tell you all, Jamie's reasons are ones that benefit himself only; he has just shown his true colours. He wants what the Suttons have: wealth and influence and he doesn't care how he gets it.'

Chapter 27

October 1825

It is chilly and although it is not raining the air is moist and everyone's clothes are covered in droplets of water. The clouds hang low and look too heavy to retain their water much longer. The weather matches my mood perfectly. I can cry no more tears and I feel exhausted with the intensity of my emotions; I just want it all to be over.

Mama is the last of us to say goodbye. She reaches up, holds Matthew's face in her hands and studies it intensely, her eyes devouring every inch. Then she wraps her arms around his chest and holds him to her. His chin rests on the top of her head and they gently sway together, their eyes closed. It is as if she is rocking a newborn baby and for the first time my own grief and pain seems as nothing to what I imagine she must be feeling. He is her firstborn, her creation, and despite not being a mother I sense that all she wants to do is to put him back inside her womb so that she can keep him forever safe. She releases him and steps back and although she must want to weep, she sheds no tears; although she must want to curl into a ball, she stands upright, head held high; although she must want to open her mouth and scream her denial, she smiles, her lips closed to keep in her wails; although she must want to grab hold of his jacket to keep him with her, she raises her hand to wave as he steps into the rowing boat that will take him out to the waiting sailing ship.

I cannot take my eyes off her; this bravest of women. She stands on the quayside watching and waving until she cannot possible identify which small dot is her son. She is surrounded by the bustle of other families saying farewell to their loved ones; the stevedores loading, unloading and moving boxes of goods from here to there and back again; the seagulls circling overhead, buffeted by the wind and crying like abandoned children, but she stands as if alone until her husband gently takes her waving hand in his, and turns her around so that her back is to the sea, to her son. She stares ahead, unseeing, still smiling. She allows Papa to lead her away and I follow, wondering when she will break down.

We pass the Docherty family and it is I who acknowledges their greetings with a nod. Someone knocks into me and I stumble and grab onto a sleeve to steady myself. He wrenches my hand off and turns quickly away and disappears into the crowd, but I know my own brother when I see him. I have to quicken my step to catch up with Mama and Papa but I decide not to tell them yet that Jamie did come, after all.

It is only when I am in my room that I notice something in my reticule that was not there this morning: a sheet of paper folded and 'Mr and Mrs Hayes' scrawled on the outside. I open it then shut it again; the letter is from Jamie to my parents, not me. I go to their bedroom but the sound of sobbing that rips at my very heart stays my hand. I will wait a bit longer.

Sutton House
Bristol
October 29th '25

Dear Mother, Father,

I hope I can still call you that despite the awful things that were said, and not said, yesterday afternoon. This is not an easy letter to write but I want to try and explain what life has been like for me as your second son, and why it is that I have chosen to remain with the Suttons.

First of all, I have always known that Matthew is your favourite. This is perhaps inevitable as he is your first son and such a paragon of virtue, but it is not easy to understand or accept when you are a small child. I both looked up to him and resented him because I was always compared to him and found wanting. You never just appreciated me for my own sake and from a very early age I realised that nothing I could ever do would put me in a better light than him, and in the end I stopped trying.

I soon knew that I would only ever gain respect and admiration from other people, never my own parents, and the one thing that would earn that respect is wealth and power. So, that has become my goal in life, to become wealthy and powerful.

I knew I would have to work hard to achieve my goal and I was willing to do that, which is why I was good at what I did working for Charles Sutton and I earned my promotions. But what the Suttons have also done is to open the door to a society where I feel most at home and know I want to be part of.

The men I meet are wealthy beyond even Lizzie's imagination but I would hazard a guess that the majority have obtained that wealth by means more foul than fair. And I find that I don't respect them any less for that. I am sure you think me a very bad person but I would rather be bad and rich than good and poor, as Matthew and yourselves will always be.

Lord Sutton has taken a fancy to me, even after yesterday's outburst, perhaps even more so because of it. He ranted and raved after you left but he shook my hand and said he was proud of me and would like to talk to me about some business opportunities that he would like me to take advantage of as he says they will benefit me greatly. I had to choose yesterday, and I chose my own ambition over yours. I am sure you will feel hurt and betrayed but I have to follow my own road in life as our destinations are very different.

I'm sorry I have been such a disappointment to you.

Kiss Dorothy for me.

James

I wish I was not here. I wish I had not had to hear Jamie's hurtful words come out of the mouth of my beloved Papa. I wish

I had not had to see the pain in my parents' eyes as they realise that today they have lost two sons, not one.

There is nothing I can say, so I say nothing.

Papa re-reads the letter to himself then folds it carefully and puts it in his jacket pocket. He looks at Mama with an expression so forlorn and dejected I want to hold him and tell him that everything will be all right, although it would be a lie.

'Were we really such bad parents to him? Is it our fault he has turned out to be so,' he struggles for words, 'so cynical and mercenary?'

Mama's voice is hoarse from her crying. 'Perhaps,' she turns to look out of the window, towards the docks, 'perhaps I did favour Matthew. He was such a good, intelligent, loving boy and James was always naughty, from the day he was born. He never seemed to be happy and he was always getting into trouble. But I did love him. Of course I did.' She turns her gaze to me. 'Were we so very bad, Lizzie? Do you hate us as well?'

'Oh, Mama, of course not. Jamie was born mean and spiteful; he was always pinching and punching me and he was only ever interested in himself, never anyone else. The bad always appealed to him more than the good. I can't remember him ever doing something kind or selfless. It is just like him to blame everyone else but himself for the way he has turned out. You have been and still are wonderful parents.' Apart from Mama's attitude towards Bobbit, of course. If any of the sons have anything to complain about, it is him.

'Perhaps I should go and see him and talk to him. We can't leave things like this. He needs to know that we love him and that he is not a disappointment to us.' Papa stands up abruptly, glad, I think, to have something to do. 'In fact there's no time like the present, I'll go now.'

He soon returns, however, his shoulders drooping with disappointment. 'He's gone back to London. He left this morning, apparently.'

'Probably soon after he came to the docks and put the letter in my bag.'

'How I wish he had joined us and said goodbye to his brother. Why did he not show himself? And why did he put the letter in Lizzie's bag and not just give it to us? Oh, he must hate us all so much.' Mama puts her hands in her face and finds more tears from her well of sorrow.

I am suddenly very tired. I just want to go home.

Chapter 28

November 1825

'It's more than four weeks since Matthew left, Bobbit. He may already be there by now. But even if he writes straight away there may be no boat coming to England for weeks, so I know it's too soon to look for a letter but I still do, every day. I just want to know that he has got there safely and what life is like.' My own life soon resumed to normal after our visit to Bristol and I am taking Bobbit for a walk, having been kept inside for many days due to persistent, heavy rain. 'We haven't heard from Jamie, needless to say. Poor Papa has written numerous letters to him but he hasn't bothered to respond at all. He really is detestable. I wouldn't bother any more if it was left to me.'

The towpath is muddy so I am treading carefully. My eyes are cast downwards watching out for water-filled holes ready to drench my boots, buried roots waiting to trip me up or piles of horse dung not yet cleared away. I do not heed Bobbit's warning whimper and don't see the boys until we are but a few feet away from them. There are six of them, standing in a line across the path, blocking our way. I know these sons of mine owners; each boy has the education and money those who have made their wealth for them can only dream of.

'Good morrow, Miss Hayes.' It is Daniel Sutton.

'Good morrow yourself, Master Sutton. Is there any reason why you and your cronies are blocking our way?'

'Of course not, mistress. Stand aside, men.'

He speaks to them like a general in the army, but they are probably all about my own age and in my eyes they are just unpleasant boys. Papa is still giving most of them, though not the Sutton boy, private tuition to prepare them for a university education they do not deserve; there is no such thing as a degree in cruelty and greed. They respond to the order from their leader and they part, grinning and chortling, allowing us just enough room to squeeze through. They are close enough for me to smell the ale on their breath and something about their insolence and smirks makes my heart and step quicken.

I am suddenly pushed forward and Bobbit's hand is torn from mine. I turn to find myself on the outside of a ring of boys, with Bobbit standing bewildered at the centre. The boys start to walk slowly round him, chanting,

'Freak, freak, can't even speak,
Should have been drowned at birth,
You ain't of any bloody worth.
Freak, freak, why don't you speak?'

The boys walk faster and faster, the rhyme keeping pace. Bobbit is spinning round and round, trying to keep up with them, his face a picture of total incomprehension and fear.

'Stop it! Stop tormenting him! Stop it, stop it, stop it!'

My shouts are lost amongst the foul words that are now being spewed out of each boy's mouth.

'Freak, freak, can't even speak,
Should never have been born,
Should never have seen that first dawn.
Freak, freak, why don't you speak?'

They all have sticks that they now start poking at Bobbit, at his chest, arms, back, legs, anywhere they can get at. 'For the love of God, stop it! Leave him alone, you're hurting him.' My voice is just a sob now and my eyes and nose are running with fear. I look desperately around for someone to help, but the place is deserted, it being that part of the day when there is no traffic on the canal. Round and round they whirl, too fast for me to identify which boy is which. Suddenly Bobbit stumbles and falls sideways and the human circle instantly becomes a jumble of arms and legs, the song replaced by curses and laughter.

I can't get to Bobbit, who is buried under the fleshy mound. Suddenly a scream rents the air, all other sounds instantly cut off, leaving just the echo ringing in my ears. 'Oh my God, what have you done to him?'

The boys slowly disentangle and stand and I see that Daniel is being held up by two others. He is holding the side of his head trying to staunch the blood that is pouring through his fingers. His face is white and his mouth open in an O of shock. He looks around in confusion but when he sees me he howls, 'He bit off my bloody ear, he bit it off!'

All eyes, mine included, turn towards Bobbit. I see now that there is blood around his mouth and as we all watch in horror he spits something pink into the canal. It bobs on the surface for a few seconds then sinks into the murk. The stunned silence is broken only by Daniel's sobs, then the sound of their muddy shuffling as they all back away from Bobbit, who is standing as still as a piece of wood, staring into the distance over the canal.

None of the boys dare look at me and, still supporting Daniel, they disappear round a bend and out of my sight and hearing. I am shivering, not just from the cold. I am rooted to the spot until Bobbit takes an unsteady step forward towards the edge of the canal. I shout a warning and rush towards him, pulling him back. 'Be careful, Bobbit. You don't want to fall into the canal; neither of us can swim. Oh, Bobbit.' What else can I say? I cannot reprimand him for protecting himself against six bullies; Daniel only has himself to blame. I feel no regret, only fear at the consequences. I spit onto my handkerchief and wipe Bobbit's mouth, then take his hand in mine and continue our walk home, both of us on unsteady legs.

We need warmth and sympathy, so I take Bobbit to the kitchen, where Mama and Sarah are preparing dinner. Dorothy is sitting under the table, playing with wooden bricks John made her. He has engraved the letters of the alphabet on each side, using a template I made for him. She looks at us and gives a smile, showing off her front teeth; she cares nothing for our dishabille. Not so Mama and Sarah, who both gasp and put down the knives they had been using to pare the vegetables.

'My goodness, Lizzie, what has happened? Why are Robert's clothes so muddy and torn?'

'Come over to the fire, Miss Elizabeth, you're both shivering. Is that blood on Robert's collar?'

I wait until we are both seated either side of the fire, our boots removed and put to dry, steam rising from our damp clothes. Bobbit is moaning to himself, his hands restlessly pushing away at things only he can see.

'Well, Elizabeth?'

'We were attacked.' The two women gasp again. 'It was Daniel Sutton and his gang of ne'er do wells. They stopped us when we were walking along the towpath, pushed me away and then tormented poor Bobbit. They shouted horrible things at him and beat him with sticks.'

'Did they hurt you, Lizzie? Did they touch you at all?'

I am impatient with Mama. 'No, it was Bobbit they were after.'

'They were just teasing, Lizzie. You know how boys are.'

'Teasing? I truly thought they were going to kill him. It was more than just horseplay, it was a vicious attack and Daniel deserved what he got.'

There is a moment's silence. 'What do you mean, Lizzie? What happened to Daniel?'

'There were six boys all on top of poor Bobbit, he was frightened and he must have just bitten whatever was closest, which happened to be Daniel's ear.'

Both women repeat 'Daniel's ear?'

'Well, not his whole ear, just his ear lobe.' I instinctively feel my own lobe, and notice Mama and Sarah doing so likewise.

177

'Bobbit spat it into the canal. The boys went then; Daniel was sobbing like a baby.'

'Was there no man around to help, Miss Elizabeth?'

'No, there were no barges, they were all being filled or emptied, so there were no horses or men around.'

'Oh God, Lizzie, the Suttons will not let this lie, nor should they.'

'But Mama, they started it. It's all right for six boys to terrify and hurt Bobbit, but not all right for him to hurt one back? They might have turned on me next.'

'But they didn't. It will be the boys' word against yours, Lizzie. They will make out that it was Robert who attacked Daniel unprovoked. Everyone knows how much you dote on your brother and they will just think you are trying to protect him. Oh dear, I must speak with your father and tell him what really happened. Take Robert upstairs, Lizzie, and get yourselves changed into clean clothes. You will need to mend his shirt and britches; it will give you good practice in darning.'

Whilst upstairs I hear Papa and Mr Whittaker come in and the murmur of voices that is suddenly interrupted by loud banging on the front door and a man's voice shouting, 'Open up, Hayes. Do you know what that monster of a son of yours has done to my boy?' There is the sound of footsteps as Mr Sutton, for it is he of course, is led into the study. Then silence.

I pace the room nervously, imagining the lies that Mr Sutton is telling Papa. Bobbit sits on his bed, fidgeting with the buttons on his shirt. I wish I could take him downstairs into the kitchen but I am frightened we might cross Mr Sutton's path when he takes his leave; I cannot imagine it would be a happy meeting. After at least half an hour I hear the study door open. I tiptoe onto the landing so that I can hear better what is said.

'I assure you Mr Sutton, I will see to this matter; Robert will not go unpunished. There is no need to take any further action.

Please send me the medical bill. Yes, yes, an institution will be for the best.'

An institution?

Chapter 29

November 1825

'I have never been so humiliated in my life!'

'But Papa, it was not Bobbit's fault. It was the boys who were the aggressors. They only pick on Bobbit because they think he is weak and cannot fight back, but he did and now they go crying home and expect him to be punished. It is they who should be punished, not Bobbit. And anyway, it was only Daniel's ear lobe.'

Papa's face goes from red to purple. 'Only his ear lobe?' He goes quiet. We are both standing facing each other like two hares ready to box but he now sits in his chair behind his desk and indicates that I should sit also. 'This is what your Mama has always worried would happen; that as Robert gets older he will get stronger and more aggressive. She is right; he has become dangerous.' He holds up his hand to silence me. 'It is not fair on him or on the whole family.'

'What do you mean?'

'After the episode with Jamie I said I would give him one more chance. Well, he has had that chance.'

I hear my voice rise hysterically. 'What do you mean? You can't put him in an institution, you can't. That's not fair. He has done nothing wrong; he was just defending himself against the bullies. You can't punish him for that, you can't.'

'We can't have him live with us any more, Lizzie. He has become a danger to others and I can't have that. As he gets older he will get stronger and start to lash out more and more and goodness knows what damage he will do. No, he will be better off in an institution. As it happens, Mr Whittaker knows of one that he understands is excellent. They care for the patients very well, he says. It will be expensive, but that is my problem, not yours.'

'No, no, no! You can't do that, Papa, please don't. I promise I'll take better care of him. I won't go down the towpath anymore. Please don't put him in one of those places, please don't.' I can't speak any more, my tears are choking me.

Papa looks at me sadly. 'You have been wonderful with your brother, Lizzie. If it hadn't been for you taking him under your wing when you were just four, he would have been sent away when he was a baby. You know that is what your mother wanted. He has had a wonderful life here, because of you, but now he needs to go somewhere else to be cared for. The place is not all that far away; you will be able to visit him.'

I am defeated. If I say anything more it will be words of anger and recriminations that I know I will regret, so I keep my silence, which I maintain throughout dinner. Mr Whittaker had returned to his digs on Mr Sutton's arrival so it is just the family at the table. How I wish Matthew was here; he would surely be on my side? On Bobbit's side?

Once I have helped Sarah clear up I sit with Mama and start to mend Bobbit's shirt. Mama keeps looking at me, whilst she darns a pile of stockings. 'I'm sorry, Lizzie, but it is for the best.'

'The best for whom? Not Bobbit, that is for sure.' I take a moment to compose myself. 'When do you think he will leave us?'

'I don't know, Lizzie, perhaps a month or so. There is a lot to arrange and Papa will need to contact your grandparents to see if they can help with the cost. I am sure they will; they have always said he should be cared for away from home. He will be taken good care of, Lizzie. I don't want him to suffer; he is my son, after all.' I manage to keep an ugly retort unsaid. 'Now, leave that shirt. Why don't you take Bobbit to bed, I expect today's events have tired him out. Tell him one of your stories; he'll like that.'

Mama's words echo in my head as I get Bobbit ready for bed. Will someone else spend every waking hour with him? Will someone else understand how much he loves animals and how he can converse with them? Will someone else have the patience of Job with him, whilst he shuffles along in his own inimitable manner, or tries to button his own shirt or put on his gloves? Will someone else tell him stories in which he is the hero? Will someone else treat him with respect and assume that he understands, even if he gives no indication that he does so? Will someone else love him as much as I do?

He lies on his back, his dark eyes looking into mine; they seem so knowing. I brush a lock of hair from his forehead and take his limp hands in mine.

There was once a farmer and his wife who were very sad because they couldn't have any children of their own. Instead, they lavished their love on the village youngsters; they let them come and play with all the baby animals on the farm, gave them gifts for no reason at all, and looked after them if their own parents were sick. One day the farmer's wife was picking carrots when she heard a strange cry and what did she find under a blackcurrant bush but a baby swaddled in a cloth of spun gold. When the farmer's wife picked him up he gave her a smile that made her feel as if she was floating on a cloud. The farmer and his wife asked everyone in the village whether anyone had lost a baby and when no one claimed him they knew that he had been left by the fairies for them to look after. They decided to call him Ciaran, which means little dark one, because already he had a full head of thick, black wavy hair.

Ciaran grew up very quickly and after just a few months he was running around and had all his teeth. He never grew higher than twenty-four inches, which is actually quite tall for a fairy. The farmer and his wife never doubted that he was fey because when they looked into his eyes they could see all the stars of the galaxy; when he smiled it was as if he had swallowed the sun and when they found him standing in the garden one night, he held the crescent moon in his cupped hand. He spoke not words but the crashing of surf on the shore and when he sang it was as a skylark.

The farmer and his wife were saddened that the children of the village no longer came to their farm because they thought Ciaran to be strange and different, but the fairy boy was not lonely. When he sat in the garden and sang, the birds flew down from the trees and joined in his merry tune. When he sat on the river bank and dangled his toes, the fishes came and nibbled them, the otters gambolled for his entertainment and the waters gurgled with delight. When he walked through the fields the rabbits came out of their holes and skittered and hopped alongside him.

Early one spring morning, Ciaran went for a walk before breaking his fast. He wanted to welcome the new lambs that had been born that night. But when he got to the field he found that hungry wolves had come down from the hills and slaughtered many of them, dragging some away to eat but leaving others. He sat by their bodies and wept, his tears a waterfall and his sobs the howling wind. When the farmer who owned the sheep came to feed them, he was horrified to see Ciaran sitting by the bloody carcasses of his lambs. The farmer did not know that Ciaran loved all animals and would never hurt them; the farmer did not know there was a pack of hungry wolves in the hills; the farmer only knew that Ciaran was a strange boy, different from all the other village children. So the farmer did what all men do when faced with something they do not understand, he attacked. He beat Ciaran with his stick until every inch of his pink skin was black and blue, until every bone in his little body was broken. The farmer was so angry that he did not notice a butterfly flutter out of the boy's open mouth and soar up, up towards the heavens, where it changed as if by magic, which of course it was, into a skylark.

The farmer and his wife were devastated by the death of their fairy boy but were strangely comforted by the singing of a bird that hovered above their farm and sang through rain and shine, until the end of their days.

Chapter 30

November 1825

I lie with the blanket pulled right up to my chin. I know Jack Frost has been overnight as I can see his fingerprints on the windows and my breath creates clouds that hover then melt away. I listen to all the early morning familiar sounds: my own heart beating; the rustle of my sheets as I wriggle further down seeking warmth; the tapping of the branch on the windowpane; the distant rattle as Sarah pours coals onto the range; the creakings and sighs of the house as it prepares for another day. There is something missing and it takes me a while to realise that it is the sound of Bobbit's gentle snore. I sit up and peer over the edge of my bed, to see that his mattress is empty, the covers neatly folded back. Sarah must have taken him downstairs. I wonder that I did not hear them; I must have been in a deep sleep.

Knowing that I don't need to get Bobbit up, I decide to stay awhile longer, putting off leaving the warmth of my bed, putting off having to face a day where plans will be made to send my fairy boy away. In one of my own stories I would have found a cure for him and he would have walked in a straight line, talked to people as well as to animals and everyone would have loved him. Or at the very least I would have saved him by running away with him to a land where such as he are normal and it would be me that was a freak.

I eventually brave the cold and quickly put on layers of clothes before going downstairs. I call a polite 'Good morning' to Papa, who is sitting in the dining room, drinking his tea and waiting for his breakfast. Before I open the kitchen door I know exactly what everyone will be doing. Sarah will be at the range frying the eggs and bacon; Mama will be dandling Dorothy on her knee and Bobbit will be in his chair, rocking gently, as always. When I enter, it is very much as I imagined except that Bobbit is not there.

'Where's Bobbit?'

Before anyone can answer I hear footsteps and Mr Whittaker's cheerful voice, 'Do you know the front door is open?'

Mama and Sarah look at each other, then at me in puzzlement. I go down the hall and re-open the door that Mr Whittaker has closed and peer out. Everything is blanketed in thick hoarfrost, except for down the stone steps and along the path where there are still the imprints made by small, warm feet.

My mind cannot make any sense of what is clear before me. Bobbit has opened the door himself and gone out into the bitter cold? I remember seeing his pile of clothes still folded neatly on top of the chest of drawers. Gone out in just his nightshirt?

Papa has joined me. 'He cannot be outside, Lizzie. He can't open the door. Sarah has gone upstairs to see if he has hidden himself away somewhere.'

My mouth is frozen shut and I point to the footprints.

Papa frowns as he slowly realises the implications of what he is seeing. He suddenly snaps out of his trance. 'My God, we must find him before he freezes to death. Come inside quickly, Lizzie, we need to know where to look. Where are his favourite places?'

I can't think; my mind is as blank as a virgin sheet of paper. Where would he go, where would he go?

'He loves fetching the eggs. It would be warm in there.' I hear Mama open the back door and crunch down the pathway to the chicken coop. 'The church! He loves to sit on one of the tombs. But it will be cold up there; maybe he has gone inside?' Where else? Where else? 'The stables by the canal, and along the canal itself, of course.'

'I'll go to the cathedral then if he is not there I'll knock up the Goodmans on the way to see if they can get more people to help in the search. Mr Whittaker, will you walk along the canal and go to the stables? Sarah, perhaps you can make sure there is some porridge and hot chocolate for our return for we will all need it when we bring him home. Which we will, Lizzie, I promise.'

Mr Whittaker turns to go and I pluck at his coat sleeve. 'Wait for me, I'm coming with you.'

'Not dressed like that you're not; you need your boots, gloves and a coat. I'll go on, catch me up.'

Mama has returned from her search and gives a small shake of her head as she hands me my coat and boots that have been drying by the range after yesterday's incident. Was it only yesterday? I catch up with Mr Whittaker before he is halfway down the street and I have to run to keep up with his long strides. We have the furthest to go and by the time we reach the canal I am overly warm and can feel the sweat trickle down my back. The mud on the towpath is frozen solid but we still need to take care not to slip. Each time we come to a clump of bushes I expect to see Bobbit huddled underneath, his teeth chattering and his whole body shivering. How long could anyone last in this cold? Especially only wearing a nightshirt. Please God, please let him be in the stable, or anywhere where it is warm and dry.

We are nearing the place where we were attacked by Daniel Sutton and his gang. Suddenly Mr Whittaker stops, causing me to bump into him. I hear him groan and think that perhaps he has twisted his ankle. But I see that he is staring into the reeds that grow along the side of the canal. There is something white tangled amongst the stems. White cloth. A white nightshirt.

'No! Get him out, get him out!'

I go to the edge and get to my knees and stretch out my arms to try and pull him out, but my fingertips just touch the edge of his sleeve and I cannot get a grip. I lean further forward until I am yanked back.

'Don't be silly, Miss Hayes. I'll go.' Mr Whittaker removes his coat and is starting to take off his boots when there is a splash and someone wades into the water, grabs Bobbit and pulls him to the edge. Mr Whittaker drags my boy out of the water and lays him on his back, and then helps John, for that is who the rescuer is, to clamber out. Bobbit's face is as white as the frost upon which he lies, with a touch of blue around his mouth and nose. His eyes are open and I think I can see a galaxy of stars reflected there.

I slap his face. 'Wake up, Bobbit, wake up. What do you think you were doing coming out in just your nightshirt? You'll be lucky if you don't catch pneumonia. Wake up, goddamn you!' I start to shake him until Mr Whittaker gently pulls me away.

'He is gone, Miss Hayes, gone to a better place.'

'He can't be gone, not just like that. He can't be.'

'Come, let's get you home.' He tries to pull me up but my limbs will not bend. Suddenly I am lifted in the air and carried like a baby in Mr Whittaker's arms. 'You, bring the boy.' I see a spasm of anger on John's face but then he bends to pick Bobbit up and he follows us as we make our way slowly back along the path, back home.

Papa promised we would bring Bobbit home, but not like this, not like this.

Chapter 31

November 1825

'I must go and sit with him, he'll be scared.'

'You stay where you are, Lizzie. Robert won't be scared, the angels will look after him. Here, drink this, you need to get warm, you're shivering.' Mama crouches by my side and puts a cup of hot chocolate in my hand. I don't have the energy to lift it to my lips. Mama strokes my arm and opens her mouth to speak, but then shuts it again.

A stab of anger sears my soul. 'Were you going to say that this is for the best, Mama? That he has gone to a better place? Were you? Were you?' I realise I am shouting. Mama shakes her head and continues to stroke my arm but says nothing. My anger subsides as quickly as it had risen. I stare into my drink and see the canal with a white body floating but it slowly sinks into the depths. I take a sip; the chocolate warms my body but not my ice-bound heart.

Mr Whittaker has gone to find Papa and John has returned home to get changed out of his sodden clothes. Poor John, he must have been freezing but he carried Bobbit all the way home and laid him gently onto the table in the parlour. I don't like to think of Bobbit being alone; he needs to change into dry clothes, otherwise he'll catch his death. I give a hiccup of laughter; of course he won't, a boy can't die twice. Sarah is standing at the range and stirring the porridge with fervour; she turns to look at me with a concerned expression. I hope she does not think I am laughing because I am happy. Dorothy is still under the table playing with a doll made with odd scraps of material. A normal, everyday scene, no different to any other morning in the Hayes' household. Except that Bobbit isn't in his rocking chair and never will be again.

Mr Whittaker and Papa come in, followed by John and Mr Goodman, but they speak in whispers and sit at the table drinking their hot chocolate and eating their porridge; they don't disturb me although each of them glances at me now and then. I hear the word 'coffin' and I shake my head. 'He'll hate being in a coffin, it's so dark and such a small space.'

'It's just for his body, Lizzie. His soul will already have taken flight and will be with God.'

Taken flight! I gasp in horror as I remember the story I told Bobbit last night about the soul of poor dead Ciaran taking flight up to the heavens as a lark. I drop my cup, the contents splattering my skirt and adding to the dried mud splashes that already decorate it. 'It's my fault, oh my God, it's my fault!' I stand and run through the door, along the hallway and into the parlour.

Bobbit is lying on a thick cloth on the table, his clothes and hair still damp, the room too cold for them to dry. I turn his face to me so that he can see me; his eyes are open but dull and vacant. I must make him understand. 'Bobbit, it was only a fairytale. I didn't mean for you to kill yourself and make it come true. Oh, Bobbit, come back, come back.' I shake him. 'Wake up, do you hear me? I didn't mean for you to kill yourself, I didn't mean it like that.' I keep shaking him until someone pulls me away and wraps me in his arms.

'Hush, Lizzie, hush. He's gone. It's not your fault. If it's anyone's it's mine. He must have heard me saying about sending him to an institution. It's not your fault. And it was an accident, Lizzie, do you understand? He did not end his own life, it was an accident.'

'But I told him a fairytale and in it the boy dies and his soul turns into a lark and flies up into the sky. Bobbit must have wanted to do the same.' Papa puts a hand gently over my mouth.

'You are not to blame, Lizzie, I don't want to hear any more about fairytales. He heard me talking about an institution to Mr Sutton, he was scared so decided to run away and he slipped and fell into the canal. It was an accident. Do you understand? An accident. He will be buried in the churchyard with his other poor brothers and sisters and we will all join him when it is our time and we'll see him again in heaven. If we tell everyone that he killed himself he will be buried outside of the churchyard in unconsecrated ground and we don't want that do we? Do you understand, Lizzie?'

I nod. I don't want him lying in the rough ground all alone. I want him to be with the other little ones whose lives were too short.

Papa takes my arm and leads me back to the kitchen. Nobody looks at me as I walk to the rocking chair and carefully sit down. Sarah has cleaned up the spilt chocolate and she hands another cup to me, as if a drink of hot chocolate will ease all my sorrows.

I stare into the flames and see Bobbit's smiling face as the others go over what must have happened. I don't listen to them. I know what happened. He understood far more than anyone else ever gave him credit for, even me. He understood that life is not fair and that the likes of the Suttons are entitled to bully but the likes of him are not entitled to protect themselves; he understood that he was going to be taken from his home and put into an institution because he fought back; he understood that the only person that ever loved him and cared for him would not be with him; he understood that he could not swim and that if he drowned in the canal then his suffering on this earth would cease and his soul would soar up to the heavens. He had not slipped. It was not an accident. He had chosen.

He continues to smile at me out of the flames and I smile back. He is finally in a place where he is not considered a freak, where he is not bullied, where he is unconditionally loved; perhaps he is already running and playing and chatting to the angels. I pray it is so.

Sarah comes to me. 'Would you like to help me dress Robert, Miss Elizabeth?'

191

I am still smiling, which I think confuses her. 'Yes, of course. I'll go and get his best suit.'

I stand by his head and peer closely at his face and am glad that it is not Bobbit's. It has his features but it is not him. I close his lids; I don't want to look into the void. I remember I shouted at Mama earlier when I thought she was going to try and console me that he had gone to a better place. But she was right. He is already there.

We remove all of his clothes and wash down his pale body, the skin wrinkled and clammy from the canal water.

'He was never easy to wash was he, Miss Elizabeth? I wonder now whether he was laughing at us as we struggled to get him clean.'

'I hope so. I would like to think he has been laughing at us all his life. He is certainly happy now, though. I know he is.'

'I am glad, Miss Elizabeth.'

I hesitate about trying to explain, but decide that I should. 'I saw his face in the fire, Sarah, and he was smiling. He has never smiled at me before, not ever. I truly believe that he was telling me not to grieve and that he is finally at peace. Does that sound silly?'

Sarah doesn't answer but tears mark the shirt we are trying to get onto his unresponsive body. We finally manage to dress him in his Sunday best and Sarah takes out the bowl of water. I am doing up the buttons on my boy's jacket when John comes in, carrying a roughly made rectangular wooden box; Bobbit sized.

'This is just for now, Miss Elizabeth. Father and I will make a good one for him ready for the burial.' His voice thickens and I realise that he is upset.

'Thank you, John. And thank you for jumping in and taking him out of the water. That was very brave of you.'

'I hoped he was still alive, I hoped we could save him.'

'He decided to save himself.'

192

He looks at me with a puzzled expression on his dear face. 'What do you mean?'

'I just mean that he decided he didn't want to go to an institution, he didn't want to remain on earth being treated like a freak and being bullied, so he decided to go where he will be loved.'

John's frown deepens. 'Do you really think he was capable of making such a decision? Could he not just have slipped?'

'He could have and I know that is what Papa wants everyone to think, but I don't believe he did. He knew to get up when we were all fast asleep; he knew how to open the front door; he knew his way to the canal; he knew he couldn't swim. He knew exactly what he was doing, John, but I will say it was an accident although it doesn't change the truth of what really happened.'

I help John lift Bobbit and lay him in the makeshift coffin. I smooth his hair and stroke his icy cold cheek. 'He looks like a Robert now, not my Bobbit. The boy that was Bobbit is gone.' I fetch a cushion I had badly embroidered when I was learning and place it under his head.

'Will you be all right, Miss Elizabeth? You loved him so much. Don't keep your grief inside; it will eat away at you. You can cry on my shoulder, if that would help.' He looks a little sheepish at his forwardness.

'Don't worry about me, John. I am sure the tears will come and I will take advantage of your kind offer, but not today. I will miss him dreadfully, of course, but how can I wish he was still here if he was going to be sent to an institution where his life would have been dreadful? That would be selfish. I only ever wanted him to be happy and to be loved by everyone; well he now is. But leave me now, John. I will sit with him for a while.'

John takes a last look at Robert and then surprises me by kissing me gently on my forehead. 'I will make him a beautiful bed, Miss Elizabeth.' He turns quickly and leaves me to my vigil.

Chapter 32

November 1825

I shake my head when Mama tells me to come with her and let someone else sit with Bobbit, because I want the person who sits with him to be here out of love, not duty. I know he is dead but with his body in front of me I do not yet miss him. There is no fire in the room, of course, but Mama brings me a warm blanket to wrap around me like a cocoon. I am aware of others coming into the room but I pay them no attention; I feel as if I and Bobbitt are in a glass dome and people may peer at us but they can't touch us and we can't hear them.

At some point during the day, I neither know, nor care, what time it is, Mr Whittaker comes and sits by me. He talks to me but he sounds as if he is speaking underwater and his words are meaningless. He takes a hand in his; is it mine? I suppose it must be, but I feel nothing. He is looking at me, not at Bobbit and I don't know why he is here. He soon leaves me in peace.

I am happy to stay here throughout the night, although this seems to cause my parents some anxiety. Eventually they leave me alone after lighting some candles, which I proceed to blow out. I don't need to see; I let the blackness envelop me like another blanket. I wonder if Bobbit would like a story?

There was once a farmer and his wife who already had three strapping sons, all of whom helped their father on the farm. When another boy was born they were all very surprised and disappointed when he grew up to be small, thin and pale and could hardly hold his dinner fork, no matter about a pitchfork.

The boy's elder brothers made fun of him day in and day out and they often practised their kicking skills on his fragile little body. The boy was desperately unhappy and longed to help the men folk on the farm but all he was able to do was to help his

194

mother by feeding the chickens and pigs and even that made him very weary.

His bedroom was in the attic, a cold, cheerless place with no curtains at the window or carpet on the floor. There was a tall tree at the side of the house and its top branches would tap, tap, tap on his window and he would hide terrified under his thin sheet. Every night the boy would pray that he would become strong like his brothers but his prayers were never answered.

An owl lived in the tall tree; he had been there before even the boy was born. He saw how he didn't grow big and strong like his brothers; he saw how mean everyone was to him; he saw the cuts and bruises on his puny little body; he saw how the boy cried himself to sleep every night. One night the owl decided he was going to interfere in the life of this little human and he flew to the window sill and tap, tap, tapped on the window. This terrified the boy more than usual and he hid even further under his thin sheet.

The owl called his name gently, over and over until the boy became curious and peeped over the top of the sheet. When he saw the owl sitting on his sill he smiled in delight and opened the window to stroke his beautiful feathers. The owl, who was very clever and could talk, told the boy to climb onto his back. The boy was not afraid and did not question how even a boy as small as he could sit astride an even smaller owl. He clambered onto the bird's back with his arms around the downy neck and the owl took flight.

The owl flew up and up and up until the boy could no longer see his empty bed, no longer see the farm, no longer see the village, until he reached the night-time playground. The boy jumped off and was surprised that he did not plummet to earth and was even more surprised when he was surrounded by baby stars and moonbeams, all of whom wanted to play with him. What a wonderful time he had, chasing and being chased by stars, sliding down moonbeams, playing hide and seek amongst

195

the clouds. No one cared that he was small; no one cared that he was thin; no one cared that he was pale. They liked him for who he was and were happy that they were able to make him laugh. Too soon the owl came for him to take him back to his cold little bed.

Each night thereafter the owl would take the boy to play with his friends in the sky and the kicks no longer hurt him; the mocking laughter no longer upset him; the mean words no longer humiliated him. Each night he went willingly to bed and no longer cried himself to sleep but lay excitedly waiting for the owl's tap, tap, tap on the window.

The boy, however, still did not grow strong; in fact he grew smaller and smaller, thinner and thinner, paler and paler. One night as the owl flew away the boy noticed that his bed was not empty as it should have been. He asked the owl who was in his bed. The owl replied, 'It is just your body. You have no need of it now.' When the owl had dropped off the boy at the night-time playground he said, 'I won't be taking you back there, this is your home now and these are your family, you are one of them.'

And the boy was surprised to see that his small, thin, pale little body was transformed into a glorious, sparkling star and he gave a tinkling laugh and sped away into the night sky, chasing a baby moonbeam.

I go to the window and pull apart the thick drapes; I can see no stars, but I know they are there behind the clouds. 'That story is for you, Bobbit. God bless you, dearest.'

It is morning; I must have slept, although I didn't mean to. Mama comes into the room, moving quietly, trying not to disturb me. 'It's all right, Mama. I'm awake.'

'You need to eat something, Lizzie. Please come and have breakfast. I will sit with Robert awhile.'

I realise I am hungry and that I no longer feel it is necessary for me to sit with the body; for that is what it is, just a body that looks a little like Bobbit. As I leave I hear Mama whisper, 'I do wish Matthew was here.' She makes no mention of Jamie.

Mr Whittaker is at the table with Papa and he glances at me with eyes dark with sympathy. 'Good morning Papa, Mr Whittaker.' Papa gets up, comes round and kisses me, a most unusual occurrence that warms my heart. 'How are you, this morning? I really don't know why you felt you had to stay there all night. You must have been very cold and uncomfortable.'

'I am perfectly well, Papa. I was quite warm and I managed to sleep. I said my goodbye. I suppose I must spend today making a black dress, for I don't have one.'

'Your mother and I have discussed this and we both agree that we will, of course, mourn Robert's death and give him a proper burial, but we will do so quietly and with decorum. We will all wear armbands,' I notice that he and Mr Whittaker are already doing so, 'but there is no need to make a show of it and make new dresses and put on a display. I hope that meets with your approval, Lizzie.'

'Of course, Papa. We want no pretence.'

Papa looks at me sharply but I leave my expression bland. Let him wonder whether I am being sarcastic or not.

Mr Whittaker takes his leave to go to the school and I ask if I may accompany him. We walk in silence for a while, heads bent against a cold wind that seems to want to force us back home again.

'I am truly sorry about Robert, Miss Hayes. It is such a terrible waste of a life and you were so devoted to him.'

'Let's be honest, Mr Whittaker, not many people felt his life was of any worth at all. Most saw that he was different to them and so assumed he saw nothing, heard nothing, understood nothing. But I am convinced, even more so now, that there was more to Bobbit than anyone thought, he just wasn't able to communicate it to us.'

'What do you mean, "even more so now"?'

'Even I, who believed he was capable of far more than anyone gave him credit for, did not think he would be able to wait until everyone was asleep, get himself up, unlock the front door and then find his way to the canal. He knew exactly what he was doing.' Mr Whittaker muses on what I have said. 'Then,' I glance at him out of the corner of my eye, 'he slips and falls in but cannot swim, so he drowns. Poor boy.'

'Indeed, Miss Hayes, poor boy. May I ask why you are walking into town? If you need to purchase something, I could do it for you to save you the bother.'

'I don't really have any plan to purchase anything, thank you, I just wanted to get out of the house for a while and get some fresh air. And very fresh it is too.' I pull my collar up which does nothing to stop the icy fingers tickling the back of my neck and creeping down my spine. I suddenly had a dreadful thought that stopped me in my tracks. 'Do you think the ground will be too hard to dig his grave? Where would Bobbit go then? He can't lie on the table forever.' I giggle rather hysterically at the thought.

'Fear not, Miss Hayes, the gravediggers will have the right tools. Robert will get his final resting place. Now, here we are at the school. Will you allow me to escort you further? Back home perhaps?'

'That is quite all right, thank you. You are needed in the school, especially as Papa will not be there today. I think I will go and visit the Goodmans. I haven't really thanked John properly for rescuing Bobbit.'

I feel Mr Whittaker stiffen at my side. 'There really was no need for him to leap into the canal in such a dramatic manner. It would have taken me just a minute more to remove my shoes.'

'He said he thought he might still be alive, that there was no time to waste.'

'I'm sorry for being blunt, but it was perfectly obvious that the boy was dead. I knew that another minute would make no difference.'

198

'Well, John saved you getting your clothes wet, unless you were going to remove them also?' I laugh at Mr Whittaker's blushes then bid him farewell and walk onto the Goodmans' workshop.

Chapter 33

November 1825

It is pleasantly warm inside and I savour the woody smells as I make my way towards the back of the workshop. Mr Goodman is bent over a long, rectangular box and John is at a workbench chiselling. Neither hears me, so intent are they on their craft. I like watching them; there is a stillness about them even when they are in motion and the love they have for the wood is apparent in their every movement and facial expression. I take a step forward; John sees me and puts down the tool with a clatter.

'Father, look it is Miss Elizabeth.' He speaks loudly to get his father's attention, who, on seeing me, rushes to stand between me and the box he has been working on, although he is not wide enough to hide it from my view.

'Please, Mr Goodman, there is no need to hide it. I realise it is Bobbit's coffin.' Although I hadn't until I glimpsed the brass handles already screwed onto the side.

John comes over, takes my elbow and leads me away. 'Come to the kitchen, Miss Elizabeth. Mother will be pleased to see you. As we all are.' The kitchen is a haven of warmth and mouth-watering smells of new bread and cakes.

'Ah, Miss Elizabeth, come in, come in, you poor thing. Sit you down and I'll make a nice pot of tea and here, I've just baked a cake to a new recipe and you can be the first to try it.' John and I share a smile at her good-natured bustling. There is only one topic of conversation. 'Such a shame, such a shame. What will you do now, Miss Elizabeth?'

I must admit that I had not thought of anything beyond the funeral, but indeed, what will I do now that I don't have Bobbit to care for every hour of the waking day?

'I have not thought on it, Mrs Goodman.'

'Well, you make sure you take your time, Miss Elizabeth, and grieve fully. There is nothing worse than bottling it all up for it will out eventually, in some form or another and all the worse for being held in. Isn't that right our John?' She does not wait for his answer. 'Now, what do you think of the cake?'

'Excellent, Mrs Goodman. You must tell me the recipe, or is it a family secret? I didn't just come to eat cake, though. I wanted to thank John again for pulling Bobbit out of the canal. Although, according to Mr Whittaker, there was no need for such melodrama as he knew there was no hope. That is why he was taking his time unlacing his shoes.' I smile at John's stiff expression and at Mrs Goodman's most unladylike snort. We chat some more and then, out of nowhere, a thought occurs to me. 'I think I will go and visit the Suttons. They probably don't know that Bobbit is dead. They think we are still planning to send him to an institution. Yes, that's what I'll do.' I stand up abruptly. 'In fact I think I'll go there now. They should be told.'

Mrs Goodman looks at me anxiously. 'Do you think that's a good idea, Miss Elizabeth?'

'Oh, I think it is an excellent idea, Mrs Goodman. The best I have had for many a day.'

'I will escort you, Miss Elizabeth. It is not right you facing them alone.'

'Thank you kindly, John. I would appreciate your company, but I don't want to take you away from your work.'

'Don't worry, I can spare a few hours. It's too far to walk in this weather, so I'll go and hire a carriage from Mr Bulman.'

'No, don't bother. We can go in your cart, if you don't mind taking the horses out?'

Mrs Goodman looks shocked, her already red cheeks even redder in indignation. 'You will most certainly not go in the cart, Miss Elizabeth, whatever will people think? You are a young lady and should travel in a carriage not a dirty old cart used for carrying wood and all sorts.'

I am tired of what other people think; it is rarely of any merit. 'You are very kind, Mrs Goodman, but I insist. I can put my hood up so that people don't see me and we can leave the cart away from the gates and walk in, if that will make you happier?'

Mrs Goodman opens her mouth to continue her objections but something in my expression closes it again. 'Very well, Miss Elizabeth, as you wish. Take this blanket to put around your legs, for the cold will creep into your bones.'

I treat myself to a second slice of cake whilst John harnesses the horses and brings the cart to the front of the workshop. It is, as Mrs Goodman foretold, extremely cold and I am grateful for the blanket. We slowly make our way through the town and out into the countryside where the rich owners have their oversized houses. Heaven forbid that they should live amongst their workers or the dirt and grime that their own factories produce.

'Your mother is a good woman.'

'She is. She fusses but means well.'

'Someone else who means well is Mr Whittaker.'

John's knuckles whiten. 'He speaks to me as if I am a pot boy.'

'I think he just wanted to be a hero and you stole his thunder.' This makes John smile.

We arrive at the gates to Sutton Hall. John hobbles the horses on the verge, takes my arm and we walk up the long, winding drive, the colonnade of young silver birches shivering in the chilly breeze. The lawns on either side are covered in sparkling frost except for the footprints of birds and rabbits. It reminds me of Bobbit's small footprints leading away from his home. It is not until we have crunched along the gravelled driveway for a good ten minutes that we turn a corner and see the house in all its glory. The newly painted white plaster glows and the windows glitter like diamonds in the weak winter sunshine.

'Goodness,' is all I can say.

John's steps slow until he stops. He says nothing but glances at his work clothes. I know what he is thinking. 'John, don't even think about leaving me alone. You are my escort and as such I need you to come with me. Through the front door.' I lead him up the stone steps and knock thrice the brass lion's head, which is almost too big to fit into my hand. I then notice a brass bell rope, which I pull three times. Nobody will be able to say that we did not announce our arrival. The door is opened by the housekeeper, whose polite smile turns upside down when she sees us.

She raises an eyebrow and looks at John. 'You're the carpenter man aren't you? What are you doing here; get round the back this instant. And take this person with you. What are you thinking of?' She goes to close the door but John puts his boot into the gap. 'This, madam, is Miss Elizabeth Hayes, daughter of Mr Hayes, the well-respected school teacher of this town, and granddaughter of both Lord and Lady Hayes of Herefordshire and Lord and Lady Adams of Inverness. I am here as her escort and we wish to see Mr and Mrs Sutton as a matter of urgency.'

I look her in the eye, nod my head in confirmation and sweep into the now open door as if I am indeed the granddaughter of such illustrious grandparents. The housekeeper scuttles after me, simpering as she goes.

'I apologise, Miss Hayes, I did not know who you were. I will go and see if either Mr or Mrs Sutton is available. Do you have a calling card? No? No matter. Please, let me take your coat and show you to the morning room.' She does not offer to take John's coat.

The room is as I imagined it would be: full of unnecessary furniture, ornaments, pictures and mirrors, all there to announce to the world that the Suttons are rich. John brushes the seat of his trousers before perching on the edge of a chair. 'I wouldn't worry, I expect there are an army of girls whose sole job is to make sure there is not one speck of dust anywhere in the whole house. You might as well give them something to do.' I smile broadly at him. 'You were very quick thinking back there. Fancy me being of the aristocracy.'

Before he can answer, the door opens and Mrs Sutton glides in, like a galleon in full, satin, pale green sail. 'Miss Hayes, this is most unexpected but how nice to see you.' She does not look at or greet John. 'I believe I was at a dinner party recently with your dear grandparents.' She does not say which fictional ones she purported to sup with. 'I'm afraid my husband is not here at the moment. May I offer you refreshments?' I shake my head; I have no desire to be here longer than necessary. 'Is this a social call or may I be of any assistance?'

'I apologise for not sending a calling card first to arrange an appointment, but I think you will agree that my visit cannot wait for the so-called proper proprieties to be followed.' Mrs Sutton's beady eyes look puzzled. 'You can indeed be of assistance, not only to me but to the whole of Wednesbury, and that is by bringing up your boys not to be bullies.' Mrs Sutton sits more upright, her powdered face takes on a look of shock and her painted lips form a perfect circle. She seems to be struggling for words, so I continue.

'You are aware, I am sure, Mrs Sutton, that your younger son, Daniel, recently received a bite on the ear from a much younger boy whom he and his friends were mercilessly bullying?'

'I am aware that my boy was severely injured in an unprovoked attack by your insane brother.' I can hardly hear her through her gritted teeth.

'Is that what he told you? He didn't tell you that there were six of them, led by Daniel, who pushed me aside and surrounded my brother, singing the coarsest of rhymes and poking at him with sharp sticks? He didn't tell you that I pleaded with them to stop because I was convinced they were going to kill him? He didn't tell you that Robert was absolutely terrified? He didn't tell you that it was only when they all fell in a heap on top of my boy

204

that he bit the ear? It could have been anyone's but it just happened to be Daniel's. It was not an unprovoked attack, Mrs Sutton, it was a desperate attempt to protect himself.'

Mrs Sutton still seems lost for words but she gives her head a shake, so small I hardly notice it.

'You will know though, that your husband, whom I assume taught his sons how to be bullies, came round to our house and made my father promise to send Robert away to an institution; away from the only home he ever knew, from the only people who ever loved him, just because he nipped the ear of someone who was tormenting him. Robert was thirteen years old, Mrs Sutton, and half the size of your son, never mind that there were six of them. Robert was different from other children, yes, but it was not his fault. He was the kindest, most gentle boy and he did nothing to warrant being mocked and hounded by your bully son and others like him.'

I can almost see my words swirling around in her head and then her face pales. 'Was? You said was?'

'Oh, didn't I tell you? He ran away that night because he was frightened of being sent away from home and,' I glance at John, 'he fell and drowned in the canal.' I wait a few seconds. 'I'm sure your husband and son will be most disappointed that Robert has escaped further suffering but they can be proud of themselves for being the direct cause of his death.' I look at John. 'Does that make them murderers?'

Mrs Sutton gets to her feet, then sits again, flapping her hands as if to shake off water. 'Oh, no, no, they are not murderers. I know Daniel can be a little rough sometimes, but he is a good boy really. He gets bored.'

I surge to my feet in anger. John looks at me apprehensively and Mrs Sutton fearfully. 'Bored? He was bored? Could he not have gone riding or shooting like other boys? Or is killing animals too boring; did it have to be a child?'

205

We are all standing now. John takes my arm and whispers, 'Enough.'

Mrs Sutton looks smaller and her tears have washed a winding path through the powder. 'Oh, my dear, I'm so sorry. But neither of them killed your brother, they didn't kill him. You said it was an accident. It could have happened at any time. Please, it wasn't their fault. Mr Sutton is a good father and Daniel a good boy, really he is. I will speak with him, tell him he mustn't bully other boys. He'll be at Cambridge in a few months. Oh dear.' She seems to deflate and sits back down, her head in her hands.

I feel nothing but contempt for the dejected figure and let John lead me out. There are no words of farewell. The housekeeper comes running into the hallway having heard our footsteps on the tiled floor. 'Are you leaving? The mistress didn't ring for me.'

'Yes. Please fetch me my coat and then go to her; she is a bit upset over some news I gave her.'

Outside, I am surprised to see that everything is exactly the same as when we entered the house, only a short time ago: the house is still glowing, the windows glittering, the frost sparkling.

'That was not well done, Miss Elizabeth.'

I did not cry when I thought Bobbit was going to be sent away; I did not cry when we found his body; I did not cry throughout my vigil. But I cry now, at John's disappointment in me.

I stand at the bottom of the steps and I sob 'I'm sorry' over and over onto his shoulders, whilst he whispers, 'There, there,' over and over onto the top of my head.

Where are so many tears stored, waiting patiently to be wept? They run out eventually and I stand back and wipe them from his coat lapels. 'I was a bully, wasn't I? I'm no better than Daniel, am I?'

Chapter 34

December 1825

The month has slipped almost unnoticed into December; Bobbit's death was now last month, soon it will be last year.

The frost has disappeared along with the sunshine and today is grey, damp and dreary; a perfect day for a funeral. Each night I have slept as soon as I have blown out the candle, with no dreams or nightmares to disturb me, yet I have not awoken refreshed. This morning is no different. I feel weighed down by the blankets; they are too heavy to push off me, so I just lie listening. I hear Sarah, or it might be Mama, banging the pots on the range; I hear doors opening and closing; I hear footsteps; I hear Papa coughing; I hear Dorothy giggling; I hear Bobbit's chair squeaking slightly as he rocks gently to and fro; I hear the creak as he turns over on his mattress; I hear his breath as he settles back down to sleep.

I whisper to myself, like a mantra, 'He's gone to a better place; he's gone to a better place.'

He's gone.

I hear my own door open and Mama comes in and sits on my bed. 'It's time to get up, Lizzie. What will you wear?'

'Does it matter? My Sunday dress I suppose. Or maybe just one of my ordinary day dresses. Bobbit won't care what I wear.'

'Bobbit won't care, no, but you will, my dear. Wear whatever you feel comfortable in. Come on, I'll help you dress and do your hair.'

I feel like a small child again as Mama passes me my clothes; she even does my buttons up for me. As she brushes my hair I look at her reflection.

'What are you feeling, Mama?'

'At this precise moment? Anxious. I want today to go smoothly. I want today to be over.'

'Do you feel sad at all? That he's dead, I mean? Or guilty?'

207

She returns my stare in the mirror. 'I tried at the start, Lizzie, believe me, I tried. When I held your brothers and you in my arms straight after you were born I felt nothing but overwhelming love. I would have died for you. But when I held Robert, even before we knew he wasn't right, I felt absolutely nothing. It was a difficult birth and I was exhausted, sore and just wanted to sleep for a month. Then he wouldn't feed, although I had plenty of milk. I tried so hard, Lizzie, but he just wouldn't take it from me. As soon as we got in a wet nurse, he suckled away. It was as if he was rejecting me.'

'Perhaps he knew you didn't love him?'

'Perhaps, although I'm not sure young babies are capable of such feelings. It was the wet nurse who said there was something wrong with him. He never cried, even when he was hungry or she stuck a pin in him by accident. He never looked around or followed people; he just stared into space. And she noticed one of his legs was not straight and the foot turned inwards. We got the doctor in and he confirmed that he was damaged and would never be a normal boy.'

'He wasn't spiteful like Jamie, or a bully like Daniel, if you think that is normal. But he was kind and gentle and I loved him.'

'I know, Lizzie, and it's all down to you. If you had not taken him under your wing when still a babe yourself, I would have sent him away. But your father persuaded me to let him stay, so long as you cared for him. And you did, Lizzie, you did.'

She coils my hair, pins it up and hands me my bonnet. 'You asked me if I feel guilty. I stopped feeling guilty years ago but, yes, I do feel sad, so very sad. Not for Robert but for you.'

There is indeed a great sadness in her eyes and I feel sorry for her.

'You have lost all three of your sons: two to God and one to the Suttons.'

She gives me a watery smile before taking my arm and we go down the stairs together, side by side. She tells me that the

Goodmans have already brought the coffin and that they are waiting for me to say a final goodbye before they screw the lid on.

It has been just three days. The room has been kept cold, bowls of herbs are scattered around the room, along with vases of lilies and late honeysuckle, and his body lies on sweet smelling wood shavings mixed with twigs of rosemary, but even so the smell assaults my senses. I stand in the doorway but cannot go any further. I don't want to see his thin little body wrapped in a winding sheet; I don't want to see his bound jaw; I don't want to see his lips, coloured pink to cover the blueness of death.

'You can cover him now, Mr Goodman.'

He lifts the lid and he and John tighten the brass screws. Only now do I come closer. The body of the coffin is plain but the lid is the most beautiful thing I have ever seen. John, it must be him surely, has carved every inch with flowers, birds, chickens, rabbits, horses, butterflies – everything that Bobbit loved.

'How? When? I cannot believe you have done this in just three days.'

'He worked through the nights, Miss Elizabeth.'

'It is a bit rough in places, but I didn't have the time to finish it as well as I wanted.'

I don't know what to say. I run my fingers along the grooves and bumps, caressing each tiny carving, trying to memorise them. 'It is beautiful as it is, John, just beautiful. He cannot thank you, but I can.' I go to him and hug him tight and whisper 'Thank you' into his shirt. Mr Goodman shuffles his feet in embarrassment; I release his son and go and hug him too. 'Thank you too, Mr Goodman, I know you have also worked hard on this.' He shuffles in embarrassment again and I'm sure I spy a tear at the corner of each eye.

The Goodmans leave to get changed and I sit with the remains of my family to eat a desultory breakfast. Even Dorothy is quiet and sits on Mama's lap whilst she pops honeyed bread into her mouth.

'Is Dorothy coming?'

'No, she will stay here with Sarah. She won't understand what is happening and I don't want to frighten her.'

We sit at the cleared table, each with our own thoughts, Dorothy sucking her thumb, until there is a loud knock on the front door.

'They're here.'

It's the Goodmans again come to take the coffin, to where? I have taken no notice of the planning that Mama and Papa have been doing over the last few days so the horse-drawn cart that stands on the street is unexpected. I thought the coffin would be carried to the church on the shoulders of bearers, but instead it is gently slid onto the back of the cart, puckering the black velvet as it goes. None of the four horses are black but there is a sob in my throat as I realise that they are the canal horses, released for a few hours from their labour to carry their friend to his last resting place. Mama has brought the flowers from the parlour and she lays them on top of the coffin.

John gets into the cart and gently urges the horses on. The load is lighter than they are used to and he has to keep slowing them down to a more sedate walk. Mama and Papa follow the cart, followed by myself. Others join us as we walk along the street up to the church: Mr Whittaker, Mr and Mrs Goodman and their daughters, the elder boys from the school, some of the bargemen, neighbours, shop-keepers, market-stall holders, all of them knew Bobbit to be a gentle soul, who did not deserve to die so young.

It starts to rain quite heavily, which causes some of the followers to scuttle back home. By the time we reach the church, where the Reverend Stephenson is standing waiting for us, we are down to just the family, the Goodmans, Mr Whittaker and his boys. Papa, John, Mr Goodman and Mr Whittaker take the coffin on their shoulders and carry it slowly to the unsheltered grave. God does not take pity on us and sheds His own tears; the rain hammers noisily on the coffin lid and drips off hats and bonnets down necks and into every opening it can find.

The gravediggers lower the coffin into the hole; there is a squelching noise as it settles in the mud and I hope the coffin is sufficiently watertight. Poor Reverend Stephenson fairly gallops through the service and there are not enough of us for our Lord's Prayer to be heard beyond our shivering party. After the final Amen, the good Reverend walks briskly away back to the protection of his church, followed by the others, but it is as if I am stuck in the mud. I am still holding a sprig of rosemary in my hand; for remembrance, as if I am ever likely to forget him, or perhaps it is so that he does not forget me? The rain pools into the carvings, mud spatters up the sides of the coffin, my feet sink deeper into the mire but still I cannot do this one final act.

Can he hear the raindrops? Is he feeling cold? He must be scared. Should I get him out and run home with him? Warm him up? Tell him a story? He'd like that. I squat down ready to jump into the pit when my arms are grabbed by stronger ones.

'Be careful, Miss Hayes, you don't want to fall in. Come, let's get you home and out of those wet clothes. Come, my dear. It's over.'

'I can't leave him here all alone. He needs me. Help me get him out. Help me, Mr Whittaker, if you care for me at all.' I struggle against his tight grip and the sprig of rosemary falls to the ground, as do I.

Chapter 35

January 1826

1 January 1826

My dearest Matthew,

It is strange writing to you not knowing if you have even received any of our earlier letters. Hopefully you have and that they are in the correct order, otherwise it will be very confusing for you! Just in case, though, I will give you a summary of events up to the present day:

<u>The most awful event</u> that has happened is that our beloved boy is no longer with us. On 27th November, a day I will never forget, he and I were taunted by Daniel Sutton and his bully boys down by the canal and for once in his life poor Bobbit retaliated and bit the nearest ear-lobe off, which happened to belong to Daniel. As far as I am concerned, Daniel deserved what he got, if not far worse, but Mr Sutton came to our house and bullied Papa (like father, like son) into promising to send Bobbit away. Bobbit must have heard because that very night he managed to get himself out of bed without me hearing him, open the front door (which he has never, ever done before) and make his way to the canal, where he jumped in and drowned himself. Papa says we must tell everyone that it was an accident but it wasn't, Matthew, it wasn't. What grieves me more than anything is that my poor boy spent his last hours being terrified: terrified of Daniel and his friends and terrified of being sent away from the only person who has ever loved him. I hope he wasn't terrified of death itself. I honestly think that he believed this to be the best course of action.

I handled his death very well at first, as I convinced myself that he was in a far better place, but at the funeral, when I saw the little coffin (beautifully carved by John) at the bottom of the muddy hole (it had been raining all day), I collapsed. Mr Whittaker carried me home and I have been in bed ever since, in fact I am writing this letter to you propped up by every pillow in the house. Doctor Peters insists that I had some sort of nervous reaction to the death but I think I was just overwhelmed and exhausted and just needed to sleep for a few weeks.

I remember different people coming in and soup being spooned into my mouth but not much else other than the night times when Bobbit visited me. He really did, Matthew. I can still hear the bed creak as he sat next to me; I can still feel his hand as he stroked my hair. I wasn't dreaming, Matthew, honestly I wasn't. He never said a word until last night, when he bent down and kissed my cheek and whispered, 'goodbye brave girl.' I know he won't come again. You do believe that God sent Bobbit to comfort me, don't you Matthew?

This morning, Dorothy came bounding in as usual, shouting 'new year,' at the top of her voice (she can be extremely loud!) and she roused me from my slumbers – both sorts. I mean to get up once I have finished this letter and I am going to ask Papa if I can now help at the school. He surely can't refuse me.

<u>News of Jamie</u> – he did come to the quay on the day you left, but he didn't make himself known to us other than by a letter secreted in my reticule. He has disowned the family in favour of the Suttons. Papa has written him countless letters pleading to meet so that they can talk man to man, but our not so dear brother is not a man, he is a spoilt brat and is breaking our parents' hearts. He and the Suttons are well suited and I don't care if I never see him again, but would you write to him and see if you can get him to grow up and agree to meet with Papa?

This letter writing has quite tired me out, what a pathetic specimen I am! But I am quite determined to get up this afternoon and start living my life again.

Please, please write and tell us that you are all right and being a missionary is everything you ever hoped for. I can't bear to think of you being miserable. I miss you so much and pray for you every night.

Come home soon,
Your loving sister,
  Lizzie

My new year energy is indeed exhausted but after a short sleep I manage to get out of bed and downstairs, with the help of Sarah on one side and Mama on the other. The kitchen is warm and welcoming and I sit down gratefully, feeling as if I have walked down a mountain rather than a flight of stairs. It has been four weeks since I was last here, sitting in this same chair and I look around as if for the first time, taking everything in with new eyes: the simmering pots on the range and those waiting to be so used suspended from hooks, their shiny bottoms like bronze mirrors; herbs tied in bundles and hanging from the ceiling; the open fire merrily dancing in the grate; the vegetables on the table, chopped and ready to be boiled alive; a dead chicken patiently waiting to be stuffed and roasted. It is all so familiar and comforting and yet there is something different; it takes a while for me to realise that Bobbit's chair is no longer in its rightful place. Mama notices where I am looking.

'We thought it best to move it.'

I nod my understanding. Sarah wraps a knitted blanket around my knees, hands me a drink of tea and strokes my hair. 'You had us worried, Miss Elizabeth, good and worried.'

'Maybe I got a chill. It was raining hard on the day, wasn't it?' I am alert enough to see Mama and Sarah share a glance.

'Yes dear, I expect you did.'

'I remember slipping and falling to the ground and Mr Whittaker being there. I don't remember much after that, until this morning when I felt I had woken from a long sleep. I must thank Mr Whittaker for carrying me; I cannot have been an easy load.'

'Yes, he was a great help. He was most anxious and has asked after you every day. He has taken on a lot of the teaching this last month. He is a good man, a very good man.'

'John Goodman has also called every day, Miss Elizabeth. You are lucky to have two fine men so interested in your health and well-being.'

I smile at the thought of the two of them trying not to be outdone by the other's show of concern. 'Talking of school, Mama, I am going to ask Papa if I can help at the school now that, well, now that I don't have so many responsibilities. That would be all right, wouldn't it? I will still help in the house and with Dorothy, but I would so love to be able to help Papa. I know I am nowhere as good as Mr Whittaker, but I can help with the young ones and leave the men to the older boys. Perhaps we could even take on a few girls?'

Mama comes and crouches by my side and strokes my arm, just as she did on the morning we found Bobbit. 'It's so good to hear you plan, Lizzie, but you have been quite unwell and you will need to take things slowly, until you get your full strength back. You know how tired even Papa and Mr Whittaker are when they come back after teaching. Just make your health the top priority for the time being.'

The heat of the fire and the hot drink make me sleepy. I fall into a deep sleep and am woken by the entrance of the men returning from the school. Mama tries to shoo Mr Whittaker out of the kitchen, no doubt thinking that seeing me with my hair loose and still in my nightgown is not a sight for his eyes. She tries to push him through the door but not before we have managed to have a brief conversation.

'It is good to see you up and about, Miss Hayes. We have been most worried about you.'

'There really was no need, it was only a chill.' He raises one eyebrow at me but doesn't challenge my diagnosis. 'I believe I have you to thank for carrying me home. I hope your muscles were not overstrained.'

Mama looks horrified at this mention of his body parts and gives him a final push and slams the door behind him. She glowers at me. 'Really, Lizzie, that is no way to speak to a gentleman. Whatever will he think of you?'

'I doubt he will think any differently of me than he has ever done, Mama.'

Papa comes over and awkwardly gives me a hug. 'It's good to see you up and about at last, my dear. But don't overtire yourself. Listen to what Mama and Sarah say; they know what's best for you.'

Mama is right. I don't regain my strength as quickly as I hoped. After a few days, however, I am able to dress and make my own way downstairs unaided and I can help prepare vegetables and mix ingredients, as long as I'm sitting, although kneading bread is still too much for me. I sit with my parents and Mr Whittaker for the evening meal and they are quite embarrassing in their concern and treat me with great kindness, far more than I feel I deserve. Mr Whittaker now speaks in a most gentle tone that I find slightly irritating; I would much rather he taunt and mock me as was his wont. Each evening when he greets me, he takes my hand in his, gives a slight bow, his mouth getting ever nearer to the back of my hand. I find that I am quite looking forward to the time he actually kisses it.

I am trying to think only happy, shallow thoughts, which is possible when I'm chatting with others, executing tasks or entertaining Dorothy as far as my frail health will allow. It is in the silent times that I cannot stop them from wandering into the darkness. I see Bobbit rocking in his chair in the corner of the kitchen, his eyes closed in a world of his own; sitting in the garden, enchanted by the butterflies; walking down the towpath, his hand in mine. I see his dark eyes shining with a knowledge he was never able to share; the piece of dark hair that always used to flop down over his forehead; his pale, thin body as he lay on the table waiting for me to dress him in his eternal best suit. I hear his breath as he slept at the bottom of my bed; the clucking he made when he collected the eggs and the strange sounds as he talked with his equine friends. I see his look of terror as he was surrounded by jeering boys; I hear the sound of the screams he never uttered; I feel the chill of the icy water on his skin as it draws out the warmth, the very life from his body.

I keep looking but I don't see his smiling face in the flames.

Chapter 36

March 1826

It is quite spring-like today and I am feeling strong enough to walk into town with Sarah. We progress slowly arm-in-arm as I delight in the feel of the breeze on my cheeks, the sight of the bobbing daffodils and the sounds of the birds a-courting.

'You take it nice and easy, Miss Elizabeth, we're in no rush.' Sarah is carrying a large basket containing jars of conserve, a packet of tea and sugar, squares of linen, blocks of butter and cheese and other items of food that she packed as I donned my outdoor clothes.

'Are you setting up a shop, Sarah?'

'Don't be silly, Miss Elizabeth. I'm just taking a few things to the Morgan family.'

'The name sounds familiar. Who are they?'

'Robert Morgan was one of the leaders of the riot a couple of summers ago, do you remember? He was in jail and then just before Christmas he was shipped to Australia, like he was a common murderer. His poor wife is left with three little ones and is in very great need. She was just pregnant when he was taken so she has twins of nearly a year old who he has never seen, and a small boy of about three.'

'But she was the lady Mr Whittaker saved from being trampled under the horses' hooves when she was following the cart containing her husband. Poor woman; poor children. Isn't the parish supporting them? That's what the Parish Fund is for, isn't it?'

Sarah gives a snort. 'Donations to the Parish Fund are from the better off families, who are mostly the mine and factory owners. They have apparently made it quite clear that the families of the ring leaders are not to be helped any longer.'

'But that's terrible! How can they do that? The money is to help families in trouble, regardless of the cause.'

'The Parish Fund Committee is made up of the wives of the owners and they have the final say.'

'But the Reverend Stephenson is at the head of the committee; surely he doesn't allow these women to dictate who gets what?'

Sarah looks at me pityingly but passes no comment on the moral strength of the good reverend.

'I know it's not right, Miss Elizabeth, but as we can't force these people to give the money, your mother and I are donating goods instead.' Sarah has quickened her step in her agitation.

'Please can you slow down, Sarah, you're walking too fast for me. How did you find out the family is in need?'

'I'm sorry, Miss Elizabeth, but it makes me so angry. It was on a market day just after you were taken ill when I saw a small boy being chased by the baker. The lad ran past me and I just grabbed at him. It was like holding a skeleton, Miss Elizabeth, his arms were that thin. I paid the man for the loaf the boy had stolen and I asked the lad to take me to his home.' She goes silent for a few seconds. 'When I told your Mama how the family is living and that they are getting little support, she very kindly suggested that we put together a few basic items each week and take it to them, but it's not enough, Miss Elizabeth, nowhere near enough.'

'Mama is always very generous.' Her only cruelty was to Bobbit. 'Does she not come with you on these visits?'

'Not as yet as she has not been able to leave Dorothy in your care during your illness.'

'I am quite well now and I will gladly accompany you today.'

'No, miss, it's no place for you, especially in your weakened state.' I begin to object. 'No, Miss Elizabeth, the mistress would never forgive me if I took you there today and you became ill again. Now, be a good girl and take this jar of conserve to Mrs Goodman and stay there until I return. She'll be glad to see you; the whole family will, I'm sure.'

I watch as Sarah strides down the street, wasting no time in looking into shop windows or exchanging gossip with other less purposeful women.

I go straight into the kitchen and Mrs Goodman welcomes me as if I were a long lost daughter. 'Oh, Miss Elizabeth, how good to see you up and about again. Come, sit you down by the fire and get yourself warm. I'll make a nice, hot drink. How are you, my dear? You've lost weight and look a little pale, if you don't mind me being so bold? You surely didn't walk here all by yourself?'

'I'm quite well, thank you, Mrs Goodman. I just had a chill, that's all. Now that it's spring I will be back to normal very soon. I walked with Sarah; she's gone on to visit the Morgan family with a basket of victuals. She says they are in dire straits since the husband was shipped off to Australia and the owners' wives are refusing to give the family any money from the Poor Fund. She is quite incensed at the unfairness of it all. Here, she asked me to give you this.'

I hand Mrs Goodman a jar of marmalade and she gives me a jar of raspberry jam to take back. This exchange has become a ritual; whether it is done in the spirit of friendship or competition I'm not sure and do not like to ask. 'Is John around?'

'He and his father are just delivering a chest of drawers to the Suttons; they should be back soon.' She looks at me guiltily. 'We almost refused the commission, but, well, we can't afford to turn away work at the moment.'

'No, of course you can't, I quite understand.'

'I can maybe understand the mine owners like the Suttons not going to the aid of Mr Morgan, but to refuse to help his poor wife and little ones just isn't Christian. What Mr Sutton paid for that chest of drawers would keep a family in food for a month of Sundays. I wish we'd said "no" now, I really do.'

'If the miners were paid decent wages in the first place then none of this would have happened. It's all about greed, Mrs

Goodman, just plain old fashioned greed. It's always the women and children who suffer, though, isn't it? Mr Morgan wasn't the only man to be imprisoned, was he? I wonder how the other families are faring?'

Before Mrs Goodman can answer we hear heavy footsteps, the door is flung open and father and son come into the kitchen, filling the space with their bodies and the smell of wood and resin. Mr Goodman greets me kindly, asks after my health then returns to the workshop. John's already red cheeks go a deeper shade as he shyly sits by my side.

'Oh, it's so good to see you, Miss Elizabeth. I have been pestering Sarah every day as to how you are doing and I have been so pleased to hear you are on the road to recovery, but even more pleased to see you sitting here looking so pr... so well.'

'Thank you, John. As I told your mother, I only had a chill but I have almost returned to perfect health.'

He studies my face intently then smiles and gives a small nod. 'A chill, yes, of course.'

'Now, John, don't you get mithering Miss Elizabeth. Make yourself useful and take this drink to your father.' She gives John two cups and follows him with fond eyes as he bids me farewell and makes his way to the work shop, carrying the coarse pot mugs as if they are made of bone china.

'He's a good lad, is John. He'll make someone a good husband one of these days. But not yet awhile I don't think.'

She carries on with her chores and doesn't seem to expect a reply, so I give none, for what can I say that will not give my own feelings away?

Before long Sarah returns and we leave the Goodmans and make for home. She looks weary and her face is set in a hard expression but she doesn't tell me of the visit. As we walk along the main street I hear footsteps running behind us.

'Oi, Miss Hayes, stop awhile.'

We stop and wait for a panting Mr Cooper, the innkeeper, to catch up with us.

'There's a letter here. It's a bit battered but I reckon it's from your brother what went as a missionary.'

He hands me an envelope that does look as if it has been trodden on by a hundred muddy feet, but the address is still legible and it is indeed in dear Matthew's handwriting.

I clutch it to my breast, holding it tight in case an impish gust of wind should steal it from my fingers. 'Oh, thank you, Mr Cooper, thank you so much. We have been waiting for this letter. Thank you, thank you.'

'Come, Miss Elizabeth. The man has only carried it down the street, not from Sierra Leone itself. There is no need for such excessive gratitude. We need to get home so that your parents can read it. Come now.'

I smile my thanks once more and then almost skip home.

CMS House
Freetown
Sierra Leone
November 21st '26

My Dearest Mother, Father, James, Lizzie, Robert, Dorothy and Sarah,

Well, I am finally here and I am writing to you on my very first day on solid ground for what seems months, but is in fact only three or so weeks. I was going to write every day during the voyage but neither I nor Mr Docherty are good sailors, (despite both being born on an island!) and every day either I was too ill or I had the care of Mr Docherty. We shared a cabin with two other men and believe me, by the end of the three weeks we were all heartily sick of the place, both literally and figuratively!

But God was with us and we all survived, which I was told today, is not always the case. I'm glad I didn't know that at the time.

We are currently housed in a building built specially for the Church Missionary Society and we will stay here for a few weeks to get acclimatised. The weather cannot be any more different from that in England. When I left it was damp and cold and perfectly miserable. Here in Freetown it is warmer than our summer and just going out of the rainy season into the dry. It is humid, which I expected, but I have already had to change my shirt twice today and fear I will need to get more made up for me. I can see the sea from my window where I am writing and it is a most brilliant blue and I can quite forgive it for making me so sick. The trees are very different than the ones in England; I will try and sketch some in my next letter. There are no great oaks but there is something called the cotton tree. We passed a giant one on our way from the harbour to the house and we were told this is of great significance because it was this tree where, in 1792, former slaves from Novia Scotia gathered and gave thanks for their liberty. This tree, so they say, is the site where Freetown was founded.

As well as merchant ships, I can see the ships of our own navy in the harbour. Their job is to capture slave ships and they bring the human cargo here to Freetown – these are the people we will be ministering to. They come from many different countries so there is a real mixture of races. I have not yet met many of the residents but those that I have are colourfully dressed and all have the widest smiles I have ever seen. They are happy to be free and, God willing, ready to hear His word.

I am truly blessed and thankful that God has chosen me.

I look forward to your letters. You can send to the above address and they will be forwarded to me if I have moved elsewhere.

I will write more in my next letter. I am not sure when this will get to you but know that I am thinking of you and praying for you.

Your loving and dutiful son and brother,
Matthew

Matthew's letter has really raised my spirits and I am resolved to do good in some small way, so I now contribute to the weekly basket that Sarah takes to the Morgan family. I make batches of biscuits in the shape of a star for the children and extra meat pies and I select the biggest, brownest eggs and the shiniest, reddest apples from the store. I retrieve a couple of half-finished shawls I had put away when its intended recipient had not survived and each evening I sit and continue to work on them. Mama considers me well enough to look after Dorothy for a few hours and she now accompanies Sarah with a second basket, necessitated by my contributions. The first thing they do on their return is wash their faces and hands and change their clothes. The banging of pots and the chopping of vegetables is always more vigorous until they have given vent to their frustrations. They are disinclined to talk and I don't want to cause them further upset by asking them about their visit.

Chapter 37

April 1826

I go for longer and longer walks each afternoon and four weeks after I first found out about the Morgan family, I am determined to go along with Sarah and Mama.

'I have spent many hours finishing these shawls and I would like to give them to Mrs Morgan myself. I feel I know her and her little boy. I am in the most robust health and I am more than capable of carrying one of the baskets. Will you now allow me to go, Mama?'

Mama looks at me intently as if to confirm that I am indeed of sound health and mind. She gives a short nod. 'I see no reason why you shouldn't go with Sarah instead of me. But Lizzie, it is not an enjoyable outing. You will see things that will upset you but it is perhaps time that you understand how these poor people live and what they suffer.'

Sarah and I walk down the familiar route to the centre of Wednesbury but then go down side streets I have never ventured down before, being where the miners and foundry workers themselves live. The wide streets quickly narrow and become darker and more oppressive. The rows of houses are black from the smoke that belches out of the chimneys that loom over us and the air itself carries small particles that settle on my clothes, hands and face. I now understand why Mama and Sarah need to wash and change when they return home. The front doors open straight onto the muddy, puddled roads that have a channel down the middle, overflowing with sewage and offal. I hold a handkerchief to my nose but it does not prevent the smell of coal, iron smelting, boiled cabbage, sewage and decay from assaulting my senses. I try and peer into the grimy windows but see only dark shadows moving in a room full of shadows. The houses seem to lean in, blocking out the light, and I have a horrible feeling that they are going to collapse on top of us.

Sarah looks at me and grimaces. 'This is where people who aren't as lucky as us live. Couples fall in love, get married, have babies who, God willing, grow up, fall in love and so on and so on. This is their home and there is no way they can ever leave, other than in a wooden box, which most of them do well before their time.'

There is nothing to distinguish one house from another but Sarah stops at one and knocks on the door. 'Maggie, it's me, Sarah.' The door opens slowly as if by magic but I lower my eyes and see a small child peeping out. 'Good morrow, young master William. How are you this fine morning?'

Young master William gives Sarah a gummy smile and steps back into the gloom, having looked at me shyly and popping a surprisingly clean pale pink thumb into his mouth. We step into the room and the air, despite it being warm outside, is cold and damp and clings to my skin, making me shiver. There is a bustle of movement when a woman comes into the room with a baby in each arm. She is thinner than when I had seen her last, almost skeletal, with cheek bones jutting out like blades, eyes that are dull and a mouth that doesn't look as if it has ever smiled. She looks older than my grandmother although she must be younger than Mama. None of the children have the plumpness that makes Dorothy so delicious and huggable; they are like wooden puppets and I half expect their bones to click as they move.

'Oh, Sarah, I'm so sorry, I was in the back. Did our William let you in? Good man, Willy.'

'We don't stand on ceremony, do we Maggie? Let me introduce Miss Elizabeth Hayes, the eldest daughter of my mistress. You have already met her, actually. She was with the gentleman who helped you when you fell on the day of the riot. She's not been well recently but she's been baking and embroidering some things for you and she wanted to come today to meet with you again.'

226

Mrs Morgan bobs a curtsey, no mean feat decked as she is. 'I remember you, Miss Hayes, and I'm right grateful to your Ma sending me this food every week. If it wasn't for these baskets, well, we'd all be starved to death by now.'

'We won't let that happen, will we Miss Elizabeth? Now, Maggie, just to let you know that my mistress has written to the vicar of the church in Derby and asked him to contact your uncle and let him know of your situation. I'm afraid she hasn't heard anything back as yet.'

Mrs Morgan's shoulders droop even lower, either from the disappointment, the weight of the twins, or both. Sarah puts her basket on the floor, there isn't a table in the room, and indicates that I should do the same. 'Will you help me take everything out, Master William? I'm sure Miss Elizabeth has some biscuits in her basket that really need eating this very minute.' The two of them squat down and unpack the two baskets. There is a squeal of glee when William finds the little bag of star-shaped biscuits and he rushes to his mother to show them to her.

'Thank Miss Hayes, Willy, then you can have one and save the rest for another day.' William looks at me under his eyelashes and gives me a small smile and whispers something I cannot hear, but I smile back and help him take one out of the bag. Before I can straighten my back he has devoured it, leaving not a crumb as evidence of its existence.

Sarah holds out the two shawls I had made. 'Miss Elizabeth made these especially for the twins, Maggie.' Mrs Morgan has tears coursing down her face. 'I'm ever so grateful, miss, I am.' She holds one of the babies out to me as if offering a thank you gift. I take him carefully, terrified I will break his bones. How light he is compared to Dorothy at one year. I wrap the shawl around him and hold him to my breast. I can feel his shoulder blades and hip bones and can hear each of his rattling breaths. I catch a glimpse of his bright blue eyes before they close and his head flops onto my shoulder.

'What's his name Mrs Morgan?'

'That one's Matilda, miss, and this here is Morris. They ain't exactly the same; Morris has a birthmark here on his cheek, see?' It looks like a smudge of coal dust. 'I tell him it's where the angel patted him because his Pa couldn't. He's too young to understand yet, though. It grieves me that Pa has never seen these two, and that they will never see him. Nor will I, never again.' Sarah manages to grab hold of Morris before Mrs Morgan slumps onto the edge of the bed, the only furniture in the room, and starts to sob uncontrollably.

Sarah deftly puts her free arm around the woman's shoulder and tries to comfort her until the storm is over. 'You must be strong, Maggie dear, strong for the children.'

'What's the point, eh? What future do we have? We might as well just curl up in a corner and die. No one will notice or care.'

'Don't you dare say that, Maggie! I care, my mistress cares and Miss Elizabeth cares. And God, of course. Aren't the other families helping you at all?'

'Aye, some. They let me have some pieces of coal and Mrs Smithers, she has a goat, and lets me have some milk sometimes. But most don't have enough for themselves and can't spare even a crumb, nor why should they? They have sympathy, but we can't eat sympathy. The Reverend comes sometimes and slips me a coin, but he hasn't been here for weeks. William manages to beg in the town but people up there are mean and more often as not chase him away, poor little blighter. If it wasn't for your baskets, Sarah, it would all be over for us. My uncle is our only hope otherwise it's the workhouse for us.'

We take our leave but all the way home I can feel Matilda in my arms, the warmth of her body and her fine hair tickling my chin. The baskets are now empty but the heaviness in our hearts weighs down each step.

'Mama has heard from the vicar, hasn't she? I remember she received a letter from Derby the other day. What did it say?'

'It said that Maggie's uncle passed away two years ago. I just couldn't bear to tell her. He was her one and only hope and I don't know what she will do when she knows he's gone.'

'She said she would have to go to the workhouse. They are meant to look after people like Maggie, aren't they?'

'I know there is the Parish Workhouse in Meeting Street. I have no experience of them but I have always known it is not somewhere anyone would choose to go. It's the last resort but maybe it's the only option for Maggie.'

We find Mama sitting in the garden under the shade of an apple tree. The sight of a plump Dorothy playing contentedly amongst the daisies overwhelms me and I run sobbing and throw myself at Mama's feet. 'It's all too awful, Mama. That poor family; they don't deserve to live like that, having to live off our charity. They live just down the road, for heaven's sake but it could be another country. They have done nothing wrong, nothing. I held one of the twins, Matilda was her name, I thought it was a boy at first but it was a girl and I held her and she was so terribly thin and she had a dreadful cough and she slept on me.' I stop to get my breath. 'They could live here, couldn't they? The boys don't need their rooms anymore and we could clear out the store room; that would give Mrs Morgan plenty of space for her, William and the twins. Maggie, that is Mrs Morgan, could help in the house and I would look after the children, you know I'm good at that.'

Mama wipes my tears. 'Oh, Lizzie, we can't help them any more than we are already doing. I know it's dreadful, dear, but if we gave a home to the Morgans, what about all the other poor families, we can't accommodate them as well. Every miner's family, every iron founder's family, is poor, is always cold and hungry. They work all the hours God sends, and more, but they get a pittance from people who have never done a day's work in their lives. The Parish Fund is meant to help these people but the one in Worcester is run by the very people that cause the suffering in the first place.' She stops talking and looks into the distance. 'Maybe I should try and join the committee, although I am not sure my voice will be heard.'

'I know we can't help every family, Mama, but we could just help the Morgans. Surely it's our Christian duty?'

'I know it's unfair what has happened to Mrs Morgan, but Mr Morgan would have known the risk he was taking when he decided to make a stand. I'm sorry you are so upset but this is the society in which we live and the likes of you, me and Sarah will make very little difference.'

'We could make a difference for one family.'

'Be realistic, Lizzie. We are not poor ourselves, I grant you, but we cannot afford to support a woman and three children for the rest of their lives. How old is the boy, Sarah?'

'Master William is three, mistress.'

'Well, in a few years' time he will be old enough to work and earn a small bit of money.'

I look at her in horror; I had almost forgotten how cruel she could be. 'Are you suggesting that a six-year-old boy should become the wage earner? Have you ever been in a mine, Mama? Jamie took me and Bobbit into one a few years back and left us there as a joke. I was only there for a few minutes but I was terrified. The miners are there day in, day out, in the dark mostly along with the rats and the boggarts. They tear at the coal with their bare hands that blackens their bodies and souls, but which lines the owners' pockets with gold. Nobody should have to work in places like that, certainly not children. If men and women have to work in mines then they should only work for a few hours but still be given a proper wage and children should be left to be children for as long as possible.'

Mama closes her eyes and gives an exasperated sigh. 'I know it is not ideal, but until the coal can be extracted by magic then it has to be extracted by men, women and children. You can't change the world by wishing, Lizzie. I'll speak to the Reverend Stephenson about the Morgans and see what he can suggest.'

I sniff my lack of faith in the good Reverend's ability to act according to his own sermons. I have a sudden idea and run inside and up to my room; Bobbit's clothes can be made into good outfits for William. I pull open drawers and throw my brother's shirts and pantaloons onto a pile on the floor. What else can I use? Of course! I rifle through my own clothes in the wardrobe and add a couple of old dresses that won't take much modification to fit Maggie. I then go into the tiny room next to my parent's bedroom that Dorothy sleeps in and take out outfits that no longer fit her; they will be ideal for the twins and Mama has assured me she has no intention of having any more babies.

Once I have finished, the pile of unwanted-but-now-needed clothes is high and I know I am faced with weeks of sewing, which is not my forte but will now be my singular focus.

Chapter 38

April 1826

There is a slight drizzle and Sarah and I hurry along the streets, trying to avoid the puddles and foul messes that litter the ground. I have managed to finish two little petticoats that I am keen to put on the twins. Even after three visits I still have no idea how to get to the Morgans' and have to trust to Sarah's good memory. When we arrive the door is slightly ajar. I recognise the door now, by a distinctive mark halfway up the frame that looks like a leaping deer. Sarah taps and after a few seconds of silence pushes it open.

The whole family are there. Mrs Morgan is sitting on the edge of the bed, holding the twins and William is sitting at her feet, clutching her legs as if he is frightened of drowning. There is another woman sitting next to Mrs Morgan, presumably a neighbour as she has the same look of shabbiness, hunger and despair. This woman looks at us sadly. 'She won't let go of him.'

The babes are tightly wrapped in the shawls I made for them but I can see their faces. Matilda's eyes are open although their blueness is dulled and her mouth is open as she tries to gulp in enough air. Morris is silent and still.

Sarah puts her basket down and goes to Mrs Morgan. She kneels and tries to take Morris but the mother has a fierce strength and will not release him. 'Oh, Maggie, my dear, I am so very sorry. Will you let Miss Elizabeth hold Matilda for you for a while?' Mrs Morgan doesn't answer but allows me to take the bundle that seems to have become even smaller since the previous week. I hold her to me and am distressed at how much thinner she is and how she has to struggle to take each breath. I feel her chest reverberating against my own and I want to hug her but dare not. Mrs Morgan burnt the chairs many months ago so I sit on the floor, rocking Matilda in my arms. William crawls over to me and curls up on my lap, sucking his thumb vigorously.

Sarah has her arms round Mrs Morgan and is whispering to her, so quietly I cannot make out the words. I rock Matilda with one hand and stroke William's hair with the other and sing softly to them both, accompanied by the baby's death rattle.

I close my eyes and imagine I am walking through a meadow full of spring flowers. I am holding the hands of two small children, a boy and a girl, who are running by my side on chubby legs. Their blond hair is shining in the sunlight and their faces are pink with health. Their blue eyes are bright and full of merriment and we are all laughing for no reason other than that we are happy and glad to be alive. We come to a stream and we sit on the banks and take off our shoes. I remove my stockings and sit with my toes in the cool water but the two children wade in and start splashing each other. I open my mouth to warn them to be careful but no words come out. I watch as they drift further and further out, to what is now a wide river. They both turn to their laughing faces to me and wave. The sun reflected on the water dazzles me but I can still make out their little faces as they drift further and further out to what is now the sea, still laughing, still waving. I look until I can't make them out any more and only then do I let the tears fall.

'Miss Elizabeth, Miss Elizabeth.' Someone taps me on the arm and I am startled out of my reverie. For a moment I don't know where I am and I look at John's face in puzzlement.

'John? What on earth are you doing here?'

'Sarah sent Mrs Albright to ask us to make two small coffins. They didn't take long and I've just brought them in the cart. Are you all right, Miss Elizabeth?'

'Me? Yes, I'm perfectly fine, thank you.'

'Shall I take the baby?'

I look down at Matilda, whose eyes are still open and whose cheeks are wet from my tears. She makes no sound. I give her one last hug and then hand her over to John, who takes her gently and places her carefully in one of the boxes. Mrs Morgan is in

Sarah's arms, the only sound is of her weeping. Even this eventually stops as she falls into an exhausted sleep. Sarah lays her onto the bed and covers her with the thin blanket. John picks up William and puts him by his mother's side.

Mrs Albright, the neighbour, is still in the room. 'I will stay with her now. My Bob has gone to tell the vicar and we'll make sure they are buried proper like. We'll look after her, don't you fret.'

'We'd like to know when the funeral is, please, Mrs Albright. Could your Bob come and tell me when you know?'

'Aye, he'll do that right enough. Poor Maggie, her luck fair run out.'

'Can you help me up please, John? I think my bones have seized up.'

I take his hand, and he pulls me up. He keeps hold and I am comforted by the warm roughness and his thick fingers wrapped easily round mine. I compare them with Mr Whittaker's hands, which are always cool, whose fingers are long and slender and have never done anything more strenuous then hold a quill.

We leave the basket of food and take our leave, Mrs Albright promising again to let us know the day and time of the funeral and that she will make sure 'our poor Maggie' is looked after.

John keeps hold of my hand as he helps me onto the cart, then he helps Sarah, who is wheezing at the exertion. She looks pale and there is a sheen of sweat on her upper lip.

'Are you all right, Sarah? We need to get back and you need to rest. This has all been too much for you. We'll be home soon and I'll make you a nice cup of tea and maybe a piece of that Madeira cake?'

Sarah tries to smile but it turns into a grimace as she suddenly claps her hand to her breast and her face turns red as she struggles to breathe.

'Sarah, Sarah! Oh my God, John. Help me, she's not well.'

John comes running round and leaps onto the cart. 'Undo her jacket buttons, make sure she can breathe properly.'

'Shall I get her some water? I saw a water pump further down the street.' He nods and I jump out of the cart and run to the pump, realising on arrival I have no container. I knock desperately on the nearest door and as soon as it is opened I shout, 'Please, do you have a cup? I need to give Sarah some water; it is a matter of life or death.' The woman looks a little shocked at my outburst but disappears for a few seconds before coming back with a cup. She wipes it with her soiled apron and hands it to me.

'I need it back.'

I nod my thanks, pump up some water, which is cloudy and has bits in it, and run back to the cart, trying not to spill any. Sarah's breathing seems a bit easier and she is no longer clutching at her chest, though she is now deathly pale and beads of sweat are trickling down her cheeks. I put the cup to her lips but they are tightly closed and I can't get her to take even a sip. I dip my handkerchief into the water and wipe her face instead, which rouses her slightly.

'I'm all right now, Miss Elizabeth. I just had a funny turn, that's all.'

'We need to get you to a doctor. John can you take us there please?'

'No, John, there's no need. There is nothing wrong with me that a sit down and a cup of tea won't fix. I don't want to be wasting the good doctor's time when he has properly sick people to look after. Just get us home please, John, be a good boy.'

John and I look at each other and silently agree to take her home but I am determined to ask John to call on the doctor afterwards and ask him to visit Sarah as soon as possible.

By the time we arrive home Sarah has dosed off but I have to waken her as she is far too heavy for even John to carry. We take an arm each and help her from the cart, up the stone steps, into the house and into the kitchen. Mama is reading to Dorothy but comes to us as soon as she sees that we are supporting a confused and weary Sarah. We seat her as gently as we can into a rocking chair. John hands me the cup I had forgotten to return and then leaves to fetch the doctor.

'What's happened, Lizzie?'

'Sarah seems to have had some sort of fit. She was clutching her breast.' I mimic Sarah's action. 'She didn't want us to take her to the doctor but I have just asked John to fetch him. She really frightened us, Mama.'

Mama doesn't ask how John happens to be there; her sole concern is for her beloved Sarah. I busy myself making a pot of tea and cutting slices of cake, casting frequent glances at the two women, the older one in the rocking chair, still pale but breathing easier and the younger, kneeling at her feet. I satisfy Dorothy's desire with a small piece of cake and then hand Sarah a cup of tea, which she takes with shaking hands.

'Thank you, Miss Elizabeth. Once I've supped this I'll be as right as rain.'

'John has gone for the doctor, Sarah. He will say whether you are as right as rain, or not. I fear it's all my fault; I should never have let you keep going to that family, it was too much for you. I ought to remember you are not getting any younger and should be taking it easy, not doing extra work.'

Sarah becomes agitated and spills her tea down the front of her blouse. 'You mustn't say things like that, mistress. Of course it's not your fault; I asked to visit Maggie, Mrs Morgan, and it was no trouble. I was just upset because the twins both died today, that's all it was, I was just upset.'

I leave Mama to reassure Sarah whilst I answer the front door, the doctor's arrival heralded by three loud knocks. Dr Peters is a short, round, jovial man and a great favourite with his patients, with whom he is both understanding of their frailties but also firm with his treatments. I lead him into the kitchen and offer him a cup of tea; he declines in favour of a small glass of port.

'So, Sarah Milligan, what have you been up to?'

Sarah manages to raise a smile but does not seem to have the energy for her usual banter.

'Let's take a look at you then. Mrs Hayes and Miss Hayes, maybe you could leave us whilst I examine the patient?'

Mama gets up reluctantly but then retrieves Dorothy from under the table where she is surrounded by a fairy circle of crumbs and almost marches out of the kitchen and into the parlour. She sits on the edge of a high, hard chair, her eyes firmly on the door as if she is trying to see through the wood and brick that separates her from Sarah and the doctor.

'I can't lose her, Lizzie, she's too dear to me.'

I don't like to say that she will have to lose her at some point; Sarah is well into her sixties and, as far as I am aware, not immortal.

'I am sure she will be fine, Mama. Doctor Peters will prescribe some medicine and rest and she will soon be back to normal. She had to be especially strong today.'

Mama doesn't take her eyes off the door. 'Why today in particular?'

'Sarah told you, Mama. Both the twins died today. Morris was already gone when we got there and Matilda,' sweet, sweet Matilda, 'died in my arms. Sarah got the neighbour, a Mrs Albright, to go and ask John to make two small coffins. That is why he was there and why he was able to bring us home in the cart.'

'That was lucky.'

'Lucky? That the twins died?'

She gives an angry shake of her head. 'No, I mean lucky that John was there to bring Sarah home.'

She shows no sorrow at the death of the twins; no concern for me who held the dying Matilda in my arms or for Mrs

Morgan who has lost her husband and now two of her children. Her only concern is for Sarah.

The grinding of Mama's teeth is the only sound until the door is flung open and the doctor comes rolling in. Mama stands up, rubbing her hands as if washing them in invisible water.

'Will she be all right, doctor?'

Dr Peters looks startled at the curt question hurled at him.

'Shall we all sit down, Mrs Hayes? Then I'll give you my diagnosis.'

Mama sits down again, still on the edge of her seat whereas the good doctor relaxes into an armchair and sighs contentedly.

'Well, Miss Milligan seems to have recovered from her seizure. She does not seem to have suffered any permanent damage but,' he gives Mama a stern look, 'it must be taken as a warning sign. She needs to slow down considerably and start to look after herself, rather than others. I suggest she rests in bed for a few days and then when she feels well enough to get up, she continues to rest.' The doctor gives me a big, beaming smile. 'Miss Hayes here is more than capable of looking after Miss Milligan.'

My mother snaps her head up. 'I will care for her, Dr Peters. She used to be my nanny then came as housekeeper when I got married, but she is more than that, she is my dear friend. Does she need to take any medicine?'

'Just a tonic but mostly rest, rest and more rest. I'll call in tomorrow but fetch me if she has another fit. I'll take my leave now.'

I show him out as Mama seems to have forgotten her manners completely.

Chapter 39

April 1826

We had to wait for Papa and Mr Whittaker to come home from school yesterday so that they could take the weight of Sarah as they helped her up the stairs and into her bedroom. Mama has been in with her ever since, leaving me to cook the meals and look after Dorothy, which I am, of course, happy to do.

There seems to be a never ending list of chores and I have little time to reflect, so full is my brain with the minutiae of daily life. It is only three days after our visit to Mrs Morgan, when I am cutting some flowers from the garden to put in Sarah's room, that I wonder why we have not heard when the funeral is. Surely the poor little mites will have been buried by now? I decide I will go and see Mrs Morgan this very afternoon, as long as Mama can spare me.

I take the flowers into Sarah's bedroom and am pleased how her face lights up at the sight of the sunny daffodils.

'They're lovely, Miss Elizabeth. They really cheer up the room.'

'Hopefully you can soon come down and sit in the garden and see them in their natural glory. How are you feeling today?'

'I keep trying to tell the mistress that I am well enough to get up and carry on with my duties. But she won't hear of it.'

Mama gives me a wry smile. 'Sarah is paying me back for all the times I used to be cheeky to her when I was a child. I'm reading Jane Austen's *Emma* to her and I have said I will consider whether she can try and get up once it is finished and not before.' She gives me a mischievous wink. 'I am reading very slowly.'

'I'm going to get some shopping this afternoon. Is there anything you want?'

Mama follows me out. 'Can you take this letter and have it posted? It's to Sarah's sister, Esther, in Bournemouth.'

'Why is it a secret from Sarah?'

'She won't want me to bother her sister, but I feel I need to tell her that Sarah is not well. I have asked if she could come and stay here for a few weeks. It would cheer up Sarah no end. It would have been nice to take her to Bournemouth but I'm afraid the journey would just be too much for her. And can you buy some material to make a new nightgown? The one she has is quite threadbare.'

'Mama, I am worried about Mrs Morgan. Someone called Bob was meant to tell us when the funeral is but he has not come with any message.'

'They will have been buried by now. She wouldn't have been able to afford a funeral, though. I doubt the vicar would even have said any words, not if he was not getting his fee.'

'Mama, don't say such awful things! They were just innocent babies. Surely they would have been buried decently, with the Reverend offering prayers for their souls. You are sometimes just too cruel.'

'It is not I who am cruel, Lizzie, it is the world. But yes, go and see her but please don't bring her back with you, do you hear me?'

'Yes, Mama, I hear you. I'll bring Dorothy up when I go.'

I write myself a list and put a pie, bread, milk and cheese into a basket for Mrs Morgan and some cake for William, along with a jar of last year's strawberry jam for Mrs Goodman. I also remember the cup I borrowed. It is a pleasant day and as I set off for the town I imagine Bobbit shuffling by my side, and me telling him some fanciful tale. I haven't made up a story since the one I told him the night I sat with his poor, dead body. Neither have I walked along the towpath, even though it was one of our favourite places. It is good, though, to see the buds bursting into life and to remember that there is always new life, even when we seem to be surrounded by death.

I go round the back of the Goodmans' workshop and knock on the kitchen door. Mrs Goodman answers, her hands and tip of her nose covered in flour, and her cheeks as red as tomatoes.

'Please come in, Miss Elizabeth. How is Sarah?'

'She is recovering well, thank you. Mama is making sure that she stays in bed and has complete rest. I think Sarah is desperate to get up and do some cooking but Mama is a strict nurse and the only thing she is allowed to do is to listen to Mama reading to her. We hope she will be able to get up in a few days.'

'Oh, I'm so glad to hear that. John had us all very worried when he told us what happened. And those poor babes; such a shame.'

'Yes, it was an eventful day. In fact I'm going to see Mrs Morgan now, that's why I can't stop but I just wanted to give you this jam. I had expected to hear when the funeral is but have heard nothing. I just want to make sure she and William are all right.'

'But you can't go there alone, Miss Elizabeth. Places like that aren't safe for young ladies on their own. I'll get John to come with you.' She goes into the workshop and doesn't wait for my opinion, although I would be glad of John's company. Her son returns with her, brushing curls of wood shavings from his shirt. I always get a warm feeling when I see him; he is such a good friend.

'I hope I am not taking you away from some important work?'

'No, Miss Elizabeth, nothing that can't wait.'

John takes my basket and we stroll together down the main street and then turn into the side streets that lead away from the brightness into the darkness.

'I am glad you are with me, John, I don't think I could have found my way to Mrs Morgan's house. I remember the first bit, right, left, right then right, but after that I get very confused. It all looks the same.'

'These aren't the sort of streets you should be wandering around in; there are some dangerous people that live here.'

'Why are they dangerous? They are just people like you and me whose lives are desperate.'

'It is their desperation that makes them dangerous.'

'The only way they will ever get away from here is to be educated. That's why I want to teach at Papa's school. I want to help the children learn so that they can get better jobs and don't have to go underground and tear the coal out with their bare hands.'

'I think they have tools, but I know what you mean. I thought your parents were dead set against you teaching?'

'They were when I still had Bobbit to care for. I was going to ask Papa once I had recovered from my own little illness, but then all this happened with Sarah and I am now needed to look after the house, the cooking and Dorothy whilst Mama looks after Sarah. It just seems that everything is against me.'

'Tush, Miss Elizabeth. Be thankful for your blessings. You have a good imagination; just imagine what it is like for girls living in places like this, with parents who work day and night in the most awful conditions but don't earn enough to buy food and clothes for their children. These girls don't have the luxury of having any choices at all; their lives are mapped out for them and all they can hope for is to marry a half decent man and have children that survive.'

This is the second time that John has chastised me over the last few months and I find that I rather like it. 'You are right, John. I'm sorry if I seem to be behaving like a spoilt child. It's just that I want to make a difference, and it is hard to do that in the kitchen.'

John laughs. 'You make a difference to everyone you meet, Miss Elizabeth. I'm always a better man having seen you.' He blushes at this revelation and quickens his pace as if to outrun his words.

We have, by now, arrived at Mrs Morgan's house, which I am now able to recognise by the deer-like mark on the door frame. John knocks, waits then knocks louder. There is no sound from inside. He turns the knob; it is unlocked and the door swings open, squeaking on its hinges. John puts up his hand to keep me back and then steps inside and disappears into the gloom. I hear him walking about and the creak of the internal door as he goes into the back.

'You can come in. The place is empty.'

I follow him into the room. It is only three days since I was last here but it has an air of desertion. The bed has been stripped bare and there is nothing that indicates that anyone has ever lived here. 'Maybe they're out. Maybe the funeral is happening as we speak.'

'No, miss, they aren't at the funeral.' It is the neighbour, Mrs Albright. 'I seen you at the door so came to tell you they've gone some two days since.'

'You never sent a message telling us about the funeral arrangements.'

She gives a grunt of derision. 'There was no funeral arrangements. They come and took the bodies and put them in a hole in the ground. That's all there was to it. Maggie never got to say a proper goodbye. When I come round later on, she'd upped and gone.'

'But where has she gone? Her uncle in Derby has been dead for two years, he was her only relative. But she doesn't know that he's dead; perhaps she's gone there?'

'Maybe, miss, though she had no money for a coach. Is it far to Derby, maybe she walked?'

'I don't know, do you John?'

He shrugs. 'I don't but it would be too far for a woman and child to walk. I suppose she might get a lift on a cart going that way. But she may be anywhere, Miss Elizabeth, there is no knowing where she's gone. Maybe she's gone to Birmingham, there might be work there for her.'

'But we must find her. I have some cake here for William. Oh dear.' I am suddenly overcome and find myself crying into John's chest. Mrs Albright tuts sympathetically until I am recovered.

'There's no need to upset yourself, miss. I know she was afeared of being sent to the workhouse. She said she would rather die than go to one of them places.'

This does nothing to comfort me and I find myself sobbing again, John patiently bears my passion and tries to comfort me by awkwardly stroking my head and muttering, 'There, there, Miss Elizabeth.'

When I am recovered again, I wipe my eyes and pick up the basket from the floor. 'We will try and find her, won't we John? She and William deserve a better life after all they have been through.'

'We all deserve a better life, miss, but deserving don't mean getting.'

'You have been a great support to Mrs Morgan, thank you. Perhaps you would like these few things I brought? It's not much.'

'Thank you kindly, miss, that's most kind.'

'Oh, and there's a cup in there that I borrowed from the lady who lives just by the water pump. She said she needs it back. I've washed it.'

'I'll make sure she gets it, miss. You take care of this one, young man, she's a good 'un.'

John blushes and then takes my arm and leads me out of the house of sorrow.

'I meant what I said, John, we must try and find Mrs Morgan. I can't bear to think of poor little William being hungry, cold and tired. Will you help me?'

'They've been gone for two days according to the neighbour. Just think, Lizzie, how many roads there are out of Wednesbury, she could have gone down any one of them. She might have got a lift with someone; she might even have managed to go some way on a barge. She could be anywhere, just anywhere. We could even ride right past her if she has gone off the road. I know you want to find her, but we have to be realistic.'

I feel the tears threatening to spill again and my heart plummets to my feet. I dab my eyes and try and smile, although my lips are disinclined to turn upwards.

'Why do you always have to be right, John Goodman? Maybe you could make some enquiries to see if anyone has seen her, or given her a lift?'

'Yes, I can do that, though don't raise your hopes, Miss Elizabeth, don't raise your hopes.'

#

Three weeks have passed and on one of my visits to his mother, John silently hands me a newspaper and points to a small entry at the bottom of a page.

Woman and child found dead

Early on April 26th, Mr Bacon, a farmer who lives on the outskirts of the town of Wednesbury, was walking through a wood by his farm when he came across a woman and child he thought were sleeping under a tree. He went to rouse them to move them on when he discovered they were both dead. Mr Bacon, being a good citizen, told the magistrate, who had the bodies removed and disposed of. It is believed they had been dead for a number of days. There was nothing on either body to identify who they were but both were of slight build and were malnourished. The boy was aged about four. There was an empty basket next to them which had only the remains of a biscuit in the shape of a star. If anyone thinks they know who these people were please contact their local magistrate.

Chapter 40

June 1826

Sarah's sister, Esther, is so very like her. She is younger but has the same positive spirit and amiable disposition that means that the three of them - for Mama is an honorary member of their sororal band - are often helpless with laughter.

Esther has been with us a month and doesn't seem to be in any hurry to leave, although she has a husband back in Bournemouth whom, she never tires of telling us, she worships. Sarah is now fully recovered but Mama won't hear of her returning to the work she used to do. 'Sarah, you have given most of your life to looking after me and my family, and it is now time for us to look after you. You may potter in the garden, bake an occasional cake and sew a button or two, if it gives you pleasure to do so, but Lizzie and I are more than capable of running this household especially now Emily Goodman has started helping in the kitchen; she is a good little worker and with your instruction will turn into an acceptable cook.'

Mr Whittaker still comes in the morning to walk to school with Papa and joins us for the evening meal. The elder women adore him and I wonder what my feelings towards him are. I enjoy his company and he is good to listen to and, I admit, good to look at. I know him to be clever and a passionate teacher, just like Papa. Recently I have noticed that he makes an effort to include me in conversations and I often find him just looking at me, which makes me blush and my heart beat faster than it needs to.

Now that things have settled down a bit and Emily has turned out to be such a treasure, I am determined to speak with Papa about the possibility of helping at the school. It is usually hard to catch him alone but this morning there is no school and he has no other lessons, the women have gone early into town and Papa is sitting over a leisurely breakfast, reading a newspaper.

'Papa, may I have a word?'

He peers at me over the newspaper, sees that I am serious and puts it down to give me his full attention.

'Of course, my dear. We don't seem to have talked much these last few months. You are fully recovered from everything that has happened to burden you?'

'Yes, Papa, thank you. I wanted to ask you whether it would now be possible for me to help in the school? There is not so much for me to do in the house now that Emily comes every day and you know it's my dream to teach. I have no desire to be a lady of leisure. You don't need to pay me. There is nothing to prevent me, is there?'

He rubs his forehead and gives a deep sigh. He avoids eye contact and stares instead at the china salt cellar.

'I have been meaning to speak to you about the school, Elizabeth. I'm afraid that I'm going to have to close it.'

I look at him in disbelief.

'Close it? But why? That school is your life.'

'No, Lizzie, it's only part of my life. I still have the private students, the ones who bring in the money.'

He looks at me quickly and then away again, his expression one of embarrassment. I wait for an explanation.

'The number of boys attending the school has dropped steadily over the last year or so, from the time the wages were reduced, do you remember?'

'I am not likely ever to forget am I? It was the wage reduction that resulted in the riot, which led to Mr Morgan being deported to Australia and ultimately to the death of his wife and all his children. But why does it mean the school has to close?'

'The families are finding that the boys cannot be spared even for a few hours each week because they need to help to earn money for their very survival.'

I look at him in horror.

'You mean that boys are being forced to work down mines and in the factories just so that the family have enough money to buy food? That is wicked, Papa, absolutely wicked. How can the owners get away with it? How can the greed of a few be allowed to ruin the lives of so many?'

Hot, angry tears course down my cheeks and Papa reaches across and pats my hand.

'I don't know, Lizzie, I really don't know. I was trying to educate just a few boys, to give them a chance of improving their prospects, but I have failed and the owners have won. Money equals power in this world and these men have no intention of giving either up, regardless of the cost to countless others.'

'Oh, Papa, you haven't failed, don't say that. Didn't young Sam Ewing go and work in a bank instead of down a mine because of his schooling with you? And there are others whose lives you have made a huge difference to. Surely it is worth keeping the school open even if there is just one boy who can be saved?'

'I learned yesterday that the last boys I had will no longer be attending. There are no boys, Lizzie, There is no one to teach.'

Papa's shoulders slump and I fear he is going to cry, but he rallies and sits upright and puts his shoulders back. 'I will close the school for now, but I will let it be known that I intend to open it again as soon as circumstances allow. In this newspaper, in fact, there is an article about how there is a group of people demanding that the government pass a law preventing children under 9 working at all. If that ever happens then I can open the school again. It may not happen for a few years, if at all, but I will be ready. Until then, I will just have to continue teaching the sons of the owners and see if I can instil morality into them, as well as mathematics.

'And honesty, as well as history.'

'Selflessness, as well as science.'

'Generosity, as well as geography.'

'Largesse, as well as Latin.'

'Philanthropy, as well as philosophy.'

Papa shakes his head and laughs. 'I can't think of any more.'

I have a sudden thought and am ashamed it has not occurred to me earlier. 'What about Mr Whittaker? What will he do?'

'Ah, well, that is another matter. He is leaving anyway.'

'Leaving? Where's he going? Why hasn't he said anything to me?'

Papa looks at me keenly. 'I am sure he has his reasons for not telling you yet. He will very soon. I think he wants you to...'

'You think he wants me to do what?'

'Nothing. I'm tired of thinking. He will tell you in his own way soon.'

He gives another deep sigh, picks up the newspaper and continues to read where he had left off.

I feel disheartened and restless and have the urge to share my anger. I make sure Emily has no need of my help and then walk into town to see her brother. Neither he nor his father is in the workshop and I am not in the mood for Mrs Goodman's bonhomie, so I carry on walking and find that my feet take me to the canal of their own accord. It has been a wet month and the towpath is muddy, just as it was the last time I walked along it with Bobbit. I hesitate; do I really want to walk along here, where I have so many memories? My heart says 'no,' but my feet say 'yes' and I continue along the familiar path.

Some of the bargemen wave and shout 'Halloa' and I wave back and find myself returning their cheerful greetings. The rushes and irises are in flower and I walk straight past where Bobbit was found, so different does it look. I realise I have missed it and force myself to turn around and go back. I stand and stare at where he floated amongst the reeds but I can't see him. There is a nest where his body had been caught and a family of ducks is paddling along the bank, enjoying the sunshine and laughing at me. I am glad I came; there is no ghost here.

I hear someone coming along the towpath and wait for him to pass, but he doesn't; he stands by my side and rocks on the balls of his feet, his hands clasped behind his back.

'Good morning, Mr Whittaker. What brings you here?'

'Good morning, Miss Hayes. I often take my constitutional along the canal. I haven't seen you here for many a month.'

'This is the first time I have come here since we found Bobbit.' I say this with no waiver, no thickening of my voice with emotion. 'I find that there is nothing to be scared of after all.'

'Good, good.'

'Papa told me about having to close the school this morning. It makes me so angry; it meant such a lot to him to teach the boys and offer them the means to a better life. I would like to send every owner, his wife and children into the mines and factories and make them work from dawn to dusk with hardly anything to eat, and then go home to a cold, dismal, tiny house and all sleep in the same lice-ridden bed. I doubt they would last for more than a day. But he says you are leaving anyway? Is it true?'

Mr Whittaker laughs loudly. 'You are always forthright, aren't you Miss Hayes? But yes, I am leaving soon. I am glad to have this opportunity to speak to you alone.' I am surprised when he takes my hand in his. 'I would very much like to be allowed to call you Elizabeth and for you to call me Nathaniel.'

'I am sure that is not quite proper, Mr Whittaker,' but I do not withdraw my hand.

'Perhaps not now, but very soon? I am sure you are aware that I think very highly of you.'

'You do? Even though I am always forthright?' His hand is cool and he easily encompasses mine in his. 'Must you joke? I am trying to be serious. I could see that we were losing boys and that very soon the school would not be viable. I love working with your father and I honestly feel we are doing some good but

I knew that I had to look for another job in the near future. Then, luckily, my grandfather died.'

'It's lucky that your grandfather died? You are too cruel, sir!' I try and pull my hand out of his, but his grip is too tight.

'He was an old man. He became both physically and mentally weak; he hated being old and incapable. He was ready to go on the next part of the journey.'

'You are not explaining why his death is lucky.'

'I loved my grandfather very much and we got on splendidly although I have not seen him much in latter years, only corresponding by letter when he was still compos mentis. That means ...'

'I know what it means, Mr Whittaker, I'm not stupid.'

'Forgive me, Miss Hayes, I know you are anything but stupid. He was a great philanthropist and it was because of him that I became a teacher and believed in education for the poor. I belong to the poorer side of the family and he has always been very supportive of my efforts and has provided a small annual income. In his will, though, he left me quite a lot of money with one caveat.'

I wait, but he continues to study the other side of the canal with great intensity. He is obviously waiting for me to ask and I feel inclined not to, but my curiosity gets the better of me.

'That being?'

'The caveat is that I use the money to open a school in London. The students must be a mixture of those with parents who can afford fees and those with parents who cannot or who have no parents at all.'

'My goodness. I don't know what to say, that is quite astounding.'

'I would like you to say that you will come with me.'

Did I hear him correctly? I look at him but he is still staring out across the canal. Did I hear him correctly?

He turns to look at me, his cheeks flushed. 'I mean as my wife, obviously.'

'Your wife? Me?'

'Oh, Elizabeth, Miss Hayes, we would make a fine couple. Isn't it what you have always wanted? To teach in a school? Well now you can help actually run it. I thought we could also take girls. You would approve of that, wouldn't you?'

'You want me to marry you so that I can come to London with you and help run a school. Have I understood you?'

He gives me a shy smile. 'I want to marry you because I admire you greatly. You are pretty, clever, amusing, kind and will make an excellent wife and mother. I think we can give each other what the other needs and we could be a great success together. We will be partners and make decisions together. You don't have to answer me now; your father said you would probably need time to think. You are rather young, but I think circumstances are such that now is the right time. I will go to London in a few weeks to start looking at premises for both a school and a house, hopefully a home for us. We could get married next spring; that is plenty of time to plan a wedding isn't it?'

I feel as if all the air has been drawn out of my lungs and I have to take deep breaths that make my whole body shudder. My cheeks are hotter than is warranted by the heat of the sun and images flit before my eyes as if someone is quickly flipping through illustrated pages in a book: me as a teacher in front of a classroom of boys and girls; me walking hand in hand with Nathaniel down a busy London street; me passing Nathaniel a jug of milk at a table decked with white porcelain and silver; me holding up my cheek and a baby for Nathaniel to kiss.

Mrs Nathaniel Whittaker. Would it be too forward to say 'yes' straight away?

'You have taken me quite by surprise, Mr Whittaker. I am, of course, greatly honoured, but this has come out of the blue. I had no idea that you had such feelings for me.'

'Did you really not realise?
Perhaps I did.

'No, I really did not. I need to think about everything you have said. Please give me some time.'

'Of course, my dear. Perhaps you could give me your answer before I go to London? You would make me a very happy man indeed if the answer is "yes".'

'I'll go home now. Please don't come with me, Mr Whittaker. I need to think.' He bows, brushes his lips against the back of my hand then releases it and walks away. 'Oh, and Mr Whittaker,' he stops and turns round, 'thank you for asking me.' He smiles and carries on walking.

Oh, and Mr Whittaker, is 'greatly admire' the same as love?

Chapter 41

July 1826

'Do you love him?'

I am surprised at John's bluntness. 'I enjoy his company.'

'That is not love.'

'He makes me laugh, he is very intelligent, and he thinks I am too.'

'That is not love.'

'He says he admires me.'

John looks at me but passes no comment, he doesn't need to.

'You are being cruel, John. We are going to make each other very happy, very happy indeed. I had hoped you would be pleased for me.'

'I am not being cruel, just concerned. I don't think you love him enough to marry him and spend the rest of your life with him.'

Do I? Do I want to spend possibly the next forty or so years with Nathaniel Whittaker? Do I want to work with him to start and run a school? Do I want to have his children? Do I want his face to be the first thing I see every morning and the last thing every night, forever? Do I? Well, yes, I do.

'He says I can help run the school and that we can even have girl pupils. That is something I have always dreamed of, you know that. It's such a good opportunity.'

'So it would be a marriage of convenience? You don't have to marry him to teach in a school, Miss Elizabeth.'

'Papa's school is closed now and he will never allow me to leave home to teach elsewhere. No, marrying Mr Whittaker is the only way.' I think I see a flash of anger in his eyes but then it is gone and I'm not sure. Why doesn't he tell me not to marry Mr Whittaker, to marry him instead? Why doesn't he show any emotion at all? Was I wrong to think he had any feelings for me?

His lack of emotion decides me. 'And to answer your original question, yes, I do love him.'

'You must do what you think is best, Miss Elizabeth. If this is what you really want then I wish you much happiness. Now, please excuse me.' He walks away, his back straight, shoulders back and his hands thrust deeply into his pockets. I am left alone under the yew tree until Mr Whittaker joins me and we start our walk home.

'It is not seemly, especially now, to be alone with John Goodman.'

'We were hardly alone; we were visible to the whole congregation. And why is it not seemly, especially now? He is just a good friend. Well, I thought he was, now I'm not so sure.'

'You are a young woman. Young women do not have young men as just good friends. Not unless that are engaged to be married, as I very much hope we are to be. I go to London in two days, Miss Hayes, will you give me your answer before I go?' He looks at me almost pleadingly.

I had imagined a pretty scene where Mr Whittaker is in the coach leaving for London looking dejected as it pulls away and I run after it shouting, 'I will, I will marry you!' But why wait? Without thinking any further, the words come out. 'There is no need to wait, Mr Whittaker, I am very happy to accept your proposal.'

He stops dead in his tracks. 'Oh, thank you. You have made me the happiest man alive.' He takes my hand and squeezes it. 'I will speak with your father this very afternoon. I have already told him I was going to ask you to marry me, of course, but I can now provide more of the details and what my plans are.'

'Our plans, surely?'

He laughs and nods his head, 'Of course, my dear, our plans.'

'We will have much to say in our letters to each other. I will write to you every day, will you likewise?'

'Of course, more than once a day if you like. I will tell you all the details about the school and the house, Miss Hayes. Or may I now call you Elizabeth? Oh, you have made me so happy! And we are going to be so happy together, don't you think?''

'I know so, Nathaniel.' Mrs Nathaniel Whittaker. I roll the name around in my mouth and it tastes good.

Sarah is the only one who does not seem pleased at my engagement. She sends Emily out to the garden to collect herbs we already have plenty of. 'I always thought you would marry John Goodman. He thinks the world of you and he has a good heart. You could do no better than him, Miss Elizabeth.'

'He is, was, my friend, that's all. He has never shown me anything other than friendship.' I feel my cheeks warm as I remember his kiss the night after Bobbit died, but that was a kiss of sympathy and concern, that is all. 'I told him about Mr Whittaker's proposal and he didn't say anything other than to wish me happiness.'

'Oh, isn't that just like him? Of course he didn't say anything if he thinks you love Mr Whittaker. Do you? All those fairytales you told when the girl refused to marry the prince because she didn't love him. You always used to say you would never marry anyone unless you loved him. So, do you love Mr Whittaker?'

I feel anger rise from the pit of my stomach and for the first time in my life I shout at Sarah. 'How dare you ask me such a thing? Of course I love him! Why do you find that so hard to believe? I love him, I love him, I love him. Is that clear enough? Any anyway, life is not a fairytale, Sarah Milligan, and my stories are just that, stories to amuse.'

Emily comes in, nervously glancing at the two of us; she obviously heard our raised voices. She hands the herbs to Sarah, who ignores them and carries on viciously chopping up the carrots; they look like long, thin fingers.

#

The whole family see Nathaniel off. It is by now quite a familiar scene with the friends and families bustling around outside the Turk's Head; cases and boxes being lifted onto the top of the coach; voices raised in laughter, farewells and reminders; the passengers gently extricating themselves from embraces and quickly forming relationships with their fellow passengers. There are no embraces; he shakes the family's hands, even mine, although he holds my hand for longer than anyone else's and he looks me in the eyes and smiles warmly. He climbs into the coach and has to sit between two other gentlemen and I can hardly see him behind his neighbour's large moustache and belly. I remember how I ran after the coach that carried Matthew off to university, but today I am content just to wave and mouth, 'Goodbye.' I am a bit ashamed that I feel relief as the coach turns a corner and goes out of view, but then I convince myself that it is relief because it is the first step of my big adventure, of my dream coming true.

We weren't able to spend much time together and when we did, Nathaniel – it takes me a while to stop calling him Mr Whittaker – spoke only of practicalities. Perhaps he will find it easier to woo me in his letters.

36 Portland Place
London
20th July 1826

My dearest Elizabeth,

I hope you don't mind that I don't call you Lizzie, it is the name of a child and you are anything but that to me; you are to be my wife. I want to go to the top of Nelson's Column and shout out 'Elizabeth Hayes has agreed to be my wife!'

You will see from the address on the top of this letter that I am ensconced with my uncle, Mr Gordon Whittaker. He is the eldest of the brothers and has done surprisingly well for himself as an importer of fine wines. He is a recent widower and he seems very happy for me to stay with him – he says he misses his wife and all his children have left home so he enjoys the company. There is a distant cousin of mine, Miss Arabella Burton, living here also but she keeps very much to herself. In fact I haven't seen her yet. I imagine she is old and frail, with a bent back and probably a hooked nose. You have a good imagination, what do you think she might look like?

The house is beautiful but far too large for him and it occurs to me that we could perhaps live with him for a while; it would save me having to search for a house for us until after the school is established. It is really very splendid, and I am sure you will find it very pleasant and comfortable. He is in good health and needs no one to care for him. Let me know what you think and if you are in agreement I will raise it with him.

I have been looking for suitable properties and there are a number that have possibilities. I have made a list of things that the building will need to have:

- *Two large classrooms, one for the boys and girls aged four to twelve and the other for those aged thirteen to twenty one.*
- *A kitchen and refectory.*
- *A room where the teachers can relax and prepare for lessons*
- *An office for myself*

The above is, I think, the least that the property needs to provide in order to be a school. We will obviously need to buy benches and tables to work at and books, chalk, slates, paper and all the paraphernalia that goes with teaching. Can you think of anything else we need to include, especially as I have no experience of teaching girls?

I am very hopeful that I will find a suitable property over the next few weeks. It will doubtless need some work doing to transform it into the school I want, or I should say, we want. When I have purchased a property I will then put advertisements

259

in newspapers and start trying to get pupils; I am very hopeful that we will have a full quota when the school opens. When I know how much the property and repairs will cost, I will then be able to work out how many fee-paying pupils we need in order to keep the school going. I really must practise saying 'we' after a life-time of saying I!

I hope all this meets with your approval.

One bit of news you might find interesting. I accompanied my uncle to the theatre the other evening and bumped into your brother, James. He was escorting a very pretty lady whom he introduced as Mrs James Hayes. He was with another two men whom he introduced as Mr Charles and Mr Geoffrey Sutton. I don't recall you mentioning that your brother had married? I am no expert but it looked to me that their family may be increased by another in the not too distant future.

I look forward to your letter.

With my fondest regards, nay, with my fondest love,
Nathaniel Whittaker

I have to read the last paragraph three times before I understand that James has got married to Lucy Sutton. He is now well and truly one of 'them.' How could he be so cruel as not to invite Mama and Papa to the wedding or even to tell them? I wonder how long they have been married? If she is indeed expecting, is this why they have married so quickly?

11 Church St.
Wednesbury
25th July '26

My dearest Nathaniel,

Thank you for your letter, it was lovely to hear from you and I am glad it was so informative. If you think your uncle really won't mind us living with him for a while (which may turn out to be many months, surely?) then I agree that it would be sensible to move in with him. But you must make sure he is happy with the arrangement; I would hate to be a burden to him.

Your list of requirements for the school seem correct, although it would be useful to have another room for smaller groups to use for activities such as drawing, reading, sewing. Is it too much to ask for a library? Thank you for asking for my opinion – start as you mean to go on!

I am glad that you are able to enjoy yourself in the evenings. You do not say what play you went to see – please tell me all about it. I have only ever been to the small theatre in Wednesbury; one of the things I am looking forward to is going to a London theatre. I am embarrassed to admit that we did not know of James's marriage. As you know there has been a falling out and he has obviously decided to disassociate himself totally from the family. Mama and Papa will be so upset if they know that there will soon be a grandchild whom they will never see. And I will never be able to be a good, kindly Aunt. It really is too cruel of James. I feel so very sorry for Mama and Papa. I am not sure whether to tell them. Do you think I should? If you happen to meet James again perhaps you can give him a slap and tell him to contact us.

Life here is very quiet and I have taken it upon myself to start to teach Dorothy to read and write; she does not seem to have any desire to do either. She loves to hear my stories and I am thinking of writing some more. I have not felt so inclined for a while but I think my imagination is coming to life again. As far as what Miss Arabella Burton might look like, is a wart likely? Poor woman, I hope we have not imagined correctly! You must have seen her by now, what does she really look like?

The weather is very wet still. The farmers are complaining and so are the miners – many of the mines keep flooding and they have to bail out the water before they can start their proper work. What a terrible, terrible way to earn a living.

261

Mama says she will have a word with the Reverend Stephenson in a few weeks to see when we can hold the wedding. She thinks after my twentieth birthday would be suitable, so that will be after June next year. It seems a long time to wait but I am sure the time will pass quickly. You do intend to come back for visits, don't you? I so desperately want to speak to you face to face and hear your laugh. Do you think me silly? We have so much to discuss that cannot always be said in a letter. Perhaps I could come and visit you in London? Would that be proper?

Please pass on my regards to your uncle and Miss Burton (regardless of what she looks like and for goodness sake do not show her this letter!).

With fondest love
Elizabeth

Chapter 42

October 1826

'Have you had a letter recently from Mr Whittaker?'

'Yes, he writes religiously almost every day still. Why?'

'You haven't mentioned him for the last few weeks. Does he say anything of interest?'

'He always says something of interest, Mama. He tells me everything he is doing with the school in great detail. It is very interesting indeed. He is overseeing all the repairs. I told you, there is a lot of work that needs to be done before it can open as a school. He is a very busy man. He also seems to go out quite a lot in the evenings with his uncle and cousin. She is a distant cousin, he says, although I don't know how distant. Her name is Miss Arabella Burton. He doesn't say much about her, just that she is quite old and a bit boring. She doesn't have a wart though, nor a hunched back or hooked nose.' I cannot help but laugh and Mama puts her sewing down and looks at me with a concerned expression.

'Distant cousins can be dangerous things. Are you excited about the wedding, Lizzie? Are you regretting accepting Mr Whittaker's proposal?'

'Of course I'm not regretting accepting him, how can you possibly ask that? I will get excited about the wedding when we have a definite date.'

'I thought we agreed it would be July next year? That is not so long away.'

'Nathaniel wonders whether we should wait a bit longer, so that he can get the school on a firm footing first. He says that he doesn't want his wife to have to face any teething problems with the school and if it is well established he will be able to concentrate on the wedding and on being a good husband.'

'Is that what you want? You surely would prefer to be married and help him establish the school rather than wait another year or so?'

'I'm sure he knows best, Mama. I don't want to be a burden to him.'

'For goodness sake, Lizzie, listen to yourself! When have you ever thought that any man knows best, and why should you be a burden? You'll be his wife, there to work with him, not to hinder him. When is he coming here again? It's hard to keep in love from such a distance, if indeed you are in love.'

'He says he will try and come before the end of the year, if not early in the spring. He is a busy man. And of course I love him, Mama; I don't know why you would think otherwise.'

'When I knew I was in love with your father, I couldn't bear to be away from him; he was in my thoughts day and night and I wrote to him all the time, even when I was seeing him the same day. He wrote to me as well, the most beautiful letters; he even wrote me poetry, it might not have been as good as Shakespeare's sonnets but, my, how I treasured them; in fact I have them still. I was never in any doubt that we both loved each other equally and that I wanted to be his wife as quickly as possible, so that we could achieve our dreams together. It does not seem to be like that for you and Nathaniel, although I suppose people experience love in different ways.'

'As you say, everyone experiences love in different ways. Of course we would prefer to be together all the time but it cannot be at the moment. He doesn't have the time to sit and write endless poetry, neither do I. Nathaniel and I are not you and Papa, so please let us just be ourselves.'

I can feel her eyes fixed on me but I don't return her gaze. I am suddenly tired of sewing and of having to justify myself; all I want to do is to go for a vigorous walk.

'I think I'll just take a stroll, if you don't mind?'

'It's going to rain, Lizzie. It's been threatening to do so all day but those clouds will burst very soon. You'll get drenched.'

'I won't be long and I'll dress accordingly. I just need some air.'

'If you are going into town pop in and say "good day" to Mrs Goodman. She was asking after you the other day; she says she hasn't seen you in quite a while.'

Not since John and I argued on the Sunday I accepted Mr Whittaker.

I put on my coat, some sturdy shoes and a hat and pick up a new purchase, an umbrella. I leave the house with relief. The air is fresh and I can smell the rain that is threatening to fall, but I don't care. I take deep breaths and long strides and feel quite exhilarated. I have missed my chats with Mrs Goodman and determine to go and visit her. If John happens to be there, well, we are both adults and should be able to act accordingly. I will hold out the hand of friendship and I hope he takes it.

As I near the Goodmans' house the earth beneath my feet trembles. There are no other people around and I wonder if I imagined it. I stand still for a few minutes but the ground remains solid. I hear shouts in the distance, but they are too far away to make out what they are saying.

Mrs Goodman is effusive with her welcome and hugs me, offers me a cup of tea and the biggest slice of fruit cake imaginable.

'Oh, Miss Hayes, I was only saying to your dear mother the other day that you had not come visiting for months. I supposed you are far too busy to spend time idly chatting with me now that you are preparing for your wedding. My sincere congratulations, if I may say so.'

I do not correct her misconstruction of the real reason for my absence. 'Thank you for your best wishes.'

'Have you set the date? Mr Goodman and I were married in the spring, a lovely time of the year. But any time is a good time for a wedding.'

'No, we haven't set the date yet. Mr Whittaker wants to get the school up and running first, which is sensible, I think.'

'Will you be happy living in London? It's such a long way away and I hear it's dirty and full of sin and poverty.'

'It is the poor we are hoping to educate so that they don't remain in poverty.'

'Well, I wish you luck although I think...'

I never find out what she thinks because all of a sudden the door to the kitchen is thrown open and a man, I don't know his name, runs in, gasping, 'Come quick, missus. There's been an accident at one of the mines. Men are trapped. Your man and son have gone in to help. Come quick.' He doesn't even look at me before he runs out, leaving the door wide open and his words echoing in our ears.

We look at each other, our faces a mask of horror.

'Blankets, they will need blankets and perhaps lamps. Can you fetch some blankets Mrs Goodman? We can pick up some lamps from the work shop. I'll put this cake and some food into a basket, bread, cheese, meat. Please Mrs Goodman, fetch the blankets then we can go. Mrs Goodman!'

She seems in a trance but my shouting rouses her and she runs upstairs to strip the beds of blankets.

It is not until we are outside that I realise we don't know which mine has collapsed, but people are running down the street, similarly laden with items of warmth and sustenance so we follow them. Mrs Goodman is a large lady and not able to run fast so, much against my inclination, I slow my pace to match hers. Her face is as red as a tomato, sweat is pouring down her cheeks and she is wheezing with every breath. Remembering what had happened to Sarah, I take her arm and try and slow her down. 'There is no need to rush, Mrs Goodman, you collapsing will be of no help to anyone, especially Mr Goodman and John. Come, we are nearly there. They are probably already amongst that crowd of men, waiting for us.' We approach them, some thirty of them, their faces almost indistinguishable under a mask of coal dust but they are not there.

We join a group of women and children standing close by, their faces taut with fear. Just then there is a flash of lightening, a loud clap of thunder and the heavens open, drenching everyone in seconds and dampening the billows of dust or smoke or both that had been spewing out of the pit entrance. The group of men are being preventing from going in by a man of authority. He has to shout to make himself heard over the rain pounding the earth and our heads. 'I have sent some men in to see what the situation is and you all going in mob-handed will just make matters worse. Just bide a while, will you? It will help if I know who is still in there. I have a list here of all the miners on shift, which I'll try and read out, though the ink is running in this rain.' I am still holding the umbrella and I run to the man's side and hold it over his head, offering some protection from the downpour.

'That's better. Right, Abrahams are you here?'

'Yes, I was near the entry and was just going off shift and as soon as I heard the bang and I just ran for it. I dragged young Morrison here with me, so you can cross him off the list an'all.'

'All right, we don't need to hear your life history. God, this pencil isn't working on the wet paper. Can you all try and remember the names that are still in there?' There is a murmur of acceptance. 'Right, next on the list is Ad, something, Adams I think.' Silence. I put Adams on my mental list. The man, whom I assume to be the foreman, goes through the list and by the end there are fifteen names I am trying to remember: Adams, Albright, Charles, Cook, Ford, Forester, Hammond father and son, Jones, James, Lambert father and son, Newton, Powell, Tindall.

The rain is now just a drizzle but I still have to shout to make myself heard. 'Were the Goodmans in there as well?' Mrs Goodman starts at the sound of their name.

'Right, of course, we need to remember the men that have gone into help. That's Goodman father and son, Collins, Williams and, who was it now, ah yes, young Walter Smith.' He looks around at everyone, men, women and children, 'We now need to wait to see how many get out.' There is a ripple through the crowd at the realisation that some may not. 'Abrahams, you go and fetch the doctor and all you women, make sure you have whatever blankets and sheets you have and we'll need warm drinks and food. Can one of you men go and tell the Suttons? Come along now, we need to be ready for when they come out which will be soon, God willing.' I am close enough to him to hear him mutter under his breath, 'Them what survive, anyway.'

People have brought lamps and the opening to the mine is well lit, but shows nothing but blackness. There is absolute silence apart from a child crying and the hiss of rain. All eyes are fixed on the entrance.

We all hold our breath as we hear coughing and shuffling footsteps coming from the mine's maw; we all take a few steps forward; we all gasp as two men come stumbling out, supporting each other. They are nearly as black as the hole from which they have just emerged but their women-folk recognise them and rush over to them. Blankets are wrapped around the men, who are scantily dressed and shivering from the cold or perhaps fear. They both look around as if surprised to see everyone. The foreman, whose name I don't know says out loud, 'Collins and Tindall, thank God.'

I readjust the list in my head: Adams, Albright, Charles, Cook, Ford, Forester, Hammond father and son, Jones, James, Lambert father and son, Newton, Powell, Goodman father and son, Williams and, who was it now, ah yes, young Walter Smith.

He goes over to the men, who are surrounded by the others shouting out, 'Did you see Eric?', 'What happened down there?' 'Is my Albert, Albert Newton, safe?' They look confused and the whites of their eyes shine in their sooty faces. The foreman shouts to everyone to shut up. 'Now, slowly, Tindall, tell me what you know about what happened and Collins you tell us what it is like down there and what needs to be done.'

One nudges the other.

'Go on, Tindall, tell Mr Grant what happened, and be quick.'

'It was firedamp, Mr Grant, one minute we was chipping away looking forward to coming off shift, and then suddenly, whoosh, a great ball of fire comes hurtling towards us. I'm one of the lucky ones; I was right at the end, but others,' his voice wobbles, 'others in front must have been burnt alive.' There are wails from the women and, I suspect from the men. I clutch Mrs Goodman's arm and that of Mrs Albright, who is standing alongside, with a gaggle of children hanging onto her skirts.

Mr Collins shakes his head. 'No, Mr Grant, There are definitely men alive down there, I heard them. The trouble is it's not safe. Some of the props have broken and the roof has collapsed in places.' That must have been the tremble I felt.

'Tindall, get yourself to the doctor who's over there and if he says you can, go home. Collins, are you willing to take some men with you and get back in there? We need to try and get everyone out.'

I can't hold my tongue any more. 'Did the Goodmans go in with you? Are they all right?'

Collins looks at me and perhaps recognises that I am not one of the miner's wives. 'Aye, they came in with me. They had just delivered some wood and when they saw what happened they both volunteered to go in. I don't know what has happened to them, as soon as I came across Tindall I dragged him out. Now please, I need to get back in. Mr Grant I think only two others,

269

no more at this point. I'll take you, Smith, and Frobisher.' I wonder if the Smith is the father to young Walter Smith.

I watch, my heart pounding in my chest, as Collins and the two miners are devoured by the deathly blackness. Many of the women are holding each other and weeping. All they can do is wait, as has always been the fate of women since time immemorial.

I take hold of Mrs Goodman's hand and squeeze it gently. 'They'll be all right, just you see. Look someone else is coming out, perhaps it's them.'

It isn't, but now I can remove three names from my memory list: Albright, Hammond father and son.

So, those still underground are: Adams, Charles, Cook, Ford, Forester, Jones, James, Lambert father and son, Newton, Powell, Goodman father and son, Williams and, who was it now, ah yes, young Walter Smith. Plus Collins, Frobisher and Smith father?

These new survivors have evidence of burns and one is limping, his legs covered in blood. I see Mrs Albright rush to her husband's side, the children trailing behind her like a wedding train. She hugs him but he grimaces; he has raw patches on his bare chest. Mr Grant goes over to them but I don't follow; Mrs Goodman and I are holding each other up and if one moves the other will fall. The three men are taken into one of the rooms where the doctor has ensconced himself, along with some of the miners' wives.

The ground beneath gives a groan and trembles. Another rock fall. Oh God, please keep John safe. There are cries and moans from the crowd, which has increased threefold since we arrived.

What seems like hours, but is probably only minutes, passes until there are shouts of joy as more men emerge like phantoms out of the night. One man is being carried by three others, his limbs hanging limply down. Mrs Goodman gasps and pulls her hand away from mine and runs towards the stumbling party. One of the bearers is Mr Goodman, thank God. But where, oh where is John?

I hurry over to where Mr Goodman is reporting to the foreman. 'It's bad down there, Mr Grant. I think all those that can walk are now out. That one we carried, Forester I think his name is, is in a really bad way, but he was still alive when we got to him. My John and a few others are still down there trying to force their way through a wall of broken rock to get to the others. I need to go and help them.'

'No!' Mrs Goodman holds onto her husband's arm and with a strength I expect she never knew she had, pulled him away from the mine. 'You aren't going back in there. Look at you! You're covered in cuts. You have done your bit but please, I can't lose you.'

Mr Grant nods his head and puts a hand on Mr Goodman's shoulder, which makes him wince. 'She's right, Mr Goodman. There are enough men down there now. You are a hero getting those three out, but you need to get yourself checked over and then wait, like the rest of us.'

Mr Goodman looks at his wife, Mr Grant and the mine entrance and back to his wife. Any energy he had seems to seep out of him and his shoulders slump. 'I don't need the doctor.' He puts his arm round his wife's shoulder, wincing again, then fixes his stare on the mine entrance and does as he is told, waits.

'Mr Grant, what are the men's names that Mr Goodman brought out?'

'They are Forester, Adams and Mr Lambert, the father, not the son.'

I recite the names of the men still underground, 'Charles, Cook, Ford, Jones, James, Lambert son, Newton, Powell, Goodman son, Williams and, who was it now, ah yes, young Walter Smith. And Collins, Frobisher and Smith father?

I can feel the Goodmans shivering, as I am. I hand them both a hot drink and a slice of cake. 'Please, you need to keep your

271

strength up. Just take one bite, that's it. And here, wrap these blankets around you. You can take them off if they are needed elsewhere, but you need to keep warm.'

All eyes swivel towards some riders who canter in. It's the Suttons and, I'm surprised to see, my father, who dismounts quickly and searches the crowd. When he sees me he runs over and puts his arms round me, his body warm and comforting, despite his coat being damp. 'Oh, Lizzie. We heard about the accident, that there are men trapped down there and you came here with Mrs Goodman. I can see Mr Goodman there with his wife, where's John?'

I can't put it into words and soundlessly point to the entrance, where all eyes have swivelled back to. There is a small surge forward as more men appear. There are six of them, two each carrying another. The men walking stumble with exhaustion and their bodies glisten with sweat and blood. They don't drop their burden, though, and carry on to where the doctor is waiting. A number of women run after them and after a few minutes there are the most dreadful wails.

Mr Grant comes over to me. 'You are remembering the names aren't you Miss?' I nod. 'Those six were Cook, Collins, Newton, Powell, Williams and Frobisher. Frobisher was with Collins when he went in again. Who does that leave?' I close my eyes and recite the re-written mental list.

'Charles, Ford, Jones, James, Lambert son, Goodman son and, who was it now, ah yes, young Walter Smith. And Smith father?'

Mr Grant nods his thanks. 'Yes, both Smiths are in there, father and son. God, what a mess.'

'Are the two men that were carried still alive?'

Mr Grant shakes his head and walks off to talk to the Suttons, who are standing away from the miners and their families, their pink, clean faces shining in the lamplight.

Eight men still underground. Please God, I know I'm not a good Christian and don't always take the Reverend Stephenson's sermons as seriously as I ought, but I am praying for John Goodman, who is the kindest, most gentle and most worthy man You have ever created. Please, please, just keep him alive.

There is an unnatural hush; even the wailing has stopped. All eyes are fixed on a bobbing light that gets closer and closer until it emerges, held high by a man whose other arm is around another, whom he is almost dragging along. Two others are carrying someone who seems to be struggling, as if he wants to get back in. I creep forward, Papa by my side, and scan each face looking for the one I hold dear. The man carrying the lamp I recognise as Smith the father and I hear him say, 'Come on son, we're almost there. Don't you fret, you're safe now, and look, here's Mother and our Vera. You're safe now, my boy.' Others take his son off him, at which the man falls to his knees and sobs uncontrollably, perhaps with relief.

The two men carrying the other are not John and I almost ignore the man being carried but look again just to be sure. He is wearing a shirt, which the miners do not when they are underground, and there is hardly any white under the coal dust and the blood. One of the arms that is hanging down is at an odd angle and where the hand should be is just a mangled, sticky mess, The bile rises in my throat. I hardly recognise his face, one half looks like an oil painting that has been smudged; the skin is bubbled and shiny and the eye has disappeared. But the other side is definitely that of John.

Chapter 43

October 1826

The three of us, Mr Goodman, Papa and I, stare at the floor, the wall, the ceiling, anywhere rather than the fire – fire that has burnt away half of John's face. We can hear the footsteps of Doctor Peters and Mrs Goodman upstairs as they tend to John's wounds; the deep voice of the doctor as he comforts and explains; the moans of the mother.

Finally they come into the kitchen; the doctor's expression one of concern rather than his usual joviality. We wait in silence whilst he washes his hands, takes a mouthful of tea and a bite of pie; it is nearly midnight and the poor man must be starving for he has been working non-stop since the afternoon.

He turns to Mr Goodman. 'Well, he is as comfortable as can be expected at the moment. I have given him a strong dose of laudanum so he shouldn't be in any pain for the rest of the night; I have explained to your good wife when and how much to give him over the next few days or weeks, until he can abide the pain. I don't know how he got his injuries but his arm is broken, his hand smashed and his face burnt.' I reach out and take Mrs Goodman's hand and don't quite manage to stifle a sob; I know all this, but hearing the doctor say it out loud somehow makes it more real. 'I have put a splint on his arm and on each finger as best I can, but I don't think the hand will ever be of much use to him. As for his face, well, I have to be blunt, it looks like his eye is damaged beyond repair and he'll have scars. I have cleansed the burnt area and applied linseed oil.' He pauses whilst he finishes his drink and pie then holds the cup out to me for a refill; I am happy to oblige, to be doing something useful.

'But he will recover, won't he? I mean everything will heal, won't it? He won't...' I can't say the word.

'My main fear, Miss Elizabeth, is if the wounds become infected. His arm and hands will need to be washed every day with soap and water and a little vinegar seems to help the healing process. The face is more difficult, but the greatest danger lies here. My suggestion is that the burnt area is cleansed at least twice a day with diluted vinegar and then covered in a poultice with either linseed oil, honey or egg whites; all these are helpful in the healing process. If an infection sets in then the wound will become red and inflamed and he will have a temperature. I will come and visit him every day but if you are worried, fetch me at any time, day or night.'

'How are the other men, Doctor Peters?'

'None that lived are as badly hurt as young Goodman, but when I left to come here they had not recovered three or four of the men. Mr Grant the foreman knows I am here; if he has not sent for me then either they have not managed to get them out, or they have and they are not injured or they have and there is no rush. Now, I must get home. It has been an exhausting time. Everyone try and get some sleep; you will need all your energy for the next few days and weeks to care for the boy.'

Papa accompanies the doctor out and I see him slip some coins into his hand. When he returns he puts his hand on Mrs Goodman's shoulder.

'Take heart, Mrs Goodman, Peters is an experienced doctor, one of the best. You need to do as he says and get some sleep tonight; there is nothing more you can do. Lizzie, I know, will come tomorrow and help in any way she can, won't you, my dear?'

I nod. 'Of course, I want to help.'

'Bless you both for staying; you are good friends. My poor, poor boy.' Mrs Goodman puts her hands over her face as if to catch the sobs that wrack her body. Mr Goodman puts his arms around her. Papa and I take our leave.

Although it is the middle of the night there is enough light from the moon as it plays hide and seek with the clouds that have

275

shed their rain and now skip across the sky, uncaring of the troubles of man beneath them.

'His life will be very different from now on; you realise that don't you?'

'As long as he has a life, Papa.'

'You need to write to Nathaniel and tell him what has happened. He may not approve of you helping to nurse John. I know he has never been comfortable with your friendship, even before the two of you became betrothed.'

'I don't care whether Nathaniel approves or not, Papa! John is my friend, the best I have ever had, and he needs me. I care more for him than I do for stupid rules about what is proper and what isn't.'

'Oh, Lizzie, dear Lizzie. Whatever shall I do with you? I will be so glad when Nathaniel takes you off my hands! Come, let's speak no more of it. But please write to Nathaniel, he deserves at least that.'

October 26th

Dear Nathaniel,

It is with a heavy heart that I write to you tonight – no, in fact it is just after midnight so it is morning. There has been the most terrible accident at one of the mines. Some of the men have died and many are injured, including John Goodman. I know you have never liked him but I need to help care for him because of the very friendship that you have never approved of. If you care for me as much as you say you do, you will understand and not try and discourage me.

I hope you are keeping well. Might you be coming to Wednesbury soon?

Lizzie

Only when I have sealed the letter do I remember that he doesn't like the name, Lizzie.

I wake early, unrefreshed and troubled with memories of falling roofs, choking coal dust and burning fire. I can hear Emily in the kitchen; how must she be feeling with her only brother so badly injured? I get up and wash and dress quickly.

'Good morning, Emily. It's good of you still to come. We can spare you if you would prefer to stay at home.'

She gives a bob as she measures out the milk for the porridge. 'Thank you, Miss Elizabeth but Pa says it would be best if I carried on as normal. 'Appen we need the wages. He says you are going to give a hand with our John, which is right good of you, if you don't mind me saying.'

'It's not good of me at all, it's the very least I can do. I had a lot of experience caring when Bobbit was still alive. Now, is that porridge ready yet? I'll have a bowl and then go.'

I eat standing up at the kitchen table, burning my mouth in my impatience. It is raining again and I remember that I left the umbrella somewhere at the mine. No matter; it earned its keep yesterday.

When I reach the Goodmans' I have to knock on the door as it is still locked. Mr Goodman opens it and I am shocked at how old he looks. His normally ruddy complexion is a beige colour and the lines on his face are more deeply etched.

'Oh, Miss Elizabeth, we're not ready for you. Mrs Goodman is still asleep in John's room and I haven't even got the range going. I sent Emily off as I thought it best but I could have done with her help to be honest with you.'

'No matter, Mr Goodman. I'm here as a helper not a guest. I'm an expert at getting ranges going and I will soon have a good breakfast ready; you and Mrs Goodman need to keep your strength up. How was John during the night? Did he sleep through?'

277

'Aye, Mother stayed with him all night although she needn't have. They were both still asleep when I looked a few minutes ago. Please, let me sort out the range, it's not right you grovelling on your knees getting your hands all dirty.'

'I'm here now and my hands will wash. It would help if you could fill up the coal scuttle.'

Within just a few minutes the range is doing what it should, and it takes me little effort to find the eggs and bacon and get them sizzling.

'I'll go and wake Mother. I want her to eat else we'll have her ill as well.'

Mrs Goodman has aged also. She stumbles in and then looks embarrassed as she sees the breakfast I have made. 'You shouldn't have had to do that, I'm so sorry, Miss Elizabeth.'

'I will only say this once, Mr and Mrs Goodman. I am here to help in any way you need. I can build fires, start ranges, cook, clean, wash, iron, sew, sit with John; whatever you need. Now I have made some porridge; do you think John could manage it?'

'I really don't know, Miss Elizabeth. He was still fast gone when I left him just now. Maybe when he wakes we can try. I need to give him some more laudanum in a while.'

'Do you mind if I go and sit with him whilst you have your breakfast? I'll let you know if he wakes.'

'He doesn't look like our John, just be prepared. I'll be up in a minute; it's not seemly you being in there alone with him.'

'Now, Mother, there's no fear of anything untoward happening, now is there?'

I hesitate before opening the door and try and prepare myself. I had seen how he looked last night before the doctor had ministered to him; it couldn't be any worse now, surely?

Chapter 44

October 1826

It is dark, the curtains still shut against the cruel world outside. There is a musty smell of old breath, vinegar, linseed oil and lavender water. I am a great believer in the healing powers of light and fresh air, so I pull open the curtains and open the window a fraction; the air may be fresh but it is also cold and damp. I look at the sleeping figure and for a moment I am certain that he is dead until I am reassured by the gentle rise and fall of his chest. His damaged arm lies by his side, forced into straightness, but his good arm lies curved across his stomach. The side of his face that is towards me is lightly covered in layers of linen. His hair is darker than I remember it being but when I tentatively stroke his curls, my finger tips come away coal black.

I sit on the chair Mrs Goodman had occupied through the night and watch him. He stirs and groans. 'John, John, can you hear me? Oh, my dear, say something.' He responds with guttural, meaningless sounds. He tries unsuccessfully to lift his head. I rush round to the other side, to his good side so that he can see me. 'John, it's me Lizzie. You've had an accident but you will get well. You have broken a few bones in your arm and your face is burnt, but that is all, John, that is all. Look at me, John, just nod if you understand.' His good eye is bright and unfocussed, rolling side to side.

'I know you must be distressed. The doctor gave you something for the pain and it has helped you sleep. Your mother will give you some more. Do you think you can eat some porridge?' He doesn't seem to understand me for his eye continues its frantic oscillation and his half-burnt mouth emits nothing but short gasps and groans. Suddenly he flings out his good arm and hits me squarely in the face, causing me to yelp and step back, knocking over a small table.

Mr and Mrs Goodman rush into the room, both looking worried. 'Is he all right? What was that noise?'

'I'm sorry, it's my fault. I was startled and I knocked over the table. He is awake but I don't think he is fully conscious. He doesn't seem to understand anything I say. Do you think he needs more laudanum? Shouldn't we try and give him something to eat first? Will he be able to manage with his lips like that?'

Neither of them answers me. Mrs Goodman becomes calm and takes control.

'Father, you can leave us now. Go into the workshop and carry on working. There's coffins that have to be made so that is where you are most needed at the moment. Lizzie, he won't manage that thick porridge, Doctor Peters says he has probably burnt his throat. Go and water it down so it is almost like a drink. There, there, my boy, don't you fret; your mother is here and she'll look after you.'

I am horrified at the stab of jealousy I feel, but go downstairs to do as I am bid.

When I return Mrs Goodman is stroking her son's head and singing softly to him which seems to have calmed him. He is looking at her and I can see tears running down both his and her cheeks; and mine.

'We need to sit him up, Miss Elizabeth. Get the pillows from Emily's bed and ours so that we can prop him up. Then go and fetch Mr Goodman; we'll need his help to raise him.'

John is a dead weight and it takes the three of us to get him into a sitting position and from the noise he makes we have not managed it without causing him pain. His good eye is closed but he is not sleeping; he cautiously raises his good hand to the poultice on his face and tries to lift it off.

'No, John! Leave it there. You have a burn that we need to keep covered up. Miss Elizabeth and I will take it off later and clean it but only after you have had something to eat and had some more opium as I think it might sting a bit.'

I almost laugh at Mrs Goodman's understatement. I offer the bowl of liquid porridge to her, but she shakes her head and tells me to try. When I put the spoon to his mouth he clamps it tightly shut and shakes his head. 'Come now, John, you must eat. It's nice and warm.' He purses his lips even tighter and looks at me with an imploring eye. I take a mouthful myself, it is just warm, slightly thickened milk. He puts his good hand to his throat and shakes his head again.

'Oh son, I understand, your throat is burnt. Miss Elizabeth, can you go and just get him a cup of milk and another of water? He can't tolerate anything warm or thicker than pure liquid.'

This time when I put the spoon to his mouth he opens it slightly, but most of it dribbles down his chin and onto his chest. I try again, with the same result. I look at Mrs Goodman in consternation. 'Just be patient, dear. He is probably finding it difficult to swallow, but just keep trying whilst I get everything ready to change his bandages.'

I sit for what seems an eternity dribbling drops of milk then water into his damaged mouth; one half is perfect, the other blistered and misaligned. His face contorts in pain every time he swallows and the effort exhausts him. After about fifteen minutes he closes his eye and shakes his head slightly.

'Now son, just one more sip of this medicine. Come on, just open your lips a little bit and try and swallow it, then you can rest. There's a good boy.'

It is about twenty minutes before John's body relaxes and he drifts off into a drugged sleep. I help Mrs Goodman unwind the bandages from around his arm and hand; these are thrown onto the floor to be washed later on. I try not to retch. There is a terrible wound on his forearm from where the broken bone in the arm has torn through the flesh and his hand looks like a piece of steak with five pieces of wood poking out. Mrs Goodman takes a deep breath and gently starts to wipe the wounds with a cloth she has soaked in soapy water into which she added some vinegar. John stirs and whimpers; she stops, her hand frozen in mid-air, but continues when John makes no further objection.

'I can see bits of dirt here and here. Do you have any tweezers, Mrs Goodman?'

'Of course, they are needed almost every day to get splinters out. I'll go and get them.' When she returns she hands them to me, 'You do it, Miss Elizabeth, your hands are more dainty than mine.'

'I really wish you would just call me Lizzie.' But, like her son years ago when I said the same to him, she shakes her head and says it would not be proper. How I hate that word.

I look anxiously at John every time I pick out a piece of debris but he seems to be in a deep, painless sleep. When I think I have found every piece Mrs Goodman cleanses the wounds one more time and then we wind clean bandages around the arm and hand; we do not make such a good job as the doctor had done.

We both stare at the poultice on John's face, knowing we have to remove it, neither daring to. Mrs Goodman takes a deep, ragged breath then picks up one corner of the linen and starts to peel it off with a shaking hand. I take heart from her fortitude and take the other corner. It sticks and we have to tug; I realise the strange noise is the two of us whimpering. Eventually the linens are removed and we are faced with a mess of blisters and raw, weeping flesh, shiny from the residue of the linseed oil that had been applied by the doctor. Where his eye should have been there is just a lump of melted flesh. Mrs Goodman finally succumbs to the horror, sits heavily on the chair and makes the most dreadful wailing sound.

I put my arm around her and just say, 'There, there,' over and over again, for what else can I say? It is clear that her beautiful boy, *my* beautiful boy, will never be beautiful again.

She eventually calms down. 'I'm so sorry, Miss Elizabeth. It's just...He's my son and it is so awful to see him so broken.' I nod my understanding then help her to stand up. She is calm and in control again. 'Now, the doctor said to wash his face with diluted vinegar, then to cover the burn with linseed oil, honey or white of egg, then lay clean linen lightly on top. We have plenty of linseed oil, of course, because the men folk use it to protect the wood, but I have brought a jar of honey; I have great faith in it.'

Having cleaned the wound, she uses a cloth to scoop out the honey and then very gently smears it over the damaged side of his face. The smell is pleasant and it reminds me of a summer a few years ago when Bobbit sat in the garden, entranced by bees flying in and out of a hive, his head tilted as if listening to them and he buzzing softly in response.

Once the burn is completely smothered she lays a couple of clean linens over it and then steps back and lets out a deep breath, as if she has been holding it in during the whole process.

'It will get easier each time we do it, Mrs Goodman.'

'He's not going to be able to do his carpentry, is he? He'll be devastated; he loved his work.'

'We can't worry about that at the moment, we just need to get him well and back on his feet.'

The doctor comes later in the day, looking more refreshed than he had the previous night. He praises us on our work and shows us how to apply a bandage properly. 'Give him the laudanum every six hours or so for the next few days or maybe a week, so that he rests; rest is the best medicine there is. Clean the wounds as you have been doing and hopefully, we can try and get him out of bed in a week or so. He's strong and healthy, he'll pull through.'

I spend the rest of the day doing the cooking, washing and cleaning. 'If you are going to stay with John through the night, then you need to rest in the day, Mrs Goodman, and let me do these chores and keep an eye on John.'

'Perhaps it would be best if Emily comes home.'

'You will have need of her wage if John is unable to work. And I...' How do I say that I want to be near John, I want to be the one that nurses him? She looks at me with something akin to compassion in her eyes as if I had said these words out loud. 'I know, dear, I know.'

Whilst Mrs Goodman rests in her room and in between the chores I sit with John. I hold his good hand and trace the veins on the back, follow the lines on his palm, and caress the nicks and cuts, marks of his trade. My hand fits so comfortably in his. I remember the feel of Nathaniel's touch, cool and somehow comfortless.

The next day and the ones after follow a pattern: once we have changed the dressings Mrs Goodman retires to her bed, leaving me to do the basic housework and to sit with John. I talk to him, knowing he can't hear in his laudanum-induced sleep. I reminisce about all the things we did when we were younger and not bound by conventions; I tell him what I know about the accident and how everyone thinks he is a hero; I admonish him for his very act of heroism; I make promises only God can keep and I tell him stories. I tell him nothing of Nathaniel and my plans.

Chapter 45

November 1826

There was once a boy called Jack, who lived in a village with his parents. They were poor but happy. Jack's father was a carpenter and the boy was following in his footsteps and was almost as good as him, although not quite yet. Jack was the kindest, most generous boy there ever was and his heart was surely made of gold.

In the village there also lived a teacher and his family, one of his children being a girl called Eliza, who was the same age as Jack. She considered herself very clever and quite pretty and wanted more than anything to do something exciting with her life. Eliza's family were much richer than Jack's and lived in a bigger house, but the two children didn't care about such things; they just loved playing together and being the best of friends.

As Eliza grew older she dreamt of leaving the small village where she lived and travelling to all the cities of the world and having great adventures. As Jack grew older he dreamed of staying in the beloved village where he lived and marrying Eliza and having lots of children who were as happy as he had been.

One day a new family moved to the village. They were very rich and had just one son called Nathan. He was not only rich but also very proud. Although he liked to play with Eliza, he refused to play with Jack, because he was poor. At first, Eliza managed to play with both boys but after a while, Nathan said he wouldn't play with her if she kept on seeing Jack.

Now, when Eliza and Jack played, they played in the fields or in the woods or by the river; they played games with stones and bits of wood; they picked wild flowers and made garlands for each other; they made up stories that made them laugh and cry. When Eliza and Nathan played, they played in his bedroom, which was as big as Jack's whole house; they played with real china tea sets and trains that moved by themselves on tracks that went all around the house; they read stories from books with leather covers, taken from a library that was so vast Eliza thought it must contain every book ever written.

Eliza, enchanted by these toys told Jack she couldn't play with him anymore because he was poor and didn't have nice things. Jack was grief stricken but tried to understand because he loved Eliza and wanted her to be happy.

So, Eliza played with Nathan in his big mansion, with his expensive toys but after a very short time she realised that she missed the open air; she missed taking her shoes and socks off and paddling in the river, laughing when the fishes nibbled her toes; she missed collecting acorns, fir cones and conkers and pretending they were a feast fit for the king; she missed telling tales; most of all she missed her friend, Jack.

When Nathan realised that Eliza was regretting her choice of friends, he offered to take her to all the cities of the world where they would have great adventures – which is what she had always dreamed of. So, she forgot about missing Jack and went gladly with Nathan.

Whilst Eliza and Nathan were away visiting the cities of the world and having great adventures, Jack carried on with his simple life, continuing to make furniture for all the families in the village and those beyond. He was happy that Eliza was living her dream but he missed her. One day there was a terrible fire in the nearby forest. Jack could hear the woodland animals screaming in fear and stampeding to try and escape the hungry flames. He ran right into the burning trees and tried to lead out as many animals as he could; he couldn't bear the thought of any of his friends dying in such an awful way. Others from the village were too scared to run into the flames like Jack was doing, but they gladly took the animals to safety and fed and watered them and made them comfortable. After many, many hours the fire finally died down and all the animals had been rescued but there was one casualty, Jack himself. A burning log had fallen on him and burned his face and hand, but still he had continued, ignoring the pain.

He did get better, but his face was terribly scarred and he lost the use of one eye and one hand. But Jack was a brave, determined fellow and he slowly learned to make things with just one hand and one eye. At first the things he made were a bit skewed but he soon got used to it and very soon he was producing beautiful furniture again. The whole village hailed him as a hero and made sure they ordered all their furniture from him but Jack was glad Eliza was not there because he didn't want her to see him so ugly and imperfect.

After a year or so, even though she had visited all the cities in the world, none of which were as pretty or friendly as the village she had grown up in; even though she had had great adventures, they never seemed as exciting as watching a chicken hatch or a lamb being born. Eliza realised that she yearned for Jack and that Nathan really wasn't as a good a friend as she had thought. So, she came home.

Her parents were thrilled to see her and they told her all the news, especially about Jack's heroic act. They warned her about his injuries but she didn't think they could be that bad and rushed to his little house to visit him. She watched him as he worked with his one good hand, and she saw how his face was burnt and he had only one eye and do you know what? She thought he was the more handsome than he had ever been before. She knew that his kindness, his generosity and his heart that must surely be made of gold, had not been damaged. But would he forgive her for choosing Nathan above him; for thinking that what Nathan offered her was in any way better than what John could offer?

'You are writing very intensely, is it a long letter to me?'

Oh, my dear Lord, it's Nathaniel! In my surprise I drop my quill and ink splatters over the story I am writing. 'Nathaniel, what a lovely surprise! What, what are you doing here?'

'I thought it was time I visited you. I was a bit disturbed by your last letter.' I can't for a minute remember what I had said in my last letter and I must look confused. 'You basically told me that, like it or not, you were going to nurse John Goodman and oh, by the way, was I coming to Wednesbury any time soon. Well, here I am and you don't seem very pleased to see me.'

'Of course I am, Nathaniel, forgive me, it has just taken me a bit by surprise seeing you standing there so unexpectedly. Shall we go into the kitchen? It's warmer there.'

'No, here in the parlour is fine. Your mother is bringing some refreshments, which will be much appreciated; I have had a long tiring journey.'

'Of course you have, you must be exhausted. Come and sit by the fire in one of these comfortable chairs.'

He sits down and stretches his legs out and sighs tiredly. 'I would like to read what you have written. Is it one of your fairy tales?'

'My goodness, you don't want to read that, it's not finished and it is just a bit of silliness; even more silly than the ones I usually write. Oh, Nathaniel, it is so good to see you. You look well. The London air must suit you. Tell me all about the school. I find your letters very interesting. How is your uncle, and your cousin, Miss Burton, isn't it? They are keeping in good health I hope?' As I speak I fold the pages of my story and slide it surreptitiously under the blotting pad.

Mama comes in carrying a tea tray and puts it onto the table. There are three cups and plates; I am thankful for her presence. Just before she sits herself down, Nathaniel holds his hand up to stop her. 'I wonder if you could be so kind, Mrs Hayes, to pass me those sheets of paper that Elizabeth has placed under the blotting pad? It is one of her fairytales but she doesn't want me to read it. I'm sure she is just being shy; I know they are always extremely entertaining. I wonder what lost cause she is supporting in this one?'

288

'Please, Mama, no! It really is childish and I am most embarrassed by it. It is poorly written and a pathetic little plot. It is not worthy of even being read to Dorothy. Here, I'll burn it right away; that's all it deserves, to be burnt to ashes.'

Mama hesitates. Nathaniel speaks in an angry voice. 'I absolutely insist, Mrs Hayes. As her future husband I think I have a right to read it, don't you?'

I am frozen at his unexpected arrogance and cannot stop Mama from taking the papers. The room swims before my eyes and I feel as if I am going to faint. Yes! If I pretend to faint, then whilst Mama is tending to me I can retake the papers and throw them in the fire before anyone blinks an eye. I must be quick, how I wish our parlour was bigger so it would take Mama longer to get to Nathaniel. I let my knees sag and begin to swoon to the ground, but too slowly, for as I fall I see Mama handing the papers to Nathaniel, who grabs at them impatiently. I think I really do faint because the next I know I am sitting on a chair and Mama is fanning me and dabbing lavender water onto my brow. Her face is inches from mine and she looks me in the eye and I know that she knows.

I risk looking at Nathaniel. He is reading my story and his face is white and pinched; he looks quite ugly. He finishes and sees me staring. 'You forgot to change the name to Jack in the last sentence.'

I swallow and find my voice only comes out in a hoarse whisper. 'It is just a silly tale, Nathaniel. I mean nothing by it. It's just a tale.'

'You are indeed a teller of tales, Elizabeth. You have been telling me a tale all along, haven't you? I am sure the Goodmans could have called on any number of people to help, if they really needed it, but no, only you would do because of your so-called friendship with their son. Ha!'

'The Hayes family have always been good friends of the Goodmans and my daughter was there when they brought poor

John out of the mine and she was there when the doctor was seeing to him that first night. She has a very kind heart, Mr Whittaker and she is happy to support the family as a friend. There is nothing improper about her actions and she is never alone with the boy for more than a few minutes.'

'I am not worried about any improper public behaviour; it is what she is feeling privately that concerns me. Here, read this, then perhaps you won't feel so inclined to defend Elizabeth. Here, take it.'

Mama gets to her feet, groaning a little as she unbends her knees. She takes my story, reads it quickly then tears it into four pieces and throws it into the fire. We all watch as the papers curl and brown, blacken then disintegrate. My mouth feels as if I have swallowed the grey ash.

'That changes nothing, Mrs Hayes.'

'Would you like another cup of tea and slice of cake, before you go Mr Whittaker? And perhaps you need to revert to calling my daughter Miss Hayes, that would be more proper, don't you agree?'

Nathaniel looks at her in astonishment. 'You condone her deceiving me? Promising to marry me whilst loving another?'

'No, Mr Whittaker, I don't condone it but I understand it. She didn't lie to you; she lied to herself. She really did think she loved you, I am sure of that. Love is a strange thing, one day you may realise that yourself, sir. Perhaps you already have?'

'What are you saying, that I didn't, don't love Elizabeth?'

'Perhaps you did at first too, in your own way, but not in the way my daughter needs to be loved. I'm sorry if you are disappointed, but it is best that you find out now, rather than after you were married.'

Mr Whittaker looks nonplussed, as indeed I am. I have said nothing since lying that the story meant nothing and I don't seem to be expected to say anything. I am partially hidden behind Mama's body and I am quite content to remain so.

'I could make things very unpleasant.' When did Nathaniel turn into such a monster? It is a side I never knew existed.

'I think not. Did you know that James finally wrote to his father the other day, quite out of the blue? Most welcome after all this time, but quite unexpected. I think marriage and fatherhood have mellowed him and he realises that family is important. He wrote a long letter as you can imagine; he had to fit in so much. He asked if he could visit along with his wife and son. I'm sure you will appreciate how thrilled we are.'

'I am very pleased for you but I am not sure I see the relevance to this current predicament.'

'At the end of the letter he mentioned seeing you a number of times, sometimes with and sometimes without your uncle.' Mama pauses, 'but always accompanying your distant cousin. Miss Arabella Burton.' Mama pauses again and Mr Whittaker takes a sip of what must now be cold tea and stares at the remains of the cake as if deciding whether to eat it or throw it. 'He said nothing more except that he wondered whether it was proper for you to be holding the lady's arm in such a way, seeing as you are meant to be engaged to his sister.' That word 'proper' again.

Mama is still standing in front of me and she reaches a hand behind for me to take, which I do as a drowning man holds onto a branch. 'Papa didn't read that bit out to you, Lizzie. We weren't sure whether to but now I think it's important for you to know.'

Mr Whittaker licks his lips. 'I am surprised you listen to gossip from your son; he is hardly a paragon of virtue is he?'

'No, he has many faults, but he has no reason to lie. I think you are very glad that Lizzie wrote that story, for it lets you off the hook because she is now the person at fault. But didn't you really come here to try and disengage yourself because you have found another; one perhaps more suited to be your wife?' Mama waits for Mr Whittaker to stop huffing and puffing. 'So, I think the best thing to do is for you to leave now and we will all be grateful that two people have not gone through with a most unsuitable marriage. We wish you all the luck in the world with your school, don't we, Lizzie?'

All I can do is nod and continue to hide behind Mama's skirts like a recalcitrant child. I feel nothing apart from something akin to relief.

Chapter 46

November 1826

It has been three weeks since the accident. The routine has changed as Mrs Greenwood no longer sits with John during the night and she was keen to get back to her role as wife and mother. She is happy for me to visit, though, so now I go just in the afternoons and sit with John for an hour or two. More often than not he sleeps whilst I am there and as yet he has not spoken, to me or to anyone. The doctor says it is because his throat needs to recover from the burning smoke he must have swallowed. His wounds are healing slowly and his face no longer needs the poultice; the burn is protecting itself with a crusty shield.

Today I am continuing with *Ivanhoe*, an exciting medieval romance that I am very much enjoying reading out loud, although my narration falls upon deaf ears. I stop at the end of a chapter for a rest, look up and find John's good eye looking at me. Is he smiling? It is hard to tell with one half of his lips still immobile.

'Are you enjoying the story? It's rather exciting, isn't it?

He continues to stare at me; I feel quite unsettled for his expression is not a friendly one. He opens his mouth and for the first time speaks. His voice sounds like charred wood and I have to bend closer to hear what he says.

'Go.'

'Did you say go? Go where? Do you want something? Do you want me to fetch your mother?'

He shakes his head impatiently and looks at me fiercely. 'Just go.'

'You want me to go?'

He gives a small nod.

'All right, I'll see you tomorrow.'

He shakes his head. 'No. Never.'

I feel as if something has slammed into my chest and I gasp for breath.

'But why? Have I done something to upset you? John, please, tell me why. I am no longer engaged to Nathaniel, I told you that. What have I done wrong?'

But he has turned his face away from me.

Mrs Goodman enters the room. 'Are you all right, dear? I thought I heard you shouting.'

'He says he doesn't want me here; that I should go and not come back.' I am almost wailing.

'Ah. Let's go downstairs shall we? We can talk better there.'

As soon as we are in the kitchen, I turn to Mrs Goodman, angry with her. 'You knew, didn't you? I thought he hadn't been able to talk yet. What has he said?'

'He hasn't talked, he wrote. Let me show you, then perhaps you'll understand.' She goes to the dresser and takes a sheet of paper out of a drawer and hands it to me. On it in barely legible hand-writing were just 4 words: Don't want her pity.

'Pity? I'm not here out of pity! I'm here out of friendship, out of love. There, I've said it. I love your son and he doesn't want to see me anymore.' I take shuddering breaths and sit down, holding the sobs in my mouth, refusing to let them out.

'You must try and see it from his point of view, my dear. First of all he lost you to that Mr Whittaker, then he had the accident, now he has to come to terms with the scars on his face and not being able to do the work he loves. At the moment he feels he has nothing to offer anyone, least of all you. Give him time, Miss Elizabeth, please just give him time.'

I feel like going upstairs and shaking him but know that it will do no good, either physically or mentally. 'I will go home but I won't desert him. I realise he has no reason to trust me but I'll write him letters; will you make sure he reads them or read them to him if he can't see properly?'

'I'll try, Miss Elizabeth, but I can't make any promises. I am ever so grateful for all the help you have given and John will be too, when he gets better.'

I feel dejected and a little embarrassed so I give Mrs Goodman a hug them make my way home, formulating my first letter in my head.

12th November '26

Dear John,

First of all, I want to say I am sorry; sorry for thinking that I loved Mr Whittaker; sorry for being so angry with you for questioning my feelings; sorry for continuing the charade for so long; sorry (but so proud) that you went into the mine; sorry that you couldn't save all of the men; sorry you were so badly hurt but most of all, sorry that I seem to have lost your friendship, something I value more than anything in this world. What I don't feel for you is pity. I feel respect, humility, admiration, warmth, friendship – but not pity.

I am going to write to you every day and I'll send you one of my stories for you to read – you always said you enjoyed them. I have marked the place we got to in Ivanhoe and I hope I can finish reading it to you in the near future.

I know everything must seem very black at the moment and you can't see what the future holds, but you are a strong, young man, physically, mentally and spiritually and you are a survivor. You have a loving family and a loving friend here waiting to do whatever you need.

I hope you will agree to see me very soon and accept the hand of friendship I am holding out to you, but until then know that I am here and thinking of you and praying for you.

With fondest regards, your friend always
Lizzie

I write a copy of one of my early stories, one I know John likes, and put it inside the letter then ask Emily to give it to her mother when she goes home later on. There is nothing written that I am not happy for her, or anyone, to read.

Once I have written the letter I go to my room, restless and not knowing what to do with myself; it is as if now I don't have the two hours with John my day seems empty; my life seems empty. I sit and stare at myself in the mirror. I am nineteen years old and unloved. I do not consider myself pretty, especially not now with my brow furrowed and my lips turned down; will they ever turn up again? What is to become of me? Will I just stay in this house, taking over the running of it as Mama gets older? Sarah will die, then Papa, then Mama and I will be left here with Dorothy. Would that be so bad? Maybe by then Papa will have opened the school and I will teach and eventually run it. That will give my life some meaning, I suppose. Will anyone ever want to marry me? Do I even want to get married? What is it that I do want? I stare and stare at my reflection but she looks mutely back at me, her dark eyes revealing nothing of her secrets.

I write to John every day, telling him amusing anecdotes of my daily life: funny things Dorothy has said; gossip I have heard in the town; news from Matthew of his life in Sierra Leone and the very bad drawings he has made of some of the strange flora and fauna; the amusing happenings during my visits to some of the mining families; outrageous things the Suttons are purported to have done – some, I admit, I make up. I always send a story, although I never rewrote the one Nathaniel read, and anyway I would never have sent it to John. I also send him a book to read every week. I tell him to let his mother know if he doesn't like my choice, for there are plenty in Papa's library and there are bound to be some to suit his taste.

I have never received one reply although Mrs Greenwood, who ostensibly comes to visit Sarah on a regular basis, says John is recovering slowly but he will never have the use of his right hand or right eye. He reads the books and my letters and has not, as far as she knows, used them to feed the fire.

'Patience, Miss Elizabeth, just bide your time.'

I have, as everybody knows, the patience of Job.

Chapter 47

March 1827

March 12th '27

My friend John,

It is spring already, how quickly the year is flying past. It is so lovely to see some blue in the sky, to hear the birds nesting in the bushes and see the daffodils peeping out of the soil to see if it is safe to come out. I hope you are taking advantage of the weather and sitting in the garden, sunshine always makes one feel so much better, don't you think, even if one feels melancholy, which your mother says you do.

As you know Jamie finally came to visit yesterday. I was surprised to realise that I was very pleased to see him and I think I surprised him too when I gave him a big hug. My anger with him seems now so very childish. Lucy looks ravishing and obviously dotes on Jamie and on their little boy, Thomas. I didn't know it was possible to love a thing so small, so very much, so quickly! He is three months old and possibly, no definitely, the most perfect baby in the whole world. Even Papa is quite smitten and was most upset when he had to hand the little bundle over to Mama to hold. They are so pleased that Jamie has come back to them. I think you will agree that they will make splendid grandparents. I think I will also make a wonderful Aunt; what do you think? They are staying with the Suttons who, I am sure, will spoil Thomas to bits; as long as they don't teach him their bullying ways.

I have got a new friend. She is called Betty – named by Dorothy – and she is a smoky grey kitten of indeterminate age. There was a basket of them in the market last Friday and they were free to anyone that wanted one. I have wanted a kitten for a while, to replace poor old Thomasina, who died of old age at the end of last year. I could have taken all of them but chose the smallest and shyest, although she seems to have already doubled in size, is no more shy than I am. She has also brought with her a whole community of fleas!

I am sending you a new story. It might make you cross; I hope not for it is written, as always, in friendship.

Lizzie

Should I send it? Perhaps it is too presumptuous of me? I read it to Dorothy and she loves it, but she loves any story with fairies in. I read it to Mama.

'Do you think he will take umbrage, Mama?'

'It is a risk, but it might just shake him up a bit. It sounds to me as if he could do with a good shaking.'

'That is most unfair. He has suffered greatly; you can't blame him for feeling down.'

She carries on darning stockings and gives a harrumph.

There was once a carpenter called Jack, who was the best carpenter ever there was. He had a real affinity with wood and used to say that it spoke to him and told him where to chisel, where to plane and where to carve. Rich people came from all around the country with orders for him to make: a chest of drawers to hold the layette of an aristocratic baby, with feet like lion's paws and handles carved to look like newly opened rose buds; a wardrobe to fit the King's clothes, including his vast selection of crowns; cribs decorated with rabbits, squirrels and badgers to hold sleeping princes and princesses; a four-poster bed for the Queen to sleep in, dreaming of whatever it is Queen's dream about. He made every piece with love and he thought himself the happiest man alive.

One day he had a terrible accident when he fell from the top of a ladder into a fire. He lost the use of one hand and of one eye. He was grief-stricken, for how could he make beautiful things now; how could he make anything? He stayed in his bed, refusing to come from under the covers, and wept tears of disappointment and misery.

People knocked on his door asking where their orders were and whether he was all right, but he just shouted at them to go away, to leave him alone. In the end they did as he asked and no one called again.

One night he was woken by strange noises coming from his workshop; it sounded like bells tinkling in the breeze. He turned over and tried to get back to sleep but even with his head buried under the pillow he could still hear the musical sound. In the end he got out of bed and stormed into the workshop. He was very surprised to see six little people, no more than four inches high, dancing a jig on his workbench! They were cavorting and leaping over his tools, which had all been cleaned and laid out ready for use.

'Who are you? What are you doing here?'

'Why, Master Jack, we are wood fairies and we have come to help you listen to the wood speak to you again.'

'I'll never make anything ever again. Haven't you noticed I have lost the use of an eye and a hand? Now go away and leave me in peace.'

But the wood fairies were the most stubborn of the fey people and laughed their tinkling laugh. 'Haven't you noticed, Master Jack, that you still have the use of an eye and a hand? Come over here and we will help you.'

Jack didn't believe they could help him but he was curious so he went over to them on the workbench. 'We will help you carve something simple, at first; how about a mouse?' One of the wood fairies brought over a small block of mouse-sized wood and another lifted up a chisel which was longer than him but he managed it perfectly, for he was magical, of course.

And with the wood fairies acting as his second eye and his second hand he managed to carve something that didn't look to him anything like a mouse, but neither did it look any longer just like a block of wood. When Jack saw the finished article he laughed bitterly. 'I told you, I can't make things any more. That looks nothing like a mouse.'

One of the fairies turned it around and said, 'It does from this angle. Look, it is a little mouse curled up asleep.'

And he was right, it did. Jack smiled for the first time since his accident.

Every night from them on, Jack would get up at midnight – for that is when fairies appear to humans – and with their help he would carve more and more complicated things and every dawn – for that is when fairies disappear from sight - he went back to bed satisfied that he was indeed beginning to hear the wood talk to him again.

After six months Jack stood back and realised that together they had made the most exquisite chest of drawers, worthy of royalty. It had three drawers, only big enough to hold socks, handkerchiefs and bibs but there was not an inch of it that was not beautifully carved with flowers, birds, butterflies woodland animals and fairies. He was so happy he cried. The wood fairies jumped up and down with glee.

'Oh, thank you, little people. I never thought I would be able to make anything beautiful ever again. I am so grateful to you. What shall we start making tomorrow? I have a long list of orders we could start to tackle.'

The chief of the wood fairies put up his hand to quieten the others. 'We won't be coming tomorrow, or ever again.'

'What? But why? How am I going to make anything without your help?' His tears of happiness turned to tears of sorrow.'

'Don't cry, Master Jack. Had you not realised that we stopped helping you two months ago? We came and we danced and sang and pretended but we never actually did anything. You did it all by yourself. You don't need us any longer. Goodbye!' And with that they promptly disappeared, although it was not yet dawn.

Jack was astounded but the next day – for he no longer had to work at night – he started on a crib for a baby that by now was probably too big for it. The wood fairies were right; he could manage perfectly all right without them!

From that day on people started coming back to him with their orders that Jack made with the same love as he had ever done.

He never sold the chest of drawers, though.

I do send it and as expected, I get no response.

I have decided to stop writing to John. My patience has finally run out.

Chapter 48

April 1827

I am sitting in the garden with Dorothy making a daisy chain. Betty is getting in the way and the backs of my hands are testimony to the sharpness of her little claws. I am trying to teach Dorothy to count and we agree that ten daisies are not enough to make a crown, we need twenty. I watch her with pleasure as she scampers about the lawn picking the daisies, 'One, two, free, five.'

'No, Dorothy, one, two three, *four*, five.'

Mama comes into the garden a wide smile on her face. 'Dorothy, can you come in for a minute? Sarah has made some little biscuits and needs to know if they are good enough to give to visitors.' Dorothy, whose tummy always takes precedence over everything else, drops her handful of daisies and rushes into the kitchen without a backwards glance. 'Oh, and Lizzie, you have a visitor. Stay there.'

Who can it be? Jamie and family have gone back to London, with promises to visit again very soon; one of the church committee, maybe, with news of another mining family to visit; or perhaps, someone from one of these families, although none have ever paid me a visit before.

I am still puzzling who it can be when someone walks through the door and into the garden. The sun is in my eyes and I can't see who it is until I shade my eyes.

'John! Oh, John!'

I stand up and brush Betty and a heap of wilting daisies off my skirt. I want to rush to him but stand demurely, not sure what I should do.

'May I join you?'

'Of course, come and sit here. Can you manage?'

'I still have the use of two legs, one hand and one eye as you took great pains to point out.'

Is he cross, upset, hurt? I glance at him and see that his good eye is crinkling and the good half of his lips is smiling.

'I didn't offend you, then?'

'Oh, yes, you did at first. I was furious and cursed you from here to kingdom come; I'm surprised you didn't hear me.' He sits by my side and I breathe in his smell of wood shavings and linseed oil. 'But I read it again, and again and again. Every time I went to screw it up, I re-read it. I have something for you.'

He hands me a box-shaped parcel, covered loosely in brown paper.

'Forgive the wrapping; I was never any good at it, even with two hands.'

The paper falls off with no help from me and I find that I'm holding a book, bound with thick wooden covers with letters carved on the front. The words blur and I have to wipe my eyes on my sleeve before I can make them out. I trace the letters with my finger and whisper each word, 'Fairy Stories by Elizabeth Hayes, A Teller of Tales'

'Your mother suggested the title. The letters are not as perfectly carved as Jack's chest but I hope it meets with your approval.'

I want to tell him they are the most perfectly carved letters I have ever seen but I can't seem to speak, so I open the cover. Inside are the fairy tales I have sent him over the last months; unedited, unchanged, as they were originally written. I turn the book over and see that he has carved his mark of the acorn, his initials JG and the date April 10th 1827.

'It is the most beautiful thing anyone has ever given me. Thank you so much, John. This means more to me than you will ever know.'

'Your stories need to be preserved, Miss Elizabeth. You can read them to your children and to your children's children.'

I decide to take one more risk. 'Don't you mean *our* children?' I hold out my hand to him.

His good eye crinkles, the good half of his lips smile and his big, warm, calloused hand takes mine.

THE END

ACKNOWLEDGEMENTS

A writer always reads what she should have written, not what she actually has. I'm grateful to my writer friend Margaret Mather, who has an eagle eye for typos and has hopefully found them all. Also to Ben Wildsmith, a freelance editor, who has read all my novels so far and always offers invaluable feedback and suggestions for improvement. And to Camilla Shestopal, my literary agent, for all her hard work and faith in the book. Lastly, my thanks go to Mike Linane; the independent publishing house he runs may be small, but he is a man with a big heart and offers a wonderful opportunity for writers just like me.

ENJOYED *A TELLER OF TALES?*

If you enjoyed reading *A Teller of Tales* could you please leave a review? Write as little or as much as you like, but it will mean so much to me.

Want to know what happens next?

Look out for *A Keeper of Tales,* book 2 of the *Grandmothers' Footsteps* series due to be published at the end of 2022. Book 3, *A Seeker of Tales,* is in progress.

KEEP IN TOUCH

Follow me on social media:

Facebook: facebook.com/marilyn.pemberton.391

Blog: writingtokeepsane.wordpress.com

Website: https://marilynpemberton.wixsite.com/author

e-mail: marilyn.pemberton@yahoo.co.uk

Printed in Great Britain
by Amazon